THE HIDDEN TOWER

JAMES E WISHER

Edited by: Janie Linn Dullard
Cover art by: B-Ro
ISBN: 978-1-945763-72-4
6920201.1

CHAPTER 1

Cold and dank: those words always flitted through Otto Shenk's mind when he reached the bottom of the basement stairs. A thin sheen of condensation covered the stone walls and shallow puddles dotted the packed dirt floor. A pair of Lux crystals rested in niches built into the wall, their feeble enchantments barely adequate for the task of illuminating the narrow hall that led to Master Enoch's workshop. The musty scent of mold lay over everything.

A wall had been built specifically to seal his master's chambers off from the dungeons and cold storage. One lonesome passage allowed entrance and exit and the door to the stairs was located as far from Otto's father's audience chamber as the castle architecture allowed. It seemed Father feared wizardry was a disease that might be catching. Certainly the looks of disdain he favored Otto with suggested he found his youngest son to be a diseased thing.

Otto shook his head, sending his mop of unruly dirty-blond hair waving about. As if to mock his, his servant's and his mother's best efforts, Otto's hair never stayed in place for more than fifteen minutes. It had been that way since he was five, and at seventeen it seemed unlikely anything would change, at least until it started to fall out. All the Shenk men lost their hair, it was only a question of when.

He stepped off the bottom step, careful to keep his new boots dry lest he draw his mother's wrath. Otto hated the cavalry boots and didn't especially care if the stiff, knee-high monstrosities got soaked. The nobles of Garenland currently favored the stupid things and even country barons had to keep pace. Or their sons did anyway. Father wore what he liked and woe to anyone that complained. Otto preferred his fawn slippers. They fit far more comfortably, not that he dared leave his room with them on.

A shadow danced on the wall beside him, prompting Otto to look up at the spider stalking a moth caught in its web. "Morning, Claud. I hope I haven't interrupted your breakfast."

The arachnid ignored him, the same way it did every morning. It was the story of his life. If he wasn't being ignored, he was getting shouted at for some infraction, real or imagined.

He left Claud to his meal and strode down the short passage that ended at an ill-fitting door sporting an iron knocker with the face of a gargoyle. Rust covered the knocker, giving it a grungy, orange patina. Since he had no desire to touch the disgusting thing, Otto rapped with his knuckle.

The door opened a moment later, revealing the gaunt form of Master Enoch. A many-times-patched brown robe draped the wizard who peered at him with watery blue eyes. Master Enoch had seen better days when Father hired him a decade ago and the poor pay, worse food, and miserable living conditions had done little to improve his state. Long gray hair and a beard jutted out in every direction, making Otto's wild mane look positively tame by comparison.

Otto bowed. "Good morning, Master."

The wizard darted a look down the hall and licked his lips. "Please, Lord Shenk. How many times have I said you mustn't call me master? If your father should overhear…"

Otto straightened and sighed. It seemed wrong not to treat his teacher with the respect he deserved. He should be used to it by now, but every once in a while he slipped into student behavior instead of noble behavior "Don't worry. Father's busy meeting with some merchant's representative. He's all excited about finding a new buyer for our cider. At least I assume that's what he was excited about. I pay as little attention to Father's ranting as possible."

"Yes, of course." Master Enoch darted one last look behind Otto and moved aside to allow him in.

"Speaking of apples…" Otto stepped into the room and dug a shiny red fruit out of his satchel. "I brought you a snack. I've seen the gruel Cook fixes. It's a shame the way they treat a genius like you."

Master Enoch bit into the apple and sighed as a trickle of juice ran down his beard. A minute later the apple was gone, core and all. His teacher spit four black seeds into the bucket at the foot of his simple cot.

If Master Enoch's treatment was a shame, his living conditions were a crime. The workshop slash living quarters held little beyond the cot, bucket, a rickety stool and a crude, rough-hewn bench covered with alchemy equipment. Three leather-bound books sat on one corner of the bench, as far from the caustic chemicals as possible.

Otto often wished for a window during his master's experiments, but Enoch's skill with wind magic proved sufficient to keep them both from suffocating. He hoped to eventually learn a bit about alchemy, but his master didn't yet deem him skilled enough in the basics of magic to move on.

"Have you been practicing?" Master Enoch asked when his apple joy had faded.

"Yes, Mas... uh, Enoch. Two hours every evening, just as you said. I know I can do more."

"You mustn't push yourself. Remember, training to use magic is no different than exercising your muscles. Do too much too fast and you might hurt yourself. You have the gift, Otto. As strong as anyone I've ever met. Be patient, build up your strength. Now, show me what you've learned."

Otto grinned and pulled his dagger. It still took him a moment to make the mental shift necessary to view the etheric currents. When the swirling, multicolored energy resolved around him he flipped the blade into the air and flicked his thumb against the iron ring on his middle finger, sending a thin streamer of energy into the dagger. The magic activated as the metal of his ring resonated with the steel dagger creating a connection between them. The Bliss when his will and the ether became one filled him for a moment.

When he'd fully linked his will to the weapon, he sent it flying around the small room. It rose and fell, spun and twisted to Otto's whim. When he'd performed every trick he knew, Otto held out his hand and the dagger settled into it.

"How was that?" Otto sheathed the blade and ended the spell.

"Excellent. You've mastered basic resonance magic in only ten years. I needed twenty to get where you are now. What about the sparks?"

Otto grimaced. When he was five, Otto had discovered when he snapped his fingers sparks would shoot out if he wished them to. He couldn't peer into the ether yet and so only called on his magic instinctively.

Since he was five and generally bored, he often wished the sparks to appear. If he really concentrated, different colors and sometimes even shapes formed. When he caught the drapes of his bedroom on fire, Father had decided he needed to learn how to control his magic properly.

When Otto recovered from the beating his father gave him, the wall in the basement had been built and Master Enoch hired.

"I can still feel the fire right there, just outside my grasp, but as you commanded"—Otto barely noticed Master Enoch's wince —"I haven't reached for it except in your presence."

"That's very good, but please, it's my suggestion. I would never dream of commanding a nobleman."

"No, of course not. Can you control fire, Master?" They'd had this discussion a number of times over the years, but Otto still didn't fully understand his master's limitations.

Master Enoch sighed and settled down on his stool. "Not well. Fire has always been nearly beyond my reach. Oh, I can light a torch or summon a cooking fire and I understand the spells just fine, but the ether refuses to obey when I ask it for anything more. I don't know why. Every wizard has different limitations. That's the reason I had so much difficulty finding work. In Garenland, wizards are valued in direct proportion to their ability to produce value. Since I can't help in the foundry or the forges my options were always limited. It was a great stroke of luck when the baron hired me as your tutor."

"That seems rather narrow-minded, considering all the things you can do."

Master Enoch shrugged. "At least in Garenland I have basic

rights as a citizen. I'm free to live as an ordinary man if I choose not to use my magic. Not that I ever would. But in Straken they hang then burn anyone that shows wizard potential. In Rolan and the other kingdoms they use us as slaves. Be grateful that you were born in Garenland. Being of the nobility would offer you no protection in the other lands. Now show me your fire."

Otto grinned. He loved this part of the lesson the most. He'd used his magic instinctively as a child, but now that he'd learned the proper way to do it, the things he could accomplish had multiplied by a hundred, as had the Bliss. It was a pleasure beyond anything imaginable to a non-wizard and Otto pitied them its absence.

He rubbed his fingers together to build up heat. Fire magic was a form of enhancement magic. Next he focused on the warmth between his thumb and forefinger and sent ether into it. A flame blossomed to life. A quick adjustment to the etheric flow and the flame started feeding on the magic.

Like the dagger earlier, the flame was fully under his mental control. Otto shaped it first into a dancing girl that pranced around on the palm of his hand. Next he made a dragon and sent it flying around the room, breathing tiny fire blasts.

The dragon landed on his finger and he considered what to have it do next.

"That's enough, Otto. I think you're ready for a new spell."

Otto snuffed out the dragon and blinked away the ether to better focus on the spell book. Finally, a new spell. Master Enoch was so stingy with his magic. He never let Otto learn a new one until he had full control of the last. "Which one this time, Master?"

The wizard didn't even bother to correct his use of "master" as he grabbed one of the books at the end of the bench.

"Since you have the knack of enhancing heat to make fire we'll see if you can enhance electricity. Here we are."

He set the book down and Otto peered eagerly at the pages. You could build up a charge capable of rendering a man unconscious by enhancing the spark you made when you shuffled your feet on a carpet. The etheric flow matched almost identically the shape he used for fire magic. The description went on to offer a number of ways to create the initial spark since there wouldn't always be a carpet handy.

Otto eagerly read and reread the pages, setting it all firmly in his mind.

"Otto."

The sooner he mastered this spell the sooner Enoch would teach him another one.

"Otto!"

He blinked and turned towards Master Enoch. "Did you say something?"

"It's time for your sword practice. If you don't hurry, you'll be late."

Otto's momentary happiness vanished. He hated sword practice, but it was a skill required of a nobleman. Never mind that he didn't have the least aptitude for the blade, much less any interest. Father expected him to show up for training and if he didn't, the beating he'd receive would keep him in bed for a week.

CHAPTER 2

The crisp fall air made a refreshing change after the stifling closeness of the basement workshop. Otto strode across the empty courtyard toward the training circle where his tormentor—or teacher as his father would have it—waited, bare chested and eager. Halfway to the circle Otto diverted to the armory to collect a padded leather jerkin and wooden sword, even though it would have made no difference if he had chosen a live blade from the numerous racks. He had no hope of landing a blow on Sergeant Graves.

Properly armed and armored for his daily beating, Otto resumed his trek. All around the yard the dark walls of the castle rose, blocking out his view of anything but the clear, blue sky. It was said that in the old times, when the Arcane Lords still ruled the world, a wizard with the knowledge and power could soar through the sky like a bird. He would have given anything in that moment to bound into the air and away from the circle. Unfortunately, he had a better chance of being struck by lightning on this fine day.

One step from the training circle Otto stopped and bowed

to Sergeant Graves. Though approaching fifty, Graves had shoulders twice as broad as Otto's. Scars crisscrossed a chest covered with coarse black hair. The wooden sword in Graves's hand looked like a child's toy.

Graves had joined the army when Otto's grandfather still ruled the barony. Father and the sergeant had trained together and become fast friends despite their differences in rank. When it came time to select a sword master for his sons, Father had come to his decision instantly. Both of Otto's older brothers had taken to the sword like a pig to filth. He wanted only to survive his daily bouts without any broken bones.

"Sergeant Graves, permission to enter the circle?"

"Permission granted, my lord." Graves always spoke perfectly politely even as his training methods remained brutal. "You showed some promise yesterday. Hopefully we can keep that up today."

Otto restrained a laugh. At this point if he went ten minutes without falling on his face it was considered progress. It wasn't Graves's fault he had an incompetent student. At least his father had ordered the yard cleared during Otto's training. If he'd had to do it with all his father's men-at-arms watching, a miserable experience would have been rendered a nightmare.

Not that he imagined Father gave the order for his benefit. He simply didn't like to advertise the fact that one of his sons was useless in the one area that really mattered for a nobleman. Otto was no warrior and all the training in the world wouldn't change that.

"Let's start with forms and get you loosened up."

Otto stepped into the circle and began an unending cycle of parries, slashes, and lunges. The minutes dragged on, broken only by the occasional, "Raise your elbow, my lord." Or "Don't overextend, my lord."

After an interminable length of time which was probably only fifteen minutes, Otto's shoulders and thighs burned and sweat plastered his dark-blue tunic to his back. He bent over, hands on knees, and struggled not to throw up.

"That should have your blood pumping," Graves said. "Let's have a couple practice bouts."

Otto straightened and joined his teacher in the center of the circle. When he first started training with Graves, Otto had asked why the sergeant didn't wear protective gear when they sparred, to which Graves had replied that as a beginner he had no chance of landing a blow and even if he did it wouldn't strike with enough force to hurt him. It seemed in eight years his assessment of Otto's skills hadn't improved.

Which only went to show how preceptive the veteran warrior was. Otto raised the hilt of his practice sword to his forehead then slashed it to the side. He'd grown competent with the salute at least.

Graves returned the gesture and raised his sword. Ten seconds later Otto's weapon went flying to the left and he went sprawling to the right. A light tap on the head ended the first bout.

"Up and at 'em, my lord. We still have an hour of sparring and half an hour of running."

It took all Otto's self-control not to scorch the smile off Graves's face. His palms already burned from grasping the sword. A little etheric energy and *whoosh*, he'd win his first match ever. Using offensive magic would also see him quickly hung and his body burned.

It would almost be worth it.

He retrieved his weapon and returned to the center of the circle. Another salute was followed by a hard slash from his opponent. Otto parried and even managed a fair riposte which Graves dodged easily.

Otto bore in, slashing left and right before ducking a counter.

"Good, my lord. Be aggressive, be a warrior."

Unfortunately, the warrior had used up the last of his energy and Graves's next slash sent his sword flying and a hard blow to the ribs crumpled Otto to the ground.

Graves sighed. "You have to do better, my lord. If this was a real fight, you'd be dead."

Otto rolled over on his back. "If this were a real fight, you'd be hung for assaulting a nobleman. Besides, in a real life-and-death fight I'd use magic."

"Bah! Magic is no match for a good sword. I've never seen a wizard I feared."

Otto's eyes narrowed and the ether appeared in his vision. "Is that right?"

He flicked his thumb against his ring, sending ether into it then out into Graves's body. The magic resonated with the iron in the sergeant's blood, rendering him rigid and immobile.

Otto climbed slowly to his feet and brushed the dirt off his clothes. He didn't bother retrieving his wooden sword, instead he drew the razor-sharp dagger at his belt.

"Did you know, Sergeant, that you have tiny bits of iron in your blood?" Otto held up his hand and wiggled his ring. "I've connected that iron to the iron in my ring rendering you as rigid as the metal band."

Otto moved closer, raising his dagger. "I know you and my father don't think much of magic. None of the true men of Garenland do. In a large-scale battle this little trick would be useless, but one on one, I think you'll agree, it's quite effective. Legal too, as the spell isn't doing you the least harm."

When the dagger rested lightly on Graves's throat Otto liked to imagine there was a hint of fear in the man's eyes. Graves couldn't speak, or even blink for that matter. He was totally helpless. Otto drew a breath to ask how the sergeant liked being the helpless one for a change when a heavy fist crashed into the side of his head and everything went dark.

CHAPTER 3

Otto blinked, groaned, and at last the world came into focus. The glowering, bearded face of Baron Shenk stared down at him, his bald head gleaming in the morning light. The side of Otto's head throbbed from the heavy blow and he'd probably have at least one black eye in the morning. It wasn't the worst clout his father had ever given him, but it hurt all the same.

As was his habit, Father dressed in all black save for the ermine collar of his cloak. The hilt of his longsword jutted out. Even in his own castle Father never went about unarmed. Whether this was a comment on the garrison or general paranoia Otto didn't know.

"Hello, Father. Come to observe my training?"

"I came to see you sparring, not threatening to cut the throat of the best man to ever serve in this garrison," Father bellowed, waving his hands in his best imitation of a grizzly bear. "On your feet."

With considerable groaning and scrabbling Otto stood,

swayed a moment, then steadied. "I wasn't going to cut his throat, Father. I simply wished to demonstrate to the good sergeant that wizards are dangerous and shouldn't be taken lightly."

Off to the side a pale Sergeant Graves had a hand to his throat. Otto coughed and when Graves looked his way said, "No hard feelings."

"No, my lord. I didn't realize a wizard could do such a thing. I thank you for the instruction."

Father slapped Otto on the back of the head, staggering him a step. "You're not here to instruct Graves in the dangers of magic. You're supposed to be learning the sword."

"So you keep telling me. Has it not yet become abundantly clear that I have no aptitude for dueling? If I ever find myself in a situation where my life depends on my skill with the blade, I'm done for. I made peace with that within a month of beginning my training. If you ordered Graves to pound on me from now until doomsday it wouldn't change a thing. Better for everyone if you stop wasting his time and let me focus on the things I'm actually good at."

"Like magic?" The contempt in Father's voice hurt worse than the blow to his head. "You will gain no respect for your wizardry and the fact of its existence will prevent you from inheriting any land or leading men in war."

Otto rubbed the side of his aching head. "I'm a third son. I'll never inherit anything anyway and the idea of me leading men into battle is laughable. Surely having a wizard in the family will be an asset to Stephan. He won't have to rely on the dubious words of a stranger should he run into arcane matters."

"You will serve the family. It's the main reason I brought in that skinny rat to teach you. Saving the castle drapery was just a bonus." Father grabbed Otto by the front of his shirt and jerked him off the ground so their eyes met. "Do not ever use magic on one of my men again."

Otto stumbled when his father dropped him but managed not to end up in the dirt.

"As for your training, consider it ended. If, in eight years, you haven't achieved even basic competence you never will. Now follow me. Stephan's wife is pregnant again and your mother wishes to know the sex."

Otto grimaced at his father's back. He hated performing such simple spells. Any midwife knew the trick to divining the sex of an unborn child. Even those without the ability to see the ether could perform minor spells. Only the knowledge that he'd never have to enter the dueling ring again made up for it. If he'd known threatening to cut Graves's throat would get him out of the training sessions, he'd have done it years ago.

He pulled off his jerkin, tossed it beside his wooden sword, and strode along beside his father. They left Graves alone in the circle to pick up. The three-story keep loomed, dark and forbidding, ahead of them. Otto had never felt welcome in the cold, drafty halls even though they were ostensibly his home.

For his entire life, Otto's brothers had alternated between bullying and ignoring him. His father beat him regularly for offenses real and imagined. The servants tiptoed around him for fear of his magic and the soldiers mocked his lack of sword skill, though never when they thought he was around.

Only Mother had shown him kindness, even if it was always tinged with pity. Pity for his weak body, his magic, and for the fact that he was a third son with no real prospects. When he thought about it, her pity seemed fully justified.

One of the guards on duty opened the heavy, iron-and-oak door at their approach. Father stepped through without comment and Otto followed. Once they were inside, the door shut with a dull, final-sounding thud.

A short passage lined with murder holes led to the main hall. Four long tables running north to south and one running east to west filled the room. A fire blazed in the massive hearth and Father's hounds lounged in front of it. The fire did little to warm the chamber, but it did push back some of the gloom. Stairs to the left led to the second-floor living quarters.

"They're waiting for you." Father stomped over to his high-backed chair and settled in before the fire.

Otto made his way upstairs. His brother, Stephan, shared the second-largest suite in the castle with his wife and two sons. A pair of blond-haired boys guarded the room; four-year-old Stephan II with his tiny wooden sword and his brother, one-year-old Mandel who wielded nothing save drool and snot.

"Halt and state your business!" Stephan II brandished his toy sword.

"Your Uncle Otto has come to visit your mother." He smiled. "May I enter?"

Little Stephan slid his sword through his belt and stepped away from the door. "You may."

The boy managed to retain his stern expression for a few more seconds before breaking into a bright smile and running over to hug Otto. "Mama's going to have another baby, Uncle Otto."

"So your grandfather told me. Grandmother Katharina wants me to see if you're going to have a little brother or sister."

Little Stephan's eyes grew big. "Can you look into Mama's tummy?"

Otto chuckled and ruffled the boy's hair. "Something like that."

The bedroom door opened and the kind, lovely face of Otto's mother appeared in the gap. "I thought I heard you. Come along, everyone's waiting."

"Yes, Mother. Stephan, back to your post."

Little Stephan brought his fist to his heart. "Yes, sir!"

Otto joined his mother inside and she shut the door. Her hand went immediately to his face. "Arnwolf at his gentle best."

"Yes, well, he did excuse me from further sword practice, so I consider it a minor price to pay. Did you not think to have the midwife perform the divination when she confirmed the pregnancy?"

"Lidda tried, but claimed she got no result." Mother smiled and took her hand away. "I thought a proper wizard might have better luck."

"I can certainly try, though I can't imagine why Lidda failed."

"Shall we move this along?" The disagreeable voice of Stephan the Elder came from deeper in the suite. "I mean to go hunting this afternoon."

Ever the caring husband. Stephan and his bride of five years, Griswalda, had fallen in hate at first sight. Not that either of their fathers cared in the least. Griswalda's father ruled a small but wealthy county on Shenk Barony's eastern border. The old count had no sons, so when he died his county would be absorbed into the barony, increasing its size by a quarter. For such a prize Father would have wedded Stephan to a goat.

"Coming, brother." Otto led his mother back to the bedroom.

Lying on the bed under a mound of blankets was the blushing bride herself. Only the woman's piggish face, surrounded by a mound of greasy, dark curls, peeked out from under the covers. Otto had on occasion wondered how his brother worked himself up sufficiently to bed the woman, but ultimately the less he thought about that the more his stomach approved.

"I understand congratulations are in order." Otto sat on the edge of the bed.

"Just get on with it." Stephan glowered from his chair in the corner.

Otto glanced at his oldest brother. Stephan was big and broad like their father. Receding dirty-blond hair hung down the front of his brown tunic. Angry blue eyes stared at the world from under heavy brows.

They'd never gotten along; too different Otto had always assumed. Over the years he'd come to realize Stephan hated everyone. That made him feel oddly better.

"Right." Otto placed his hand over the blankets and shifted his perception, so the ether became visible.

"The ring!" Griswalda's shrill voice cut the air like nails on slate.

Mother held out a silver chain with a gold ring dangling from it.

"That's not necessary." Otto refrained from reaching for the bauble. "I can read the ether directly."

"It's tradition." Griswalda heaved herself up higher on the pillows. The blanket fell away, revealing her massive bosom.

Otto shuddered as she covered herself back up. He took the chain from his mother and dangled it over Griswalda. A thread of ether swirled down into her abdomen at his command. Otto followed the thread in his mind and soon found the shape of the baby. Etheric energy caressed the tiny form, revealing everything. A faint resonance vibrated between them as Otto's blood reacted to that of his partially formed niece.

He smiled. It would be a girl.

He set the chain to swing left to right and prepared to withdraw the magic. He pursed his lips. There was something else, something in the tiny, still growing brain. Otto wasn't well versed enough to recognize the nodule beyond knowing it didn't belong.

"It's to be a girl then?" Griswalda's shrill voice broke his concentration.

Otto blinked. "Yes. Congratulations."

"Isn't that wonderful, Stephan? A little sister for the boys."

"Yes, wonderful." Stephan heaved himself out of his chair. "I'll be back this evening."

"I should go as well." Otto straightened. "Would you walk with me, Mother?"

"Of course, dear. I'll be back shortly, Griswalda."

She nodded and snuggled deeper into the bed, still beaming at the idea of having a daughter. Otto and his mother left the suite and walked down towards his small bedroom. When they were well away from the suite Otto stopped.

"I know why Lidda didn't get a result with her test."

Mother raised an inquiring eyebrow.

"The child is malformed. I don't know if she's going to lose it, but if she doesn't…"

"Are you certain?" Mother's forehead wrinkled in concern.

"As certain as I can be. I know there's something wrong, but this early in the pregnancy I can't tell what, exactly. My guess is Lidda's spell recognized the child wouldn't live which caused it to fail. I wasn't certain if I should say anything. There is a small chance I'm mistaken."

Mother patted his arm. "We'll keep this to ourselves. Miscarriages happen all the time. Should the angels will the child not be born, there's nothing we mortals can do about it."

Otto nodded and left his mother in the hall. Hopefully he'd made a mistake. Magic wasn't perfect after all.

CHAPTER 4

Axel Shenk sat tall and straight in his saddle as he rode at the head of his patrol. A cool breeze sent a chill down his spine and he cranked his broad-brimmed hat down tighter on his head. On Garenland's northern border, fall was coming to a rapid end. The sun hid behind thick clouds and the air held a hint of moisture. They'd have a dusting of snow by morning, he knew it.

Back home, Axel would have enjoyed another three weeks, possibly a month, of decent weather. He also would have had to share it with his family. Given the choice of sitting beside a warm fire and drinking a mug of ale with Stephan or having the bitter wind blowing down the collar of his heavy cloak, he'd take the breeze. He pitied Otto having to deal with Father and Stephan both, but the runt was used to getting slapped around, so he'd survive. Mother wouldn't let them do too much damage.

He still remembered the day he gathered up his few possessions and rode out before dawn to join the army. He hadn't said goodbye to anyone, not even Mother, though he left her a note. He'd lived a relatively easy life as a baron's son, certainly compared to the average man. But Axel simply refused to stomach another day of his father's orders or his brother's arrogance.

Any man who wished it, noble or common, had the right to apply to join the Garenland army and so answer to no one but his officers and the king. Axel had been accepted at once, due to both his noble birth and skill with the sword. Luckily, he was a second son, so Father had no recourse to complain. As heir, Stephan would never have been permitted to walk out.

Axel received the rank of lieutenant and an assignment to the Second Legion on the northern border in the hopes that he might help end the bandit raids that had been plaguing the area for the past ten years. That was two years ago and he'd made little progress in his mission. If anything, the raids had intensified.

Axel adjusted the cross guard of his longsword so it wouldn't dig into his hip with each step his horse took along the goat path that passed for a road in this part of the kingdom. His command currently rode through a thick pine forest on their way to check the next village. The locals were mostly loggers and trappers that made their living in the wild places far from civilization. Their remote homes made them easy targets for bandits looking for unguarded victims.

Easy targets, but poor ones to say the least. Maybe they'd get some coin for the traps, furs, and other equipment in the villages, but it seemed little enough for the effort. Whatever their motivation, his job was to find them, kill anyone that resisted, and bring the rest back to base to hang. It sounded so easy, yet not a single raider had swung since he began the campaign.

He turned to the thick-set, bearded man riding beside him.

Sergeant Cobb had lived in the borderlands his whole life and knew the land and the people like the back of his hand. Axel had found him a great asset since assuming his command.

"What do you think, Cobb, do we stay over at the next village or check one more before dark?"

"Best stop at this one, Lord Shenk. We won't reach the next one until well after dark."

Axel nodded. "It's Lieutenant Shenk when we're on duty, Cobb. How many times do I have to tell you that?"

"Sorry, my lord."

The fifteen men behind them in a double column chuckled at the resumption of their long-running argument. At this point Axel only brought it up to draw a laugh out of the men. He'd long since given up hope of convincing Cobb to call him by rank rather than title.

Cobb stopped short and cocked his head. Axel had seen that pose often enough to loosen his sword in its scabbard.

After a moment Cobb relaxed. "Scouts returning, my lord. Riding hard too."

"Damn it all!" Axel took his hand away from his hilt. The only thing that would bring his men riding like that was another raid.

Two men in mottled brown and green scout uniforms came thundering around a bend on galloping horses. They slowed as soon as they spotted the column and approached at a more sedate canter.

The scouts reined in and saluted, fist to heart.

"Report," Axel said.

"Another burned village, sir," said Colten, the senior scout.

"Survivors?" Axel had little hope, but you never knew.

"We only made a quick survey, but no one presented themselves. The cabins were still smoking when we arrived. We missed them by a day at most." Colten's voice held the same rage that filled Axel to bursting.

"We'll have a closer look." Axel shook his reins and clucked his tongue, setting his mount in motion.

Colten fell in beside him in case he had any more questions. Axel had many questions, but none that the scout could answer. At the top of his list was who had attacked the people he was sworn to protect and where were the bastards hiding?

Fifteen minutes later the column rode into the smoldering remains of a ten-house village. Bodies in simple homespun clothes lay scattered about, some in the center of the cabins, others just outside their doors. There was no rhyme or reason to it, just chaos and death.

The villagers had plenty of firewood stacked up against a cold winter. That would make his final task here a little easier.

"Squad, gather wood and bodies and prepare a pyre. Cobb, Colten, with me. Let's see if we can't make some sort of sense out of what happened here."

A chorus of "yes, sirs" was followed by the men dismounting. It wasn't the first time they'd had to perform this sad task and Axel feared it wouldn't be the last.

The corpse of a large, bearded man lay near the center of the village. He had a double-bitted axe frozen in his hands. Axel bent down for a closer look. Red ice covered half of one blade. At least he had gotten in a good lick.

Frozen blood caked the front of the dead man's shirt, fusing it to his chest. Axel sent a silent apology to the dead man's soul and ripped the shirt open. A single round wound had been punched in the corpse's chest.

Cobb crouched beside him. "Arrow wound looks like."

Axel agreed. "Why would the bandits bother to retrieve the arrow?"

"Not a lot of civilization around here." Cobb straightened and looked around the rest of the clearing. "Steel arrowheads aren't easy to come by."

Colten stood a short way off studying the ground. The dirt had frozen as hard as stone, no way he'd find tracks. Even when they did find tracks, they usually lost them after a mile or two. The raiders knew their woodcraft, that was certain.

Axel loosed a shrill whistle. When everyone was looking at him, he said, "Keep an eye out for any wounds that might have been made by an axe."

He waited for the "yes, sirs," then went to join Colten. "What is it?"

"Blood trail." Colten pointed to a dark line running along the ground. "It goes to the trees. Looks like the raiders took their dead with them."

"Horses?" Cobb asked.

"The forest is too thick—they're on foot. Look here." Colten bent down and picked up a charred piece of wood. "Give it a sniff."

Axel took the stick and held it to his nose. He smelled the acrid, charred scent of burned wood, nothing remarkable in that. "What am I missing?"

"The blood of the earth, don't you recognize the stink?" Colten asked. "They used the stuff to accelerate the fires. I'd like to know where they got it. There are no wells in this part of the world."

Axel frowned. If Colten was right and the bandits had used the thick, black ooze to start their fires it added yet one more mystery to this madness. The nearest wells lay hundreds of miles away.

An hour later the bodies of the fallen had been gathered and a massive pyre built. Axel said a short prayer, lit the pyre, and they rode on. Only two hours of light remained, but no one wanted to make camp in the burned-out village.

None of his men feared spirits—at least he hoped none of them were that faint hearted—but it somehow seemed disrespectful to camp in the remains of the village. Foolish perhaps, but when Axel gave the order to mount up, no one complained.

Cobb led them to a clearing three miles down the road. A low pile of half-rotted logs lay to one side, but they still had plenty of room to set up their one-man tents and get a fire going. The men went about their nightly routine with their heads down and none of the usual banter.

The lack of progress was dragging everyone down, Axel included. Some days he wondered if he had the right to lead men. He seemed to accomplish nothing beyond riding around and cleaning up bodies.

A heavy hand landed on his shoulder as he set up his tent.

"Don't let it get you down," Cobb said. "The men need to see their commander with his head held high, confident that he knows what to do."

"I wish I did know what to do. The attacks seem random, so I can't predict when one might come and set a trap. Garenland lacks the resources, or at least the willingness, to put a small garrison in each town. I'll discuss it again with the commander when we get back, but frankly, I'm at my wit's end."

"I wouldn't waste your time trying to get soldiers stationed in the villages." Cobb dug his pipe out and started packing it. "The reason folks live up here is to get away from authority. Soldiers are only a little less welcome than raiders."

"That's madness."

Cobb shrugged. "Madness to you maybe, but to the people living in this part of the country it's their preference."

One of the men had a fire going and had started getting a stew put together. Axel and Cobb ambled over and Cobb used a burning brand to light his pipe. Colten joined them and held his hands out to the flames.

"Pickets in place?" Axel asked.

"Yes, sir," Colten said. "In place and the rotation set."

Axel nodded. He wished the bastards would attack the camp. Anything would be better than finding another burned-out village.

CHAPTER 5

Otto lay in his feather bed and stared up at the ceiling. After four blissful days without sword practice, Sunday had arrived. It was Master Enoch's day off. Though he would have preferred to study every day, Otto understood that the master needed a bit of rest now and then. Since Otto had little in the way of responsibilities, Sundays were his to do with as he pleased. Especially if he escaped the castle without his father spotting him.

He agitated the ether, causing a ball of light to appear. Once the room became visible, he rolled out of bed, dressed in a soft, brown tunic and leggings, and put on a well-worn pair of shoes. Damned if he was going hiking in those horrid cavalry boots. With the addition of his satchel and dagger he was set.

The hall outside was silent and empty when he stuck his head out. So far so good. He slipped out and tiptoed down the hall. As he passed his brother's room, he tried not to think about what he'd seen earlier in the week. There was nothing to be done about Griswalda's unborn daughter, so best not to dwell.

A quick glance over the railing revealed a great hall devoid of hounds and relatives. He sighed. Father and Stephan must have gone on an early morning hunt. Part of him wanted to feel indignant that they hadn't asked him to join them, but he didn't have it in him.

Otto had never cared much for hunting. As far as he could tell it was just an excuse for the men to get drunk and ride around. Heaven help any farmer's daughter out this morning. Stephan's appetites were well known amongst the country lasses. No doubt more than one Shenk bastard wandered the barony.

When he reached the ground floor he turned toward the kitchen. Otto planned to be gone all day so he'd need lunch. Heat from the spits and ovens washed over him as he stepped into the room. Cook bellowed orders at his assistants, his three chins jiggling. His white shirt sported a splash of blood stains along with a coating of flour. Two girls in faded blue smocks chopped vegetables while a third pulled loaves from the oven.

Cook finally spotted him standing in the doorway and hurried over. "Morning, my lord. Something for breakfast?"

"I'll grab an apple or two on my way. I need bread, ham, and a skin of ale."

Cook offered a little bow and bellowed for the girls to fetch his food. While they were gathering it he asked, "Anything else, my lord?"

Otto shook his head. "Did my father go out hunting this morning?"

"He did indeed. I believe the plan was for boar up on Oak Ridge. Will you ride out to join him?"

"No, I'd never catch up."

One of the girls in blue ran up with a cloth-wrapped

bundle and skin, handed them to him, curtsied, and rushed back to her chopping.

"Thanks. I'll be back for dinner so set me a place."

"Of course, my lord." Cook bowed again and returned to his work.

Otto left the kitchen and walked out into the courtyard. Now he knew which way not to go. Oak Ridge was two hours north of the castle, so he'd head south. There was a pond he'd found years ago in a little glen three miles away. That would be a nice place to while away the day and practice his new electricity magic. Maybe he'd zap a fish to go with his lunch.

Fifteen minutes later found him clear of the castle town and on his way. Most of the people had packed into one of the three small temples. The Shenk family had never been overly religious and Otto considered most of it superstitious nonsense. His father ostensibly prayed to Branik, the King of Swords, but the archangel was largely honored on his two holy days and ignored the rest of the time, barring an upcoming battle.

Otto sometimes wondered if the many archangels and demon lords ever grew bored with the self-serving prayers of men. Most people he knew only cared about them when they needed something. For Otto, the wisest path seemed to be to ignore them all and hope they returned the favor.

He'd barely left the outskirts of the village when two blond boys, perhaps ten and twelve, wearing torn trousers and battered tunics of tan wool emerged from the newly harvested corn field at the edge of the road. The panting children spotted him and raced over.

Both took a knee and bowed their heads. "Lord Shenk," the elder said. "Please, my lord, our sister is missing."

So much for his morning hike. "On your feet, boys, and start from the beginning."

The youngsters scrambled up but refused to meet his gaze. "We were playing with our sister near Rock Creek, my lord. We got bored and started up a game of dares. One thing led to another and we dared her to go into the Haunted Forest."

"It was your dare," the younger boy said.

"Was not."

"Was so!"

"Quiet, both of you." Otto rubbed the bridge of his nose. "So your sister went into the forest and hasn't come back out. And you two are clearly too frightened to go looking for her."

They hung their heads. "Yes, Lord Shenk."

"Very well. Show me where she went in and I'll see if I can find her. What are your names?"

"I'm Walden," the older said. "And this is my brother Danen. Our sister's Jessa. She's eight."

"What's she look like?" Otto followed the boys back across the field.

"Small, blond, red dress," Walden said over his shoulder.

"She's always dragging a doll around with her too," Danen added.

"So basically a girl version of you two." They stopped twenty feet from the tree line. "The red dress should make her easier to spot."

"As long as the ghosts didn't get her." Danen shivered and hugged himself.

"She went in there, my lord." Walden pointed to a deer trail a little way to their right. "We'll wait for you here."

"Best head on home." Otto examined the ground for tracks. He wasn't as good a woodsman as his older brothers, but he'd learned the basics. "Heaven knows how long it will take me to find her."

"We'd just as soon wait, Lord Shenk," Walden said.

"Yeah, if we come home without Jessa, Ma'll give us an awful spanking." Danen rubbed his rear end for emphasis.

Otto grinned. "Suit yourselves. I'll be back as soon as I can."

"Good luck, my lord." Walden sketched a fair approximation of a formal bow.

"And watch out for ghosts," Danen said.

CHAPTER 6

The air was cooler in the shade of the forest. Otto followed the trail even though there were no clear tracks. He assumed that a little girl in the woods would take the easiest path. This patch of woods had a pack of feral dogs, some boars, and its share of black bear, but no ghosts. That's why they warned the people against having their children play in the area. Why the parents had chosen to warn them with a ghost story was beyond him. If anything, the idea of seeing a ghost would tempt kids, not keep them away.

He stepped over a dead and rotting cedar. Still no sign of tracks or Jessa. He had to have come at least a quarter mile. He'd thought to find the girl huddled behind a tree just out of sight of the field. Perhaps something had startled her into running and she got lost. Hopefully she wouldn't run into anything too aggressive. Otto really didn't want to have to carry her body back to her parents.

He frowned and shifted his perception. Maybe the girl had left some path through the ether. The currents were disturbed, but not in anything resembling a line. Instead of its usual smooth flow, the ether swirled around a central point deeper in the woods. The path he followed ran in the same general direction. Perhaps he could solve two mysteries in one go.

Three hundred yards further along, the first black apparition appeared. It startled him for a moment, but he knew there was no such thing as ghosts. There had to be a rational explanation for the thing. Otto blinked away the ether, but the translucent figure remained. It floated around and let out a low moan, but otherwise made no aggressive move. It would certainly do the job of convincing any of the more superstitious souls that saw it that the forest really was haunted.

He shifted his sight again and studied it closer. Four etheric threads entered the... whatever it was. The threads emanated from the same central point around which the currents swirled. He drew his dagger and slashed the ghost several times, meeting no resistance and feeling neither heat nor cold.

He nodded once. An illusion. He'd read about them in Master Enoch's books, but had never seen one. Satisfied that the apparition posed no threat, Otto continued on his way. If Jessa had seen the "ghost" he might well find her fainted nearby.

Half an hour later a thick stand of jack pine blocked his way. Not more than twenty paces beyond them waited the center of the etheric vortex. He tried to peer between the trunks, but the branches grew too thick. It almost looked like they'd been woven together to form a screen. The deeper he went into the forest the less natural it became.

Damned if he'd let a patch of evergreen stop him. Otto circled left, hoping to find a gap. The weave remained tight and impenetrable. It took him a full five minutes to make a complete circle around the stand. There wasn't even a half-inch gap between the needles. If he'd required further proof that something unnatural waited beyond those trees, he needed it no longer.

He grabbed one of the branches. If he couldn't find an opening, he'd bloody well make one. Otto yanked with all his might, but the branches didn't so much as flex. While he wasn't the mightiest man on the planet, he refused to believe he lacked strength enough to flex a one-inch-diameter pine bough.

Enough of this!

He took a step back and searched the forest floor for a fallen branch. He snatched a foot-long stick the size of his pinky off a pile of yellow needles. His tap sent etheric energy through the twig and created a link between it and a branch. The moment the etheric tendril touched the pine branch the whole barrier opened up like a lily in the morning sunlight.

His jaw dropped along with the stick. Beyond the opening stood a simple twenty-foot-tall stone tower in perfect condition. An iron-banded door filled the arched entrance. Not a hint of rust showed on the metal.

Otto shook himself, closed his mouth, and stepped through the opening. He paused, coiled and ready to spring back should the branches show any sign of closing, but they didn't so much as twitch. He chewed his lower lip for a moment then shrugged. He'd come this far, might as well have a look inside.

A step from the entrance the door opened all on its own, without a sound, as though on well-oiled hinges. His stomach did flips as he stepped through the doorway and into an empty chamber. He'd seen more magic in the last half hour than in his whole life previous.

There was nothing on the first floor beyond a set of stone stairs to the second. He started up them, his hand trailing on a wall completely free of dust or cobwebs. At the top waited another room nearly as empty as the first. The sole decoration consisted of an oval mirror, perfectly flat and smooth, like you might find in a wealthy lady's dressing chamber.

He turned a slow circle just to be certain he hadn't missed anything. Talk about disappointing. After all that buildup he'd expected to find a library filled with tomes and artifacts. Or maybe a treasury heaped to the ceiling with gold and gems.

He sighed. Best get back to hunting Jessa. Her brothers had to be frantic by now.

"Do not be so swift to leave."

Otto spun back to face the mirror so quickly he stumbled and almost fell. The clear glass had filled with black mist. A woman's face, her skin tinged green and translucent, appeared in the center of the mirror. A halo of ghostly hair floated around her.

"Who are you?" he asked.

"Do you not recognize me?"

He looked closer and racked his brain. "I'm sorry. Should I know you?"

"No, I suppose not. Six hundred years is a long time to you mortals after all. I am Karonin and at one time I ruled this continent."

Otto gaped like a rube at his first fair. "Arcane Lord Karonin? But you're dead."

"Indeed. For long centuries I've waited for a wizard to approach my sanctuary. I expected one of my apprentices and long before now. What has happened and who are you?"

"I'm Otto Shenk, my father rules these lands. As for what's happened, well, that's a long story."

CHAPTER 7

Otto recited the history of the last six centuries as he'd been taught it. He felt like a schoolboy standing in front of the teacher. When he arrived at the part about the wizard purges Karonin stopped him.

"All the wizards were killed?" Disbelief rang in her voice.

"Perhaps not all, but all the ones that were known to have served, well, you. The books make it sound like a great bloody mess. The wizards killed many soldiers, but in the end were badly outnumbered and eventually they grew so exhausted they couldn't hurl spells anymore. Once that happened the war came to a swift end."

"Surely new wizards were born. You're here after all."

"True. For many generations anyone showing signs of magic was killed at once. That's still the law in the Kingdom of Straken to the north. In Garenland, the kings eventually realized wizards would be of use in the forges, helping create high-quality steel and more importantly, working mithril. The law still imposes many limits on what a wizard can do, but at least here we are no longer murdered out of hand."

Her lips twisted. "How high-minded. Our kind has been reduced to little more than slaves to the people we once ruled. Damn Valtan and his betrayal."

Otto blinked in surprise. "I hadn't thought about it, but it's only natural that you'd have known him. It's easy to forget that the last living Arcane Lord has been around for centuries. Lord Valtan is quite highly thought of, for a wizard. It was in large part his efforts that brought the many wars to an end three centuries ago."

"Oh? And how did the pig manage that?"

"He reactivated the portals, but only for those countries that signed the Portal Compact agreeing not to invade or otherwise harm the other members. We've become dependent on them for swift, safe travel and trade. They've made us rich and soft, or so my father claims."

"So there are no more wars?" she asked.

"Not between the nations of this continent. We have little knowledge of the other lands as none of them agreed to join. There are enough internal squabbles to keep the ground well watered with blood. Lucky for Garenland, as our main export is weapons."

"Bah. Enough history. Show me your magic."

Otto brightened then trembled faintly. To cast before an Arcane Lord was a great honor. Even if the world regarded them as monsters, that didn't change the fact that they were amazing wizards.

He drew his dagger and sent it flying around the room. After a handful of passes he switched to fire again to no comment. Time to try his new spell. He pulled a glass rod and a small square of sheepskin.

He'd barely touched them together to begin building up the

necessary spark when Karonin said, "What in the world are you doing?"

"Building up a charge for an electrical spell."

"What ignorant buffoon has overseen your training? The reason lightning is the most common offensive spell used by wizards is that the body produces a constant flow of electricity. It's what allows you to control your physical functions."

Otto held up his hand and looked at it. "Truly?"

"Of course, truly. Send your thread into your hand then shape the electricity into lightning."

He did as she said and immediately the crackling power grew in his palm. A moment later blue sparks danced around his fingers. Why hadn't Master Enoch taught him this method?

"Good. Now hurl the lightning at the wall. Only a single thread's worth as I don't wish my home damaged."

"I don't understand. How do I throw the lightning?"

She closed her eyes and shook her head. "Don't tell me you've only mastered single-thread spells?"

"In all honesty I didn't even know it was possible to wield more than one thread."

"Ha! An Arcane Lord had the ability to control over a hundred threads at once. Even a regular wizard can weave multiple-thread spells."

Otto's head spun. A hundred etheric threads at once? What could he accomplish with that much power?

"Will you teach me?"

She opened her eyes and smiled. "I will. Two-thread lightning is simple. With the energy gathered around your hand, draw a second thread and use it to connect your finger to the spot on the wall you wish to hit. Finally, will the energy along the thread."

Otto nodded. That did sound simple. He was surprised he hadn't considered the possibility on his own.

He focused on the wall opposite him and conjured a second thread. His body trembled at the increased stress even as the Bliss increased to a degree he'd never experienced. The ether obeyed and a moment later a sparkling line ran from his extended hand to the wall. He centered himself and sent the energy he'd gathered racing down the thread.

The lightning bolt slammed into the stone and blackened it. Otto's smile nearly split his face. He spun back to the mirror. "I did it!"

"Yes, and it only took you half a minute. You'd be dead ten times over in a real wizard's duel. Still, now that you know the technique it's only a matter of building up speed. You will practice and when you return, I expect you to have the casting under five seconds."

Otto slapped his forehead. "Damn it! Jessa. I was so excited to meet you I forgot all about her. I will practice, Lord Karonin, on my honor, but I have to go. There's a girl missing and I was searching for her before I found your tower."

"Ah, she would be the first person I detected today. She stopped moving about a quarter mile from here. I'll guide you, but first, on the wall to your right you'll see four triangular stones that meet at a round, slightly raised pebble. Touch the pebble."

It took only a moment for him to pick out the pattern she mentioned and tap the central stone. A vibration ran through the wall and the pieces slid apart, revealing a book bound in red, scaled leather.

"My first spell book. It's probably not well known, but I was born not far from here, likely within the boundaries of your father's barony. I built this tower a century before I became an Arcane Lord."

Otto ran a gentle finger over the smooth, cool cover. Everything in him screamed to grab it and dive into the secrets within, but the rational part of his mind balked. "Your gift is most generous, Lord, but if it should be found the book will be at risk. Books of dangerous magic are often destroyed. It will be safer here. When I return, I'll bring my journal and copy as much as I can."

She muttered something about ignorant peasants and shook her head. "Do as you think best. This new world is a mystery to me. When will you be back?"

"I can only visit safely on Sundays. Any other time my absence will be marked."

"Once a week is fine. It's not like I have a great deal else to occupy me. When you get outside, follow the etheric light, it will lead you to the girl." The hidden compartment ground shut. "Practice hard, Apprentice. I trust I don't need to warn you against mentioning this place to anyone."

"No, Lord. It's been an honor to meet you and an even greater honor to have a chance to study under you." He bowed to the face in the mirror. "Until next week."

He retraced his steps to the clearing surrounding the tower. A glance at the shadows revealed it was only a little past noon. A bright, blue light appeared in the ether and moved quickly away from him and out the opening in the pines. Otto jogged after it, his mind awhirl. A million questions battered him and left him reeling.

He would have time to explore them when he returned next week. All that mattered for now was that one of the most powerful wizards to have ever lived had agreed to teach him. So much had been lost since the time of the Arcane Lords, but she probably knew every secret in the universe. That she was dead didn't trouble him in the least.

Ten minutes later a faint whimpering reached him. The spark he'd been following hovered over a juniper bush. He stepped around it and found a little blond girl in a torn red dress lying on the ground, clutching her left ankle.

"Jessa?"

She sniffed and looked up at him. "Who are you?"

"I'm Otto. Your brothers asked me to try and find you. Are you okay?"

"I tripped, then I fell. I lost my dolly and I want to go home." She burst into a fresh bout of crying.

He winced at the loud wailing. "I know the way out of here. Can you walk?"

"No, my foot hurts."

"Let me see." He bent down and examined her swollen ankle. It didn't look broken at least. He spun around. "Can you climb on my back? I'll give you a piggyback ride."

She scrambled around and finally wrapped her arms around his neck, half choking him. He hitched her up a little higher and took a breath. She weighed more than he thought. Luckily, he didn't have too far to go.

"Ready?"

"Yes." Jessa whimpered a little but didn't start crying again.

He set out for the field where he left the boys. He hit the deer trail five minutes later and followed it all the way back to the corn field.

"Lord Shenk! Jessa!" Walden raced up to them, his brother right on his heels.

"We thought the ghosts got you," Danen said.

"I didn't," Walden said.

"Did so!"

"Boys! How about you show me the way to your house? Your sister isn't getting any lighter."

"Yes, my lord. This way." Walden set out in the lead. He led them to a modest three-room cabin near one of the many sprawling orchards that dotted the barony. A thin trickle of smoke rose from the chimney.

Otto rapped on the door and a moment later a portly woman in a pale dress and stained apron opened the door. "Who are…"

She trailed off and her eyes grew wide. "Lord Shenk. I meant no disrespect."

Her eyes went to the ground and she bobbed a curtsy.

"I take no offense. If you'd be kind enough to remove your daughter from my back, I'd be grateful. She appears to have twisted her ankle."

A moment later the weight was removed and he straightened. Otto sniffed and his mouth started to water. "What is that delightful aroma?"

"Bean and tomato stew, my lord." She held her daughter in one arm, the girl hugging her neck. "It's almost ready if you'd like a bowl."

"I'd be delighted, madam. The tradition is for a guest to bring something for the pot, isn't it?" He dug the ham from his satchel. "Perhaps this would make a good addition."

"Meat!" Walden grinned and punched his brother lightly on the shoulder.

"Oh, boy!" Danen hit him back.

Whether this was genuine excitement or an excuse to beat on each other, Otto didn't know. He liked to think it was the former and when the boys' mother invited him in he happily accepted.

CHAPTER 8

A cold, drenching rain fell outside as Otto made his way down the stairs to Master Enoch's workshop. It was one of those fall storms that would soak the land for hours, swell the creeks, and generally make the apple pickers' lives miserable. The basement air was redolent with the scent of decay and rivulets ran down the stone wall.

A faint scream penetrated the dividing wall. Father must have been amusing himself with one of the prisoners. A patrol had brought in a pair of highwaymen an hour after he returned home yesterday afternoon.

Poor bastards.

If he had nothing better to do, Father would drag out their punishment for hours. At least if Father made an example of them the next desperate men might think better of robbing the people of Shenk Barony. Otto very much suspected their fresh corpses would be hanging from the castle walls come morning.

He glanced up at the corner, but Claud must have found a warm place to hunker down for the day, as the spider was nowhere to be seen. Larger-than-usual puddles covered the floor, leaving only a narrow path for Otto to pick his way across. He rapped on the door and his master opened it a moment later.

"Good morning, Lord Shenk." Enoch sneezed and wiped his nose on his patched robe. Otto half expected to find clumps of moss growing on it, so damp was the interior of the workshop. "Did you practice your lightning magic yesterday?"

"Yes, Master." Otto dug the wool and glass out of his satchel and cast the simple spell. He didn't dare skip the unnecessary components lest his master ask too many questions.

"Very good. The spell gave you no trouble then?"

"No, in fact it's almost identical to the fire spell you taught me." Otto steadied himself. Time to take a risk. "Once I became comfortable with the spell, I did a little experimenting on my own and discovered something interesting."

Otto sent his dagger flying with one hand and conjured the fire dragon with the other. He was about to have them fight when Master Enoch grabbed his arms, breaking his concentration and sending the dagger clattering to the floor.

"You must never let anyone see you using two threads at once." Master Enoch's voice was as hard and commanding as Otto had ever heard it.

"Why? Being able to use two threads opens up so many more options for spells. I'd been thinking for a while now that a single thread was far too limiting."

Master Enoch released him and sat on his rickety stool. He gestured toward the cot.

When Otto had settled in, Master Enoch scrubbed his face with his hand and sighed. "It's my fault, my lord. I should have cautioned you from the beginning, especially once I saw your curious and eager nature. I allowed myself to imagine if I didn't teach you multi-thread spells you would never attempt them on your own. Foolish of me."

"I don't understand, Master."

"It's less about the technique than displaying your power. If anyone should see you performing a feat of potent magic it puts you at risk and potentially all other wizards along with you. We're not so far from the purges after all."

Otto chewed that over for a minute then leaned forward. "You think I could be killed for making a dagger fly while conjuring a flame?"

"No, those simple tricks wouldn't cause enough consternation. My worry is about the future. Today it's two threads, but next month it may be three, then four or five. Once you reach that level you have the potential to do real wizardry. While I doubt I can convince you not to learn it now that you know such magic exists, I do want to caution you about using it. It risks more than your own neck."

Otto leaned back and nodded. "How many threads can you conjure, Master? It's only the two of us. Please?"

"This one time only."

Master Enoch stood and spread his hands. Multicolored threads sprang from each finger until ten of them danced in the air. He only maintained the display for a few seconds before slumping back onto the stool.

"Ten, Master!" It strained Otto's credibility and if he hadn't seen it with his own eyes he wouldn't have believed the ragged figure before him capable of such a display.

Master Enoch rubbed his eyes. "That's my maximum and it exhausts me rapidly. I can use up to five with no trouble, though I never do."

"Can all the wizards, like those working the forges and advising nobles, perform such feats?"

46

"Many can. Understand, Otto, since the time of the purges, from master to student, the warnings have passed. Never show them your true power. Never give them an excuse. Magic frightens people in direct proportion to the power displayed. The weaker we seem, the safer we are."

"I understand, Master." And he did. Men like his father respected power, but they also needed to control it. And magic was something they'd never truly control or even understand. "Surely when we're alone you can teach me more than sparks and flying daggers."

Master Enoch finally cracked a smile. "Very well, though it will have to be from memory as I dare not write any of my stronger spells down."

"Fair enough." Otto rubbed his hands together. Now he had two wizards willing to teach him high-level magic. That should accelerate his studies considerably.

ↄ

Otto shivered in the predawn gloom as he slipped through the woods toward Lord Karonin's tower. The temperature dropped more and more each day. He pulled his fur-lined cloak tighter about him. Soon the snows would come, trapping Otto in the castle with his family. He shuddered at the thought. Winter was the worst part of the year as well as the longest.

A quick glance at the ether confirmed his direction. He'd taken a different route today as he didn't wish to run into the boys and their sister. In his experience kids liked to talk and he had no desire for his weekly treks to become a topic for gossip. Even if no one knew he went to the hidden tower, he didn't want to risk drawing attention to his weekly strolls lest a curious soul come searching for him.

At his side, the journal he brought weighed down his satchel. The spell book she'd showed him must have been three hundred pages thick so he doubted he'd get more than a quarter of it copied before the snows, but even that much would provide an excellent distraction for the coming long, dark months.

Ahead of him, a thick patch of evergreens rose up, blocking his path. Otto looked around then grinned. Once Master Enoch had accepted the inevitable, he'd been more forthcoming with his instruction. Otto wove three strands of ether together and slashed it through the branches blocking his chosen route. The invisible thread sliced through the small branches like a hot wire through wax.

According to his master the minimum number of threads required to directly affect an object was three. He touched the smooth stubs as he walked past, letting the whip fade as he did. Otto didn't know what only two threads would do, but three worked like a charm. He couldn't wait to discover the power of four or five. His master assured him that since he'd been training with a single thread for so long, he should be able to add a few more relatively quickly.

He reached the circle of trees which opened up when he applied etheric energy to them. Inside the tower he bounded up the stairs and found Lord Karonin waiting in her mirror. Otto bowed then shrugged off his cloak and satchel.

"Have you been practicing?" she asked without preamble.

"Yes, Master. I've also learned some new tricks from Enoch —he's the wizard my father hired to train me. When I showed him I knew how to use two threads it convinced him to be more generous, though not without offering a warning first."

"What warning?"

When Otto had explained, Lord Karonin's frown was so deep her lips almost touched her chin. "The masters of this time are training their students to feign weakness? If I still lived, I'd have them flayed. Their ideas are an insult to all wizards since the dawn of magic."

"If you still lived there'd be no need to hide our power as no one would dare do anything to us for fear of your wrath. As it stands now, we need to survive."

"Simple survival isn't enough. Wizards are, and always have been, the strongest and the smartest. We should rule ordinary men, not be ruled by them."

Otto shrugged. It was easy for a centuries-dead wizard to make such claims. For the still-living wizards matters weren't so simple.

"Show me your lightning."

Otto obliged, using two threads to gather power to speed the process. In less than a second power crackled around his hand. The targeting thread shot out followed by the blast which enlarged the black spot he'd made the week before.

"Under two seconds, much better. What else has your other master taught you?"

The way she said "other master" made his stomach do somersaults, but he set it aside. For now, he needed both his teachers. He hadn't actually learned a great deal beyond the etheric whip. When he started to describe it she stopped him.

"Three strands may be enough for small pieces of wood, but it won't dent flesh or metal."

"Metal I can understand, but why not flesh?" Otto asked. "Surely an arm is no harder to cut through than a branch."

"When you're using pure ether, an arm is harder to cut than metal. Even ordinary people, when attacked by magic, will instinctively use the ether to protect themselves. It's not something they can control, but it will blunt your attacks just the same. To penetrate the etheric barrier your target raises requires at least six threads and eight would be better."

Otto stared for a moment. "But I used a single thread with resonance to bind a man without any trouble."

"That's different," Lord Karonin said. "I'm talking about affecting them directly like you did those branches. Spells like Iron Bind, or the lightning bolt you've improved so much will affect them with less energy."

"I don't understand." Otto's head started pounding. "Why should one sort of magic work and not another?"

"Did your master not explain the fundamentals of magic?"

"Before this week, Master Enoch didn't even acknowledge that multi-thread spells existed."

Lord Karonin sighed. "Very well, I shall relieve your ignorance. What we call spells—fire, lightning and that sort of thing—utilize energy magnified or altered by the ether, not the ether itself, to affect the target. A single thread is used to direct the energy and that thread is so weak that it doesn't register as a threat, so no instinctive barrier. When you try to use the ether in its unaltered state, you're using something with no real substance, so you need to use more of them which makes it easier to recognize as a threat. That triggers people's barrier. Clear?"

"Yes, Master," Otto lied. He found her explanation as clear as mud, but he took her at her word. "Would it be all right if I copied some of the spell book?"

"By all means."

Late afternoon had arrived and Otto's wrist had cramped so bad it bent back like a claw. He'd managed twenty pages which included a number of illustrations. His were crude by comparison, but they got the gist across.

"I think I'll call it a day."

"Keep practicing. The harder you work the faster your power will grow."

"I will, though it's difficult when you have to be so sneaky about it."

"Overcoming challenges is what wizardry is all about."

CHAPTER 9

The wind screamed and fat flakes of snow soaked Axel from head to foot. After another two and a half weeks they'd finally finished their patrol and set their sights for base. By some minor miracle none of the remaining villages on their route had been attacked.

At each stop he'd warned the locals to be on guard against the bandits prowling the area. Scowls and sullen silence greeted his announcement. It seemed Cobb hadn't exaggerated the locals' general dislike of soldiers, even soldiers trying to protect them. Axel had been giving the same talk for the past year and a half and the glares seemed to get sharper each time. Maybe if he'd managed something beyond talk, he'd have garnered more respect.

After his little speech, Axel led his men back out onto the road with the silent hope that the next time he visited the village he'd find it still standing.

He raised his hand to block the snow and tried to peer through the blizzard. The fort had to be close, but in this mess, he wouldn't know it until his horse ran into the bailey wall.

"Cobb! Can you see anything?"

"I can't even see my horse's ears, my lord. We have to be close. We've been riding long enough to have arrived already."

Axel frowned. He'd ordered the men to tie themselves together as soon as the snow picked up. At least he didn't need to worry about anyone getting lost. He turned right and squinted. If the trees were still there, then they hadn't yet reached the clearing surrounding the fort.

The thick screen of evergreens might have been ten feet away or ten miles for all he knew. Cobb yanked on his cloak.

"What?"

"A light, my lord." Cobb pointed ahead and a little to his left.

The height looked right. It had to be the signal lantern in the highest tower. The commander must have ordered it lit so any patrols in the area could find their way out of the storm. Axel had always held the level-headed son of a duke in high esteem and this only raised it.

"I owe Commander Braddock a bottle of whiskey." Cobb's grin was barely visible through the snow.

"I'll chip in. Let's hurry before my nose falls off." Axel snapped his reins and his horse broke into a trot.

Half an hour later, having seen the horses to the stables and rubbed down, Axel changed into a dry uniform and marched through the keep to the commander's quarters. The warm halls with their rough-hewn board walls and timbers visible in the ceiling had never felt so welcoming as they did after escaping that storm.

He knocked twice and a muffled voice said, "Come in."

Axel pushed the door open and found Commander Braddock seated behind his plank-and-timber desk. The commander was twirling his trademark bushy gray mustache and humming a bawdy tavern song. Axel had no trouble understanding why he'd chosen a life in the army. Armin Braddock would have stuck out like a corpse in a choir at any noble party. Axel's fist came to his heart in the traditional salute.

"Lieutenant Shenk reporting in, sir."

"Glad you made it, Axel. Your squad was the last." Commander Braddock stopped twirling and sighed. "Well, let's hear it."

"I wish I had better news, sir. Three villages burnt, twelve unharmed, and no raiders killed or captured."

"Damn it!" The commander slammed his fist on the desktop. "How do the bastards do it? Are they wraiths, able to appear and disappear at will?"

"No, sir. We found a bloodied axe at the last battle site. Whoever got hit was solid enough. The raiders took their dead with them. Also, Colten found traces of blood of the earth."

"Where in this frozen hole did they find blood of the earth?" Commander Braddock leapt to his feet and stomped around his quarters muttering imprecations and looking like he wanted to strangle someone.

"Sir, have you passed my suggestions up to the capital?"

"Of course." The commander dropped back into his chair. "I've written, sent messengers to the generals, hell, I even wrote my brother Duke Braddock. I was roundly ignored. The northern borderlands are too far from everything to rate any help."

"What are we to do, wait until everyone's dead then head south?"

"Close enough. When spring comes, you're going to the capital to make your case. I've never had a gift for diplomacy. Maybe you'll have better luck."

If the commander was counting on Axel persuading anyone, the North was doomed.

CHAPTER 10

Otto stared out the arrow slit as snow fell from the leaden sky. He'd been overly optimistic in his hope for a full month before winter arrived in force. After his initial visit with Lord Karonin, he'd managed another two trips out to the tower. His journal held only fifty pages copied from the spell book, far less than the hundred he'd planned.

On the positive side, he found he understood most of what he'd read so far and he'd worked a fourth thread into his practice sessions. He couldn't maintain it for more than a few seconds, but he'd done it. Unfortunately, he couldn't cast any of the offensive spells he'd discovered for fear of the noise drawing unwanted attention.

Worst of all, Griswalda spent most of every day moaning and writhing in her bed. Despite the midwife's best efforts to comfort her, the woman found no peace. It wasn't so bad when he went to the basement with Master Enoch, but when night rolled around the noise made it almost impossible to sleep. Stephan had abandoned his bedroom and moved into the hall, sleeping in front of the hearth with the hounds. To say this did little to improve his brother's mood would be an understatement.

The malformed child growing in Griswalda's womb had to be the problem. At this point he didn't believe it would survive to be born. On a practical level he wanted to suggest she drink the tea that purged unwanted pregnancies, but he knew how badly she wanted a daughter. A practical suggestion wouldn't receive a happy welcome no matter how well intended.

A faint moan reached him even this far from the living areas. He sighed and pushed away from the wall. It was going to be a long winter if this kept up.

The halls were quiet as Otto made his way to the basement entrance. A few hours of peace and quiet would steady his nerves. Master Enoch had been helping him with physical enhancements. Infusing his body with etheric energy allowed for an increase in both strength and toughness. It made for a nice change of pace, being strong, even if for only five minutes at a time.

On his way to the door he swung by the kitchen. They had a bent spit that needed straightening and he meant to do it bare-handed. If his magic made him strong enough to bend iron that would be quite a thing. He found the spit leaning against the outside wall and grabbed it.

He snuck away from the kitchen unnoticed and made his way to the basement door. At the bottom of the steps he found Claud dining on a fat fly. He nodded to the spider and continued on to the workshop. Master Enoch had his beakers set up and a small etheric fire burning under one bubbling flask. Enoch hadn't done much alchemy since his arrival, though Otto had seen some formulas in his books when he paged through them.

"Master?"

Enoch's head snapped up. So focused had he been on his work that the wizard apparently hadn't heard Otto enter.

"Lord Shenk. Forgive me, I was distracted."

"So I see. What are you brewing?"

"A sleeping draft for Lady Griswalda." Enoch adjusted the flow of ether to the fire, lowering its heat.

"She asked you for it?"

"No, my lord, your father did. He said he needed a night of peace before he went mad. I suggested the sleeping potion for him, but he said he wasn't downing any magical slime."

"That sounds like Father. How does he plan to convince the mother-to-be to drink it?"

"He said she'd drink it or he'd pour it down her throat and pinch her nose shut until she swallowed. Do you mind practicing on your own? I have another hour before it'll be ready."

"Certainly. I have an experiment I want to try."

Otto put Master Enoch out of his mind and focused. He sent two threads into his chest, weaving the energy through muscle and bone. Like the first time and every time since, the power sent a thrill through him, like lightning in his blood. Another thread went into each arm, enhancing them as well.

The first time he'd cast the spell he'd only used it on his arms. Master Enoch had quickly stopped him, explaining that if he strengthened his limbs and not his core he'd likely hurt himself.

When his entire upper body pulsed with energy Otto picked up the bent spit and pulled. The iron protested, but slowly yielded to his efforts. In two minutes, he'd straightened it enough that the forge master would only need to make a few minor adjustments to get it back in service.

He'd never bothered to ask Cook how it had gotten bent in

the first place. Otto suspected the fat tyrant had thrown one of his tantrums and slammed it into the wall. Lucky for him he served the finest food in the kingdom since his personality left much to be desired.

Otto released the spell and grimaced at the sense of weakness that followed as surely as night followed day. The problem didn't come solely from the lack of enhancement. Directing the magic inward sapped him faster than when he sent the power outward. This made no sense to Otto and when he'd asked for an explanation Master Enoch had shrugged and said it just worked that way. If there was rhyme or reason behind it he didn't know the secret.

The worst of the aftereffects of the spell had passed when Master Enoch said, "Done. Would you hold the silver flask for me, Lord Shenk?"

Otto took a step toward the flask then realized if he held it by hand the near-boiling liquid would burn him. Lately Master Enoch had been giving him little tests like this to see if he was paying close attention to the task given.

The first couple instances had annoyed him, but as time went on, he realized his master was simply trying to teach him to think through the consequences of his actions. That was an important skill for a wizard and showed his mentor took him more seriously.

Otto wove three threads into a tendril ending in a pincer which he used to hold the flask upright and steady. His master smiled and wove a similar construct to grasp the beaker and pour the steaming liquid into the flask.

"There. I'd best take this to your father." His master's voice held a slight tremor.

"Want me to tag along?"

Enoch's sigh of relief brought a smile to Otto's face. "If you wouldn't mind, my lord."

○

A shrill, piercing scream woke Otto from the first peaceful night's sleep he'd had in weeks. What in the world had happened now? Master Enoch's potion should have kept Griswalda quiet through the night. While he didn't know the time, Otto doubted morning had come yet.

Let Stephan deal with it. She was his wife after all. Otto threw an arm over his eyes and tried to get back to sleep.

Another, longer scream thwarted the effort. He groaned and rolled out of bed. Clearly he would sleep no more tonight. Otto dressed by a conjured light and stepped out into the hall in time to see his brother thunder out of his room and down the stairs.

Now what was that about? Otto shrugged and hurried down to the open door. He poked his head in and found his mother sitting beside Griswalda, holding her hand and making soothing, nonsense sounds.

When she looked his way, Otto raised an eyebrow. Mother patted the distraught woman's hand once more then came to join him.

"She miscarried," Mother whispered.

Otto grimaced, but the news didn't surprise him. He'd known the child wasn't viable the moment he felt it in the ether.

"She blamed the potion your teacher prepared. Stephan has gone to extract vengeance from his hide."

"Damn it! Father made him prepare the sleeping potion and we both know it had nothing to do with the miscarriage."

"Yes, well, I doubt your brother would listen to reason if we explained." Mother glanced back over her shoulder at the now-quiet Griswalda. "What will the wizard do if he's attacked?"

That was a good question and it worried Otto that he didn't know the answer. "It won't come to that. I'll stop Stephan."

He couldn't restrain a smile at his mother's incredulous stare. He deserved it. If he'd announced a plan to swim across the ocean to the western continent it wouldn't have sounded any less likely.

"Don't worry, Mother. I've learned a few tricks since the last time Stephan decided to use me for a punching bag. It won't go the same way this time."

"Be careful." She kissed him on the cheek. "You know how your brother gets when he's in a rage."

Otto nodded and took his leave. He knew exactly how Stephan got. Their last encounter had left Otto in bed for three weeks and limping for two more. He also knew that if Master Enoch's life was on the line, he could kill Stephan with no trouble at all.

Whether he could kill all of Father's soldiers or not Otto didn't know. Either way it would make life hard for all wizards the kingdom over and it wouldn't bring his brother back to life. But whatever it took, Otto had to stop Stephan.

A pair of servants in their nightgowns had made their trembling way into the halls, no doubt the screams had woken them the same as they had everyone else. Otto had no time to reassure or explain. He brushed past them, ignoring their wide, frightened eyes.

When he reached the door to the basement workshop loud crashes filled the air and the door hung on one hinge. He took the stairs two at a time, sending etheric energy to his muscles.

At the bottom he found Stephan kicking the door to Master

Enoch's workshop. Threads of ether reinforced the wood and iron, keeping his brother from doing any harm. Given enough time though, Stephan would wear Enoch down.

"Enough, brother!"

Stephan spun. His face burned red and his lips were drawn back in a mad snarl.

"Stay back, runt! I'm going to kill your wizard like he did my daughter."

Stephan kicked the door again.

"It wasn't his fault, Stephan. The girl was never going to survive. I saw it when I determined her sex. Master Enoch just did what Father ordered."

His brother turned to face him once more, slowly this time. After several panting breaths he said, "You knew and yet said nothing?"

"What would it have mattered? Nothing could change the child's fate and if I'd made a mistake so much the better. It's no one's fault, Stephan. Sometimes children just die."

Stephan's fist came so fast Otto didn't have time to react.

He staggered back a step as blood from his split lip filled Otto's mouth.

"You should have told me!"

When the second blow came, Otto was ready. He caught Stephan's fist in his enhanced grasp and squeezed. The bones ground together, drawing a pained hiss from his brother.

"Maybe you're right. Maybe I should have told you. But it changes nothing tonight. Past is past. Go to your wife and leave Master Enoch in peace."

Otto released him and Stephan took a step back, shaking his hand.

"You're right, past is past. Unfortunately, my sow of a wife will give me no peace unless I bring her the wizard's head.

She's convinced it's his fault. Now get lost before I decide one wizard's head will serve as well as another."

Stephan turned his attention back to the sealed door, prompting a shake of Otto's head. He released his physical enhancements and flicked his ring. An etheric thread shot into Stephan, binding him in place.

"I'm sorry, brother, but I can't let you kill an innocent man. Master Enoch, open the door please."

The etheric threads reinforcing the door vanished and it opened enough to reveal his master's face. The skin above his beard had gone pale and sweat dripped down his beard.

"It's okay, Master. He's bound."

"What have you done, Lord Shenk?" Enoch's voice held an uncertain quaver.

"What I had to. Do you have any coin?"

"I have everything your father's ever paid me. All my needs are provided for after all. Why?"

"I fear you won't be able to live here anymore." Otto glanced at his brother whose face had grown redder as he strained against the spell. "I'm sorry."

Master Enoch waved his hand. "These have been good years, my lord. I am grateful and sorry for any trouble I've caused."

"And I appreciate all you've taught me. Hurry, now. I doubt Father will rouse the garrison, but I'm not certain."

"Yes, yes." Master Enoch ducked back into his room and the sound of rustling came to Otto.

Two minutes later Enoch emerged with a large carryall over his shoulder, a walking stick in one hand and his books in the other. He held the books out to Otto.

"Take these. I have them mostly memorized anyway."

Otto hesitated then accepted the books. "Thank you."

Enoch nodded. "I'll send you a message through the ether when I'm well away. Goodbye, my lord."

"Goodbye, Master."

Enoch rushed up the steps and out of sight. Otto listened for sounds of combat, but heard only silence. He had no idea how long it might take for his former master to escape the castle, so Otto went into the workshop and fetched the rickety stool. He sat facing his silently fuming brother.

Half an hour later a ripple ran through the ether around him. It was no natural phenomenon, so he assumed it came from Enoch. He should have a good enough lead by now. Otto stood, enhanced his strength as much as possible, and released Stephan.

His older brother slumped for a moment then rubbed his stiff legs. When he met Otto's gaze his eyes held nothing but hate.

"I will find him, runt. If I have to hunt every square inch of the kingdom, I *will* find him."

"No, Stephan. You'll never find a wizard that doesn't wish to be found. Let it go, for everyone's sake."

"Do not underestimate my determination." Stephan stomped up the stairs bellowing for the garrison to assemble.

Perhaps his brother would catch up to Enoch in some distant, lonely glade with no witnesses. Should that happen, he doubted he'd see Stephan again.

CHAPTER 11

The long, bitter winter came to an end and none too soon for Otto. He strode through the castle gate and out into the clean, fresh air. Down in Castle Town people had their doors open, airing out their houses, and sweeping up the dirt that had collected over the winter. People paused to bow as he passed and Otto gave a nod in return.

He didn't offer to stop or talk however. He'd mastered six threads practicing on his own over the winter, but he needed to talk to Lord Karonin. After reading everything he'd copied as well as everything in Enoch's books, he had many questions.

Getting out of the castle and away from his lunatic brother would be a welcome respite as well. Every clear day for the first month Stephan had ridden out to search for Enoch. Sometimes he'd take a patrol, other times he went alone. The snow and cold conspired against him, seldom allowing the search parties to travel more than a few miles before the snow reached the bellies of their mounts.

Eventually, Father had wearied of Stephan's foolishness and

ordered him to end the search until spring. Otto had hoped his brother's anger would cool over the frigid months, but if anything, the time he spent cooped up with Griswalda whispering in his ear made his madness worse.

Otto took comfort in the idea that Enoch had a good six-month head start. The snow would have been no barrier to a wizard. With any luck he'd reached a fair-sized city far from Shenk Barony and found himself a new position.

When the town had disappeared from view, Otto stepped off the road and turned toward the forest. The evergreens had survived the winter with minimal damage. New branches littered the ground, but none of the trunks had fallen. The walking was easy and invigorating. Soon he stood before the barrier that protected the tower. From the look of it, the enchanted jack pine had suffered not so much as a needle out of place.

A quick shot of ether and the branches opened for him. He rushed up the stairs to the second floor where Lord Karonin's face waited in the mirror.

Otto bowed to the Arcane Lord. "Master. I hope the winter didn't pass too slowly for you."

She laughed, a chill humorless sound that sent needles dancing up his spine. "I have dwelled alone in the netherworld for centuries. A few months is nothing."

Otto cocked his head. "Are the other Arcane Lords not there with you? Surely there are spirits you can chat with."

"Your ignorance is amusing. Most spirits that dwell here are mindless things incapable of rational thought. As for the others, I'm sure they're here somewhere, but I can't go looking for them."

"Why?"

"This mirror serves as both an anchor and a window into the realm of the living. My spirit is bound to this location. The only way I could leave this spot is to sever the anchor and if I did that, I'd no longer be able to use my window."

He marveled that someone so powerful and immortal would even consider the possibility that they might die. "Did you suspect Valtan's betrayal?"

"No." She spat the word with more disgust than he'd ever heard. "I believed him as devoted to our group as I. The Soul Mirror's original purpose was to house my spirit in the eventuality that my body was destroyed. As an immortal being, my physical form would have eventually regenerated and I'd have been free to inhabit it once more. The one possibility I hadn't considered was being forcibly shifted, body and soul, to the netherworld."

"If your body remained intact when it shifted, why do you not still have it?"

"The netherworld is a realm of the spirit. Nothing physical exists here. I became disembodied in the moment of transfer. The pig Valtan did his work well. No other course could have so completely removed us from this reality."

"Amazing. Is there any way to bring you back?"

"No. My body is gone and my spirit would be unable to affect anything, even if a path existed to bring it to the mortal world. Worst of all, as a wraith I wouldn't be able to touch the ether. As things stand now at least I can see it and even control it in the vicinity of my tower, but nothing more. You can't imagine the frustration for a wizard to be unable to weave spells."

Otto tried to imagine never feeling the Bliss again and his whole being rebelled at the idea. Nothing in the world could be worse than to remember the magic but be unable to still use it.

"I'm so sorry, Master."

"Save your pity! I need it not. You have questions? Ask them."

Otto did as she bid and in exchange received a wealth of information. For several hours they discussed magic. Spells and theory, ideas simple and so complex he barely fathomed them, no subject was off limits. Lord Karonin seemed to take some pleasure in at least being able to discuss magic.

Or perhaps his company eased her loneliness. Not that he'd ask. She seemed overly sensitive about anything that spoke of weakness on her part. He'd take what she offered and if he made her feel less alone so much the better. He could conceive of no fate worse than the one inflicted on her. Valtan must have truly hated his former allies.

When he at last reached his capacity for new information Otto said, "One last question, Master, before I take my leave. Is it truly possible to form the ether into shapes other than threads?"

"Of course it is. The ether is nothing but an energy field that responds to our will. Threads are versatile and an easy way to inject energy into people and objects, thus making them the first sort of spell taught to new students. That said, they are hardly the be-all and end-all of magic. Take one of the most common offensive spells, Fireball. You are familiar with it?"

"I've heard of it, certainly."

"The spell is created when you form a sphere of ether and fill it with fire magic. The strength and diameter of the sphere determines how much energy your spell has. You should practice it without letting the spell detonate."

"How do I do that?" Practicing fireballs inside the castle struck him as a dangerous idea.

"I keep forgetting how little you know. You can pull the energy out of your spell by reversing the flow. As long as you take your time the danger is minimal."

Minimal, well, that was a relief.

CHAPTER 12

Otto returned to the castle, his mind spinning with the knowledge Lord Karonin had shared. They'd spent so much time talking he hadn't gotten around to copying a portion of her spell book. Drunk on secrets, he almost walked right past the black-and-white piebald mare tied to the post outside the stable. It wasn't one of theirs. Shenk horses were all brown. Who would have braved the sketchy roads this early in the spring?

He shoved the keep door open and marched into the great hall. Father and Mother sat chatting with a pudgy, balding man in mud-spattered wool pants and a black tunic. He carried no weapon and Otto hadn't seen one in his gear outside. Traveling alone with no weapon, the man was either very brave or very stupid.

His attention shifted to his parents. They were both dressed in their finest clothes, silks and lace for Mother, black leather with brass accents for Father. How did this man convince his normally indifferent father to dress up? Usually nothing less than a duke would garner such treatment.

"Otto, come here." Father waved him up to the main table to join the group.

He felt out of place with his hiking clothes on, but he didn't dare ignore his father. He nodded to the stranger, kissed his mother on the cheek and sat beside her.

"Son, this is Mr. Cotton. He came to visit us last fall. Do you remember?" The way Father looked at him told him to say yes.

"Of course. Nice to have you back, sir."

"Thank you, my lord," Mr. Cotton said. "And please, call me Alaric."

"Alaric is the representative of Master Merchant Edwyn Franken. During his visit last fall we discussed a potential deal and his employer is so eager to proceed he sent Alaric as soon as the roads cleared."

"I see," Otto said, not really seeing at all. "If there's nothing else I should go clean up."

"Good idea," Father said. "When you're finished, pack your things. We're going to the capital in the morning."

Dumbstruck, Otto could only blink and stare at his father. He must have misunderstood. "Why are we going to the capital?"

"So Master Franken and I can conclude our negotiations face to face. Assuming we come to an equitable arrangement, you'll be marrying his daughter within the month."

If his father had possessed a sense of humor, Otto would have assumed he was joking. Granted, as the son of a noble he'd always known his future, as far as wife and family went, would be out of his control, but he'd always assumed he'd at least get a bit of a warning before Father simply made the announcement.

Unable to summon a coherent reply Otto nodded and half

walked, half stumbled toward the stairs. At that moment you could have knocked him over with a feather. He'd never given women much thought; his first and only true love was magic. Oh, he'd tumbled one of the serving girls in the town tavern a time or two, but that was just a way to pass a Sunday afternoon before he found the hidden tower.

Good heavens, Lord Karonin!

He'd have to find a moment to sneak out and tell her what had happened. If Father meant to marry him off to some merchant's daughter, he'd be away from the castle for at least a month, and likely longer. It wasn't like the Arcane Lord could run away on him, but since she'd been generous enough to share her knowledge, Otto felt he should at least tell her he'd be away for a time.

When, was the tricky part. In an hour or two night would fall and if Father intended to leave at dawn there'd be no chance in the morning.

He slammed his door behind him, only vaguely aware of the action. He threw his dirty clothes in a pile for the servants and pulled clean ones out of his drawers and dressed. His parents had bought him a travel trunk for his birthday six years ago, why he had no idea as they seldom went anywhere. The bulky black thing had been stuck under his bed for the past six years and however many days collecting dust.

He dragged it out and opened it. It wouldn't take long to pack as he only had four changes of clothes and two pairs of boots. Even if he packed everything he owned, including his books, he'd still have space to spare.

The last tunic went in and he shut the lid. That was that. He sat on the bed and sighed.

Someone knocked on his door and a moment later it opened. Mother poked her head in. "Want to talk?"

Otto shrugged and she came in, closing the door behind her. Mother settled on the bed beside him.

"Have you met her?" Otto asked.

"No, neither has your father, though Alaric has assured us she's very beautiful."

Otto snorted a laugh. "He's selling her. Probably best to take his words with a grain of salt."

"Given the dowry on offer I doubt Arnwolf cares. He'd marry you off to Master Franken's long-dead grandmother for ten thousand double eagles."

Otto found himself struck dumb for the second time in an hour. A single double eagle held enough gold to pay a good soldier's wages for two years. Ten thousand constituted a fortune beyond imagining.

"Where did Father find someone foolish enough to pay that much to marry his daughter off to me?"

"He didn't. Alaric rode up to the castle last fall and made the offer. He'd made it at four other noble houses and they turned him down flat. No one wanted to marry a son off to a commoner, not even for a fortune that vast. Of course, the houses he visited before us only had first sons."

"Ah, lucky Father had a third sitting around waiting to be sold. What does the merchant get out of it? If he's that rich he's obviously not looking for wealth."

Mother's laugh resembled more of a satisfied purr. "Master Franken wants the one thing a commoner can't simply buy, no matter how rich: a lordship. By marrying his daughter into a noble family, he earns the right to be called Lord Franken. He still can't own land or collect taxes, but his grandsons will have that right."

"What do you think of Father's deal?"

She took his hand and squeezed it. "It's a good bargain. We

need the gold and as a third son you'll never have a better prospect. He didn't even care that you were a wizard."

"Generous of him. Very well, Mother. I'll make the best of it. I suppose you need to go pack as well."

"I won't be joining you. Though I regret missing your wedding, someone has to stay here and keep Stephan from running the barony into the ground." She looked into his eyes and smiled. "I can't believe when next I see you, you'll be a married man. My little boy's all grown up."

Otto found sleep impossible after his father's revelation, so he settled in to read. Night had fallen hours ago and no opportunity to slip out had presented itself. Everyone had been in good spirits during dinner, even Stephan. No doubt the fact that his future treasury would soon expand by a large margin had improved his sour mood.

For his part, Otto had sat quietly, nibbling at his food and listening to the happy, indifferent people discussing his marriage like he wasn't even there. The meal had ended, mercifully, after an hour and Alaric excused himself to rejoin his guards at the town inn. The fact that he traveled with six mercenaries raised Otto's opinion of his intelligence several points.

Father had proceeded to order everyone to bed as they had an early morning ahead of them. He'd been only too happy to escape the table. Though he'd made his peace with marrying a woman he'd never met, Otto still didn't fully understand what his future held. If Father had more plans for him, he kept them to himself.

Otto turned the page and stared. It held a spell that

74

allowed you to extend your senses through the ether. He vaguely remembered it from his first reading of the book, but the details escaped him. If he extended his hearing and voice, he could talk to Lord Karonin without leaving the castle.

He read the page, then read it again, and a third time before he felt confident enough to attempt the spell. It took three threads per sense, so he had just enough power to do what he needed. First, he connected a trio of threads to his eyes and closed his lids. He saw his room as clearly as before and the ether looked even brighter.

Now the tricky part. He willed his senses outward toward the wall. It appeared to get closer followed by a moment of blindness when he passed through the stone.

His heart raced as he had the sense of floating in midair. It passed soon after as his rational mind remembered he was lying in his bed safe and sound. Since he was now literally connected to the ether it took little effort to follow the currents to the hidden tower.

As he drew closer the view grew hazy. Otto added another thread to the link and his vision stabilized. Apparently, he'd reached the outer range of that many threads.

He continued on, adding a fifth thread before he finally slipped through the wall of the tower. Lord Karonin's face appeared at once and her lips moved. Otto cursed his limited power and left a single thread to mark the location before returning sight to his physical eyes and switching the link to his throat.

Quick as thought he returned to the end of the guide thread. "Lord Karonin, I can only extend one part of my body at a time so I'm afraid I can't hear you. I will be leaving tomorrow and fear I may be gone for some time. It seems I'm to be married. As soon as I can, I'll return. I apologize for leaving you alone again."

Nothing remained to be said so he let all the threads dissolve and returned his full awareness to his body. Using that many threads for an extended time left him exhausted and he soon fell into a deep sleep.

CHAPTER 13

The clamor of something heavy pounding on his door dragged Otto back to the waking world. A faint glow came from hall. He groaned and rubbed the sleep from his eyes. He hadn't slept nearly long enough.

"Get up, Otto!" His father bellowed through the door. "We're burning daylight."

"I'm up. Give me ten minutes to dress and I'll be down."

"You have five." Father stomped away, taking his meager light with him.

Otto wanted to ask if they intended to leave without him, but discretion proved the better part of valor. More likely Father would drag him out to the horses with his night clothes on. That was an indignity he'd as soon avoid.

A light blossomed at his will and Otto rolled out of bed. He had his clothes ready from the night before, so he only needed to throw them on. He pulled his door open with seconds to spare and dragged his trunk down the hall to the stairs. Father and ten members of the garrison stood waiting in the great hall along with Mother and Stephan.

Griswalda hadn't bothered to stir herself, which suited Otto fine. The woman had never liked him and after the miscarriage her dislike turned to open hate. Otto had been thrilled when he found a spell that allowed him to check his food for poison.

"Finally," Father said. He had his heavy cloak on already and the moment Otto reached the bottom step he turned for the door, his men falling in behind him.

"Good luck, dear," Mother called as he joined his father.

Otto waved and followed along out into the yard. Not the merriest of sendoffs, but it could have been worse. Breakfast would have been nice, but he'd missed meals before.

Outside the servants worked at hooking the sixth horse to the family carriage. Otto stopped in his tracks. They hadn't used the carriage in years. Was the creaky piece of junk even fit for travel, especially over the spring roads? Father must really want to make an impression. He hated the thing.

A servant hurried over and relieved him of his trunk while Sergeant Graves and his men mounted the nearby horses. Father climbed up into the carriage and Otto had no choice but to join him. He suppressed a grimace as he settled into the hard seat. A week cooped up in a tiny space with his father. Certainly nothing could go wrong in that scenario.

Father stuck his head out the window. "Let's go!"

Reins snapped, tack jingled, the carriage lurched, and they were on their way. Otto and his father stared at each other, neither willing to break the silence.

Two agonizing minutes later and they stopped again, this time in front of the town's only inn. Alaric and his mercenaries waited out front beside their horses. The guards sported scars and stubble in equal measure. Fortunately, their swords and mail appeared well cared for. All the mercenaries that had ever passed through the barony held identical priorities: weapons and armor ahead of personal hygiene.

The pudgy agent mounted up and his men followed suit. He guided his mount over beside the carriage. "Morning, Lord Shenk. Are we ready to go?"

"We are. Your men will ride point, mine will follow and surround the carriage."

"Do you expect trouble, my lord? I assure you our trip here was perfectly safe."

"I always expect trouble." Father leaned out the window. "Let's be on our way."

The carriage rattled and lurched, then they took off. Otto held in a sigh and dug a book out of his trunk. At least the trip wouldn't be a total waste of time. He'd only read Enoch's three spell books once. A second look might reveal new insights, like the spell he discovered last night.

Three hours later Otto gave up and shut the book. The bouncing, rattling, and creaking made it impossible to focus. He'd just have to enjoy the scenery and try to read when they stopped for the night.

"Where's your sword?" Father asked.

"In the armory where it belongs."

"A nobleman shouldn't be out without a weapon."

If Otto's life were ever truly in danger a sword would only make it harder for him to run away. He doubted Father would appreciate that argument.

"If I understand the law correctly," Otto said. "Any nobleman wearing a sword can be challenged to a duel by another nobleman. Me wearing a sword is just asking for trouble."

"My son the coward." Father shook his head. "How can you

be so different from your brothers? Neither Stephan nor Axel would dream of leaving the castle without a blade."

"Axel's a soldier and Stephan's a lunatic. I'm a wizard and more than capable of protecting myself should it become necessary. If I were you, I'd worry more about what Stephan's going to do to the barony after you're gone."

Father sat back and closed his eyes for a moment. "Your brother will hardly be the worst man to rule Shenk Barony. If the people survived Mad Ulick, they'll survive Stephan."

"Mad Ulick tortured and burned innocent people alive for entertainment. You're not setting a very high bar for Stephan."

"I fear it's the only bar he can clear."

Half a day out from the castle and he and Father had already found something to agree on. They were off to a more auspicious start than Otto dared hope.

⟳

Three days from home and Otto's father hadn't tried to strangle him yet. By that measure things had proceeded better than he'd feared. By silent agreement they made no further mention of swords or Stephan. In fact, they seldom shared more than ten words from sunup to sundown.

The carriage made so much noise that after his first attempt at conversation Alaric had given up, instead urging his mount forward to ride with his men. Otto wanted badly to reach the capital if only to escape his wretched conveyance. He hoped at some point to discover the secret to flight. Anything would be better than riding over these roads.

As if to mock him the carriage went through a particularly deep hole and bounced Otto a foot off his seat. He brushed the curtain aside and looked out. Nothing but mud, dead grass, and a stand of evergreens. At least the sun had finally burned through the clouds.

A flash caught his eye and he squinted, trying to get a better look. He shaded his eyes to cut the glare, but still made out little beyond the shadows of the trees.

When a second flash appeared Otto said, "Something's out there. At the tree line."

"It's just your imagination." Father didn't even bother opening his eyes.

"It's not. I'm telling you there's something shining out there."

Father grunted, leaned forward, and brushed the curtain on his side back. "Where?"

"Just inside the tree line, it keeps moving." A third flash, this time a little way ahead of them. "Did you see it?"

An arrow thunked into the side of the carriage.

Screams from both men and horses came from the front of the column.

"Ambush!" Sergeant Graves shouted.

More arrows rained down on the carriage roof, the steel heads poking through into the cabin. Horses screamed and the carriage slewed left.

It tipped, and Otto had just time enough to brace himself before it rolled over on its side.

Father reached for the door just as three more arrows slammed into it. "We have to get out of here. Graves!"

No reply from the veteran. Otto hoped he was okay. Despite the misery he'd inflicted, Otto wished the sergeant no harm.

"Where is everyone?" Father asked.

"Probably looking for cover. I can get us out of here if you'll allow the magic."

The muscle in Father's jaw bunched, but he nodded.

Otto turned his attention to the roof of the now-flipped-over carriage and tried to ignore the arrows raining down on them. He wove six threads together and set them spinning. When the etheric construct touched the roof, it sliced through the wood like nothing. Seconds later a three-foot-diameter disk fell on the ground.

He darted through and his father joined him a moment later. Graves lay behind a horse that resembled a pincushion. The sergeant noticed them and waved.

Father motioned him over, but a fresh volley of arrows clattered down. Otto shifted his construct into a pair of tentacles and set them to waving in the air along the path Graves would have to take to reach them.

"Come on, Sergeant," Otto said.

Graves looked at him, tensed, and broke cover. Three arrows streaked in, but the tentacles smashed them aside. Graves slid to a stop beside them and Otto ended his spell and gasped for breath. Six threads still took it out of him.

"Report," Father said.

"I make at least twenty men in the trees. No idea on the condition of our people or the mercenaries."

Father snarled and reached for the hilt of his sword like he planned to go out there to kill them all on his own.

"I'll check for survivors." Otto closed his eyes and looked through the ether.

He extended his sight toward the rear where their men were positioned. Six survivors huddled behind their dead mounts. Next he went forward. The mercenaries all lay dead, pierced through by multiple arrows. Alaric still breathed, but his horse had crushed his left leg and the shaft of an arrow protruded from his right shoulder.

When Otto finished relaying this his father asked, "And the enemy?"

Otto sent his sight racing across the field. Sixteen men and three women stood amid the trees. They wore a motley collection of skins and rusty armor. Thirteen carried longbows and they'd send an occasional arrow at the trapped men, but with no clear targets they seemed content to hold their fire.

"Bloody bandits," Graves said. "I wonder if they know who they've attacked."

"After this winter I doubt they care." Otto ended his spell and looked to his father. "It's a standoff. What are we going to do?"

"Not much we can do for now. We're safe from their arrows so it's only a matter of time before they close in to finish us off."

"We'll make the bastards bleed, my lord," Graves said.

"We're outnumbered two to one and I can't tell for sure if any of the others are injured. I know it's against the law, but a little offensive magic might make the difference."

Father gave him a speculative look. "What did you have in mind?"

"A fireball. When they're halfway across the field I'll throw one in the center of the group. The shock will disorient them and the soldiers can attack."

"You can do that?" He understood Father's doubt considering the piddling spells he'd demonstrated over the years.

"It was the last thing Enoch taught me before Stephan chased him off."

"We can use every advantage, my lord," Graves said.

Otto nodded his appreciation for the backup.

Finally, Father said, "Very well, but we need some way to tell the survivors what we intend."

"I'll take care of it." Otto adjusted his thread to connect his voice to the ether.

To the men it would have sounded like the wind whispering in their ears. Since they all knew he was a wizard hopefully they wouldn't think they'd imagined his voice. When the fireball detonated, they needed to be ready.

CHAPTER 14

I t felt strange, shaping the ether into something other than a thread. Aside from the mental challenge, making an etheric sphere didn't take any more effort than forming a thread. Otto had made seven of them while they waited for the bandits to work up the nerve to attack. It took him less than a second now but filling it with power would be another test altogether and he'd only have a single chance to get it right. Failure probably meant death for them all.

So, no pressure.

Graves crouched at the edge of the carriage to watch the enemy. He hadn't flinched since Father gave him the assignment and Otto doubted he'd move for anything less than an arrow through his eye.

"They broke cover, Lord Shenk." Graves ducked back down.

Otto formed his sphere and rubbed his fingers together. When the heat had built he sent two threads to carry the fire into the sphere. The moment he did an orange ball appeared before him.

Father hissed and moved a few feet away. Otto ignored him and kept pouring power into the sphere. The glow went from orange to blue, causing the binding to shiver. He dared not infuse any more power.

"Say when, Graves." It took all Otto's focus to hold the spell together.

The sergeant resumed his position. "They're in the field, thirty more yards. Twenty. Ten. Now, Lord Shenk!"

Otto popped up and sent a targeting thread out into the center of the ragged collection of humanity. The fireball raced along and, in the blink of an eye, struck.

The explosion stunned him and the flames made Otto's eyes water. The three closest bandits went flying in pieces. Those further away were blown off their feet. At the outer edge a handful of bandits remained standing, though all they seemed capable of was staggering around and staring.

Graves leapt to his feet. "For the baron and Garenland! Charge!"

He raced out toward the field. The other men joined him a moment later. Father gave Otto one last look, drew his sword, and marched toward the enemy.

To call what ensued a fight would be overly generous. A slaughter was more like it. The bandits were so stunned by the blast most never even raised a rusted sword in their own defense. The soldiers had the day won before Father even reached them.

No wonder offensive magic was illegal. If a rank beginner like Otto could do something like this, what might the masters of old have been capable of? If Lord Karonin possessed the power to wield a hundred threads at once even an army would pose no threat to her.

With the field secure, Otto left his hiding place and

marched out to join the others near the edge of the road. As he walked past the line of soldiers, each of them touched fist to heart and murmured, "Lord Shenk."

No sign remained of the condescension that tinged their words in the past. Pity for his lack of sword skill vanished, replaced by respect mingled with no little fear. Otto found the change suited him a great deal.

He stopped beside his father and Graves. "Now what?"

"The nearest village is half a day further down the road," Graves said. "There are six missing horses, but the rest are either dead or too injured to ride."

"Alaric is alive, but in bad shape," Otto said. "He couldn't ride a horse if we had one to spare."

Father stroked his beard for a moment. "What about the carriage?"

Otto shrugged.

"No idea, my lord," Graves said.

"Hmm. Graves, take three men and examine the carriage. I'll check on Alaric while the others find the horses."

"I can find the horses, Father. You'll need help to get the dead horse off Alaric's leg. Once I locate them, I'll mark their location."

"Good enough." Father marched off toward the downed merchant, three men falling in beside him.

Graves took his allotment and went to try and learn how to repair a carriage. Otto stayed behind and closed his eyes. He sent his sight flying out through the ether. A bird's eye view should give him the best chance of locating the horses and sure enough a mile west of their position he found them cropping grass at the edge of the road. To his relief, none bore wounds.

He tagged one of them with a thread and returned his sight to his body. He had about as much skill with horses as he did with swords, so trying to herd the beasts back on his own would be a waste of time.

Otto walked over to join his father who stood watching the soldiers attempt to heave the dead horse off the moaning Alaric. They'd shifted it some, but not enough to free the unfortunate man's leg.

"I found the horses."

"Where?"

The soldiers grunted and strained to limited effect. They slumped to the ground, exhausted by their effort.

"About a mile back the way we came. None of them appear injured. Do you need a hand with this?"

Father flicked a look at him. "Shifting heavy loads isn't your strong suit."

Otto's lips twisted and he bit back a retort. "I thought perhaps I might lighten the load."

"If you think you can do something useful, go ahead."

He motioned the soldiers aside and they scrambled to move out of his way. He sent a thread through the horse, surrounding Alaric's pinned leg. With that as a reference, Otto wove three more threads into a whip and slashed it through the dead horse six inches from Alaric's foot. A second slash removed three-quarters of the remaining haunch.

Otto let the spell dissolve and tossed the last bit of horse flesh aside revealing the twisted, broken leg trapped underneath. He turned back to his father.

"There you are. Healing the unfortunate gentleman is beyond my current skill."

"Many thanks, Lord Shenk." Alaric's still-pained voice held a note of relief. No doubt getting half a ton of dead horse off your broken leg did wonders for your outlook.

The men stared at the dismembered horse. It must be

disconcerting to watch an invisible force slice up an animal like it was soft butter. Otto found it a little nauseating and he controlled the magic doing it. Combined with the exhaustion of using so much magic all at once, Otto badly wanted to sit down.

Graves ran up, breaking the moment. "Lord Shenk, the carriage appears road worthy if not fully intact. Assuming we can roll it off its side and recover horses enough to pull it, it should get us to the village."

"Good," Father said. "I don't want to spend the night out here, so you'd best get started."

CHAPTER 15

A battered, bruised, and weary group reached the outskirts of the capital three days behind schedule. Otto gaped like a country bumpkin from his seat on the carriage bench. He'd been forced outside to make room for the injured Alaric.

Ahead of them, the city of Garen sprawled over several square miles. Even from half a mile away the crash and clatter of the many forges reached them. No wonder it was nicknamed the City of Steel. With the noise came the smoke and stink of coal. Otto's eyes watered and his lungs burned. How did people stand living here?

Three walls divided it into concentric circles with the royal palace in the center, the wealthy and upper-middle class in the second ring, and everyone else, along with the business district, in the outer ring. A haze of smoke hung over the poor part of the city but didn't extend into the interior.

Otto blinked and focused on the ether. A wall of etheric energy swirled around the inner wards. That explained why the smoke stayed out. He tried to imagine how such a casting worked, but the power involved overwhelmed him. Given that this had once been her imperial capital, he suspected Lord Karonin had handled the spell.

And speaking of overwhelming power, a mass of swirling energy surrounded the Great Portal. Even from a distance, the power vibrated in his bones. The portal consisted of a semicircle of silver metal twenty feet high and thirty feet across. Every once in a while, it flashed and the ether straightened as someone passed through. Despite his limited experience, Otto doubted he'd ever see a working of magic to equal it.

Beside him, Graves flicked the reins and sent the carriage rattling on its way. The right front wheel wobbled and Otto expected it to fall off at any moment. Of course, he'd been thinking that for the past four days and it hadn't given up yet. Father was going to have to spend a couple of his new double eagles on a new transport before they went home.

On the carriage roof, the surviving soldiers rode with their feet dangling over the sides. If they had any complaints about traveling like luggage one look at his father's scowling face convinced them to keep their peace.

"Have you been to the capital before, Graves?"

"Once, my lord. I came with your father to a gathering of nobles when the last king died. It's quite a place. They say you can buy anything in Garen, assuming you have the coin."

A line of wagons, horsemen, and pedestrians had formed in front of the outer gate. Graves reined in their horses. A moment later Father poked his head out the hole Otto had cut in the roof.

"What's the delay?"

"There's a line, my lord," Graves said. "It's moving quickly, we should be through in a few minutes."

Father grunted and disappeared back inside. Slowly but

surely, they made their way closer. As they drew nearer Otto studied the fortifications. The outer wall had to measure at least sixty feet tall and thirty feet thick. An iron portcullis with bars as big as his arm hung above, ready to crash down at the first sign of trouble.

He'd expected to find guards, but the gate was unmanned. When he mentioned it to Graves, the sergeant said, "Everyone's welcome in the business district. When we reach the inner ward, you'll see more guards."

Otto laughed. "They'll probably take one look at us and refuse to stand aside."

Graves almost smiled. "Lord Shenk has a way with people. I doubt there'll be any trouble."

Father had a way with people alright. Otto pitied any guardsman that gave him grief. The poor sod would find himself patrolling the northern border so fast he wouldn't know what happened.

At last their turn came and they passed through the gate. Murder holes lined the interior. Were there any guards inside waiting to strike should an enemy present himself? Otto almost extended his sight to find out, but ultimately decided against it. The answer didn't matter enough to make the effort worthwhile and besides, he had only just fully recovered from his efforts during the ambush.

Inside the gate, a long, wide thoroughfare led straight to the center of the city. Graves fell in with the traffic. Hundreds of men and women made their way here and there. A pair of boys that didn't look much older than Little Stephan ran across the street, narrowly avoiding a wagon loaded with bricks.

The people dressed much the same as the commoners back home, trousers and tunics for the men and dresses for the women. Most everyone wore sturdy boots, though he spotted a group of ragged men with their feet wrapped in scraps of cloth.

At least the cobblestone street provided a smoother ride than anything they'd experienced so far. If he'd had to bounce along for much longer on the rutted roads Otto feared he'd end up pissing blood for a month.

It took nearly fifteen minutes to reach the second wall. This one was a good deal less impressive. Perhaps forty feet tall and fifteen feet thick. It had wooden doors instead of a portcullis.

As they approached, a pair of guards in polished, silvery mail held up their left hands while their rights reached for the longswords belted at their waists.

The elder of the two, a man in his midforties with a gray, drooping mustache said, "Hold there. What's your business in Gold Ward?"

Before Graves had a chance to reply the carriage door slammed open and Father leapt down.

Here we go. Otto said a little prayer that this didn't escalate too far.

"My name is Arnwolf Shenk, Baron Shenk to you, and I have business with Master Merchant Edwyn Franken. Now move aside before I ask your names."

That was fairly diplomatic for Father. He didn't even reach for his sword.

"Apologies, Lord Shenk." The older guard sketched a little bow. "Your conveyance isn't what we're used to seeing enter Gold Ward."

"We were attacked by bandits on our journey. It's bloody lucky you're seeing us enter at all. Now stand aside. I've tarried here as long as I care to."

So saying, Father climbed back into the carriage. The

guards, having chosen the easy path, moved quickly out of the way.

Graves flicked the reins then glanced at Otto. "Told you he had a way with people."

♁

Franken Manor sprawled over a full acre a stone's throw from the royal palace. A ten-foot-high iron fence surrounded manicured grounds patrolled by mercenaries. These men had better gear than the ones they'd left on the side of the road. Each man wore a clean, blue tabard marked with a silver rune Otto didn't recognize. He was impressed the royals allowed another armed force outside of their control inside the city walls. Should an enemy appear, mercenaries weren't above taking a bribe. Father would have no sooner let soldiers other than his men in the castle than he would a rabid dog.

The mansion itself stood two stories tall, whitewashed, and fitted with clear glass windows. The structure was bigger than Shenk Castle. Six large outbuildings were scattered around the grounds. Even from a distance the clang of hammer on anvil rang clear in the air.

Another pair of warriors standing beside a closed gate halted them outside the grounds. These two didn't wear armor as fine as the city guards', but they looked like they'd seen a fight or two if the scars indicated anything.

One of them, a pockmarked fellow missing his left eye, glared up at Graves. "Get this rolling pile of kindling out of here before the master sees it."

Otto winced and waited for Father to burst forth and beat the guard senseless. Instead Alaric said, "Is that you, Samson?"

The guard frowned and walked around to the side of the carriage. He peeked inside the window. "Mr. Cotton?"

"Yes. We ran into a bit of trouble on the road back. Kindly open the gates. Baron Shenk is eager to clean up and meet Master Franken."

"At once, sir. My apologies for the delay."

The mercenaries hastened to push the iron gate open and move aside for the carriage. Graves got the horses moving. Once they'd passed, the mercenaries shut the gate behind them. A cobblestone path led through the grounds to a large dirt clearing.

On one side, a stable long enough to hold thirty horses butted up against the yard. At a ninety-degree angle to the stable was a blacksmith shop where a sweating, bearded man pounded a horseshoe into shape. The smith didn't so much as look up at their arrival.

A little blond boy perhaps ten years old and wearing a tabard like the mercenaries came running down from the house as Otto and the men climbed down from the carriage. Otto grimaced and limped around for a minute, trying to work the feeling back into his legs. That unpadded board seat really did a number on your backside. Two of the soldiers helped Alaric out and supported him once he reached the ground. Father came around the carriage to join them.

The boy ran up to Alaric and bowed. "Mr. Cotton! What happened?"

"An unfortunate encounter with some bandits. Timothy, this is Baron Shenk, his son Otto, and their men. I trust the guest suite is prepared as we discussed?"

"Yes, sir. The butler was getting anxious as he expected you days ago."

"Travel can be difficult. Now, send a messenger to the

House of Coins and fetch the priestess. My leg and shoulder need tending. You'll have to guide our guests to their rooms as I'm in no shape to do it. Alert the master to their arrival. The noon meal is about an hour away. That will be an excellent time to do introductions. I believe that's all. Run along now."

Timothy dashed off but wasn't more than five minutes returning. "I sent Jobby, he's the quickest."

"Good boy," Alaric said. "Lord Shenk, may I impose on you for the loan of these men until I reach my chamber?"

"Certainly." Father nodded to the two men holding Alaric up.

"Thank you. The rest of your soldiers can find spaces in the barracks. Timothy, you'll tend to our guests for the time being."

"Yes, sir." Timothy bowed. "If you'll follow me, my lords. I'll send someone to fetch your luggage shortly."

Otto fell in a step behind his father as they strode along behind the boy. Instead of the main entrance, Timothy led them to a side door. Inside, the hall had silver-marble-tiled floors with red veins running through it.

Everywhere Otto looked he found signs of wealth. Gold-framed paintings covered the walls. The doors they passed were oak inlaid with silver. Each of those doors held enough wealth to feed a family for a year.

The passages were empty of servants and when Otto mentioned it Timothy informed him that most of the staff was busy preparing the noon meal and the others were cleaning upstairs. Timothy finally stopped and pushed open one of the fancy doors.

"Your suite, my lords. I'll fetch some boys to bring hot water for your baths. Do you require anything else right now?"

"No." Father stepped through the door without a second glance at the boy.

Otto shrugged and followed him in. Soft, leather-covered chairs and a table filled the main chamber. A large, cold hearth jutted from the far wall and four doors led off into other rooms. He didn't dare sit on anything for fear of getting it dirty.

Father held no such concern. He unbuckled his sword and dropped into the nearest chair, indifferent to the puff of dirt that rose off his clothes.

"How much wealth does this merchant have?" Otto asked.

Father turned to look at him, a predatory smile on his face. "A lot and I mean to get as much of it as I can."

CHAPTER 16

Bathed, rested, and dressed in clean clothes, Otto and his father followed a fully healed Alaric down the marble hall. Whoever the temple sent must have been highly skilled to have repaired his leg and shoulder so quickly. He didn't even walk with a limp. When he finally returned home, Otto would have to ask Lord Karonin how priestly magic worked.

Beside him, Father adjusted his sword. Even here he refused to leave it behind. Of course, if Father wore it in his own castle, why wouldn't he wear it in a stranger's home? Otto only carried his dagger because Father insisted a nobleman must always be armed. After his display with the bandits Otto thought he'd made it clear that regular weapons were unnecessary, but he'd thought wrong.

"What's for lunch?" Otto asked when they'd walked a hundred yards with no sign of a dining room.

"A little of everything, my lord," Alaric said. "Master Franken likes variety at his meals."

Father grunted. As long as he found meat, potatoes, bread,

and ale, he'd be satisfied. Otto hoped for fish. He hadn't had any fresh fish since last fall.

Ahead of them the hall opened up into a sprawling dining room with a sixty-foot table. Above it a gold chandelier glowed with the light of sixty Lux crystals. Otto shifted his vision and found each crystal swirled with its own little pool of ether. The enchantments appeared much fresher than the weak ones in the basement back home.

Despite the massive table, only two people stood waiting for them. At the head was a man around his father's age if not a little older. A great belly hung over the belt that held up his white pants. A white silk tunic embroidered with gold thread strained to cover his girth. Even from a distance the stink of perfume rolled over Otto. He restrained a cough with the greatest of efforts.

Beside the man waited the most beautiful woman Otto had ever laid eyes on. She had long, golden hair, and flawless curves accentuated by a clinging blue silk dress. She held her head down, hiding her face, but if it matched the rest of her it would surely be stunning. If she was to be his bride, Stephan would be jealous.

Alaric cleared his throat. "Master Franken, may I present Baron Arnwolf Shenk and his son, Otto Shenk."

Father waited as their host and his daughter made their way over. The fat merchant managed a credible bow despite his bulk and the girl bobbed a curtsy before finally looking up at Otto. Bright blue eyes sparked with rage. Smooth, pale skin held a faint blush he suspected had more to do with anger than excitement. It seemed the lady didn't look on her future with enthusiasm.

"Lord Shenk!" Master Franken held out his hand but Father

ignored it. However rich he was, the merchant was still a commoner. "This is my daughter, Annamaria."

She curtsied again. "A pleasure, my lords." Her tone held all the warmth of a midwinter night.

Master Franken turned his attention to Otto. "And you must be my future son-in-law. So good to meet you."

Following his father's example Otto simply nodded an acknowledgement.

The merchant's smile grew strained. "Shall we dine?"

Father strode over and took the merchant's seat at the head of the table. Their host grimaced a moment then smoothed his expression. He took the seat to Father's left and Otto the seat to his right.

Annamaria started towards the chair beside her father, but he shooed her over to the seat next to Otto. The daughter took her turn to grimace before reluctantly obeying.

Before the silence grew too strained six men in livery bearing laden trays entered from another door. Each platter held a different meat surrounded by a mixture of vegetables. The savory scent of roast meat mingled with spices, causing Otto's mouth to water. Any of the presentations would have made a fine meal on its own, but together they overwhelmed his senses.

At first Otto thought the merchant had arranged this to impress his guests, but there was no way he could have known when they'd arrive. If this meal represented Master Franken's regular diet, it explained the man's girth.

The trays were set on the table and the men remained behind to serve. Otto had salmon with asparagus and potatoes. More servants arrived with flasks of wine and pitchers of ale.

Everyone save Annamaria dove in and ate with enthusiasm.

About halfway through Otto asked, "Where did you come by such fresh asparagus, Master Franken?"

"The Kingdom of Rolan. It came through the portal just yesterday. And please, if we're to be family you must call me Edwyn. At least until you can call me Father."

Otto nodded and offered a polite smile.

Father cleared his throat. "Let's not get ahead of ourselves. We still have matters to discuss."

"Just as you say, Lord Shenk. But not until we finish our meal."

Forty-five minutes later the finest meal of Otto's life came to an end with a small lemon tart. He sighed and took a final swig of wine.

"Now to business," Father said.

"Of course," Edwyn said. "Why don't you show Otto around the gardens, my dear? Lord Shenk and I have matters to discuss."

She stood. "As you wish, Father. My lord?"

Otto joined her and she led him out a third door. They walked in silence through the empty halls, her a step ahead of him, never looking back. He didn't blame her for being upset, but in their position, you had to accept that your life wasn't always your own.

They finally left the mansion and went out into a perfectly maintained garden. The shrubs and many of the trees still hadn't budded, but the evergreens appeared freshly trimmed. A stone path meandered through the garden, past benches and statues.

Annamaria marched down one of them, seeming not to care if he followed or not. Otto sighed and hurried to walk beside her. They'd barely moved out of sight of the mansion when a slim, handsome man stepped out from behind one of the cedar hedges.

He wore the armor and tabard of a house mercenary. His hair was short and slicked back from a rugged, chiseled face.

He pulled his sword and pointed it at Otto. "Annamaria is coming with me."

Otto looked from one to the other. He felt no great threat from a single man. If necessary, Otto could bind him in an instant.

"Who are you?" Otto asked.

"Lothair, we talked about this." Annamaria went to him and put her head on his chest. "My fate is decided. You mustn't do anything foolish."

"I refuse to accept that." Lothair glared at Otto. "I love you, Annamaria. We can run away together. This nobleman can't stop us. He doesn't even wear a sword."

Otto had heard about all he cared to. "Take her if you wish. This marriage wasn't my idea."

Lothair and Annamaria just stared at him for a moment.

"You would give her up?" Lothair's sword wavered for a moment.

Otto shrugged. "She clearly has no interest in me. Just understand that while I'm perfectly willing to let her go, our fathers may have different thoughts."

"What do you mean?" Annamaria asked.

"I mean that if you run off with this man without your father's permission, under the law he'll be guilty of kidnapping. That's a hanging offense, as is drawing your sword on a nobleman, but I'll overlook that for the moment."

"They can't hang me if they can't find us." Lothair turned his gaze on Annamaria. "We'll hide in the wilds. It'll be romantic."

Otto laughed and sat on one of the benches. "Romantic? I assure you, having just traveled through the wilderness, there's nothing romantic about it. Assuming you don't enjoy dirt, mud, rotten food, and bandits. Oh, and bounty hunters, mustn't forget the bounty hunters."

"Bounty hunters?" Annamaria's voice came out in a squeak.

Otto nodded. "If you cost my father ten thousand double eagles, he'll put a bounty on your boyfriend so big every idiot with a sword will be looking for him."

Lothair moved Annamaria to one side. "Maybe I should kill you. Then there won't be any witnesses to tell your father who to look for."

"Lothair!"

Otto rubbed his fingers together and conjured a pair of threads. He sent fire through them into the sword pointed at his face. The hilt turned red hot.

Lothair hissed, dropped it, and held his burned hand.

Otto got up and kicked the sword a safe distance away. "Why don't you go away before I get angry?"

Lothair raised his fists. "Wizard or not, I'll fight you bare-handed before I let her go."

Otto summoned lightning around his hands. Hopefully the threat would be enough to scare the fool off. So far he'd only used his magic defensively. If he did anything more he'd be the one facing the noose.

Annamaria stepped between them. "Enough of this. Lothair, I love you, but this is madness. I've known my whole life Father would choose my husband one day. Being with you was a pleasant fantasy, but that's over now."

"But—"

She shook her head and turned to Otto. "If you let him leave and forget his foolishness, I promise to be a loyal wife."

Otto let the lightning vanish. "Very well, but I don't wish to lay eyes on him again. Should he appear before me just once more I'll see him hung from the nearest tree."

"You won't see him again." Annamaria took a gold ring from her finger and gave it to Lothair. "This will tide you over long enough to get safely away from Garen. Take it and go."

"Annamaria?" The pain in Lothair's voice cut Otto.

A tear glimmered in the corner of her eye, but Annamaria turned away from Lothair and offered Otto her arm. "Shall we retire, my lord?"

Otto didn't take his gaze off Lothair. Hate and rage burned in the man's eyes with frightening intensity. He should kill Lothair right here and now. Nothing but trouble would follow if he kept his word to Annamaria.

He turned his back on Lothair, linked arms with his bride-to-be, and walked with her back to the house. Father would say he was a sentimental fool, but Otto wanted at least a chance to be happy with his future wife. If he killed Lothair, any hope of that vanished.

○

When Annamaria and her bastard fiancé had moved out of sight, Lothair collected his sword and sheathed it, though not in the noble's heart as he would have preferred. To think her father would force her to marry a wizard. Disgraceful.

Perhaps some enchantment had been used to force his dishonorable act. He would have liked to believe that, but Master Franken had made his plans to marry off his daughter to a nobleman clear long before he'd ever heard of Baron Shenk.

Lothair tried to do as his beloved said, but no matter what, he found no way to silence his mind. He loved the woman and deep down knew she loved him. Circumstances may have separated them for now, but he believed with all his heart that somehow, they'd find a way to be together.

First, he needed to leave the grounds before the wizard informed the master that he was no longer welcome here. Lothair caressed the ring before slipping it on his little finger. He'd hold on to it until he had the chance to return it to her. He had coin enough saved to tide him over for a week or two, maybe.

Lothair fled the garden, retreating to the barracks to collect his meager belongings. Several of his comrades gave him long, sad looks, but none of them spoke. His love for Annamaria was well known amongst the other guards, though none ever said anything.

It took only five minutes to empty his footlocker into a canvas sack. Ten minutes after the fateful encounter he walked away from the manor for what he vowed wouldn't be the last time. Next time he left he'd take Annamaria with him, even if he had to remove the noble's head to do it.

Lothair soon left Gold Ward behind. He dearly wanted to stay close to the mansion, but his limited wealth wouldn't allow it. In fact, he'd be lucky if his funds would cover a one-room garret for the month.

He shook his head. Details, irrelevant details that would sort themselves out in time. With love on his side nothing else mattered.

Twenty minutes later brought him to his favorite bar, The Thirsty Sprite. Smoke poured from the chimney of the three-story wood and brick building. The lunch rush had ended, and the common room was almost empty when he pushed through the door.

He used to hang out there all the time before he got the job working for Master Franken. He'd known Allen, the bartender, since they were children. He hoped to parlay that old friendship into a discount on the attic room.

A stranger with a thin, drooping mustache that didn't connect in the middle stood smoking a cigar behind the bar. He polished a glass and watched Lothair with a look of blank disinterest. Lothair frowned. If Allen had found a new job his plans were up in smoke.

He walked up to the bar and sat on a stool near the end. The new bartender ambled over and raised a bushy eyebrow.

"I'm looking for Allen. He used to serve here?"

The bartender shrugged and blew smoke in Lothair's face.

"We grew up together. I haven't seen him in a while and hoped to catch up. Does he not work here anymore?"

The bartender yanked a pull cord hanging off to one side. Lothair didn't remember it from before.

"What is it, Ulf?" a familiar voice asked from behind him.

Lothair hopped off his stool and spun around. Allen stood there, hands on hips, his long blond hair tied back in a ponytail, not looking a day older than when last they saw each other.

"Lothair?" Allen closed the distance between then and took Lothair in a tight embrace. "It's been too long. What brings you here? I thought you'd found work at the Franken estate?"

They parted and Lothair smiled despite his heavy heart. "I did and it was a wonderful eighteen months, but my circumstances have changed."

"We'll have a drink and you can tell me all about it," Allen said. "Ulf, a bottle of the good stuff and two glasses."

Ulf grunted and rummaged around under the bar before coming up with a bottle of amber liquid and two crystal glasses.

The bartender wandered off to a far table, leaving the old friends to talk. Allen poured two measures of liquor into each glass then picked one up. Lothair took the other and they clinked. The fiery amber drink burned its way down and settled into his stomach.

Lothair sighed. "Wonderful, I needed that."

"I could tell. So what brings you to my door after all this time?"

Lothair debated for a moment then told Allen everything. When he'd finished, he asked, "Is the attic apartment empty? I need a place to stay for a little while."

"It is and you're welcome to it, no charge." Allen poured them another drink. "I know you're determined to rescue your woman, but have you considered she may not wish to be rescued?"

Lothair drank again. "She's only going through with this because her father commands it. Annamaria would be with me otherwise. I will find a way to make it happen or die trying."

Allen raised his glass a second time. "To love."

CHAPTER 17

Otto and Annamaria sat together on a bench in the garden. True to her word she'd been as pleasant a companion as he might have wanted, distant perhaps, but what could you expect? They'd only known each other for three days after all.

He restrained a sigh. Three days and Father still dickered over the dowry. You'd think what Master Franken had offered more than enough, but Father meant to suck every drop of marrow from the merchant's bones.

A cool breeze sent a chill down his back. Despite the sun, the days remained brisk. While Otto enjoyed whiling away his days in the capital, he wanted very much to get back home and resume his studies with Lord Karonin. Though he spent several hours every day in his room practicing, without a master to guide him Otto's progress had slowed. On the positive side, he'd added a seventh thread to his best spells, only for a second or two, but still.

"You have a faraway look, my lord," Annamaria said.

"Sorry, I was thinking about home. You know, assuming

our fathers ever get tired of haggling, we will marry at some point. Perhaps you could try calling me Otto."

"Yes, Otto, I guess I don't feel I know you well enough to call you by your given name. This is all very sudden."

"Did your father not warn you either?" Otto asked. "I walked in on a conversation between my parents and Alaric. Father promptly announced he'd found a wife for me and we were setting out to meet you the next day."

"I knew he sought a noble husband for me, but I had no idea who he'd settled on. I wasn't thrilled about it." She laughed, flashing perfect white teeth.

"Yeah, I got that impression when we first met."

"I'm sorry about that, truly. It never occurred to me that you were forced into this every bit as much as I was. Did you have someone...before?"

"No. I've always known and accepted my fate with regards to marriage. My true love has always been magic. I meant to ask, why is your father called master merchant?"

She smiled. "You'll appreciate this, being a wizard. Our family has the royal charter for the portal. We oversee the opening and closing of it and sell the rights to pass through to the highest bidder. We keep ten percent of the payments for our services. Even without Father's other businesses, that income would make us rich."

Otto stood up and offered her his hand. "Would you like to go for a walk? I find I'd like a closer look at the portal."

She took his hand and let him pull her to her feet. "Why not?"

They left the garden and walked hand in hand toward the front gate. They passed mercenaries who nodded to them—to her, if Otto was honest. He might be noble, but her father handed out the coins.

Outside the gate they strolled along the sidewalk. Two hours had passed since noon and the streets teemed with traffic. Elaborate carriages that made Father's look like a farmer's hay wagon even before the attack rattled down the street. Few people took the sidewalk yet for some reason he would have sworn someone was watching them. A quick look around revealed no one paying them the least attention. He'd have to be careful lest he become as paranoid as Father.

No one called to them which surprised Otto. He thought someone would stop to chat with Annamaria, given how well known her family was.

When he mentioned it she looked away. "We know many people but have few friends. The other merchants view Father as little more than a tax collector and they resent him for it. It's as if they forgot where we came from. My great-grandfather started with a wagon, two mules, and his wits. Everything we have, we earned."

"Success breeds jealousy," Otto said, thinking of all the wizards had accomplished only to have it cast down by those that resented them. "It's one of the universal truths of this world."

Ten minutes later found them fifty feet from the portal. Up close he realized the metal wasn't silver but mithril. It was the hardest metal in the world and a pound cost a hundred double eagles. The gate had to weigh a ton.

Runes ran around its length. Dull now, but he knew they'd burn with etheric energy when it activated.

"You could equip an army with that much mithril," Otto said.

"Right after the purge, the king at the time tried," Annamaria said. "They didn't have anything that so much as scratched it. It worked out though. When Lord Valtan reactivated it and created the Portal Compact it made Garenland even richer."

Otto wasn't surprised they'd failed. Mithril could only be worked if you heated it with magic; an ordinary forge didn't get hot enough. That was why Straken did no business in mithril weapons despite having huge veins of it running through their mountains. Killing all your wizards was bad for business, but the lords of Straken didn't care. They hated wizards more than they liked gold.

A moment later he sensed power building in the portal. The lowest rune burst to life followed by the next and the next as the power worked its way around the perimeter. Otto shifted his vision and had to squint against the blazing of the ether.

When the final rune lit up a tunnel of etheric energy formed. A laden wagon appeared followed by another and another. He'd expected the horses to be panicked as they arrived, but the animals appeared calm as they walked up the street to make room for the next merchant.

"It's two bells," Annamaria said. "From two until three is the Kingdom of Lasil."

After the tenth wagon passed through, the light of the gate died and the tunnel collapsed. Otto's pulse raced. He had no idea what it might take, but he would gain the power to create such wonders.

"Must be a slow day." Annamaria turned back toward the mansion. "Usually at least fifteen wagons arrive from Lasil."

Otto gave the portal one last, loving look and walked along beside her. "When do our merchants pass through?"

"Noon to one. Father and his agent hold an auction every morning for spaces. The gate only stays open for one hour at a time so on a busy day prices can climb quite high."

"What happens after an hour?"

"It shuts down for an hour then the next kingdom gets a turn. It alternates like that every day from morning to night, twelve hours on and twelve off. I haven't the least idea why it works that way, but it does, as regularly as the rising and setting of the sun."

They retraced their steps and had barely reached the estate grounds when Alaric came running up to them.

"Where have you been? Your fathers have been looking for you. They've finally struck a bargain. Now it's simply a matter of choosing a date."

Otto and Annamaria shared a look.

"No getting out of it now," she said.

"No, I'm afraid we're stuck with each other."

CHAPTER 18

Axel led his squad down the ragged road toward the army's northern command post. They still had a mile to go, but even from this distance the huge, granite fortress appeared to loom over the surrounding landscape. He hadn't visited command headquarters since he joined up and received his current assignment from General Leonhard Varchi. According to the commander, General Varchi still oversaw the entire Northern Army, all three legions of it. Hopefully, since he and the general were passing acquaintances, he'd be more apt to listen to Axel.

Not that Axel held any great hope for it. He had nothing to add that the commander hadn't included in his letters. The facts were the facts, regardless of the messenger.

Axel's gaze darted from one side of the road to the other. Bandits seldom attacked this close to the fortress, but seldom didn't mean never. He didn't intend to let his guard down until he had forty feet of stone between him and anyone that wanted to kill him.

"Why did you have to drag us along on this trip, my lord?"

Cobb asked. "It's not like we can add anything to your testimony."

"You're not along to talk, you're here to step in front of an arrow for me," Axel said.

Cobb grunted and several of the men behind them laughed. The others liked to joke that Axel and Cobb acted like an old married couple. Axel considered that an insult. He'd never marry anyone as ugly as Cobb.

"All kidding aside, you're here because one man traveling alone is a target, but a squad of soldiers is a threat to be avoided. I prefer to hunt bandits, not be hunted by them."

"I second that, sir," Colten said.

The column rode up to the raised drawbridge. A thirty-foot-wide moat filled with sharpened stakes protected the fortress. A guard on duty looked down at them.

"Identify yourselves!"

"Lieutenant Shenk, First Scout Company, Second Legion, to see General Varchi. We're expected."

A few seconds of silence then, "So you are. Hold a moment."

Iron clanked and the drawbridge lowered revealing a portcullis in the process of rising. When the path had cleared Axel led his men inside. A handful of young men wearing black tabards emblazoned with a golden griffin rushed out to take their horses.

"Well, you're here in one piece," Cobb said. "What are we supposed to do now?"

"I recommend retiring to the barracks and enjoying a hot meal. I need to hunt up the general."

"Lieutenant Shenk?"

Axel turned to find a lean, wiry man in black and gold facing him. The bars on his uniform indicated his rank as sergeant.

"That's right."

The sergeant touched his fist to his heart. "Welcome, the general's eager to talk to you."

Axel returned the salute and followed the man into the main keep. The dark walls held weapons and banners taken from the many victories the legions had won before the peace treaty of three hundred years ago. Nothing much had changed since Axel's first visit and they soon stood before the door to the general's office.

The sergeant knocked and a moment later a gruff voice said, "Enter!"

"There you are, sir." The sergeant opened the door for him.

Axel nodded his thanks and stepped into the small, square room. A bare, oak desk dominated the area. A single bookcase filled with a collection of military manuals stood along the left-hand wall and the general's banded mail hung from a rack on the right.

General Varchi himself stood behind his desk. Though well into his sixties, the general's massive shoulders still strained his black uniform. A long, gray mustache drooped down around his mouth.

Axel saluted. "Good to see you again, sir."

"At ease, Lieutenant."

Axel clasped his hands behind his back.

"So, what have you to tell me that Commander Braddock didn't?"

"Not a thing, sir."

A thick, gray eyebrow went up. "Then why are you here?"

Axel took a deep breath. "I've come to plead in person for the people of the borderlands. We can't track down the bandits with soldiers on only one side of the border. We either need permission to cross the border or to work with the Straken army on a joint sweep. It's the only way to stop the killing short of abandoning the area."

General Varchi ran his fingers through his short, gray hair. "I appreciate your passion for the people under your care. Unfortunately, I've spoken with King Von Garen himself on this matter and it's simply impossible. The Straken ambassador refuses to cooperate. I'm sorry, Axel."

Axel ground his teeth so hard his jaw ached. "What am I to do then?"

"The same thing you've been doing, the best you can."

"The best I can do is burn the bodies of the dead."

"Be that as it may, I have my orders and you have yours."

The general's tone made it clear the discussion had ended. Axel saluted again. "Yes, sir."

"On another matter, do you plan to attend your brother's wedding?"

"Stephan married five years ago." He stared at the general for a moment. "Otto?"

"Indeed. It's the talk of Garen. It seems your little brother is marrying the daughter of the richest merchant in the city. If you wish to attend, the wedding's in two days. I'll give you a five-day pass."

"Thank you, General." Axel hadn't seen or spoken to his family since the day before he rode out of Shenk Castle. He had no idea what sort of reception to expect, but maybe it would be worth trying to find out.

CHAPTER 19

The wedding was tomorrow and Annamaria feared she might throw up. Her father and the baron had decided that sooner was better and they'd only given her five days to prepare for her new life. Behind her, Mimi, her body servant, tugged again on the corset she'd been trying to wriggle into for the past ten minutes.

To celebrate the event, Father had announced a party tonight along with an all-day celebration tomorrow. Fortunately, she only had to attend the first half of tomorrow's festivities. After the ceremony, tradition demanded that the newlyweds consummate the union while their family and friends got drunk nearby.

She shuddered to think of it. Not that Otto wasn't reasonably handsome, he just wasn't Lothair. Her sigh turned to a groan when Mimi tugged again. At first, she'd feared he'd be another arrogant, obnoxious nobleman of the sort that often approached Father for a loan, but so far she'd found him to be quiet and polite, gentle and kind. Perhaps she'd gotten lucky after all with Father's choice for her husband. Annamaria knew women stuck with far worse men.

"There, miss." Mimi tied off the corset and helped her into the next piece of her dress.

It took another ten minutes for Annamaria to get all the layers of her fancy gown draped in the correct positions. Next she put on three pieces of her finest jewelry and called that good.

"You look lovely, miss," Mimi said. "Your husband-to-be is lucky."

"Thank you, Mimi." Annamaria almost hugged Mimi. Of all the people in the world, she was the only one Annamaria knew for sure was on her side. "I suppose I should be going. The guests will start arriving soon."

"Yes, miss. Can I do anything else for you?"

"No, thank you, dear."

Annamaria gathered her skirts and headed for the door. She pushed it open and stepped out into the hall. Her rooms were only a short walk from the great hall so she only had a minute to mentally prepare herself.

She heard the party before she saw it. Voices and laughter mixed with the clinking of glasses. At the end of the passage the great hall opened up before her. Only a few guests had arrived, perhaps twenty of the hundreds Father invited. The guests wore their finest outfits. Everyone he asked would show up at some point. After all, no one wanted to insult the richest man in the kingdom.

From a distance she saw no one she knew. That didn't surprise her. Father had invited even the most casual acquaintances.

A heavyset merchant wearing a turban and his companion, a woman thirty years his junior, moved to one side and Annamaria spotted her fiancé. She had a moment of jealousy when she saw the simple black tunic and gray trousers he wore. It couldn't have taken him five minutes to get ready, damn him.

maria spotted her fiancé. She had a moment of jealousy when she saw the simple black tunic and gray trousers he wore. It couldn't have taken him five minutes to get ready, damn him.

He spotted her a moment later and smiled. Otto crossed the room and bowed. "You look stunning."

"Thank you. Between you and me, my stomach is such a mess I fear I won't be able to eat a bite. How did you sleep?"

"I only got a few hours," Otto said. "I hate things like this. Too many people."

The main doors opened to admit more guests. This one was a weapons merchant she recognized from her occasional trips to the daily auctions. He probably wanted to suck up to Father in hopes of getting a better price on his access. She wished him luck; he'd need it.

Annamaria took Otto's hand. "It'll be over soon enough. Let's go greet our guests."

For the next hour she and Otto stood near the door smiling and shaking hands. She felt a little bad for him. Otto knew no one that entered, though he maintained a game, if stiff, smile.

Finally, a lone man dressed in a crisp, black and gold uniform marched up the stairs. Otto's grip tightened on her hand.

"Axel," he whispered.

The soldier went right up to Otto. "Hello, little brother. Surprised to see me?"

⌒

Otto stared at his brother for a moment, unable to speak. How was it possible Axel was here? He darted a look around but saw no sign of Father. He doubted they'd come to blows with all these people present, but with Father you never knew. He finally realized his brother had his hand out and Otto shook it.

"I suppose this is a surprise," Axel said.

"That's putting it mildly considering we haven't had word of you in two years. What brings you here?"

"Chance. I was at the Northern Army's headquarters making a report when the commander informed me of the happy news." Axel turned to Annamaria and bowed. "My brother is a lucky man."

"You're very kind."

"Forgive my manners," Otto said. "Annamaria, this is my brother Axel. Axel, my fiancée, Annamaria Franken."

"You!" Father's voice rang out over the gathering. Everyone fell silent as he stomped across the hall toward them.

"Uh-oh," Otto muttered.

"Always the talent for understatement." Axel moved away from them toward Father.

"You've got some nerve showing up after all this time."

Axel dodged the right cross and ducked a backhand. "I only came to offer Otto my congratulations, not to get in a fight with you."

Father reached for his sword.

Otto flicked his ring and forged a connection between it and the blade of Father's sword. Unless he allowed it there was no way the weapon could be drawn.

Father dragged on his hilt, his face getting redder and redder. He turned his wrath on Otto.

"Release my weapon. I'll have his head here and now."

"Are you really going to try and kill him in front of Garenland's best and brightest on the night before my wedding?" Otto favored his father with an incredulous look. "Really?"

Father finally relaxed. "Perhaps not. We'll see each other again, Axel."

He stalked off, leaving Otto and the others alone. The conversations slowly resumed and Otto breathed a sigh of relief as he released the spell.

"That went better than I'd feared," Axel said.

"Are you kidding?" Annamaria stared from Axel to Otto.

"No, Axel's right. Walking out of here still breathing is a win for him. That said, it might be best if you retired early, brother."

"Agreed. I believe I'll skip the ceremony tomorrow as well. I have no gift to offer you, Otto, beyond my well wishes."

Otto smiled. He'd never been close to Axel, but at least his middle brother hadn't bullied him the way Stephan did. It was good to know he was still alive. "I'll give Mother your love when I see her."

"Thanks, little brother." Axel nodded to Annamaria and beat a hasty retreat.

When he'd gone, Annamaria said, "You have an interesting family."

Otto's smile twisted. "Lunatics and killers for the most part. I think you'll like Mother, though."

She got a wistful look. "I wish my mother had lived to see this day."

"What happened, if you don't mind me asking?"

"There was an accident. She was walking to our favorite bakery to pick out some snacks when a carriage went out of control and hit her. The healers could do nothing. I was six at the time."

She sniffed and Otto put his arm around her. "I'm sorry."

Annamaria nodded her thanks.

Outside, a black-lacquered carriage pulled up. On the door

the Von Garen griffon waved its claws. Two soldiers in mail and black tabards emblazoned with the same symbol leapt down and opened the doors. A slender, handsome man in black and gold with short, oiled hair and a goatee leapt out ignoring the stairs. At his hip hung a longsword with a jewel-encrusted silver hilt.

Annamaria brightened and waved. "Wolfric!"

Otto's eyes about bugged out of his head. Wolfric, as in Crown Prince Wolfric Von Garen, future king of Garenland.

He bowed low at the prince's approach. His fiancée, on the other hand, rushed over and hugged the prince.

"Rise, please." Wolfric had a warm, kind tone to his voice. "No need for such formality outside of court. I merely come to pay my compliments to an old friend on the eve of her wedding."

Otto straightened and out of the corner of his eyes saw the other guests doing the same. Cold, hard blue eyes bore into his when he met the prince's gaze. That stare made a stark contrast to the warm voice.

"We are honored that you'd grace us with your presence, Highness," Otto said.

Wolfric laughed. "For the love of heaven, please call me Wolfric. I have enough people back at the palace to kiss my ass, I require no one else to do it."

"I wasn't sure you'd come," Annamaria said. "It's been, what, five years since you completed your studies?"

"Four and a half, far too long to go without seeing my favorite childhood playmate." Wolfric turned his gaze back to Otto. "Did you know Annamaria and I had the same tutor growing up? We've known each other since we were five. If only she'd been a princess, I'd have married her myself."

Otto had no idea what to say to that, so he kept silent. It

seemed impossible that the crown prince and a commoner, no matter how rich her family, should have the same tutor. Otto assumed that sort of thing happened inside the palace. Not that he was any sort of expert on the coming and going of royalty.

"Since you're marrying an old friend of mine," Wolfric went on. "We shall have to be friends as well."

The prince held out his hand.

Otto stared at it for a moment. To touch a member of the royal family, even for another nobleman, broke all protocol, but refusing might be an even bigger insult.

He steeled himself and shook. He wasn't struck down on the spot by the soldiers standing near the doors so he must have made the correct choice. It seemed his new situation came with a number of pitfalls. Having a friend in the future king should make them easier to navigate.

Or harder, depending how many enemies the prince had.

CHAPTER 20

The common room spun in Lothair's vision, one minute in focus and the next blurry. He'd hoped to be passed out by now, but Allen's brandy didn't seem up to the job. Tomorrow, or maybe today, he wasn't certain of the time. Regardless, soon Annamaria would wed the noble prick and he'd done nothing to stop it.

Some hero he'd turned out to be. Lothair groped around for the bottle Ulf had given him, but it seemed beyond his reach. When he attempted to lift his head off the bar the throbbing caused burning acid to crawl up the back of his throat. Had there ever been such a miserable wretch as him?

You might find one in some deep, dark dungeon somewhere, but he doubted it. Mere physical pain paled before the despair that crushed his soul.

"On your feet!" Allen's voice was an ice pick to his brain.

"Go away. Can't you see I'm trying to wallow in my misery?"

"You've wallowed long enough, time to pay me back for some of the brandy you've swilled on credit."

Lothair groaned and pushed himself up off the bar. When the room stilled and came back into focus, he found Allen and Ulf were his only companions. That explained the quiet at least. He'd feared he'd gone deaf before Allen's shout.

"What time is it?" Lothair looked around again and finally spotted Ulf near the fire stirring a pot.

"Three bells after midnight. I require your services for an hour."

"You don't want me, I'm worthless."

"Be that as it may, I need another sword, and yours is the only one available at this hour. Ulf, bring the cure."

The bartender left his spot beside the fire and joined them at the bar, bringing his pot along with him. Ulf poured the contents into a tin cup and held it out toward Lothair.

One sniff set his stomach to roiling. He'd smelled month-dead fish sweeter than Ulf's concoction. "I'm not drinking that."

"Yes, you are." Allen's voice had lost all its former good cheer. "You can do it willingly or Ulf can pour it down your throat. I recommend the former."

Lothair thought for a moment his old friend was joking, but one look at Allen's grim, unsmiling face put paid to that theory. "What is it?"

"As I said, it's a cure. The potion will remove the effects of alcohol as well as exhaustion with no long-term side effects. Remarkable stuff really. Ulf learned to make it in his home-land. Now drink up, time grows short."

Lothair took the cup and looked inside. The tavern lacked sufficient light to reveal any details. Probably just as well. He shrugged and guzzled it down in one go. It tasted as vile as it smelled, but his head began to clear at once. Energy filled him and he felt he could run for hours.

"Wow!"

"Told you," Allen said. "Now grab your sword. If we don't hurry, we'll be late."

"Late for what?" Lothair hunted around for a moment before spotting his sword dangling from the end of the bar. How did it get there?

"For a meeting. If you're going to drink my brandy, the least you can do is help me when I have a job."

Lothair settled his sword on his hip. "I thought running the tavern was your job?"

"It is, but the real money in this city is in information. You wouldn't believe the sorts of things drunk merchants or more precisely drunk drovers will reveal when they think no one's listening. And don't get me started on the secrets people share with the whores."

Allen marched toward the door with Ulf hard on his heels. Lothair still didn't understand what was going on, but he hurried to catch up. It was clear to him that if he wanted to continue living rent free he needed to play along with whatever Allen had planned.

Magic streetlamps glowed with pure white light on each corner, shedding just enough illumination for them to see where they were going. Allen set a brisk pace toward the foundries and away from Gold Ward.

Lothair sent a longing look over his shoulder. She was probably in bed right now, tossing and turning, unable to sleep as the horror of the situation settled over her. His dear Annamaria. He would save her from her fate, somehow.

"Eyes forward, Lothair," Allen said. "I'm not paying you to daydream."

"You're not paying me at all."

"Free room and board not enough for you? If you think you can do better, by all means go your own way."

Lothair growled away his annoyance. Allen had him and he knew it. There was no way he could hold down a regular job and continue to keep an eye on Annamaria. He'd made up his mind to watch over his beloved as much as possible. He turned away from Gold Ward and focused on the task at hand, whatever it was.

Ten minutes after their departure from the tavern Allen led them to an alley between a foundry and a smithy. The meager light from the nearby lamp did nothing to dispel the darkness of the alley.

Allen stopped and removed a small cylinder from his pocket. He twisted it and a light flashed. A few seconds later another light flashed from deeper in the alley. Allen flashed three, one, three.

A lantern was unhooded, revealing four men at the far end of the alley. Allen advanced and met the strangers in the middle.

Up close they were a rough crew. Scarred men in ragged leather armor, the hilts of daggers poking up at every angle. They looked like street thugs and Lothair figured that's exactly what they were. What business Allen might have with such men escaped him and honestly it made no difference. All Lothair had to do was stand behind his old friend and look intimidating. That had been his job in one form or another since he turned sixteen.

"You have the information I requested?" asked the central figure, a bald man with a patch over his left eye and a pair of hatchets thrust through his belt.

"I do, Crane," Allen said. "And you wouldn't believe what I had to go through to get it."

Crane fingered one of his hatchets. "I know you're not stupid enough to try and renegotiate the deal, so how about we trade so I can get home to my wife?"

Lothair stared at the bald man. He had a wife? What sort of woman would be desperate enough to marry a bruiser like him?

Allen dug a scroll tube out of an inner pocket of his cloak and held it up with his right hand. Crane returned the favor, producing a heavy-looking pouch. Both men took two steps forward and at the same moment set their respective items into the other's left hand.

They stepped back, exchanged nods, and led their groups back the way they'd come. Lothair had no idea exactly what had just happened or what part he'd played in it.

When he asked Allen, his friend said, "The deal went off without a hitch. Whether or not your presence played a part I can't say. Crane respects strength and an extra sword is never a bad thing. Three against four is a lot better than two against four after all."

"So do I get a share of the coin?" Lothair asked.

Allen laughed. "For taking a short walk and standing in an alley for five minutes? Hardly. Look on the bright side, you still get to live above my bar for free. And if you should prove yourself useful, perhaps, at some point, a paying proposition will pop up."

Lothair grinned in the dark. He liked the sound of that.

CHAPTER 21

Otto woke after a fitful five hours of sleep. He'd spent a good bit of the previous night chatting with the crown prince. Wolfric was fascinated with Garenland's history as well as wizardry. They were two subjects Otto had studied a fair bit and the prince seemed intent on dragging everything he knew out of him.

The other guests had kept darting glances at them. When Otto mentioned it, Wolfric had laughed and said they were jealous. Many people waited months for half an hour of the prince's time and Otto had been talking with him for hours. Wolfric had then warned him that others would try and use him to ferry messages for them. His advice was to charge enough to make it worthwhile.

Otto rolled out of the luxurious bed and stretched. Father's snores came, barely audible, through the connecting wall. When they returned to their suite Otto had gotten an earful about using magic on his father, and pointing out that he'd only used it on the sword hadn't helped at all. Only the fact of today's wedding had spared him a beating.

According to the schedule, guests were to arrive starting around mid-morning and the ceremony would happen at mid-afternoon. When Edwyn had asked Father if he had a preference for the presiding priest Father had only shrugged. At this point, Otto doubted his father cared about anything besides getting his gold and returning to the barony.

Otto knew how he felt. He was heartily sick of the parties and wanted nothing so much as to get back to his studies. Speaking of which, he had a few hours before he'd have to put in an appearance, perhaps he could get in a little practice.

What should he work on? Nothing aggressive, the furnishings were too expensive to risk. The books said the best way to quickly increase his power was to infuse his body with ether so he'd grow ever more sensitive to it.

Taking that suggestion to heart, Otto settled on the floor, legs crossed, and focused his mind. He called eight threads and sent them weaving through his body. Otto tried to picture the ether charging every cell with energy.

It didn't take long for his flesh to vibrate and tingle. When he tried to push past eight threads, something in his mind balked and the spell broke. Otto leaned forward, panting. Another failure. For a moment he'd believed he'd break through to nine threads, but it wasn't to be.

He made two more attempts before Father's door slammed open. He expected Otto to be ready the instant he emerged from his room and wasn't shy about reminding him. Otto hopped to his feet, slipped his shoes on, and went out into the main part of the suite.

Father glanced his way. "You're up, what a surprise. You and the crown prince hit it off last night. What did you discuss?"

"History and magic, His Majesty is something of a scholar."

"Well, even royals aren't perfect. Did you strike up a friendship with him? That could be a huge benefit for our family."

The beginnings of a friendship had taken root, maybe, but he didn't want to encourage his father too much lest he later end up disappointed.

"I think one conversation is far too minor a thing to base a friendship on. He did say he wished to continue the discussion later."

"Good." Father rubbed his hands together. "You must cultivate young Wolfric. His patronage will send much wealth our way. If I can build up the barony enough, even Stephan won't be able to tear it all down."

"I don't think you give my brother enough credit. If he put his mind to it, Stephan could destroy almost anything."

Father barked a laugh. "Let's hunt up some breakfast."

When they arrived, the main hall bustled with activity. Runners came and went, pausing only long enough to whisper in their host's ear and get a quick reply in return. Edwyn sat at the head of the table surrounded by a spread of food to make a sultan envious. Of Otto's blushing bride there was no sign.

Father walked over to the table and Edwyn started to heave himself out of the head chair, but Father waved him back, instead taking the seat to his right. The merchant slumped back into his chair in time to receive another messenger, a boy of perhaps thirteen years.

When that conversation concluded Edwyn shoved a roll in his mouth and chewed with enthusiasm. After he swallowed Edwyn said, "Gentlemen, please dig in. My daughter won't be joining us this morning. Too nervous I suppose."

"What's with all the messengers?" Father asked before helping himself to a slice of bread and covering it with honey and bacon.

"Ah, I apologize for that. With the wedding today I didn't wish to leave the estate for the morning auction so I'm trying to run things from a distance. It isn't going as well as I'd hoped. I should have trusted Alaric to handle it and just gone for the ritual of opening."

Otto forgot all about his eggs at the mention of magic. "May I join you when you depart? I'd very much like to see what happens when you activate the portal."

"Another time, my boy. It wouldn't do for the groom to be absent from the wedding party. Besides, there isn't really much to see. I touch the portal key to the gate, the runes light up, and wagons proceed through. It's actually quite boring."

Otto considered and quickly rejected explaining that much more happened in the ether than a non-wizard could see. No matter how much he explained, the half-blind merchant would never understand.

"I will be leaving in two days," Father said.

"So soon?" Edwyn voice rose in surprise. "I hoped you'd stay with us at least another week."

"My son can handle the family business in Garen. I need to return home."

Otto almost choked on his eggs. Father expected him to remain here? How would he continue his studies with Lord Karonin?

◯

After breakfast Otto and his father returned to their suite to prepare for the arrival of the first guests. They expected largely the same crowd as the night before, though Prince Wolfric had offered his regrets and said matters of state would prevent him from attending. Annamaria had been disappointed, but at this point what was one disappointment more or less?

When the door closed behind them Otto asked, "Do you not think we should introduce Annamaria to Mother?"

"At some point you can bring her home," Father said. "Perhaps when you have a grandson to show off."

Otto frowned. He needed to take a different tack. Of course, there was only one thing Father truly worried about.

"Will you leave the dowry behind?"

Father stared at him as though he'd lost his mind. "Of course not. The coins are going straight to the Shenk treasury."

"Oh, I assumed since you didn't want me along you intended to leave the gold here. It would be a shame if you ran into more bandits on your way home, especially with only six soldiers."

Father's brows drew down and Otto almost heard him mentally convincing himself that bringing Otto home was his idea. "I hadn't considered that. Perhaps it would be a good idea to introduce your new wife to Katharina. Yes, three or four days at home, show her the barony before you return to the capital. That's a fine idea."

He'd thought it might be. "Excuse me, Father." Otto ducked into his bedroom and thrust a fist into the air. Surely between them he and Lord Karonin could think of a way for him to continue studying with her.

Ten bells arrived and with it the first of the hundreds of guests. He stood at the entrance to the garden and shook hands until he feared his skin might slough off. Annamaria hadn't yet put in an appearance and when he'd asked one of the servants, he'd been told that she wouldn't come out until the ceremony, that way she'd make the biggest entrance.

Otto thought she just wanted to avoid the crowds and he

didn't blame her. If he could have skipped out on the gathering, he'd have done so in a heartbeat. Pity he didn't know how to conjure a thunderstorm. That would send the overdressed guests running.

A temporary altar had been constructed not far from where he'd had his unpleasant encounter with Annamaria's lover. Otto had feared the lovestruck fool might try something stupid, but so far, the day had been mercifully quiet. In fact, a maniac swinging a sword might liven things up a bit.

He took his place in front of a priestess wearing a necklace of gold coins and a white robe. The Frankens made generous donations to the Queen of Coins' temple so the high priestess herself had come to oversee the joyous event.

A small band sat off to one side and when the mansion door opened, they struck up a solemn tune. Annamaria emerged in a stunning white silk dress. Behind her three maids carried her train as she made her way down to the altar.

When she reached him, Otto held out his hand and the band fell silent. He looked into her eyes in hopes of finding something, anything, to encourage him, but there was nothing but resignation.

So be it. This didn't fit in with his plans either. They'd just have to make the best of it. If love was impossible, perhaps respect and eventually affection weren't.

The priestess launched into a mercifully brief recitation. Otto heard every third word until she asked, "Do you accept this woman as your wife, to love, honor, and protect for all your life?"

"I do." The words were out before he thought better of it.

Turning to Annamaria the priestess asked, "Do you take this man as your husband, to love, honor, and respect for all your life?"

For a moment he imagined her saying no and running off. It might even be a relief. If she broke the contract Father would still keep the dowry. It might—

"I do."

And that was it. He'd gotten married.

A cheer went up from the crowd prompting Otto and Annamaria to turn and wave to the guests.

"You may kiss your bride," the priestess said.

Otto leaned in, their lips brushed, and she broke away. That feeble effort wouldn't get a mention in the book of amazing kisses. It concluded the ceremony however and that was enough for Otto. Not that things got any less awkward from here.

Next it was off to the bedroom.

Edwyn raised his hands for quiet. "I know it breaks with tradition, but I wanted to offer my gift to my new son early."

A servant handed him a long, thin box of ebony. "This is a relic of my family, passed down from father to son for the past six centuries. It was used in the War for Freedom and the Great Purge. While my name ends with me, my blood continues on with my daughter. I hope when the time comes, Otto, you can pass this on to your own son."

Edwyn opened the box, revealing a sheathed broadsword with a basket hilt made of silver. Otto's eyes widened. Not silver, mithril. A mithril blade was almost priceless.

"Don't be shy," Edwyn said. "Take your gift."

Otto reached in and removed the weapon. He pulled the blade and raised the shining metal. The mithril flashed in the sun drawing a chorus of oohs and aahs.

"You have my most sincere thanks." Otto sheathed the blade. "I'll do my best to be worthy of it."

Edwyn clapped him on the shoulder and winked. "You and my daughter need to be on your way."

He turned to his new wife and found her lip trembling. They walked together to the door where Annamaria had emerged a little while ago. Servants had covered the tile in rose petals. The path led to a room Otto hadn't seen before today.

It was a single chamber with a huge bed in the center. White sheets had been strewn with more petals. Not exactly subtle.

Otto closed the door and sealed the sword in its sheath with a thread of ether. Not that he thought Annamaria would do anything crazy, but better not to take chances. He leaned the sword by the door and they walked over to the bed.

"I suppose you want to sleep with me now." She reached for her topmost button. Before she could undo it Otto took her hand and guided her to the bed.

He sat beside her. "If you don't want to do it we don't have to."

"We don't? You're my husband and that comes with certain rights."

Otto sighed. "I'll make a bargain with you. We're only seventeen and we'll—"

"I'm actually nineteen."

"Fine. The point is we're going to be together for a long time. I really don't want the first thing that happens between us is me raping you." He raised his hand to stop her when she tried to speak. "I know the law wouldn't consider it rape, but that doesn't change your lack of interest. We have time. Perhaps when you know me better this will be less of a burden."

She stared at him as if not quite believing what he'd said. "Are you truly not going to claim your rights as my husband?"

Otto stood up, crossed to the corner of the room, and sat cross-legged facing her. "I want nothing from you that isn't freely given."

So saying he closed his eyes so she could change out of her extravagant gown.

CHAPTER 22

The trip back to Shenk Barony went off without a hitch. The chain gangs had repaired the worst of the ruts during their time in the capital so the ride didn't even threaten to rattle Otto's teeth out. Annamaria hadn't been thrilled when he told her about their upcoming departure, but she packed with a minimum of complaint.

Ahead of them the castle towered over the town. Graves guided them through the gate and into the courtyard. Father pushed the door open before any of the servants reached them and leapt down. Otto followed then reached back to help Annamaria. At least the yard had dried after the early rains.

Mother, Stephan, and Griswalda emerged from the keep, each of them dressed in their finest outfits. Everyone's gaze went to Annamaria and each look held something different. Surprise from Mother, envy from Griswalda, and most troubling, hunger from Stephan. It wouldn't do to leave his new bride alone with his brother.

Otto hoped Stephan would keep himself under control, but

he held little optimism. Self-control had never been Stephan's strong suit.

Mother rushed over and hugged him. After a moment he whispered, "Axel sends his love."

She stepped back and stared. "You saw your brother? He's well?"

Otto nodded. "Army life seems to agree with him. We didn't have much time to catch up before Father spotted him."

She shot Father a glare which he ignored. Otto introduced Annamaria who made a little bow to the group.

"No need to be formal." Mother hugged her. "You're part of the family."

"Thank you." Annamaria almost sighed the words. It seemed she'd been more nervous than he'd thought.

Stephan and Griswalda approached and Otto moved over closer to his wife. The sneer Griswalda wore said this might turn ugly. Stephan's leer wasn't much better.

"My new sister." Stephan looked her all over then turned to Otto. "Father certainly did better for you than he did me."

Griswalda sniffed. "At least you married a true noble-woman and not some jumped-up fishmonger's daughter."

"Yes," Stephan said. "Lucky me."

"Enough chatter!" Father said. "Stephan, help me."

Between the two of them they wrestled the heavy chest of gold out of the carriage. It had to weigh a couple hundred pounds. A pair of soldiers hurried over to help, but Father waved them off. It seemed he didn't plan to let the chest out of his grasp.

The current and future barons lugged the chest into the keep. Griswalda gave Annamaria one last, dismissive glance and followed them.

"Friendly, aren't they?" Annamaria said.

"Don't mind them, dear," Mother said. "They weren't expecting you to be so beautiful. Griswalda isn't the most secure woman in the world. And Stephan... Stay away from Stephan if you can."

Mother snapped her fingers and the soldiers set to unloading their luggage.

An hour later Otto and Annamaria sat together in his tiny room. Compared to what she was used to it must have been like living in a cave in the side of a mountain.

Trying to break the awkward silence Otto asked, "Can I get you anything?"

"I'm fine, thank you. Your family is interesting."

"That's one word for them. Don't worry, we'll be heading back in three or four days. Father wants me to ingratiate myself with the prince and rich merchants in the capital, so he won't stand for much delay."

"Why did we come here in the first place then?"

Because he wanted to talk to the spirit of a long-dead Arcane Lord did not strike Otto as a wise answer, so he said, "I wanted you to meet my mother. She's the only sane member of the family and I thought the two of you might hit it off, especially after what you told me about your own mother."

"She does seem nice. Very well, what's the plan for tomorrow?"

"I thought you and Mother could spend the day together while I went for one last hike in the forest. While I won't miss many of the people in Shenk Barony, I will miss the land itself."

"It is beautiful country. So different from the city." Annamaria nodded. "Alright, you can have tomorrow all to yourself. The day after, you'll take me on a ride around the country, then we head back. Deal?"

"Deal."

◯

Lothair paced the tavern floor. She'd left. Annamaria had gone away with her wretch of a husband and abandoned him. How did she not know he'd remained in the city to watch over her? She must have felt his loving gaze on her whenever she left the estate.

What should he do now? He paused and darted a glance at Ulf, but the enigmatic man didn't so much as twitch and Lothair had yet to hear him speak a word. Putting the silent bartender out of his mind, Lothair resumed his path through the empty tavern. With all the chairs up on the tables he had plenty of room to walk his chosen route.

The sun had risen an hour ago and they wouldn't open until noon. He had hours to kill before a distraction presented itself.

Maybe he should go after them. If he followed, Lothair could watch over her during her time in Shenk Barony. He dismissed the idea as soon as he had it. A stranger would stand out far more in the rural barony than in the city. He doubted Otto would let him walk free a second time.

The door to the back room slammed open and Allen emerged, his clothes rumpled and his hair going in every direction. He stood directly in Lothair's path.

"Please stop with the pacing. The thump of your boots is driving me mad."

"Sorry, but when I stop moving, I can't escape thoughts of Annamaria and her husband. It's driving me out of my mind. What should I do, Allen? I fear if I go after them, I'll be caught, but if I don't something might happen to her."

"I don't care what you do as long as you do it quietly. I have an important job this morning and I need to be clear-headed."

"Can I come with you? This is just the thing to take my mind off Annamaria."

"Fine, a lookout might come in handy. We leave at nine bells. If I hear a peep out of you before then you can rot here." Allen spun on his heel and stomped back into his room.

Three hours later the temple bells struck nine and Allen emerged neatly dressed in tan trousers and white tunic. A saber dangled from a baldric at his hip.

"Let's go."

Lothair belted on his own sword and fell in behind his friend. They left the tavern and turned up the street toward the portal.

"What's the job?" Lothair asked.

"We're meeting someone, she'll have an item for me. I collect it and deliver it to Crane tonight, at which point I get paid."

"Who is she and what's on the scroll?"

Allen stopped and turned to face him. "You learn quickly in this business that the fewer questions you ask the healthier you'll stay. Your task is simple. Find someplace out of the way and keep your eyes open. Be ready to step in if there's trouble. I doubt there'll be any in the middle of the morning in the crowded area around the portal, but better safe than sorry."

They set out again and Lothair kept silent. It became clear to him exactly how little Allen knew about the people he dealt with. Perhaps it was for the best. He didn't have enough experience to say for sure one way or the other, but Lothair would have liked some idea who they met and what their intentions were.

As Allen said, the area around the portal teemed with people. Burly workers stood behind men in rich clothes. A handful of soldiers kept watch in pairs, ready to act should things get out of hand. Judging by their lax expressions the guards expected no trouble. Lothair found a bench that afforded a good view of the area and settled in to wait while Allen moved closer.

When ten bells rang out the first rune flared to life. Soon the entire circumference of the portal glowed. A moment after that the first wagon emerged. Three more followed it before the portal died again.

He looked closer at the wagons and spotted a small emblem affixed to each one. The symbol of a red dragon was well known to the people of Garenland. It represented the Kingdom of Straken, Garenland's oldest enemy.

A dark-haired woman in a blood-red dress climbed down from one of the wagons and Allen walked over to her, his arms raised in greeting. She waved and when they came together, she hugged him. After a brief exchange they parted ways. If Lothair hadn't expected it, he never would have noticed when she passed Allen a small cylinder.

The pair of them handled the exchange with smooth precision and before he knew it Lothair and Allen were on their way back to the tavern. Lothair still hadn't the slightest idea what the whole thing was about and neither did Allen. His old friend seemed a good deal less worried about it than Lothair considered wise.

CHAPTER 23

Otto found the tower exactly as he left it. After an awkward night sleeping back to back with Anna-maria, he'd gotten up early and left, pausing only long enough to belt on his new sword. He didn't really need it, but he also didn't want to leave the valuable item lying around where his lunatic brother might stumble on it.

When he slipped out of bed his wife simply groaned and rolled into the center of the mattress. Being married to a heavy sleeper might not be a bad thing for him. He'd drawn no notice as he slipped out of the castle. The servants were all working at fixing breakfast and the sweet, savory smells from the kitchen almost convinced him to put off his expedition. In the end he decided his stomach would have to wait. He needed to talk to his master.

An etheric thread opened a path through the trees and he bounded up the stairs into the second-floor chamber. The tower felt like a timeless space, as though nothing would ever change.

Lord Karonin appeared in the mirror and he bowed. "I have returned, Master."

"I can see that. Have you improved your skills?"

"I seem to have reached a plateau. I can wield eight threads with little trouble, but when I try and push to add a ninth everything falls apart. No matter how hard I try I can't make the leap."

"You've reached your natural limit. It happens to every wizard eventually."

Otto's heart leapt into his throat. Eight threads couldn't be his limit. He wanted to do so much more. "That's it then? I'll never get any stronger?"

"Possibly. My natural limit was twelve. It took me over a year to find my way through that barrier. Once I did I mastered forty in another year. This, more than any challenge you'll face as a wizard, will determine your future."

Otto slumped with relief. He wasn't doomed. For once it seemed he held his fate in his own hands. "How did you overcome your limit, Master?"

She laughed. "The same way I overcame every obstacle I ever faced: sheer stubbornness. I kept pushing and pushing, some days until I passed out and blood ran from my eyes. I decided I was either going to succeed or die trying."

Did he have that sort of willpower? Otto wanted to be a great wizard more than anything in the world, but would he die for it? His life wasn't so bad, especially now that he'd live a week away from his family.

No!

Simply living wasn't enough. He would be strong, strong enough that Father and Stephan would shy away from him for a change.

"What can I do to improve my chances, Master?"

"You must become one with the ether. Infuse it into your body until it pervades every cell. Make it an extension of yourself. Only then can you truly call yourself a wizard and gain access to the most powerful magics."

He nodded and settled on the floor. He'd been on the right track when he tried to force ether into his body, he just needed to push it further.

He shifted his perception and called eight threads to him.

"No!" Lord Karonin said. "Stop thinking in terms of threads. Embrace the ether as a whole."

Otto frowned. How did one embrace an insubstantial energy field?

He let the threads diffuse into mist and breathed it in. He pictured the energy entering his blood and circulating though him. The Bliss nearly overwhelmed him. He'd never felt it this intensely.

"Good." Lord Karonin's voice came, soft and encouraging. "Now a little more. Keep adding to the power in your body. Push it out into your hair. Enhance your senses. See everything. Feel everything."

He took another breath, drawing more ether into his body. Overwhelming pain burned away the Bliss.

Otto choked back a scream and fought to hold on to the power. He managed for a few seconds before it became too intense.

He moaned and the ether flooded out of him.

He trembled, every inch of his body raging at him. Panting and trying to force the pain away, Otto curled up in a ball on the floor. In her mirror Lord Karonin shook her disembodied head.

"You are weak. Until you discover true strength you'll never break through your wall."

Otto tried twice more and both times he ended up abandoning the power at the same point, the pain and his desire to live forcing him to give in. He heaved himself up off the floor, his body aching and his stomach complaining about the lack of breakfast and lunch.

"I believe I'll call it a day, Master." Otto considered the best way to approach his new living situation and decided straightforward was the best path. "My father has commanded that I'm to leave the barony and live in Garen with my new wife. I don't know how often I'll be able to visit for training."

She pursed her lips. "Go to the compartment and fetch my book. You'll find a spell on the last page."

Otto retrieved the book and flipped to the end. The final spell was teleportation. He read it over twice before lowering the book. "Is it really possible to travel instantly through the ether between two known places?"

"It is. This spell is the basis for the magic that powers the portals. To use it you must first become one with the ether. Until you've broken through your wall, I can teach you nothing more."

"What purpose does the rune serve?"

"It serves to help you fix a target location in your mind. There are other ways, traveling to the vicinity of a blood relative or even simply to a place you've been many times, though that one can be dubious for a beginner. The important thing to remember is that without a firm destination in mind, however you mark it, you can become lost in the ether, wandering forever unable to escape."

Otto swallowed. No one ever said magic wouldn't have

risks. "May I carve a rune in your tower? When I overcome my limits, I want you to be the first person that sees me."

"You may. The center of the chamber is safest."

He moved to the middle of the room and drew his sword. The mithril would cut stone easily enough.

"That sword," Lord Karonin said. "Where did you come by it?"

Otto held it up to allow her a better look. "It's a wedding gift from my new father-in-law. An old family heirloom, or so he claims. I'm no fighter but given its value I thought it best to keep it close."

"Do you not know the purpose of mithril?"

"Uh, to make swords strong enough to cut through steel?"

"Damn your ignorance! Mithril's true purpose is to magnify etheric energy, not make toys for warriors. If you channel your spells through the metal, it will increase their effect by fifty percent."

He looked at the sword with new respect. "I had no idea. In fact, I doubt anyone living has any idea."

"It's a powerful tool, but don't rely on it unless you have plenty of time for your casting as the extra step slows the process down even as it increases its power."

Naturally there was a downside. It seemed everything in life hid one. He lowered the tip of the sword to the stone and carefully sliced out the shape of a marking rune. As he expected, the blade cut the stone with almost no resistance.

"Good," she said. "Now channel energy into it until the rune glows in the ether like a beacon. If you do it correctly the marker will last until you destroy it."

"Why would I want to destroy it?"

"You wouldn't want to destroy this one. Since I control the ether in the vicinity of the tower, I can stop anyone else from finding it, but if you mark a different spot and don't want another wizard to find it when you're done, you'll need to erase your mark."

Otto scowled and began the flow of energy. He wasn't in the habit of thinking his every move out the way Lord Karonin did. If he wanted to last long as a wizard that needed to change.

CHAPTER 24

Annamaria woke alone in a strange bed. For a time the night before she hadn't been certain she'd ever fall asleep. Having Otto lying beside her was simply too strange. Not that he'd done anything. To say that he'd surprised her with his statement that he wanted nothing she didn't willingly offer would be an understatement. That he'd stuck to it for the last ten days surprised her even more.

In her experience, noblemen expected their whims to be obeyed at once by commoners and their desires satisfied at the drop of a hat. She'd seen it in his father during their journey out to this backwater holding as well as during his time as her father's guest. How his son had avoided all these character flaws defied understanding. She just thanked the angels that it was so.

She rolled out of bed and cracked the door to allow enough light so she could see to dress. When her morning preparations were complete, she went downstairs to the great hall, if you could call a thirty-by-thirty room filled with hand-cut tables and dogs a great hall. A fire burned, taking away most of the chill.

"Good morning, dear," Lady Katharina said. "Did you sleep well?"

Otto's mother sat alone at the table, a steaming mug of something held between her palms. She wore a simple dress of tan cotton. A gold clasp held her hair up away from her elegant face. When Annamaria imagined the ideal noblewoman, someone like Katharina came to mind.

She offered a curtsy which drew a chuckle from the older woman. "I slept fine, thank you, though I didn't expect to wake up to an empty bed."

Katharina patted the bench beside her and motioned to one of the servants standing along the back wall. The girl nodded and hurried away.

"Otto has always liked the quiet of the forest," Katharina said. "He's probably under a tree somewhere, reading."

The servant returned with a tray of bread, fruit, and cheese as well as a second steaming cup. She placed the treats in front of Annamaria and resumed her place at the back of the room. Annamaria took a bite of apple and found it sweet if a little softer than she preferred.

"Your son is an odd man for a noble. He has a gentle way and seldom speaks. If I didn't know better, I would doubt he was related to his father."

Katharina laughed again. "No, Otto certainly doesn't share Arnwolf's aggressive nature. I think it comes from being a third son. No one ever expected anything of Otto, so he didn't feel the need to prove himself."

Annamaria took a sip of her drink and found a pleasant, slightly fruity mulled wine. "I believe my husband wished us to spend the day together so we might get acquainted. Do you have any plans?"

"I have a pile of needlework that requires my attention. Do you sew?"

"Not well."

"As long as we close up the holes in the socks, the stitches don't need to be pretty."

"Don't you have servants for that?" Annamaria refused to believe the wife of a baron had to mend her own socks.

"We have many servants, but there's only so much each one can do in a day. Besides, I find it oddly satisfying to watch the pile of torn clothes grow smaller and smaller."

It sounded horrible to Annamaria, but she'd play along. It was only for a day after all.

When she'd finished her food and wine Katharina led her upstairs to the sewing room where a pile of clothes lay between two chairs. A square frame holding a section of canvas sat off to one side, directly in the sunlight. A spread of blue flowers had been sewn into it. The beautiful, delicate design rivaled anything back home.

"Is this your work?" Annamaria asked.

Katharina smiled and settled into her chair. "It is. Sometimes I run out of socks."

They worked their way through the damaged outfits, pausing for lunch. As they puttered away Katharina told stories of Otto as a child. As the day progressed her growing understanding of Otto's childhood horrified her. That he had turned out to be a decent human being considering what his father and older brother had done to him over the years was a miracle.

"Excuse me, Lady Shenk." Annamaria stood up. "I need to wash up before dinner."

"Of course, dear. If you'd like, feel free to call me Kat."

She nodded and slipped out the door. Otto was right about her liking his mother. Annamaria could easily imagine Kat as her own mother. She hadn't had an older woman in her life for far too long.

"Hello, little sister."

Her blood went cold.

Annamaria turned to find Stephan standing a few feet away. She hadn't even heard him approach. He wore the same twisted leer as yesterday. Her gaze darted to the sewing room door.

Before she even considered yelling for help he lunged closer and slapped a hand over her mouth.

Stephan leaned in, his lips inches from her ear, his breath hot on her neck. "Now, now, we wouldn't want to upset Mother."

She twisted and tried to wriggle free.

He shook her and his hand went back.

⟳

Otto trudged back to the castle. The magical training had left him as weary as if he'd actually spent the day hiking through the woods. At his side the satchel he'd brought dragged at him. He'd finally accepted Lord Karonin's offer to take the spell book with him. Heaven alone knew how long it might take him to break through whatever block kept him from fully embracing the ether and he wanted the book with him as he practiced.

The great hall was empty save for the hounds and they didn't even stir when he entered. Father must still be holed up in the treasury counting his new wealth. He'd haggled Edwyn up to twelve thousand double eagles.

He hoped Mother and Annamaria had spent a pleasant day together. It would be nice for his wife to see at least one of his relatives wasn't insane. He yawned and glanced up at the second floor.

Adrenaline rushed through him. Stephan had Annamaria pinned to the wall, his hand over her mouth.

Otto raced for the stairs

She fought and Stephan's hand went back.

Otto flicked his ring and bound Stephan in place.

Annamaria's gaze darted to him, though Stephan's frozen hand still held her in place. Otto sent ether into his aching body, grabbed his brother by the front of his shirt, and hurled him down the hall to slam into the wall.

Stephan slumped to the floor, his body still frozen stiff.

"Are you okay?" Otto asked.

Annamaria nodded, tears running down her face. "I thought he…"

"I know. We'll leave first thing in the morning. Go to my room. I need to talk to my brother for a moment."

Annamaria dashed down the hall and closed the bedroom door behind her.

The door to the sewing room opened and Mother stuck her head out. When she saw Stephan lying on the floor she sucked in a breath. Otto held a finger to his lips. Mother nodded and closed the door again.

Otto stalked down the hall, releasing Stephan as he got close. His eldest brother had always scared him to death, but right now anger so consumed him that fear didn't even enter his mind.

His brother slumped for a moment then sprang to his feet. "You dare lay your hands on me?"

Stephan swung and Otto caught him by the wrist. The moment he had a firm grip he summoned lightning. Stephan's jaw clenched as he spasmed.

When the lightning ended Otto let him collapse back to the floor. "If you ever touch my wife again, brother or not, heir or not, I'll kill you. Do you understand, brother?"

Stephan still twitched from the shock, apparently unable to speak.

"Nod if you understood me." Otto let the electricity dance around his fingers in an unsubtle threat.

Stephan's head jerked up then down.

Close enough. Otto let all his threads fade away and staggered to his room. They'd take their meal together and leave at first light. If he'd gotten home a second later things might have ended much worse. He refused to put Annamaria at any further risk.

CHAPTER 25

She had returned!

Lothair wanted to dance in the streets. His beloved Annamaria had returned from the backwoods barony and appeared none the worse for the experience. How he longed to see her, talk to her, hold her. And he would, but he had to take his time and make a plan. To the patient man went the prize.

With that end firmly in mind, Lothair slunk along ten yards back from the bastard Shenk as he made his way to the auction house. He'd invested the few coins Allen had paid him for his efforts in the finest clothes possible, so he'd better blend in with the rich residents of Gold Ward. So far, his investment had paid off. The broad-brimmed hat with the peacock feather thrust into the band made an especially nice touch. It also cast a shadow across his face making his features harder to discern.

Not that Otto so much as glanced his way. The arrogant noble never looked left or right, so confident was he in his privilege. Or more likely the confidence came from his magic. Lothair couldn't deny that one on one he had no hope of defeating his rival. Happily, there existed more than one path to any destination. Lothair's lay around rather than through the man in his way.

Otto crossed the street and went into the auction house. Lothair stayed on the opposite side. He'd been following the nobleman for the past three days and so far the routine never varied. An hour at the auction then three hours at the palace.

To be safe he intended to follow Otto for a full week to be certain nothing changed on any given day. He found a bench a comfortable distance from the auction house door and settled in to wait.

A little over an hour later, right on time, Otto emerged from the building along with Annamaria's father. They set out for the mansion, chatting and laughing just like the best of friends. Lothair followed them from the opposite side of the street until the pair entered the gate to the estate grounds. He made sure to keep his distance lest one of his former comrades see him and call out.

He had another hour to kill, so Lothair fell back to the intersection that led to the palace. A little outdoor tavern sat on the corner of the street. He settled down at one of the tables and ordered a small beer. Horrid stuff, but the cheapest item they sold and the owner wouldn't let Lothair sit at a table for free.

As he sipped his bitter refreshment Lothair's mind whirled. Assuming the pattern didn't break, he had a three-hour window to safely approach Annamaria. He didn't know if Master Franken had altered the patrol routes after he left, but he doubted it. No one had any reason to believe he'd try and sneak back in.

Lothair clenched his jaw. Damn it, he couldn't make assumptions. He'd have to scout out the mansion grounds with the same attention to detail that he tracked Otto. No mistake could be allowed to prevent his reunion with Annamaria. Better to spend an extra few days and get it right the first time as he doubted he'd have a second chance.

Two beers later Otto strode around the corner and headed up the street toward the palace gate. Lothair watched him pass but made sure not to stare too hard. Some people sensed it when angry eyes looked their way. That seemed the sort of thing a wizard might be able to do.

Lothair whiled away the time with a light lunch and some people-watching. The rich merchants in this district carried themselves so differently than their workers down in the business district. Where the poor hurried everywhere, the rich strolled as though they had all the time in the world.

Perhaps they did. When you didn't have to worry about earning coin enough to pay for your next meal it freed you to enjoy life a little.

He rubbed the gold ring Annamaria had given him. She was different. His dear Annamaria never looked down on him for serving as a guard. She loved him for who he truly was. That's how he knew she'd welcome him back with open arms.

At three bells Otto returned from the palace and set out for the mansion. He'd stayed longer today, though not enough longer to affect Lothair's plan.

With his reconnaissance work done, Lothair left Gold Ward and returned to the tavern. Allen had another job and he expected Lothair back by four bells.

〇

The auction house where Edwyn sold off daily rights to pass through the portal held seats for one hundred bidders and in every one of them sat a merchant. Twenty-five more leaned against the back wall in hopes of snagging a bargain slot. The accumulated wealth represented in that room staggered Otto's mind. If a group of robbers ever got it in their heads to hold up the place they'd make off with a fortune.

He stood at the front of the room with his father-in-law and a pair of mercenaries. The auction would begin when the Temple of Coins rang eight bells. The bidding would last until every slot had been filled or the merchants ran out of gold. Edwyn assured him that the latter had never happened.

He and Annamaria had arrived the day before after leaving Castle Shenk at first light a week ago. Only Mother had come to see them off and that suited both of them fine. After Stephan's little stunt he doubted he'd convince Annamaria to return. Not that Otto had much interest in going back to the castle. His sole desire was to get back to the tower by way of teleportation. If he arrived any other way, he doubted Lord Karonin would let him in.

"Nervous, my boy?" Edwyn asked.

"Not overly, sir." The soft, perfumed, robed men sitting in front of him didn't exactly intimidate, especially after dealing with Father and Stephan. "Good crowd today."

"Hmm, typical I'd say. We always have more loads in need of delivery than we have portal time. That's why we make so much at the auctions."

Eight bells sounded and Edwyn stepped up to a lectern with a ledger open on it. "Gentlemen, the bidding opens at five crowns a wagon for slots to Rolan. Who'll start me off?"

Ten hands shot up and the auction was under way. Edwyn

called out bids and counterbids until he rapped a knuckle on the lectern and wrote down the winning bid and began a new round.

The whole process went far faster than Otto had suspected and in under an hour the process was complete. He glanced at the ledger and did a quick calculation. They'd cleared a little over one hundred double eagles for one day. Even after the crown took its share that was still ten for less than an hour's work. It almost seemed illegal.

They returned to the mansion and Otto went to the suite he now shared with Annamaria and settled in to train. He sat on the floor rather than in the far-too-soft chairs. He'd barely begun to infuse ether into his body when someone knocked.

Grumbling, he got back up and opened the door. Thomas bowed and held out a scroll for him.

"What's this?" Otto took the scroll. It had a wax seal with the royal griffin on it.

"The courier didn't say, Lord Shenk, but it came from the palace."

"Thank you, Thomas."

The boy left and Otto shut the door again. He broke the seal on the scroll and unrolled it. It was short and to the point. Wolfric wanted him to come by for lunch. He need only present the letter to the guards at the palace gate.

Training would have to wait. An invitation from the crown prince wasn't something he could ignore. Besides, he found the prince excellent company and was curious what he wanted. After a quick change of clothes Otto left the mansion and turned up the main road to the palace.

There wasn't much traffic and five minutes later found him standing in front of an iron portcullis. The wall surrounding the palace grounds measured forty feet tall and thirty feet thick. Bowmen patrolled the top of the wall and four more men in mail and carrying spears and swords waited beside the closed gate.

One of the men, the oldest if his gray beard was any indication, handed his spear to the guard beside him and approached Otto.

"What business brings you to the palace, sir?" the guard asked, both his tone and manner perfectly polite.

He held out the scroll. "Otto Shenk to see Crown Prince Wolfric."

The guard read the brief message. "Welcome to the palace, Lord Shenk. His Highness said we should expect you. You'll just need to bind your sword and you can head right in."

Otto accepted a foot-long piece of string and tied one end to the hilt of his new sword and the other to the scabbard. The peace binding only slowed the draw of a sword by half a second, but it served as a reminder that violence wasn't permitted inside.

When he finished, the guard nodded and motioned to his comrades. A moment later the portcullis clanked open until he could pass through without hitting his head. The guards all saluted as he passed.

Beyond the wall, a wide, open killing field waited. Should the outer wall be breached archers could fire from both directions, catching any invader in a lethal crossfire. How many lives would it take to conquer the city of Garen? He shuddered to consider it.

Across the killing field loomed another wall, this one with the gate open. He went through and looked around. The palace sprawled over an even bigger area than Franken Manor and rose three stories. Wolfric said to meet him for lunch, but he didn't say where, or offer directions.

He spotted a boy wearing a black and gold servant's smock lugging an armload of firewood. Maybe the youngster knew the way.

"Excuse me!"

The servant glanced his way, dropped the firewood, and bowed. "How may I be of assistance, my lord?"

"I received an invitation to join the crown prince for lunch, but the note neglected to provide directions. If you'd direct me to the dining room, I'd be grateful."

"Of course, my lord." The boy gathered up his bundle again. "I'm on my way to the kitchen anyway. His Majesty's preferred dining hall is only two doors away."

Relief coursed through Otto and he fell in beside his guide.

CHAPTER 26

Wolfric's preferred dining room turned out to be a modest chamber with a square table and four chairs. Two places were set and a carafe of white wine waited between them. The prince stood as Otto entered.

"Welcome, Otto. Thank you for joining me."

"Thank you for the invitation, Highness."

Otto bowed and stepped over to the empty chair. He waited a breath until Wolfric had resumed his seat before joining him. Since no servant attended them the prince poured wine for each of them. The whole situation was a hideous breach of protocol, but Wolfric seemed not to care.

Wolfric sipped his wine. "Otto, if we're going to be friends you need to relax. There are scores of people available when I want to be sucked up to. In fact, I nearly have to burn the leeches off my ass to get them to leave me alone."

Otto smiled at Wolfric's turn of phrase. "Relaxing in the presence of the future king of Garenland is easier said than done. Nevertheless, I shall do my best."

"That's the spirit. Now, how's Annamaria doing? I understand you took her home to meet the rest of your family."

Talk about starting with a rough subject. "She and my mother hit it off. Unfortunately, we couldn't stay too long. I'm currently studying the business with her father. Assuming the Crown sees fit to let us keep the portal contract, I figure I'll need to know how it all works."

"Father and I are both very happy with the coin Edwyn brings in. I see no reason for that to change in the future."

Otto half bowed in his seat. "Edwyn will be pleased to hear it. And how is His Majesty? Your father hasn't made an appearance in some time."

"He's well, thank you for asking. Father spends most of his time in conference with ambassadors from the other portal nations. They constantly complain about something or other. It's tedious and I spend as little time on it as I can."

A knock on the door was followed by a pair of female servants carrying platters entering the room and setting them on the table. Both women bowed to the prince and withdrew without removing the covers.

Seeing Otto's surprised look Wolfric laughed. "I prefer to eat without servants hovering around. I'm a grown man, yet the way they fuss you'd think I was still four years old."

The prince removed the cover from one platter and Otto removed the other. There was roast chicken, vegetables, fresh bread and cheese. It smelled wonderful and his mouth started to water.

"Dig in."

They ate in silence, Otto savoring every perfectly prepared bite. Whoever ran the palace kitchen could give Cook a run for his money.

When the last drop of juice had been sopped up Wolfric sighed. "Thank you for that."

"For what?"

"For not jabbering nonstop and spoiling the meal. I often have guests and to a person they're incapable of just shutting up and enjoying the food."

"Ah, well, back home if you pester my father during a meal, you'd best enjoy the taste of blood as you'll have a mouthful of it shortly."

Wolfric winced. "That's a bit harsh."

"Harsh describes Father well. Not a bit of warmth or gentleness in the man."

"He sounds the exact opposite of my father. On the rare occasions he was around, Father doted on everything I did. My every whim was indulged instantly. Still is in fact. You have no idea how tedious it is to be surrounded by people who only tell you what they think you want to hear. Have you ever tried to debate someone that always agrees with you?"

Otto laughed. "I don't know a single person that always agrees with me. My brothers would argue with me about the color of the sky. And when I was proved correct Stephan would beat me black and blue."

"Perhaps being an only child isn't such a bad thing after all."

"Sounds like heaven to me."

They moved on to less personal subjects until they finally came around to magic. Wolfric leaned across the table. "What's it like to be a wizard?"

Otto cocked his head. "How do you mean?"

"I mean it must be wondrous to have power at the tip of your fingers. To wield fire like an ordinary man does a sword. To bend the natural world to your whims."

The prince's misconceptions were equally amusing and

dangerous. Perhaps Otto could steer him in a less threatening direction.

"I think you misunderstand what a wizard is capable of. We can only amplify what already exists. A wizard doesn't bend nature so much as nudge it. We make the fire hotter, the arm stronger, and the eye sharper."

"But I've read the histories. In ancient times wizards rained death upon their enemies, slaughtered armies and moved mountains."

"Perhaps," Otto said. "No one alive today can say for certain, but I suspect a lot of the histories are just stories. The fear they create is used to limit and, in some places, kill or enslave wizards. Better that, some would say, than to risk them running amuck."

"Do you resent the laws?" Wolfric leaned back and finished his wine.

No way would Otto answer that honestly. "I think Garenland's laws are more just than those of any other nation. The limits serve a useful purpose. They allow the regular folks not to fear wizards. The laws and those who enforce them keep everyone safe. That isn't a bad thing."

Wolfric's smile turned predatory. "You didn't answer my question."

"No, Highness, I suppose I didn't."

They ended the meal and Wolfric walked him out of the palace. When they reached the outer gate the four guards all took a knee.

"Jorvik," the prince said.

The oldest guard looked up. "Yes, my prince."

"Otto here is to be allowed entry to the palace any time, no questions asked. And he need not bind his sword. Understood?"

Jorvik bowed his head. "Yes, my prince."

"Good. Spread the word." Wolfric thumped Otto on the back. "Any guard that troubles my new friend will answer for it. Until next time, Otto."

He watched the prince make his way back to the palace. All around him the guards regained their feet.

"I didn't know you and His Majesty were such fast friends, my lord," Jorvik said.

"Neither did I."

Every day for a week Otto had been visiting the palace for the midday meal. Today, after their usual lunch, Wolfric led Otto from the little dining room, down a long hall to the biggest library Otto had ever seen. The books had to number in the thousands. He stared, mouth hanging open.

"Impressive, no?" Wolfric strode through the door. "I've spent many pleasant afternoons lost in these books."

"Do you have a favorite subject?" Otto asked. He followed Wolfric to the center of the room where a collection of tables and chairs waited. The two men settled into buttery leather seats.

"History, especially from the time of the Arcane Lords. Did you know, once all the little countries were part of a single nation ruled by a woman?"

Otto nodded. "Lord Karonin. She was a mighty wizard. The casters of our time are like children compared to her."

"I sometimes imagine what it might be like to rule such a vast empire. The power, not to mention the wisdom such a task would require boggles the mind."

"Indeed. It helped that the Arcane Lords were immortal.

When you have forever you can simply wait for most problems to go away on their own."

Wolfric laughed. "I doubt the lords were so passive. Let's have a game."

"A game? What sort of game?"

"A game of questions. I'll ask a question and if you don't know the answer you have to show me a magic trick. Then you ask a question and if I don't know the answer you can ask me for any favor."

"That's quite a bet. You must be confident in your studies."

Wolfric grinned. "I'm quite well read. I'll go first. What was the capital of Lord Karonin's empire?"

"This was, the city of Garen, though she called it Arcanium."

"Correct! I'm impressed. Your turn."

"What's the energy wizards wield called?"

"Ether. You'll have to do better than that if you want to stump me." Wolfric laughed like a little boy.

They went back and forth a couple more times, neither able to think of a question the other didn't know. At last Otto said, "Where was Lord Karonin born?"

Wolfric pursed his lips, scratched his chin, and did everything else you could think of to avoid admitting he didn't know. Finally, he blew out a sigh. "I give up, where?"

"Shenk Barony, it's something of a local legend. Since I can't show you any written evidence, what do you say we call the contest a draw?"

"Agreed, though I would have liked to see some magic."

Otto looked around, but it was only the two of them in the library. He held out a hand, wove four threads into a single strand, and used it to grab a book off a nearby shelf. He pulled the book to his grasp and held it out to Wolfric who was staring.

"Just a simple spell, but since you were kind enough to show me your excellent library, I thought it was the least I could do."

Wolfric took the book. "Thank you. I've never seen a wizard casting up close before. Not that there was much to see. Will you join me again tomorrow?"

"I'd be delighted, Your Highness."

CHAPTER 27

Annamaria knelt in front of the daisy bed and hacked out a weed. The air held a hint of summer and her work blouse was stuck to her back with sweat. In the two weeks since she'd returned with Otto from his father's barony—she shuddered at the memory—the newlyweds had fallen into a comfortable if dull routine. Her husband spent his mornings learning the family business from Father and his afternoons at the palace with Wolfric.

For her part, she'd settled into her old habits. Putter in the garden, maybe practice her harp, and generally make sure the household ran smoothly. That had been her responsibility since she turned thirteen. Despite Father's talent for business, he simply had no idea how to manage the servants and deliveries.

At least he pretended not to. She suspected the reality was he liked leaving the work to her. Someday down the road she'd be running the house for Otto. Women couldn't inherit property after all. Everything she'd helped Father build would go to Otto.

She slammed her spade into the dirt. It wasn't fair! First, she had to marry against her will and eventually she'd end up totally dependent on her husband's goodwill.

Annamaria picked up her spade and sighed. All her raging and bitterness changed nothing. The law was what it was and had been for hundreds of years.

"Annamaria."

She leapt to her feet, heart racing. It couldn't be.

Lothair stepped out from behind the cedar shrubs. He had on such a ridiculous broad-brimmed hat that she almost laughed. Only the fear that someone might hear and investigate stifled it.

"What are you doing here? You should be on the far side of the kingdom by now."

He moved closer so only a step separated them. "Did you think I'd abandon you to the wretch, Shenk? I've been searching every moment for a way back to you."

"If Otto finds you, he'll kill you."

"I've been watching him. Every day's the same. We have hours before he returns." Lothair raised his hand and wiggled the ring she'd given him. "I knew you meant this as a promise that we'd be together again."

She looked around the garden, but no guards showed themselves. Annamaria trembled. If Father or Otto discovered that Lothair had returned...

"You must leave before you're discovered. Hurry."

He closed the distance between them and put his hands on her shoulders. Heat rushed through her.

"I won't leave you alone, not like your foolish husband."

He leaned in and her breath caught. How many times had she dreamed of this since the wedding?

Their lips touched and she dropped the spade. Time lost all meaning as they kissed in the garden.

She didn't care if they got caught or her father kicked her out. In that moment nothing mattered but him.

When they finally came up for air she said, "Let's go inside."

An hour later, lying in bed beside him, Annamaria came to her senses. What they'd done was madness. Wonderful madness, but madness all the same.

Lothair stroked her arm. "Crown for your thoughts."

She rolled over to face him. "I wonder what will become of us. I should throw you out and refuse to see you again."

"But you won't. I love you, Annamaria. You know we belong together."

Did she know that? Certainly she cared more for Lothair than Otto. Even if he was a better man than she'd expected when Father announced her engagement. She didn't love him and doubted she ever would.

"Perhaps, but the situation hasn't changed since that day in the garden. If we run away, we'll be found and you'll die. I can't stand the idea of anything happening to you."

"Then we'll steal what time we can." He kissed her. "Your heart belongs to me and mine to you. You may be married to Otto in name, but in your soul, you know it's you and me forever."

Two bells sounded, drawing a sigh from Lothair. "I have to go, but I'll return tomorrow. Meet me in the garden?"

She should refuse. Today had been a wonderful thing, but nothing good could come from continuing down this path.

"I'll be waiting."

Lothair left the grounds as easily as he entered. Lightning raced through his blood and he wanted to shout his joy to the world. Not now though. As he'd suspected, the guards' patrol routes hadn't changed, and their attention remained as lax as he remembered. While that made his sneaking in easier, he worried for Annamaria with such poor protectors watching over her.

He left Gold Ward with no trouble and made his way through the crowded streets back to the tavern. Even the jostles of the crowds and cursing of the wagon drivers failed to dent his good cheer. Lothair doubted anything short of a foot of steel in his gut would ruin the day.

When he arrived the tavern was nearly empty, only a single party eating and a pair of ragged men at the bar nursing half-full mugs of ale. Ulf stood in his usual place, as sullen and silent as ever. Their gazes met and Ulf jerked a thumb toward the office.

Lothair ambled over, knocked, and pushed the door open. Allen sat behind a desk cluttered with paper. He motioned Lothair into the only other chair in the room. Lothair closed the door behind him and sat.

"What's on your mind?"

"We have a job tonight."

The prospect of more coin brightened an already glowing day, at least until he noticed Allen's scowl. "You seem less than thrilled."

"Yes, well, tonight's work is more complex than a simple delivery and more dangerous. I hate jobs like this, but the coin is too good to pass up. I take it from your shit-eating grin your assignation went well."

"Well is an understatement. So what, exactly, are we doing tonight?"

"We're retrieving information, but what we need is in an estate in Gold Ward. Are you familiar with the Kunitz family?"

"Only in passing. Their mansion is on the opposite side of the ward from the Frankens'."

"Correct. The family deals in swords and the rumor is their master smith has devised a new alloy that's stronger and more flexible than any created without the use of mithril. The sole copy of the formula is kept in a safe at the heart of the mansion."

The more he heard the less Lothair liked the sound of this business. "Wait, I thought you were an information broker, not a thief."

"I am whatever I need to be to get paid. We pull this off and it's ten double eagles for each of us."

Lothair gaped. That was more gold than he made in five years at his old job. "The security must be tight."

Allen grinned. "It is, but the three of us can do it. Ulf has a potion that will put a man to sleep within seconds of inhaling it. It only lasts for ten minutes, but that's plenty of time for us to get in, make a copy of the formula and get out."

"I thought we were going to steal it."

"No, our employer doesn't want anyone to know we were there. In addition to knocking them out, the potion leaves the target horribly nauseous. Anyone we use it on will think they got food poisoning."

"Sounds like you've got it all planned out."

"Hardly. Let's take a walk. I need a closer look at the grounds."

Allen left Ulf in charge of the tavern and the two men set out for Gold Ward. Lothair insisted they use a different gate from the one he entered that morning. He didn't want the guards to get curious about why he came and went so often.

The Kunitz estate looked about two-thirds the size of Master Franken's. Not a single shrub grew anywhere and even in passing Lothair counted six guards walking the grounds which implied at least six more he couldn't see.

As they continued their stroll he asked, "Do you know the layout of the mansion?"

"Not in detail," Allen said. "But I do know the safe with the formula is on the second floor. I'm more worried about sneaking across that yard. There's nowhere to hide. What sort of merchant doesn't have a fancy garden?"

"A security-conscious one. Do you have a plan B if we can't sneak in?"

"Ulf's working on something, but I'd hoped not to have to use it. I've seen enough. Let's go back."

Lothair gave the estate one last backward glance. They'd earn their coin tonight, that was certain.

CHAPTER 28

The last of the patrons left the tavern half an hour ago. Lothair, now dressed in plain servant's garb, joined Allen and Ulf in the common room. Allen hadn't bothered to inform him why he needed to change his clothes, but Lothair assumed his old friend had a reason.

In his right hand Ulf held a six-foot tube and in his left a needle with a tuft of hair on the end. The silent bartender proceeded to slide the needle into the tube, raise it to his mouth, and blew. The dart shot out and stuck in the wall a quarter inch. Ulf pointed at the dart then tapped his neck. Allen nodded.

Lothair was pretty sure he got the gist as well. "So we dart the guards and then go in while they're out, right?"

"Right." Allen eyed the tube. "Ever used one of them?"

Lothair laughed. "I've never even heard of such a thing. I think friend Ulf is going to have to do the darting."

Ulf tapped his chest and gave a thumbs-up. He set about loading a small box hanging from a shoulder strap with darts and a sealed vial.

"Are you sure about this?" Lothair asked.

"Not at all, but I'm not about to pass up ten double eagles." Allen gave him a hard look. "What about you?"

Lothair shrugged. "I'm broke. The coin from this job will hold me over for a year at least."

Ulf shouldered his gear and nodded toward the door.

"Okay, let's go." Allen led them outside to a fancy carriage he'd rented for the night. The guards wouldn't dare refuse entry to someone riding in such a rich-looking rig. No clouds obscured the three-quarters moon, so they had enough light to see by, if only just. "Up you go."

Allen and Ulf climbed in the back and Lothair climbed up in the driver's seat. Now he understood why he was dressed like a servant. Well, he'd played worse roles over the years. A flick of the reins got the horses moving.

Ten minutes later brought them to the eastern entrance to Gold Ward. The guards on duty raised their hands and Lothair reined in.

"What's your business here this late at night?" the nearest guard asked.

"Just bringing my passenger home after a late-night slumming, sir." Lothair shook his head as if to say, what can you do?

"What's the hold up!" Allen's slurred voice shouted from the carriage. He sounded every bit the drunken fop. "I have to piss!"

"Please, sir," Lothair said. "If I don't get him home soon, I'll have to spend the rest of the night cleaning my employer's carriage."

"Off with you then." The guard waved and the gates were thrown open.

"Thank you, sir." Lothair managed a credible bow from the

seat and urged the horses through. One challenge down, plenty more to go.

He parked the carriage across from the Kunitz estate, but well back from the front gate. The moment he pulled the brake Allen and Ulf climbed down. Ulf crossed the street, pulled a dart from his ammo box, dipped it in the poison, and loaded the tube. He crouched by the fence and watched.

Lothair turned to Allen. "What are we supposed to do?"

"Be patient and let Ulf do his work. He'll signal when he's cleared the way."

A chuff of air followed a moment later. Ulf reloaded and chuffed again. The bartender looked back and held up two fingers.

"That's a start," Allen said.

"Do we have a plan for when we get inside?" Lothair asked.

"First we're going to strip those guards then we'll walk right in like we own the place. The helmets will keep anyone from knowing we aren't who we're pretending to be. How long could it take to search the top floor?"

Another chuff announced the downfall of a third guard. Three more and this side of the grounds would be clear.

"Didn't you say Kunitz kept the plans in a safe? I don't know about you, but I'm no safecracker."

"Never fear." Allen reached down the front of his shirt and pulled out a large key. "An acquaintance of mine is a locksmith. When I mentioned the type of safe we needed to open he made me a skeleton key."

"You told someone we were robbing this place?" Lothair failed to keep the disbelief out of his voice.

"Relax, this particular locksmith isn't exactly legitimately employed, if you take my meaning. I also paid him three crowns for the key and three more for his silence. We have nothing to fear on that end."

Two more quick chuffs were followed by Ulf twisting and shooting a third dart. He waved them over, pointed inside, and gave a thumbs-up.

The three men made the hundred-yard dash down to the gate, slipped inside, and ran back to the closest unconscious guards. Between them it took only two minutes to strip off the guards' mail hauberks and helmets and don them. Allen added several items from his satchel to his pants pockets.

When they were ready Allen said, "Keep an eye out. We don't want anyone stumbling over the bodies."

Ulf nodded and Allen led the way up to the mansion. They didn't go to the main entrance, that would be asking for trouble. Instead they marched up to the servants' entrance, shoved the door open, and entered like they knew where they were going.

The interior was mostly dark and after a quick search Lothair found a lantern and fire starter. He scratched the flint against the steel and a stream of sparks landed on the wick. He squinted against the glare until his eyes adjusted.

"Let's go," Allen said. "Keep your eyes peeled for a flight of stairs. There must be one nearby."

It didn't take long to find the stairs and they climbed them quietly, but not furtively. Lothair kept his role at the front of his mind. They were guards doing their job. They had to search the office, but they didn't want to wake the whole house.

At the top of the stairs they found a long hall running left and right. Lothair raised an eyebrow and Allen shrugged. They went right, peeking in each room as they passed. The first four were bedrooms, three empty and one occupied by a snoring lump.

"This is taking too long," Lothair whispered.

Allen touched his finger to his lips and went on to the next door. This one revealed a garderobe, thankfully unused. Lothair glanced up the way. A weak glow emerged from under one of the doors. He tugged Allen's sleeve and pointed.

Allen snuck over and looked through the keyhole. He straightened at once and motioned Lothair a little way away.

"That's it," Allen said. "But Kunitz is in there reading."

"So what now?" Lothair remained acutely aware of the time rushing by. Every second increased the chances of them getting caught.

"We have to take him out." Allen dug a scrap of cloth and a vial out of his pocket. "You knock and when he comes to the door, I'll get him."

"Okay." At this point Lothair would have agreed to almost anything if it got them moving. "Ready?"

Allen nodded and stood on the opposite side of the door. Lothair blew out a breath and knocked. Kunitz's muffled grumbling was followed by his chair creaking. The lock clicked and the door opened.

"What is it?" Kunitz asked.

With the light behind him Lothair couldn't make out much beyond the merchant's bulky figure. Hopefully the dark hall limited Kunitz's sight as well.

Lothair eased back and barely above a whisper said, "There's been some unusual activity outside, sir."

"What?" Kunitz took a step closer.

The moment he cleared the doorway Allen pounced, clamping the rag on Kunitz's face. The merchant struggled for a second, but soon drooped to the floor.

Lothair looked all around. The encounter had been nearly silent save for Kunitz's words. Hopefully they hadn't drawn any attention.

"Help me carry him inside." Allen grabbed Kunitz under the armpits and Lothair lifted his legs.

The unconscious merchant weighed every bit as much as Lothair had feared. It took everything the two men had to maneuver him back into his office. They dropped him the moment his body cleared the door.

Lothair grunted and rubbed his back while Allen went to the desk.

"We're in luck." Allen went through the desk drawers until he came up with pen and paper. "It seems our host was studying his secret formula. We won't have to open the safe after all."

Allen set to work copying while Lothair chewed his lip. After what seemed a long time, but probably wasn't more than three minutes, Allen spread drying sand on the paper, rolled it up and tucked it away in one of his pockets.

"Let's get out of here." Allen headed for the door.

Lothair followed behind, grateful to have finished their business without getting caught. No one stirred as they retraced their steps, picked up Ulf, redressed the guards in their armor, and boarded the carriage.

☌

When they cleared Gold Ward, Lothair found he could breathe freely again. They left via a different gate and the guards didn't give them more than a passing glance. They were paid to keep people out not in after all.

When they'd put some distance between them and the gate Lothair asked, "Where to now?"

"The tavern. We'll leave the carriage and walk to the meeting. This rig will draw too much attention where we're going."

Lothair made no comment, as he adjusted their course. It didn't take long for them to reach the tavern since the streets were empty this late at night. He guided the carriage into the alley beside the building and climbed down from the driver's seat.

When Allen and Ulf had climbed out, they headed toward the foundry. Allen set a brisk pace, seeming as eager as Lothair to complete their business. Lothair wanted the document out of their possession as soon as possible. If anyone came looking there'd be nothing to connect them to the break-in.

The path to the foundry was as empty as the streets and ten minutes later they stood in the alley facing Crane and his cronies. In addition to their daggers a pair of the thugs carried cocked and loaded crossbows. Lothair tensed and loosened his sword in its scabbard. Something stunk and he meant to be ready.

"Did you get it?" Crane asked as he stepped two paces in front of his men.

"I wouldn't be here otherwise." Allen joined him in the middle of the alley. "You've got my gold?"

"Ten double eagles, as agreed."

"Ten for each of us you mean." Allen's voice held an angry edge.

"No, ten total. How you share it is your business."

"That wasn't the deal, Crane. You promised me ten for each man that helped."

"Bullshit! Don't blame me if you misunderstood. You might

have invited ten men to help you. Do I look like I'm made of gold?"

Allen shook his head. "I'll find another buyer."

The thugs behind Crane tensed and the crossbows went up. A phantom stab went through Lothair's chest when the bowmen aimed at him.

"You can walk out of here with the gold or be dragged out by the guards in the morning." Crane rested his hands on the hatchets thrust through his belt. "Either way, I'm taking that formula."

Allen raised his hands and patted the air. "Easy, Crane, easy. We've been doing business for two years. You really want to end it this way?"

Crane's shrug held nothing but indifference. "My master wants that formula and he's not the sort of man you disappoint, not more than once anyway. If I have to kill you to get it, well, there are other information dealers in the city."

"Okay, okay. Maybe I did misunderstand. We'll take the coin and be on our way."

When Crane smiled Lothair relaxed a hair. "Good decision. I'd have hated to kill you, Allen."

Crane gestured and one of the thugs tossed a heavy pouch at Allen's feet. It landed with a lovely clink. Even three double eagles would be as much money as Lothair had ever held at one time.

"Now the formula." Crane held out his hand.

Allen pulled the paper out and handed it over. Crane studied it in the feeble light and nodded. "Good. Until next time."

Crane spun on his heel and marched out the back of the alley, his men falling in beside him. When they'd gone out of sight Allen let out a string of curses.

"I should have run him through. Cheating bastard! How dare he suggest I misunderstood?" Allen bent down and snatched the pouch.

"Let's just go back to the tavern. It's been a long day and I'm beat." Now that the adrenaline had worn off, Lothair's legs felt like toffee and his hands shook. He hadn't come this close to death in a long time and he had no desire to do it again.

"Good call." Allen led them back the way they'd come.

"Will you do business with him again?" Lothair asked.

Allen looked at him like he'd lost his mind. "Of course. Crane's my best customer. A few death threats is no reason to end such a profitable arrangement."

No rebuttal came to Lothair. When you had to deal with people like Crane it was probably good business not to take the odd threat too seriously. And they had received a nice chunk of change for an hour's work.

CHAPTER 29

The morning sunshine shone through the windows and into Annamaria's bedroom. Summer had arrived in earnest and new blossoms flooded her garden. Every afternoon for the past month Lothair had snuck into the garden. At first, she'd had trouble reconciling the illicit meetings, but now she no longer cared. She could even look Otto in the eye without cringing. His absolute cluelessness made her subterfuge far easier.

A wave of nausea rolled over her and she made it to the chamber pot without a moment to spare. Her days of easy lying would soon end. The midwife should arrive shortly, but she had no doubts. Lothair's child grew inside her. Soon she'd have to make a decision.

She gagged again. Not right now though. Right now, she had to survive the morning bout of sickness. Her sole good fortune was that the nausea passed after she'd been awake for three or four hours.

Someone knocked and Annamaria crossed the room. Mimi

stood waiting in the hall. She bobbed a curtsy. "I heard you gagging, miss. Can I do anything?"

"No, thank you. Is Madam Kohen here yet?"

"Not yet." Mimi sucked on her lower lip. "Will you tell Master Lothair about this?"

Dread overwhelmed nausea. She grabbed Mimi and dragged her inside. "How do you know about him?"

"I see him coming and going now and then, miss. And we all know that Lord Shenk has moved back into the guest suite. Even a servant could put those two pieces together."

"Does anyone else know about Lothair?"

"No, miss. I only see him since I stay nearby in case you need me."

Annamaria grasped her maid by both shoulders. "You must never let even a hint of what you saw slip. Lothair's life is in your hands."

Mimi gave her a shy smile. "Your secret is safe with me, miss. I think it's romantic. You finding a way to be with your true love. I always thought it was wrong of your father to force you to marry Lord Shenk. Though I find him to be a kind man whenever he speaks to me."

She pulled Mimi to her and gave her a hug. "He is kind and he deserves a wife that loves him, but Otto has me instead and we're just going to have to make the best of it."

"Yes, miss. How are you going to explain…" Mimi gestured at her still-flat stomach.

Annamaria sighed. How indeed? "I'll think of something. Perhaps I just have the stomach flu."

Mimi tittered at the suggestion. "Perhaps. I'll go wait for Madam Kohen."

Twenty minutes later the midwife entered her bedroom. Madam Kohen had to be pushing eighty; her skin sagged and

wrinkles covered every bit that poked out from her volumi-
nous black robe. The harsh scent of herbs hung in the air
around her.

She peered at Annamaria. "When did the sickness start?"

"Three days ago."

"And your courses?"

"A week late."

"Hmm." Madam Kohen made a shooing motion toward the
bed. "Lie down and we'll find out for sure."

Annamaria lay on top of her heavy blanket. The midwife
stood over her, a gold ring suspended from a silver chain in
her hand.

"Just relax. Close your eyes." She held the ring over Annamaria's abdomen.

Relax? At that moment she could no more relax than she
could fly. She closed her eyes for a moment but opened them
up again. She had to know.

The ring wavered then swung from side to side.

Madam Kohen let it go for a moment then nodded. "Congratulations, you're going to have a daughter. Aren't you?"

Annamaria understood what she was asking at once. The
midwife knew about more than how to bring a child into this
world.

Whatever happened, Annamaria was no more capable of
harming Lothair's child than she was the man himself.

"I am."

The wrinkled face broke into a broad, toothless smile.
"Good. I have herbs for the sickness."

"Heaven bless you." Annamaria would have sold her soul
for something to stop the nausea.

Madam Kohen left behind a bundle of herbs and instructions to make a tea with them once a day for the next six

weeks. Mimi guided her out leaving Annamaria alone with her troubles.

She knew what she had to do. Only one thing could secure her daughter's future. While she loved Lothair, when her father died Otto stood to inherit everything. She needed to convince him the child was his. It wouldn't be difficult, assuming she could force herself to do what needed to be done.

⌒

When Otto left the palace following his daily visit, the sun hung low in the sky, casting long shadows across the killing field. He and Wolfric had gotten into a game of chess following a lengthy debate about the pluses and minuses of the Arcane Lords' rule. It would have amused his master no end to hear the prince breaking down her style of empire.

He nodded to the guards as he left, drawing a salute in return. The palace soldiers all knew him by sight at this point and they also knew he was friends with their future king. That garnered him more respect than his meager rank as the third son of a rural baron.

Otto didn't mind the formal treatment at the palace, but he wished his wife of two months would relax a little around him. He'd done his best to be patient and understanding, but he'd about reached the end of his string. A lifetime of being treated like a visitor in his own home didn't suit him at all.

He'd been considering simply moving out of the mansion and finding a place of his own for a few days, but that would be inconsiderate of his father-in-law. There were certain expectations that a father had to meet and one of them was that when

188

he chose a husband for his daughter said husband didn't leave the daughter after two months.

Otto sighed. He'd gut it out for another week. If things hadn't improved by then he'd look to make other arrangements. Perhaps Wolfric had a spare room at the palace. Some of the serving girls were quite attractive and friendlier than his wife. Moving out might make everyone happier.

His mind had been so busy he didn't remember the walk back to the mansion. The gate guards saluted as he passed, bringing a smile to his face. Everywhere he went it seemed he got nothing but salutes. There were worse gestures, but a handshake and pat on the back would have made a nice change of pace.

A servant stood beside the door when he entered and helped him off with his outer jacket. He kicked off his boots and slid on his soft, fur-lined slippers. His sword he kept on until he reached his rooms. The weapon was too valuable to leave hanging by the door.

In the dining hall only two places had been set. He frowned. Was she unwilling to even take a meal with him now? Moving out looked better by the moment.

He went deeper into the mansion, eager to be rid of his sword and change out of his formal clothes. He wouldn't bother with them in the first place, but visitors to the palace had to observe certain standards, stiff, uncomfortable outfits being one of them.

Annamaria's maid stood outside the door to his room. She bobbed a curtsy. "My lady has arranged a private dinner for the two of you. If you'll return to the dining room when you're ready, she'll join you shortly."

Another bob and she took off like a scared rabbit. So Annamaria wanted a private dinner. What did she have in mind now? The woman hadn't spoken more than a handful of words to him in the last two weeks and now this. He sighed and entered his room.

Fifteen minutes later Otto made his way back to the dining room. The space had undergone a transformation. Someone had extinguished the magical lights and lit candles instead. Annamaria waited beside the table wearing a rose-colored silk gown that revealed her pale shoulders. Long blond hair cascaded down her back.

Otto couldn't speak for a moment. When he'd gathered his wits he asked, "What's all this?"

"I've been thinking a lot the past few weeks." She motioned him to his chair and when he'd settled in sat across from him. "Especially about what you said on our wedding day."

He racked his brain trying to remember what he'd said. In truth, the day had been a blur and the details escaped him. "What did I say?"

"That we'd be together for a long time. I've been sulking like a petulant child these past weeks, pining for something I'll never have. I'm your wife and it's time I start acting like it. Tonight is my first effort to make things right between us."

While he had no idea what had made her change her mind, Otto didn't plan on complaining. Servants brought out a single platter covered with his favorite roasted salmon and vegetables. Annamaria served him herself then poured wine.

They ate in silence for a moment then he asked, "Where's your father?"

"He went to his club for dinner with some old friends. I told him we needed a little time to ourselves."

It seemed she'd thought of everything. When the meal had ended and the last of the wine drunk, she took his hand and led him to their bedroom for dessert.

CHAPTER 30

Summer on the northern border should have been the best part of the year for Axel and his patrol. The sky was blue, the breeze warm, and a hint of perfume from blooming flowers scented the air. Only three villages remained to be checked before they returned to base for their week off. Unfortunately, two more burned villages spoiled things for him.

Blasted nobles and their politics. The villages on the Straken side had to be suffering as much as the ones on the Garenland side, yet they refused to allow a joint patrol or even a temporary alliance so he could pursue the raiders in Straken territory.

How did anyone expect him to do the job given such unreasonable restrictions?

Cobb yanked on his tunic. "My lord, look."

Axel dragged his mind back to the moment and followed his second's finger. Black smoke rose in a thick column, far more than you'd expect from a cooking fire.

"Bastards! They won't get away this time." He whipped his

horse with the reins and thundered down the road, his men in hot pursuit.

Heart racing, Axel bent low over his horse's neck, urging it to more speed. The next village was only half a mile away. This might be the break they'd been waiting for.

He rounded a bend and there was the village. Small log cabins blazed as figures ran around in front of them. A woman's scream was cut short.

Someone loosed a piercing whistle and the raiders turned toward the nearby forest. They ran hard and vanished into the shadows.

Not this time. Axel refused to let them get away again. "Two men check for wounded, everyone else with me. Colten, on point."

The well-trained soldiers sorted themselves out in half a minute. Colten leapt off his mount and ran for the edge of the woods. Seconds later he motioned the others to join him. The moment Axel reached him the scout jogged into the trees.

Axel studied the broken branches and scuffed dirt. He could have followed the trail without Colten to lead him. Even though they'd startled the raiders, no skilled woodsman left a trail this sloppy by accident.

"On your guard, everyone." Axel drew his sword. The solid heft offered him some comfort. "We might be walking into a trap."

The sound of steel clearing leather reassured him as they continued deeper into the forest. Colten made his way in the lead without a moment's hesitation. Despite their reckless pace no sign of the enemy appeared.

"Colten, do we gain?"

"Perhaps a little, sir, but not much. They set a brutal pace."

Axel growled in the back of his throat. He didn't dare push

the men any harder. If it was a trap, out-of-breath soldiers would make easy targets. The raiders must have intended to cross the border. He had to catch them before then. He didn't intend to let the slaughter of people under his protection go unanswered, not this time.

Their pursuit continued until Axel lost all track of time. Behind him all his men gasped for breath. If they didn't catch up with the raiders soon, they'd be in no shape to fight.

Up ahead the trees thinned. They left the forest and found themselves at the edge of a village. The buildings were made of rough-hewn logs. A few trickles of smoke rose from stone chimneys.

A scream went up. Axel turned to find a girl of ten staring at them. A stout woman in a brown homespun dress came running, snatched the girl up, and fled into the nearest house.

"This is a Straken village, my lord," Cobb said. "We've crossed the border."

Axel swore at the sky. "Colten, this is the way they came?"

"No doubt about it, sir." The scout retreated from the edge of the village. "What do we do?"

"What can we do?" Axel slumped. They'd been so close. "We retreat, bury our dead, and try harder the next time."

He led his men back into the forest. Why hadn't the raiders troubled the Straken villagers? For that matter why weren't the villagers already cowering in their homes? They couldn't have missed a band of armed men bursting from the trees.

Had the bastards made a bargain with the raiders? A cut of whatever they took for safe passage through Straken? That would explain a lot.

Axel had many questions and few answers. The little he knew for sure left him cold inside.

CHAPTER 31

The throne room held only Wolfric, his father, and ten royal guardsmen. The Straken ambassador had requested an early morning audience and Father decreed it important for them to show a united front. The benches in front of the throne that usually held petitioners and advisors sat empty. Wolfric hadn't the least idea what the ambassador wanted to discuss, but clearly Father intended to keep the matter quiet.

When he commanded Wolfric to attend him this morning Father made it clear that all Wolfric had to do was stand beside the throne and keep quiet. The whole thing was a pointless exercise, like many he engaged in as crown prince. He'd given up keeping track of how many times Father asked his advice only to ignore it. The two men had totally different ideas about Garenland's place in the world and it made it difficult for them to find common ground.

Wolfric adjusted his sword and glanced down at his father. At fifty years old the king had lost much of the strength of his youth. His thin, haggard face wore the simple gold crown like it weighed as much as a mountain. Despite the warmth of the day Father pulled his purple cloak tighter about him.

Father looked up and caught Wolfric staring. Wolfric looked quickly back toward the door. While he may have lost much of his physical strength, Father's will remained strong. Some days he gave off an aura of unflagging determination. Today, however, he looked like a tired old man.

The throne room doors opened and the herald announced, "The Straken ambassador!"

A mountain of a man stomped into the room like he owned the place, not a hint of deference on his bearded face. The ambassador made no effort to dress in clothes appropriate for a court appearance. In fact, the leather and fur jacket and trousers he wore looked cut out for a hunting trip not a diplomatic mission. Not that the ambassador had ever been overly diplomatic in his dealings with Garenland.

The ambassador made a halfhearted bow. "Your Majesty, I bring word from my king, Uther. You are summoned to a Kings' Council in Lordes to answer for a breach of the compact."

Wolfric stared in disbelief. Father held the compact sacred. He would never do or order anything done that anyone might consider a violation. There had to be some misunderstanding.

Straken's ambassador reached into his fur jacket and withdrew a rolled and sealed scroll. Father snapped his fingers and one of the guards hurried down to fetch it. The moment it hit his hand Father broke the seal and started reading.

Wolfric followed along over his shoulder. The Kingdom of Straken accused Garenland soldiers of crossing the border in violation of the Portal Compact. It went on to describe a squad of soldiers entering a border village. No mention was made of injuries or deaths. It ended by summoning the king to a council in one month's time.

Father looked up from the scroll. "You have proof of these accusations?"

"Over a dozen witnesses. I assure Your Majesty that King Uther takes these actions extremely seriously. Do you have any words you wish me to carry to my king?"

"Anything I have to say to Uther, I'll say to his face at the council. You may go."

The ambassador bowed, turned on his heel, and marched out. When the doors had slammed behind him Wolfric's father turned to him. "What do you know about this?"

"It's the first I've heard of it. There have been raids on the border and our commanders have requested permission to cross over in an effort to bring them to justice."

"I know that. I'm the one that denied the requests. Find out who's responsible and bring them to me. We must find out more if we're to formulate a response."

Father rose and strode out of the throne room, his guards falling in place around him. Wolfric found himself alone, his mind racing. He'd best get in touch with General Varchi. As commander of the northern legions he'd know what was happening. He gave the throne one last, long look.

Someday.

○

Otto sat across from Wolfric and nibbled a delicious stuffed pheasant. The two men ate in the small, private dining room where they'd met each day since the prince first summoned him to the palace. The simple furnishings and rustic food would have fit in at any home in the kingdom. It never ceased to amaze Otto how ordinary Wolfric's tastes ran. His ambitions, on the other hand, would have done an Arcane Lord proud.

A smile creased Otto's lips as he considered his change in fortune. The last week with Annamaria had been among the happiest of his life. While he had no way of knowing how long the change would last, he intended to enjoy every second of it. Wolfric, on the other hand, hadn't taken more than three bites as he scowled down at his plate.

"What troubles you, my friend?"

Wolfric gave a little shudder and forced his expression to smooth. "Father has been summoned to a Kings' Council next month in Lordes. Straken has accused us of breaking the compact."

"That's madness. Garenland would never do something so foolish."

"Father's words precisely. However, upon further investigation, it seems some of our soldiers may have accidentally crossed the border. They did no harm and retreated as soon as they realized where they were, nevertheless, the word of the contract was broken."

"What a mess. What will the king do?"

"He will acknowledge the mistake but claim that since no harm was done there should be no penalty. If they accept his argument, we'll have no trouble, if not, well, let's hope it doesn't come to that."

Otto pushed his plate away, his appetite gone. "Will you join your father?"

"Yes, and I'd like you to come as well."

Otto's eyes widened. "Me? I'm honored, Wolfric, but why?"

"Two reasons. One, I value your judgement. Two, your brother is the one that led the soldiers across the border."

Axel, you idiot!

"I am, of course, at your service. When are we leaving?"

"Twenty days from today. Your brother arrives from the north in ten days, leaving ten to figure out an argument that might save us from the worst-case scenario."

Otto shuddered. The worst case would see them cast out of the compact and their portal deactivated. It would be a death sentence for their merchants' businesses.

"Can I share this news with my father-in-law, or do you wish it kept secret?"

"You can tell Edwyn, but no other. We don't want to cause a panic. Impress upon him the importance of keeping quiet. I only permit you to share with Edwyn because as master merchant he has the most to lose should the portal be shut down."

"I appreciate that and Edwyn will too." Otto got to his feet. "If you'll excuse me, I need to inform him as soon as possible."

Wolfric waved him away. "Go. I fear I'd make poor company today anyway. Think hard, my friend. If ever a wise solution was needed, this is it."

Otto bowed and withdrew. His mind raced as he rushed through the halls and out into the street. Beyond the walls he turned toward the portal. Edwyn should be at the gate preparing for the noon activation.

Five minutes from the portal it flashed to life. Otto rounded a corner and reached the end of a line of fifty wagons. He ignored the inching line and walked straight toward Edwyn. The master merchant had a guard on either side of him as he motioned the next wagon through.

He spotted Otto approaching and waved him over. "Your meeting with the prince ended early today I see. You're welcome to hang around, but I have nothing for you to do."

Edwyn was in such good cheer Otto almost hated to tell him, but he needed to know.

"His Highness has brought something important to my attention and I thought you should know right away."

Otto leaned closer to ensure no one would overhear. When he finished the blood had drained from Edwyn's face. "How are our chances?"

"Prince Wolfric doesn't appear optimistic. We are ordered to say nothing about this matter to anyone. He was emphatic about that."

Edwyn nodded. "I understand completely. I'll breathe not a word. That said, once I complete the day's shipments, we must hurry home to make plans."

"I'll go at once," Otto said. "Maybe I can come up with some ideas."

☊

Annamaria lay in bed beside Lothair and tried to think of the best way to tell him about both the baby and her plan for Otto. What she was doing was necessary to secure her daughter's future, but he'd hate it all the same. Why did men so seldom understand that sometimes you had to do the practical thing?

Maybe she should just close her eyes and go to sleep. The bed felt soft and the silk of the sheets smooth against her skin. A quick nap before she said anything. Would that be so bad?

Yes, it would. The longer she waited the harder it would be.

At last she took a breath, steadied herself, and said, "I'm pregnant."

Lothair stiffened beside her then his arm slipped around

199

her. He kissed her neck and whispered, "That's fantastic. Is it a boy or girl?"

She relaxed against him. That took care of the easy part. "A girl."

"I bet she grows up as beautiful as you." He kissed her again.

Now the hard part. "I've begun preparing Otto to accept that the child is his."

Lothair stiffened again. Part of her wanted to roll over and see his expression and another part, the larger part, didn't want to know.

"And how are you doing that?" The barely controlled anger in his voice sent a shiver down her spine.

"By playing the dutiful wife. In two or three more weeks I'll tell him about the baby and he'll believe it's his. Once that's done, I can beg off, maybe say it's too uncomfortable now that I'm pregnant."

"So now you're sharing your bed with him. How long until you cast me off and become his wife in truth instead of just make-believe?"

She rolled over. "Don't give me that jilted lover nonsense. You know I love you, but my fate as well as our daughter's depends on Otto not finding out about us. There are penalties for what we're doing, harsh ones."

"Please." His lips twisted in an ugly sneer. "The nobles jump in and out of bed with each other's wives all the time and the merchants are worse. None of them ever get into trouble."

"Idiot! Nobles bedding nobles or commoners bedding commoners is fine, but a commoner and a nobleman's wife? You think there would be no consequences, for either of us?"

His expression softened. "The thought of you and him together pains me. I can't shrug it away and say no big deal."

She stared in disbelief. "You think this is no big deal to me?

I'm the one that has to smile and pretend to love someone I was basically sold to. I'm the one that has to lie with a man I feel nothing for because it's the only chance I have to provide a comfortable future for my daughter. I have to bear these things, not you. All you need to do is hold me and say you love me anyway."

Annamaria sniffed and tried to will the tears away.

Lothair squeezed her tight. "I love you now and forever, no matter what. Nothing will ever change that. I swear it."

He leaned in to kiss her when frantic pounding sounded on the door.

She groaned. "This is not a good time, Mimi."

"Lord Shenk has returned home, miss." Mimi's muffled voice barely penetrated the door.

Her eyes widened and Lothair said, "He never comes back this early."

"Never say never. You need to get dressed and out of here." She leapt out of bed and swirled a robe around her shoulders. "I'll keep him distracted so you can slip out the back."

Lothair ran around collecting his clothes and dressing as he went. "I'll return tomorrow, but not until I see him leave."

She shivered. "If Otto is changing his schedule, we'll have to be extra careful."

It never occurred to her to suggest not seeing him. Without Lothair she doubted she'd survive a week with Otto.

CHAPTER 32

Otto looked at his brother and shook his head. Axel had arrived an hour ago to receive a thorough bawling-out from the king. Otto listened to the whole thing from the back corner of the throne room. To say His Majesty hadn't been kind would be an understatement. At least Axel escaped with his head still attached to his neck.

When the king finally wearied of yelling, he ordered Axel out of his sight. Wolfric had taken Axel by the arm and dragged him to the war room which was where the three of them now stood as they tried to make sense of what had happened.

A huge table covered with a map of the continent filled the center of the room. It was a relic of the days when the nations still regularly fought wars. Otto studied the northern border. Garenlanders had built villages within a mile of it. That in and of itself struck him as a risky idea.

Wolfric stalked around the room, every once in a while shooting lethal glares at Axel. Frankly it did little to help Otto concentrate. For his part, Axel simply stood in silence, hands clasped behind his back.

"Show me again where the village you found under attack lies," Otto said.

Axel studied the map a moment then stuck a pin in it. A mile and a quarter from the border.

"Okay, now where was the Straken village?"

Axel stuck in a second pin. "That's approximate. I could be mistaken by half a mile or so in any direction."

"That's close enough, thank you." Otto adjusted a compass and measured out the distance between the Straken village and their capital. Almost three hundred miles. "With a good horse how long would it take you to cover that distance?"

Axel frowned and Otto could almost see the wheels spinning in his head. At last he said, "Ten days or so, depending on the roads. What are you trying to figure out, little brother?"

"The timing. Prince Wolfric, what day did your father receive the summons to Lordes?"

Wolfric finally stopped pacing and came to join them beside the map. "July twenty-ninth. You have a theory?"

"Maybe. Axel, which day did you cross the border?"

"The fifteenth maybe?" Axel shook his head. "I'm not certain."

"That's close enough. We'll give them the benefit of the doubt and assume the best-case scenario. If someone from the village left that day for the capital it would have taken at least until the twenty-fifth for him to arrive, agreed?"

Axel nodded. "At least. The twenty-sixth or twenty-seventh would be more likely."

"Okay, let's say the twenty-sixth then." Axel glanced at Wolfric. "How long would you say for our theoretical commoner to get his message to the king?"

Wolfric pursed his lips. "At least two days. Where are you going with this, Otto?"

"You'll see. At the absolute best the king of Straken got the news about the border crossing on July twenty-eighth. Your father received the summons the next day. What are the odds of everything coming together exactly like that without some preplanning?"

"None." Wolfric bared his teeth. "It was a setup from the beginning. I'd wager Father's crown Straken, Rolan, and maybe Tharanault are in this together. Those three have always resented Garenland for our wealth and success."

"How could they have known I'd cross the border, Highness?"

"That it would be you is irrelevant," Otto said. "Eventually, the ongoing raids had to prompt one of our soldiers to ignore the border and try to put an end to them. No nation could tolerate the ongoing murder of its citizens."

"We gave them all the information they needed." Wolfric slammed his fist on the table. "This is why Straken refused to work with us on the border raids. Our stupid attempts at diplomacy warned them and they laid their plans and waited for us to walk into the trap."

"And so I did," Axel said. "Should we tell His Majesty?"

"This is all speculation," Wolfric said. "Well reasoned and most likely correct, but speculation nonetheless. I will speak to him tonight, but even if he believes us, theories carry no weight at the council."

"Especially if half of it is already set against us," Otto said. "Assuming you're right about Rolan and Tharanault our country is doomed no matter what we do."

CHAPTER 33

Otto lay back in their bed and stared at the ceiling. Annamaria had gone to take a bath, but she said she had something important to share with him when she finished. He didn't know what was on her mind, but he was eager to find out. He was due to leave for Lordes with Wolfric and the royal party in the morning.

Wolfric had explained their theory to the king and he had agreed they were most likely correct in their assessment. The king also, unfortunately, agreed that it would make little difference to the council. Garenland had broken the rules of the compact. No amount of theories or excuses changed that. The only hope they had was that they were wrong about the other kingdoms working with Straken. If that turned out to be true, then nothing would help them.

Well, that was trouble for tomorrow. He intended to fully enjoy tonight in the hopes that the memory would sustain him during what would no doubt be a difficult trip. Otto smiled at the idea of Annamaria being the source of any happy memories. Whatever caused the change that had come over her, he thanked heaven for it every day. He couldn't have asked for a more loving and attentive wife. To think he'd considered moving out only a short time ago. Now it felt like he was living a dream.

The improvement in their relationship, combined with the coming trial—and it was a trial, whatever the other monarchs called it—had even distracted him from his training. He hadn't made a single attempt to break through his personal barrier since the night before that first private dinner. It wasn't that he'd given up, Otto still intended to become the most powerful wizard possible, it just didn't seem as important as before.

The bathroom door opened and Annamaria emerged wearing nothing but a thin silk robe. He sat up, eager to meet her, as she crossed the room. She smiled in a way that set his blood to racing.

He tried to calm his pulse and focus. "You had something to tell me?"

"Yes." She sat on the bed beside him, took his hand, and placed it on her abdomen. "You're going to be a father."

His mind went blank as he stared at Annamaria.

A father.

Him.

Nothing else she might have said could have surprised him more. "Are you sure?"

She nodded. "The midwife confirmed it."

Otto swallowed. He was going to be a father! He kissed Annamaria and they fell into bed together.

Later that night he lay awake, staring into the dark. Warmth and joy filled him to bursting. Wait until Mother found out. She'd be so excited to have a little granddaughter.

Annamaria's soft breathing drew a sigh. So much had changed in such a short time. Soon they'd be a real family. Otto resolved in that moment to be better than his father. He'd be patient and gentle. Wherever their daughter's passion took her, he'd do his best to support her.

The midwife had confirmed a daughter which should mean the baby was developing properly, but after what happened with Griswalda, he had to know for sure. He reached out with a thread of ether and slid it into Annamaria's womb. The energy encircled and caressed the tiny life forming inside her.

He frowned. When the ether had touched his malformed niece, he'd felt a faint resonance as blood called to blood, but between him and his own daughter he felt nothing. Otto added a second and third thread, hoping a stronger connection would give a different result.

It didn't.

The gentle feelings in him turned to ice and the light in his heart went dark. Whoever's child his wife bore, it wasn't his.

The threads dissolved along with his focus. Whose was it? The question consumed him.

Who?

He'd find out. When he returned from Lordes he'd devote his every waking moment to the task. Whatever it took, he'd learn who had done this and when he did, heaven help them.

Heaven help them both.

CHAPTER 34

Otto didn't wake early so much as he never got to sleep. He lay awake all night, his mind consumed by his wife's betrayal. He now knew there was never any love between them, despite the fact that he'd always tried to treat her with kindness and respect. That should have bought him at least a little loyalty, shouldn't it?

He snarled away the question as the first ray of light appeared in the sky. He had more pressing concerns than his whore of a wife. She and her lover would keep until he returned from Lordes. Though he had little hope, Otto needed his mind clear so he could help Wolfric or, failing that, keep his brother from a noose.

Annamaria groaned and rolled over. He caught a hint of the lavender soap she used. Once, the scent had excited him, now it took all his self-control not to reach out and strangle her. Until he knew everything, he would give her no cause for concern. Let her believe him the clueless dupe. His eventual revenge would be that much sweeter.

Otto slipped out of bed, careful not to wake her, and dressed. When he'd buttoned the final button on his best black tunic, he took up his sword. Weapons weren't allowed in the Kings' Council, so he'd have to leave the weapon behind. For a moment he thought to put it in his old rooms, but that might tip Annamaria to his awareness. He should leave it here.

He started to set it on the dresser then caught himself. He'd been wearing it every day. Annamaria wouldn't notice if he took it somewhere. Best not to risk the precious mithril blade getting stolen.

Sword in one hand and boots in the other Otto tiptoed out of the room. He'd barely eased the door closed when Mimi came down the hall. The maid always seemed to be nearby. Did she know the identity of Annamaria's lover?

It wouldn't take a great deal of effort to compel her to speak, but if she knew nothing, he'd tip his hand. He wouldn't risk it, not when he had other options.

"Good morning, Lord Shenk." Mimi gave her customary curtsy.

He held a finger to his lips and whispered. "She's still sleeping. I assume you know about the baby?"

The maid nodded. "I fetched the midwife for her. Congratulations, my lord."

No deception seemed to lurk in her polite expression, but Otto had known servants to lie to his father with a perfectly innocent expression. He was certain all servants practiced the look in a mirror.

"Thank you. I have to leave early today and didn't want to wake her. Can I trust you to take good care of Annamaria while I'm away?"

"Of course, my lord. It's my job after all."

"So it is. See you later then."

Otto continued deeper into the mansion and Mimi retreated back the way she'd come. He glanced back and found the maid out of sight. Good. He hurried down to his old rooms and tucked his sword in the back of the closet. No one would think to look for it there.

Satisfied, he pulled on his boots and strode into the dining hall. Edwyn sat at the huge table, alone and surrounded by plates of food. The moment he spotted Otto he waved him over. His father-in-law had deep, dark bags under his eyes and his normally pink skin had turned sallow. His concern over the fate of his businesses wasn't doing the merchant's sleep any good. Did he know about Annamaria's lover?

Otto doubted it. Edwyn had a blind spot when it came to his daughter. The idea of her doing anything inappropriate probably never crossed his mind.

"Sit down, my boy." Edwyn stuffed a piece of bacon in his mouth. "We just have to convince them not to do anything rash. Without the portal we'll be ruined."

Otto doubted he'd even be allowed to speak. "I'll do what I can, but no one is optimistic. Have you been making arrangements in case we fail?"

"Of course. I've purchased extra wagons and teams so we can ramp up our internal distributions as well as—" Edwyn shuddered "—caravans. Do you have any idea how difficult overland, long-distance caravans are?"

"I'm sure they're nothing you can't handle. For hundreds of years before the portals we traded that way. Surely we can do it again until we're reinstated into the compact." Otto made himself a ham and egg sandwich and poured a flagon of wine. "We need to focus on survival now."

After breakfast Otto and Edwyn climbed into a waiting

carriage and made the five-minute trip to the portal. The royal entourage waited a few yards away. A carriage with the royal seal on the door was surrounded by four guards in heavy mail. In keeping with the rules of the council, the king was allowed an honor guard of four soldiers as well as his advisors.

Standing beside the carriage waited two of the king's advisors, Wolfric and a dour fellow dressed in all black and holding a thick tome under his arm. Axel stood off to one side. He was along to testify and hopefully not serve as a sacrifice.

Otto and Edwyn climbed down and hurried over. Otto took his place beside Wolfric while the merchant walked up to the portal.

"Are you ready, Your Majesty?" Edwyn asked.

"Activate the portal." The king's voice emerged from the carriage.

Wolfric and the man in black climbed in with the king, leaving Otto to walk beside his brother. Edwyn drew the portal key from his tunic pocket and touched the rune for the Kingdom of Markane. The rune lit up and etheric energy ran around the portal, powering the others until the entire half circle glowed. As far as Otto could tell, the rod hadn't actually done anything.

Edwyn bowed. "Best of luck, Your Majesty."

The carriage driver cracked his whip and the horses surged ahead, vanishing into the portal. Otto and Axel followed at a walk. The moment he stepped through, a tunnel of streaming light appeared around him. It lasted only for a moment and then they were standing in an open area in front of another portal.

Otto looked up at the runes. They were the same save for their positioning.

"Hey!" Otto turned at Wolfric's shout. "Climb on the back runner. We need to get going."

Otto and his brother climbed up on the six-inch board and grabbed the handle on either side. Not the most comfortable ride he'd ever had, but better than walking. The whip cracked again and they were on their way to the council building.

CHAPTER 35

The council building was a modest, single-story structure built out of gray stone. A short flight of steps led to a set of oak double doors guarded by six soldiers in mail carrying halberds. They wore tabards colored crimson and featuring an open book. It said something that the kingdom used Lord Valtan's personal sigil as their official heraldic symbol.

The carriage clattered to a stop in front of the door and Otto hopped down. His forearms ached from gripping the railings. It was more nerves than anything since the ride had been smooth enough. They hadn't hit a single pothole the entire way.

The carriage door opened and Wolfric climbed down, followed by the man in black and at last the king. It didn't appear that His Majesty had slept any better than Edwyn. The king's thin, narrow face was wan and he had dark ridges under his eyes. He wore a black tunic and black pants trimmed with gold with his purple cloak.

The king favored Axel with one last glare before marching up to the doors. The guards on duty had the door open before the group arrived and they bowed as the king passed. Otto walked beside Wolfric but didn't dare ask any questions while they were in the king's presence.

Immediately inside the building was a lounge filled with comfortable chairs and low tables. In the far wall was a closed door seething with etheric energy. Otto didn't recognize the weaving and couldn't count the individual threads, but he estimated at least fifty had been used in the casting.

The king looked around the empty room, his scowl deepening by the moment. "Where is everyone? The summons said eight bells."

As if on cue a nearby temple rang out the hour. Their group was the only one present and they knew no more than the king. After one more annoyed glance around the empty room the king stalked over to a handy chair and sat down. He waved the man in black over and the moment he sat the two began poring over the tome he'd brought.

"Who is he?" Otto asked.

Wolfric favored the man with a dismissive glance. "He's the king's lawkeeper, an expert in both Garenland's law as well as the Portal Compact. The two of them have had their heads together for the past two weeks trying to find anything that might persuade the other rulers not to invoke article six and banish us from the compact."

"How's that going?" Otto asked.

"About as well as you'd expect. Their theories aren't any more valuable than ours, at least none of the ones I've heard."

"So is there a plan, or will he make our weak arguments and hope for the best?"

"It's hard to make a solid plan until we see what the other kings have to say." Wolfric went to a chair a comfortable distance from his father and sat.

Otto joined him, leaving his brother the odd man out. Axel didn't seem especially troubled. He leaned against the wall in a dark corner without comment.

"Will your father offer Axel as a scapegoat?"

"If he thinks it will do any good, which it won't." Wolfric shrugged as if Axel's fate meant nothing to him, which it probably didn't.

An hour later the clatter of hooves on cobblestone heralded the arrival of another monarch. The doors opened and in swept a pale, dark-haired woman about fifty wearing a simple blue dress and a gold necklace set with a diamond as big as Otto's eye. He'd never met Queen Philippa Mir of the tiny kingdom of Lux, but she could be no one else.

Behind the queen came a man and woman, also in blue, and both middle-aged. A Lux crystal was embroidered on the breast of both their outfits. Otto knew less about the queen's advisors than he did the woman herself.

King Von Garen rose and went to meet her. She held out her hand and he bowed over it. The two fell into a seemingly agreeable conversation, the details of which were spoken too softly for Otto to hear.

"Those two seem to get along well," Otto said.

"Yes. Garenland and Lux have always had a good relationship. After my mother died there was talk of Father and Philippa marrying, but there was too much internal dissent in both countries so they called it off. I believe we can count on their support when the vote comes."

"It's reassuring to hear we'll have one in our favor at least."

Over the course of the next half hour the rulers of Rolan, Tharanault, and Lasil all arrived along with their various advisors. The kings of Rolan and Tharanault made a show of ignoring King Von Garen while the king of Lasil offered a polite shake of his hand before distancing himself from both groups.

"The battle lines are drawn," Wolfric said. "Just as we guessed."

Wolfric had barely spoken when perhaps the biggest man Otto had ever seen stepped into the room. Uther of Straken had to stand near to seven feet tall and dressed in leather and fur. His thick brown beard hung down to his chest and arms bigger than Otto's legs bulged under his shirt sleeves. He looked every bit the warrior he was rumored to be.

Beside Otto, Wolfric tensed and reached for the sword he wasn't wearing. Uther had only a single advisor with him, a stunning woman of perhaps forty years dressed in all red. Her lips and fingernails had been painted to match the dress. She wore no decoration and needed none. Her beauty was such that anything else would have been pointless.

"Who's the woman?" Otto asked.

"No one knows her name," Wolfric said. "We only know her as the Lady in Red. She serves as Straken's spymaster. She may be—"

"Francis!" King Uther's deep bass voice filled the room, cutting off all the other conversations. It sounded beyond strange to hear someone call the king by his given name. Otto wasn't sure he'd ever heard it before. "I hope you haven't been waiting long. I'm sure you're eager to learn your fate."

"Uther." King Von Garen didn't bother to get up. "No doubt you're behind this farce. When the others learn the truth, instead of whatever twisted story you've dreamed up, we'll have this sorted in no time."

"Ha! We'll see, won't we?" King Uther went over to the lords of Rolan and Tharanault and was greeted with a round of backslapping and laughs.

"If they're united, we have no hope," Otto said.

"No, none whatsoever." Wolfric eyed the group and disgust warred with rage on his face. "They'll pay for this. Mark my words."

Five minutes after King Uther's arrival the door opened once more and two men entered. A hush fell over the room. Not for the first man, a soft, pasty fop with a drooping mustache, nervous gaze, and ridiculous hat decorated with dozens of colored feathers. King Eddred of Markane didn't cut an impressive figure.

The man behind him, on the other hand, was another matter. So much etheric energy seethed around Arcane Lord Valtan that Otto had to switch his vision back to normal to get a clear view of his features. Valtan had bronze skin, a neat beard, and hard gray eyes that even the stoutest warrior would have trouble meeting. He dressed in all crimson save for a gold chain set with a single ruby the size of Otto's fist. The Arcane Lord didn't appear a day over thirty-five. Not bad for a man that had to be pushing a millennium.

"Gentlemen and lady." King Eddred's squeaky voice snapped everyone out of their trances. "Shall we begin the council?"

Without waiting for a response Valtan strode over to the sealed doors and brushed the ward aside with a wave of his hand. The doors opened without a sound. Beyond them waited a round table with seven seats. Etheric lights sprang to life, filling the room with a pale, otherworldly glow.

The kings and queen all stood and led their various entourages into the council room. Otto, Wolfric, and Axel went in behind King Von Garen. The time had come to learn their fate.

CHAPTER 36

The formalities and introductions took over an hour. During it all Otto stood behind the king along with Wolfric and Axel. He didn't know why they went to all the trouble. Everyone there knew everyone else and had known them for decades. While the opening ceremony droned on Otto kept darting glances at Valtan.

He'd never seen so much power gathered around a single person. A thick tendril of ether rose up out of Valtan's body and disappeared out of sight. If he had time later Otto hoped to trace it and see where it went. Judging by the direction he suspected it connected to the portal.

During one of his many glances his gaze met Valtan's. Those eyes that had seen so much bored into his, seemingly read all that he was, and dismissed him over the course of half a second.

The simmering rage that Otto had been keeping under a tight rein during this delicate meeting bubbled up to the surface for a moment. At that moment, deep in his heart, Otto vowed that one day Valtan would look in his eyes again and on that day he'd acknowledge Otto as an equal. He had no idea how he'd make such a miraculous thing happen, but he swore he'd find a way.

At last King Eddred thumped the table and everyone fell silent. "Let us get to the matter at hand. King Uther has brought before this council a matter of serious import. Uther, would you state your case for those who may not have heard it yet?"

Uther stood to his full, imposing height. "Fellow monarchs, some weeks ago soldiers of Garenland knowingly crossed the border into Straken in full violation of the first article of the compact. Straken demands the invocation of article six, a complete ban on Garenland's use of the portal network for ten years."

Uther sat back down and Eddred turned to King Von Garen. "How does Garenland respond?"

The king rose and smoothed his tunic. "Fellow monarchs, Garenland acknowledges an unwitting crossing of the border by a small patrol pursuing a band of raiders. As King Uther well knows, the northern border between our nations is long and poorly marked. The moment our soldiers realized their error they withdrew."

"They entered one of my villages with steel bared!" Uther shouted.

King Eddred made a calming gesture. "Please King Uther, King Von Garen has the floor."

Otto didn't know what was worse, King Uther's feigned outrage or King Eddred refusing to call him out on it. If the Markane king was supposed to be in charge of this gathering he gave no sign of it.

"That may be true," King Von Garen said. "But they withdrew without shedding a drop of blood. I apologize if my men startled some of your frailer citizens, but in the end, no one was harmed. Surely a minor misunderstanding like this doesn't rise to the level of invoking article six. It was put in place to prevent wars between nations, not punish minor infractions."

Their king made Garenland's case calmly and rationally, a direct contrast to King Uther's bluster. It made him appear the more reasonable one. It would have been an excellent showing if the others hadn't already made up their minds.

Once the initial arguments had been made the monarchs fell to arguing minor points about both the encounter and the law. Otto tuned most of it out and after three hours King Eddred called for a break.

By the law of the council the rulers weren't allowed to leave the council chamber. Food would be brought in for them. The advisors, on the other hand, were free to come and go. Right then Otto wanted very badly to go.

"Want to go get something to eat?" Otto asked.

Wolfric shook his head. "I need to stay with Father. You go ahead, but don't be too long. The break probably won't last over an hour."

"Okay." Otto looked to his brother. "How about you?"

"I'll pass," Axel said. "All this politics has spoiled my appetite. Life would be so much easier if we could settle this with a sword."

Otto grinned. Typical Shenk thinking. "If we settled things that way it would most likely be your neck under the blade."

"That might be preferable to all the chatter."

The king glared back at them. "Silence, all of you. I'm trying to think."

Otto bowed. "Apologies, Majesty."

He nodded to Wolfric and Axel then took his leave. The moment he cleared the doors he took a deep breath of air. Not exactly fresh since they weren't that far from the docks, but the hint of salt and rotting fish was better than the stale air of the council room.

A quick glance up showed the path of the etheric tendril that ran from Lord Valtan. Otto retraced his steps back to the portal and, just as he thought, the thread was woven all around the portal. Valtan had clearly bound himself to the artifact. The weaving was far too complex for Otto to understand. Perhaps Lord Karonin could explain it.

He looked around and spotted a restaurant serving fried fish and wedges of potato. Otto ordered a serving and settled in on a bench to eat. Maybe he could find some paper and charcoal to sketch the design. Aside from the placement of the runes the design seemed identical to the one in Garen.

A third of the way through his meal, the Lady in Red sat on the bench beside him. She had a serving of the fish and potatoes as well. How had she approached without him noticing?

"Quite remarkable isn't it?" She had a warm, melodic voice that sent a shiver down his back. "Though I expect a wizard like you can see more than I."

No surprise that the Straken spymaster knew he was a wizard. It wasn't exactly a state secret. The question was, what else did she know?

Otto took a bite of fish to buy a moment to think. "I see a great deal, unfortunately I understand very little of it. The skills of an Arcane Lord outstrip my meager abilities by many orders of magnitude."

Her laugh was a throaty purr. "You're far more self-depre-cating than most nobles I've met. You're going to lose, you know."

Otto nodded. "We've figured that much out. It's the why we're having trouble with."

"Really? I should think the why is obvious. Straken has hated Garenland for most of our shared history. Just because peace was forced on us doesn't mean we're happy about it. The reason you lost this battle was because your king forgot the war hadn't ended just because the fighting did."

He took another bite and studied the woman beside him. What did she play at, following him out here and telling him things it might be best he didn't know? Was she simply toying with him, enjoying his pending doom, or did she play a deeper game? Otto had no idea. Spycraft lay far outside his area of expertise.

"Did you want something in particular or did you follow me to gloat?"

"I wanted to gloat a little. When you tell your friend Wolfric what I said his anger will be most amusing, at least in my imagination. The main reason I followed you was curiosity. I've never had the chance to speak to a wizard. We kill ours young. I wanted to see what you were like. Imagine my dismay when I discovered you were no different than any other man." She shrugged and stood up. "Life is just full of disappointments. See you inside."

He watched her until she moved out of sight. He'd make the harpy pay for underestimating him. She may believe she told him nothing of value, but now he knew for sure she had agents in Garen, it was the only way she'd know about him being a wizard. Finding them would be his second task when he got home. First, he'd hunt down the bastard sleeping with his wife, then the spies. He'd see them roast in the same vat of boiling oil.

After Otto finished his lunch, he found a merchant selling charcoal drawings of the portal. It seemed they were a popular item with visitors to Lordes. After taking a moment to confirm its accuracy Otto happily paid the three pennies the merchant wanted. He rolled up the paper and tucked it in his pocket before hurrying back to the council chamber.

The moment he returned Otto motioned Wolfric aside and related the Lady's taunts. The prince's anger was revealed only by the tightening around his eyes. Apparently, life at court had taught the prince how to control his emotions. Ten minutes after Otto returned King Eddred called the council back to order.

Across the table from them King Uther wore a broad smile that didn't portend anything good for Garenland.

Eddred rose. "My fellow monarchs, the facts have been presented and the law discussed. We come now to the vote on article six punishment. How votes Straken?"

"Straken votes yes," Uther said to the surprise of no one.

"How votes Rolan?" Eddred asked.

"Rolan votes yes," King Villares said. Again, no surprise. Straken and Rolan had been allies for centuries.

"How votes Tharanault?"

"Tharanault votes yes," King Liatos said. Otto had suspected the result considering the king's warm greeting of Uther.

"How votes Lasil?"

This was where things grew interesting. The measure had already passed so now the question was how much support did Straken really have.

"Lasil votes yes," King Kasimir said. Disappointing, but no

great shock to Otto. King Kasimir the Coward would never go against the majority.

Now for the real test.

"How votes Lux?"

Queen Philippa looked from Uther to King Von Garen, the pain on her face plain to all. At last she drew a deep breath. "Lux votes yes."

King Von Garen slumped a little in his chair. That one had hurt. All his peers stood united against him. How could a man not take that personally?

King Eddred raised his hands. "The council has spoken. Garenland will be banished from the compact for a term of one decade after which the council will gather once more to decide if the punishment should be lifted or renewed for another term."

During King Eddred's speech Uther's smile grew ever wider. Otto would have enjoyed burning the smug expression off his face, but this was neither the time nor the place. A time would come though, he didn't doubt that for a moment.

"Out of respect for those of other nations," King Eddred continued, "that might wish to return home we will allow a grace period of one week before the portal's deactivation—"

Uther leapt to his feet. "No! The council has voted. Close it now and make the faithless dogs sail home."

A single glance from Lord Valtan put Uther back in his seat and shut him up. Someday that would be Otto standing there, silencing kings with a look. Someday.

King Eddred cleared his throat. "As I was saying. While we respect the council's decision, the portal is under the control of Markane and we will carry out the council's will in our own good time. I call this gathering to a close. Thank you all for comporting yourselves like the rulers you are."

Eddred bowed to the group and King Von Garen stood. "Fetch my carriage. I wish to be gone from this place."

Otto caught his brother's eye and nodded toward the door. The Shenk brothers joined the stream of advisors going to fetch the rulers' transports. The carriages were parked in an empty space across from the council building.

As they crossed the street Axel said, "That went well."

"It went as expected, save for Lux voting with Straken. We never had a chance. You'd best be ready, brother. I suspect the borderlands are going to get a lot busier."

⌒

The moment they reached the palace in Garen the king left them to huddle with his ministers to try and devise some way to mitigate the damage the loss of the portal would cause. The Temple of Coins' rang two bells as Otto, Wolfric, and Axel strode across the grounds to the palace door. It was hard to believe the whole world could change in six hours. At least they'd been allowed to return by portal. It would have taken weeks to get home by conventional means.

"What is to become of me?" Axel asked.

Wolfric stopped and turned to face Axel. "You will return to your post to guard against Straken incursions. And they will be coming, make no mistake."

"That's it then?" Axel's face twisted in confusion. "No punishment, no demotion, just a dismissal?"

Wolfric shook his head. "This wasn't about you, Lieutenant. Straken had been planning to betray us for a long time. You simply had the misfortune to serve as the catalyst."

Axel saluted. "As you command, Your Majesty. If the bastards cross the border we'll be ready."

"Excellent." Wolfric turned to go then turned back to Axel. "For the record, Lieutenant. Your mistake wasn't crossing the border, it was leaving those villagers alive to serve as witnesses."

Otto left his silently staring brother behind and followed Wolfric through the palace halls to the war room. When the door was closed behind them Wolfric loosed a primal scream and slammed his fists on the map table.

Otto said nothing, content to let his friend's anger run its course. When at last Wolfric turned to him, red faced and gasping, Otto raised an eyebrow. "Better?"

"Not really. The only thing that will make me feel better is Uther's head on a spike atop the palace walls."

"With the Lady in Red's beside him."

"Hear, hear. How do we make it happen?" Wolfric asked.

"That's the question, isn't it. I'm sure there are Straken agents in the city. I'm equally sure they won't be leaving before the portal closes for good. The bitch in red will want eyes on us. I suggest we wait a week for the honest merchants to leave before I begin the search. It will make the job of hunting up the spies easier."

"Before you begin?" Wolfric's disbelief came through loud and clear. "I had thought a door-to-door search might be best."

Otto leaned on the map table. "If you do that, it will only bother many innocent people, people whose good will you and your father will need in the coming years. It will also alert the spies who will probably burn anything of value."

"Can you find them?"

Otto wanted to offer reassurances, but he had no idea if he'd succeed. "I'll do my best, Wolfric, I promise you. Besides, I have means at my disposal that others lack."

"I hadn't given your magic much consideration. Perhaps it

will serve as the key to our success. It would certainly serve the Straken spies right if a wizard found them out. Very well, is there anything you need from me?"

"Not at the moment, but at some point, I'll need a group of loyal men and a secure place to keep any prisoners I take."

"I'll make the arrangements," Wolfric said. "When the time comes all will be ready."

Otto made a shallow bow of acknowledgement.

"Speaking of readiness." Wolfric's expression lightened a bit. "Has your father-in-law made preparations for the coming difficulties? Edwyn's business will suffer more than most."

"He's made what arrangements he can, but this is uncharted waters for us all. Don't worry, the Frankens are not without resources. If there's nothing else for now I should get home."

"That's fine. Will you join me for our usual lunch tomorrow? We still have much to decide."

"Of course. Good afternoon." Otto bowed once more and took his leave. Maybe he'd get lucky and find his wife in bed with her lover. That would make a fitting end to the day.

CHAPTER 37

Otto woke early the next day. It had taken all his self-control to remain in bed beside his wife. She had showed no interest in sex, especially after he finished informing her and her father what had transpired during the meeting. He'd closed his eyes as soon as his head hit the pillow. The exhaustion wasn't wholly feigned. The kings' council had taken a lot out of him mentally.

This morning he felt rested and his anger fully stoked. He had six days to hunt down Annamaria's lover before he needed to turn his attention to the Straken spies. Hopefully it would be enough time. He also had to help Wolfric plan for whatever their enemies had in mind for Garenland. That wouldn't be simple since neither of them really knew what to expect.

He left Annamaria dozing in bed. Before he left their bedroom, he conjured an etheric thread across the threshold. Should anyone break it, he'd know at once. It would be a simple matter to send his sight back to check things out.

Otto adjusted his sword as he descended the stairs. He

found Edwyn at the table, once more surrounded by a mountain of food. In addition to the food was a rolled-up scroll.

Edwyn looked up from his breakfast. "The king sent out a proclamation this morning announcing the portal shutdown. He says that even though we have been cast out of the compact, Garenland will continue to abide by its rules in hopes of showing our goodwill toward the other nations. Or some such rubbish."

Edwyn thrust the scroll at him. "Here, read it yourself."

Otto grabbed a piece of buttered bread and set to reading. Edwyn had summed it up perfectly, rubbish for sure. Wolfric wouldn't be pleased.

He tossed the scroll back on the table. "What will you do?"

"I'm not certain. I'm going to meet with the other merchants this morning. We'll have to put some caravans together. I know about ten loads headed to Tharanault, six to Rolan, and eight to Lasil. I generally just broker deals and send the occasional load of swords. We'll have to expand our direct shipments since brokering isn't going to be much use without the portal."

"Wolfric and I are trying to think up ways to help mitigate the damage to the merchants. If you could keep me informed of your peers' thoughts on things it would be a great help."

"I'll do what I can, my boy." Edwyn chewed his lip and refused to meet Otto's gaze. "But the Franken clan isn't the most popular with the other merchants. Now that they don't need me to open the portal for them, I fear some of the bad feeling may come to the surface."

"Be sure to remind them that we're all in this together. If Garenland is to survive this trial, we'll have to work with each other not against each other." Otto pushed away from the table. "I'll see you at dinner."

Five minutes from the mansion Otto sensed Annamaria pass through the thread he'd left. It was working correctly, so far at least. There'd be no auction this morning, so he set his path to the business district. It would be interesting to see how the city was reacting to the king's announcement. Not panicking was the best he dared hope for.

Everywhere he went groups gathered around the scrolls nailed to tavern doors or stuck to lamp posts. The general consensus was that Garenland was doomed. Despite the dire nature of their predictions, the people making them seemed calm enough.

As noon approached Otto turned toward the palace. He hadn't felt anyone enter the bedroom since Annamaria left. Perhaps she intended to take the afternoon off. Either way he could wait, but not too long.

The guards saluted as he passed through the gate and walked up to the palace. He found Wolfric in their usual dining room. A half-empty bottle of wine sat on the table in front of him. The prince waved him into a chair and poured a mug of wine.

Otto took a polite sip and set the mug back down. "Are you well?"

Wolfric looked at him with bloodshot eyes. "Have you read Father's proclamation yet?"

"Yes, he seemed overly generous considering the others unjustly kicked us out of the compact. I can't see Rolan or Straken treating us like we were still members."

Wolfric snapped his fingers and pointed. "My exact argument. Father would have none of it. He said if we did the right thing and bided our time the other kings would vote us back in when the decade was over. Ha! It's a bad joke."

While Wolfric downed another glass of wine Otto debated

how best to redirect his drunk friend. "I spent the morning walking around the city. The merchants are concerned, but not panicked, not yet anyway. That's a good sign."

Wolfric belched and wiped his mouth with the back of his hand. "Give them time. After a month and the reality sets in, then you'll see real panic, assuming we're not fighting a war with Straken by then."

"You're just full of good cheer this morning. Has Axel left yet?"

"At first light carrying orders from my father not to do anything that might antagonize our neighbors to the north. You know, like defending ourselves."

In the back of his mind Otto sensed two people pass through his thread in quick succession. His heart raced. This was it.

He grabbed his stomach. "Excuse me a moment, Wolfric? I'm not certain that fish I ate in Lordes yesterday agreed with me."

The prince waved his hand and tried in vain to hit his mug with another splash of wine. Otto hurried out and up the hall to the garderobe. He slipped inside, his mind so consumed with what he might find at home that he hardly noticed the stench.

He closed his eyes and sent his sight soaring through the ether. Moments later he reached his bedroom where he found Annamaria and Lothair sitting on the edge of the bed talking and stroking each other.

Lothair!

He should have killed the mercenary when he had the chance. Well, that was easily remedied. He could go home and take care of it right now. Wolfric certainly wasn't in any condition to accomplish much today.

CHAPTER 38

Otto marched back toward the mansion, his rage building with each step. He'd left Wolfric passed out in the dining room and gave the nearby servants instructions not to bother him. Maybe if the prince slept it off, he'd be of some use tomorrow.

Several people took one look at him and crossed to the other side of the streets. Just as well as he may have blasted anyone that slowed him down.

How could she have done this to him? Annamaria had begged him to spare Lothair's life and like an idiot he let the man go in the obviously futile hope that it would earn him some goodwill from his wife.

What a joke.

She'd never intended to honor the bargain she made. The pair had put on a show for him and he swallowed it like a fat fish. He'd give them a show when he got home, a lightning show.

Three-quarters of the way back to the mansion he slowed. Killing them wasn't enough. Once they were dead their suffering would end. No, he needed more. He needed to make Annamaria suffer the way he suffered.

How best to do it?

Otto reached the mansion gates and the guards pulled them open for him. He nodded in passing, his mind otherwise occupied. How best to make her wish she hadn't betrayed him?

No answer came to him as he drew the ether around himself and wove a spell of invisibility. Perhaps the loving couple would inspire him. He turned to one of the side doors and slipped inside. No servants came running, so his entrance must have gone unnoticed. So far so good.

Silent and unseen as a winter breeze he snuck through the mansion. Down the hall from his room Mimi stood silent guard. So, the servant did know her mistress's secret. That gave him one more name for his list.

Otto sent a thread of ether down the hall past Mimi then made it flash. When the girl went to investigate Otto snuck into the room next door to his. He closed the door and released his invisibility. The walls were thick and he heard nothing.

He drew his mithril blade and cut a small rectangle in the wall. Soft gasps and moans flitted out. Otto looked through. Lothair's back was to him. All he could see of his wife was her legs wrapped around him.

The rage went hot again. He grabbed a chair and settled in. He'd burn this moment into his mind. Should he ever feel a moment of doubt or pity for them he would remember today.

Otto's fists clenched and unclenched. He drew the ether to him until the pain almost blinded him.

Through burning tears, he watched Annamaria's betrayal. With each sound of their pleasure he forced more ether into his protesting flesh. In the back of his mind he wished the power would consume him. Take him away from his pain and despair.

At last, when he feared for his sanity, the pain broke and the Bliss returned. The ether flowed through him like never before. He forgot, for a moment, the betrayal unfolding yards away. Nothing existed for him in that moment but the wonder of magic.

The ether swirled around him, brighter and closer than ever. He reached out with his will and a dozen threads responded as, effortless as breathing, he bent the power to his will.

Curious now, Otto focused. Twenty threads danced to his whim before a faint pressure rose in the back of his mind. He released the ether and reeled.

Twenty threads!

His power had more than doubled. This must be what Master Karonin meant when she talked about him breaking through his personal wall.

An especially loud cry drew his attention back to the matter at hand. The happy couple lay panting side by side, her head resting on his chest. They were the very image of joy.

Perhaps he should thank them. Without their betrayal Otto would never have found the strength to achieve the next step on his journey. He felt oddly grateful, but he wouldn't spare them.

Lothair turned toward Annamaria. Otto strained to hear. "You're certain he suspects nothing?"

"No, his happiness when I told him about the baby was real. Otto believes the child is his. We're safe."

Otto's lips curled in a humorless smile. Safe, you slut? Safe is the last thing you are. Once I'm finished you two will beg for death.

They talked for a few more minutes. Nothing but meaningless chatter mostly regarding Annamaria's concern for her father and his business. When they finally dozed off Otto replaced the piece of wood he cut out and pinned it in place with ether. When he finished no one would be able to tell the wall had been damaged.

He turned invisible again, marveling at how easily the magic flowed. A spell that had taken his full concentration now felt as simple as taking a deep breath. It was time to visit Lord Karonin and begin the next step of his training.

Otto extended his sight out into the hall and found Mimi gone. That was a bit of luck. He snuck out of the spare room and down to his old suite. He'd hidden the spell book he took from the tower in the back of his closet at the bottom of an old trunk of clothes.

On the last page, he found the teleportation spell. He read it again, drew a slight variation of the marking rune on the floor, and charged it with ether. He'd have no trouble finding his way back now.

With his preparations complete, Otto returned the spell book to its hiding place. The ether swirled around him and he called out. Energy poured into him until the ether grew so bright, he no longer saw the closet. According to the book that meant he'd become one with it.

He called to mind the rune he'd drawn in the tower and willed himself to go to it. The ether changed from a swirl of colors to straight lines like at the portal. The next thing he knew he stood in the tower chamber.

Lord Karonin's smiling face filled the mirror. "A little over three months. Very impressive. Are you prepared to resume your training?"

Otto bowed his head. The transition had left him exhilarated rather than tired. "Master, I am."

☌

Otto sat on the floor facing the mirror. Nothing of Lord Karonin's appearance had changed during his long absence. He nearly laughed. Long absence; she'd been in the netherworld for over six hundred years and he'd been gone three months. That was the blink of an eye for her.

"So how did you manage it?" she asked.

He hesitated to reveal his stupidity, but in the end what difference did it make to a long-dead Arcane Lord? So he told her everything.

When he finished Otto said, "If stubbornness worked for you, anger did the trick for me. I'm not sure I would have cared if the power killed me in that moment."

"Anger is useful, but it can also be dangerous. If you fail to harness it properly it may destroy you. What else is happening in the world? I find now that I've had a taste of what's happening out there, I hunger for more."

Otto had much to tell her and she listened with a rapt expression until he reached his encounter with Lord Valtan. That tidbit drew a hiss. She truly despised the man.

"The giant thread that bound him to the portal, it never wavered? You're certain?"

"Yes, Master. I watched it for most of an hour and it never flickered. Is that important?"

"Extremely. It means Valtan has tied himself to the portal permanently. He's constantly powering the entire network on his own. That must have reduced his strength to a shadow of

237

what it once was. If only I still lived. I'd destroy him like the pig he is."

Yes, she certainly despised him. "He means to banish us from the Portal Compact. The nation is in a state of perhaps not yet panic, but concern for sure. The king's response has been weak. I fear Garenland is in for hard times."

Her snarl smoothed into a quirk of amusement. "Hard times can be valuable. Fearful people are easier to manipulate if you promise them a return to what they knew, or something better. Keep your eyes open for opportunity, Apprentice."

"The only opportunity I want is one to leave Annamaria and Lothair in ruins."

"Do not be so obsessed!" He flinched at her sharp rebuke. "I've done a great deal of thinking over the last three months. I'm not just entrusting you with my legacy, but with the future of wizards all over the world. Returning our brethren to their proper place in the world is your responsibility."

"The world is a big place, Master. It will be a wonder if I can simply restore our rights in Garenland in my lifetime."

"True. If you had only a single mortal life to accomplish my task it would indeed be impossible, but it would be a worthy task for an Arcane Lord."

His heart leapt. An Arcane Lord, him. "Is that possible?"

"You've taken the first step on the path. I didn't wish to raise your hopes, but becoming one with the ether is the first skill a wizard that wishes to undertake the transformation must master. If you had failed in that simple task there would have been nothing more for us to discuss."

"So I can do it."

She laughed. "You've made the tiniest bit of progress. It will take you years if not decades to complete the transformation. Amet Sur, the first and greatest of us, spent twelve hundred years mastering the skills to achieve true immortality. Luckily you have something he didn't."

Otto's mind spun at the idea of spending that much time on the task. "What is that?"

"A guide. I know everything that must happen for you to make the change. You will take on my mission and if you do well, I'll teach you everything I know. The more you accomplish, the more I share. When the time comes you will kill the pig Valtan in my name. He will know who cast him low. And you will raise wizards back to their proper place as lords of this world."

As much as he wanted what she offered, her price was impossible. "Ordinary men will not accept wizards as their masters. They are too many and we too few. The best I can do is get them up on equal footing. After that wizards will have to sink or swim on their own merit."

She laughed again. "I accept your terms. Raise our people out of their servile position and I will begin your training in earnest."

Her face vanished and a glowing rune appeared in the mirror. "Memorize this and when next you enter the ether seek it out. It will guide you to one of my sealed armories. There you will find what you need to carry you further down your path."

Her face returned and Otto bowed. "I will not fail you, Master."

"Return in three months to update me. I expect great things from you, my apprentice."

Otto entered the ether, called the rune to mind, and vanished.

An instant after he entered the ether Otto reappeared in a cool, dark place. The air smelled stale and close. It was so quiet he almost feared he'd gone deaf. Little was visible beyond the glowing rune at his feet, and that illuminated nothing save a twenty-foot-diameter circle of bricks. Where in the world was he?

He agitated the ether and bright light burst to life. All around him sprawled a huge vaulted chamber filled with all matter of wonders. To his left were six suits of armor sized for giants along with swords as long as Otto was tall. To his left stood a score of bookcases filled to bursting with tomes. Directly ahead was a long, wide table covered with coffers, pouches, and containers of all sorts. He felt like a child in a sweet shop.

He went to the table and opened a dark wood coffer. Inside he found a row of twenty mithril rings, their interiors covered with tiny runes. Engraved on the inside of the lid were two words: Apprentice Rings. There were nine more identical boxes. He moved on and opened one of the pouches. It held a blue crystal with a slip of paper tied to it. This one was labeled The Heart of Ice. Neither artifact had directions. Not surprising since Lord Karonin no doubt already knew how to use her items.

Once he'd closed the mystery containers back up Otto went to the bookcases. Where to begin? He took his time studying the spines. Many were written in languages he didn't recognize. After the third shelf he found one that might be of immediate use. *War Magic.*

That one he'd bring with him. The rest would have to wait until later. He'd lost track of time, but it had to be getting late. With his book tucked under his arm, Otto entered the ether and pictured the rune he empowered back at the mansion.

An instant later he appeared in the closet. He tucked his new book behind a row of boots, turned invisible, and ducked out into the empty hall. A quick walk brought him to the front door where he turned visible and ambled into the house like he'd just arrived.

A servant entered the foyer and her eyes widened. "I'm sorry, Lord Shenk. I didn't hear you enter. Do you need anything?"

"The time, please?"

"Between four and five bells, my lord. Dinner should be ready in an hour."

"Thank you." For the life of him Otto couldn't remember the woman's name. "Is Edwyn home?"

"Yes, sir. The master is in his office." The servant looked around to make sure it was just the two of them. "Forgive my gossiping, sir, but when he and Mr. Cotton returned from their meeting both of them appeared quite agitated."

"I appreciate you letting me know."

Otto left the foyer and made his way to Edwyn's office in the back of the house. After three months it was one of the few rooms in the mansion he hadn't visited. He and Edwyn usually had their discussions at the dining room table.

He paused outside the silver-inlaid door and knocked.

"I said I didn't wish to be disturbed!"

Agitated indeed. "Edwyn, it's Otto. I've just returned from the palace."

The door opened partway and Edwyn's pudgy red face appeared in the gap. "I'm sorry, my boy. I thought you were Bartholomew coming to check on me for the tenth time. Come in, come in."

Otto stepped into the richly appointed office, the primary occupant of which was a mahogany desk covered with papers. Edwyn dropped into the soft leather chair, motioning Otto into one of the two smaller chairs in front of his desk.

Once Otto took his seat Edwyn asked, "How go things at the palace?"

"Not well, at least not from Prince Wolfric's point of view. His Majesty is determined that we'll behave as if we're still a member of the compact even if we can't use our portal. The prince favors a more aggressive approach to the other nations, but his thoughts go unheard."

"That may have to change." Edwyn rested his hands on his belly. "I spoke to some friendly merchants that came through the portal from Lasil. The other nations are planning checkpoints on all roads in and out of their kingdoms as well as a, at minimum, twenty-five percent tax on all Garenland goods. Do you understand what that means?"

Otto understood all too well. "It means there's no way for our goods to compete."

"Exactly! Between the costs of a caravan and the tax, only our highest-quality items have any hope of turning a profit. And even then, most merchants don't deal in premium items. I don't know how we'll survive."

Maybe this would be enough to convince the king to change his position. "How did the others take the news of a border tax?"

"They panicked, of course. The forges can't compete with Straken steel with all the extra costs. There may be a few opportunities for grain sales in Lux, but a deal here and a deal there won't keep hundreds of merchants in business." Edwyn hung his head. "I don't know what we're going to do."

"I'll tell the prince tomorrow. In the meantime, maybe we

should shift our forges away from making swords and toward ordinary items we can sell within Garenland. It might not be as profitable, but it's something."

Edwyn gave an enthusiastic nod. "Good thinking, Otto. We'll make it through this yet, mark my words."

When the bell rang calling them to dinner Edwyn looked as determined as Otto had ever seen him. He took it as a good sign. Now if they could just convince the king to do his part to help, maybe Garenland had a chance.

CHAPTER 39

The sight of the fortress's palisade brought a sigh of relief to the weary Axel. His horse snorted and shook its head as if agreeing with him. If he'd needed any reminder of why he left his family and joined the army, his journey to Lordes with the royals and his brother took care of it. He still didn't fully understand how he'd escaped with his head, much less his rank, intact, but he'd take it as heaven's mercy and do his best to be worthy of the reprieve.

Not that he'd have an easy row to hoe if General Varchi's interpretation of the king's orders were to be followed. In all honesty interpretation might have been an overgenerous description. Axel had read what His Majesty wrote to the general and he'd read the scroll the general prepared for Commander Braddock. The connection between the two sets of commands was tenuous at best.

For his part, Axel wholeheartedly agreed with the general. The king's order made it impossible for Axel and the other soldiers to keep the people under their protection safe in the event of Straken aggression. Sometimes Axel liked to imagine there wouldn't be any raids, then he'd wake up. Prince Wolfric had warned him before he rode north that Straken would be coming, the only question was when and in what numbers.

The gate guards spotted him as he approached and after confirming his identity, opened the foot-thick oak double doors. He'd no sooner rode into the bailey when Sergeant Cobb came ambling down to greet him.

"Welcome back, my lord." Cobb grinned. "Still in one piece I see. That's a relief. I had five crowns on you returning alive."

"Then I guess the drinks are on you." Axel climbed down and a page came to collect his mount and lead it to the stable. "Anything happening here?"

Cobb's good cheer vanished. "We've had running skirmishes with the Straken border guards as well as their elite ranger units over the last five days. Some injured, no deaths on our side, yet. Braddock's pulling out his hair waiting for new orders."

Axel pulled out the scroll the general gave him and waved it at Cobb. "Might be I can do something about that."

"How bad is it?" Cobb asked.

"Bad. We're in for a bloody run I fear and heaven knows what we can expect from the capital."

Cobb winced. "I'll spread the word."

Axel clapped his sergeant on the shoulder. "I'll see the commander and meet you in the barracks."

Cobb nodded and marched back the way he'd come. Axel watched the veteran for a moment before turning toward the fort. Hopefully Cobb and the others would survive whatever was coming, but he doubted everyone would.

It took only minutes to reach Commander Braddock's office and the moment he announced himself the commander called him in.

"You look terrible," Axel said.

Braddock had dark circles under his eyes and his uniform was a crumpled mess. "Three hours of sleep a night will do that to you. Please tell me you have good news."

"Sorry, sir." Axel handed over the scroll.

As Braddock read it his expression grew ever dourer. Finally, he dropped it and looked back at Axel. "How the hell am I supposed to aggressively defend Garenland, but not cross the border? The bastards slip back and forth like ghosts. They hit our patrols then flee home. It's like they already know we can't follow."

Axel didn't know what to say. "I'm just a messenger, sir. If it's any consolation, General Varchi isn't any more pleased with our orders than you. He did his best to interpret the king's commands as widely as possible and Prince Wolfric made it clear that as far as he was concerned, we could cross the border, we just couldn't leave any witnesses."

Braddock slumped in his chair. "It wouldn't matter if we had permission. I don't have men enough to fight the enemy on this side of the border, to say nothing of taking the fight to them."

"What about the villagers?"

"We pulled everyone out that lived within ten miles of the border. The other commanders are doing the same. For all intents and purposes Garenland's new border is ten miles closer. We still make patrols into the area, but we don't control it."

Axel's jaw clenched. Things were worse than he'd expected. "Orders, sir?"

"Rest and recover. Your squad goes out in the morning."

"Yes, sir." Axel saluted and turned to go.

"Axel."

He turned back. "Sir?"

"Straken's playing by a new set of rules. Be extra alert tomorrow."

"Will do, sir."

Axel took his leave. The enemy was playing by new rules and they were stuck with the old ones. It didn't strike him as especially fair. Well, if the Shenk family had a motto it was "Rules are made to be broken."

◯

At first light Axel led his patrol out of the fortress and down the rough, narrow road they'd traveled more times than he cared to count. Everyone was tense and hands seldom strayed far from hilts. His archers kept their bows strung despite the danger of them losing their power over time. No one cared if their bow shot a little weaker three months from now as long as they survived to use it.

As soon as they moved out of sight of the fortress Axel said, "Colten, take point. You see anything even a little off get back here double quick, got me?"

"Yes, sir." Colten motioned the other scouts to join him and urged his mount on.

When they'd rounded a bend out of sight Cobb asked, "Is it a good idea letting those boys get ahead of us? They might stumble into trouble."

"Better if three men get ambushed than twenty-five. Don't worry, Colten knows his business. There isn't a better scout in the legion."

Cobb grunted, seeming unconvinced. Axel valued Cobb's opinion, but right now he didn't dare let the veteran's concern for their youthful scout keep him from doing his job.

An hour later the column caught up to Colten and his men. They had dismounted and the head scout knelt at the edge of the road.

Axel reined in. "What is it?"

"Tracks, fresh ones, not more than three hours old." Colten straightened. "Looks like a ranger patrol from the tread of their boots."

"What the hell are they doing this close to the fortress?" Cobb asked. "They haven't come within ten miles of the place before this."

"I'd say they're setting a trap," Colten said. "Rangers aren't clumsy enough to leave signs like this unless they want to be found."

Axel knew the elite soldiers' reputation well and was inclined to agree with Colten. Unfortunately, he couldn't just leave an armed band wandering the woods this close to headquarters.

"Suggestions. Besides ignoring them," Axel added when he noticed Cobb about to speak.

"We could try flanking them," Colten said. "Make a big, wide circle and come at them from the rear. The trick is knowing how far to go before we swing back."

"Figure it out." Axel pointed at his two youngest men. "You two, take charge of the horses. Lead them up the road and find a secure place to hunker down. If we haven't reached you by sunset head back to base and alert the commander. Understood?"

He read a bit of disappointment on their faces, but both men saluted. "Yes, sir."

Axel nodded and dismounted along with the rest of his men. The two rookies would get their chance soon enough, but sneaking through the woods to try and ambush rangers wasn't the place for them to begin.

"Colten, take the lead. Cobb, you're on rear guard. Ten-yard spread and watch where you put your feet. We'll only have one chance at this so let's not screw it up."

Axel couldn't have been prouder of his men as they slipped through the hardwoods. No one made more than a faint rustle. A little way ahead of him, Colten resembled a ghost, only quieter. He didn't know how the scout managed to almost disappear into the forest. Axel considered himself a good hunter, having spent most of his life in the forests back home, but Colten made him feel like an amateur.

For two hours they kept their course before Colten eventually led them on a slowly bending curve back toward where Axel assumed the rangers had hidden. Their pace grew slower and slower as the sun rose higher into the sky. Sweat plastered Axel's armor padding to his back and dripped down his face.

Ahead of him Colten stopped and waved him up. Axel glanced back and raised his fist. The signal passed down the line until everyone had fallen still. Axel sidled up beside the scout.

Colten didn't speak, instead he pointed up into the branches of a stout maple. Axel studied the leaves for half a minute before he spotted the archer. The man's brown and green armor blended in so well that Axel doubted he would have seen him without Colten's warning.

He leaned in so his lips were inches from the scout's ear. "Where are the rest?"

Colten held up three fingers then pointed out three different locations. Next he made a fist, held up one more finger, and shrugged. Rangers always worked in squads of ten, but they'd only marked four. Not ideal, but if their archers took the four they'd spotted, the rest should reveal themselves. That was Axel's theory at least.

He looked back at the waiting men and found every gaze on him. He touched his finger to his lips then crooked his finger. Once more the signal got passed back and the squad started working its way up to him. It took five minutes, but they didn't make more than a whisper of noise.

Colten got their archers on target while Axel and Cobb divided the rest into two strike teams. When the scout nodded their readiness, Axel pointed at the rangers.

Four bows twanged as one and three hidden figures came crashing to the forest floor. A fourth man shouted but didn't fall. The leaves on the floor shifted. That was where the other rangers had hidden.

Axel drew his sword and charged, his men right behind him. Five rangers leapt up in a flurry of leaves. Each enemy carried a pair of double-edged shortswords which they drew with such speed that the weapons seemed to appear in their hands like magic.

The nearest ranger met Axel's overhead chop with a cross parry and the battle was joined. The crash of steel on steel filled the clearing.

He didn't dare take his eyes off the man in front of him. His opponent darted in and out with quick slashes before dodging Axel's counter. What the ranger lacked in power he made up for with speed.

A bow twanged from the far side of the clearing bringing a shout from one of Axel's men. From behind him Cobb shouted and charged the hidden archer just as they'd practiced during the scouts' training missions.

With the enemies all revealed Axel went from defense to offense. When the ranger darted in this time, he swept the short blades aside and stepped in, bringing the pommel of his longsword crashing into the ranger's temple.

The man spun away from the worst of the impact, but he still staggered a moment. An arrow whistled in and pierced his throat.

Axel spotted a hard-pressed soldier and waded in from behind. His thrust took the ranger through both lungs.

He ripped his blade free of the dying enemy and twisted around, ready to rejoin the melee. Axel lowered his sword. The rangers all lay unmoving in the leaves.

In fact, the only movement came from one of his men writhing with an arrow sticking out of his right hip. The company medic rushed from the edge of the woods and slid to a stop beside the injured man.

From the opposite side of the clearing Cobb emerged, dragging a body behind him. He dropped the corpse beside the others and kept coming.

"Anyone else injured?" Axel asked.

"One of my boys got nicked along the ribs, but nothing serious. How did you know there'd be another hidden archer?"

"I didn't, but better safe than sorry. Let's check them for intelligence while Garrett fixes up our wounded."

After fifteen minutes of searching they turned up nothing beyond the standard equipment you'd find in any wilderness combat unit's kit—no orders, no indication of what Straken intended. Well, it had been overly optimistic to imagine they'd find a scroll laying out their grand strategy.

Axel picked two men to ferry the wounded back to base and fill in the commander. If the rangers were scouting this close to the fortress, they'd need to beef up local patrols. Axel led his squad to rejoin the rookies. It looked like they were in for a long deployment.

CHAPTER 40

Otto stood in the shadow of two small shops and watched as Lothair entered a little dive of a tavern. He'd had no trouble tracking his wife's lover through the city when they finished their business. After his daily visit with Wolfric he'd left the palace and caught up with his target just outside the gate to Gold Ward. He'd trailed Lothair for half a mile before he finally entered the tavern.

A small part of Otto wanted to simply walk in behind him and see the man's reaction. As satisfying as that might have been, it wouldn't serve his plan well. He backtracked to a bar he'd noticed in passing and went inside.

Most of the local businesses hadn't closed for the day yet and only a handful of hardcore drinkers occupied stools at the bar. No one but the bartender so much as looked Otto's way. He ignored the tables scattered throughout the common room and took a booth in a shadowy corner. He'd barely settled in when a blond barmaid whose best years had come and gone long ago sashayed over.

"Get you a drink, handsome?"

He flinched as the stink of her rotting teeth rolled over him. "A mug of wine, please."

"We don't get many fancy boys like you in here. You meeting someone?" She winked at him.

Otto slapped a silver crown on the table. "I needed some time away from my wife. This struck me as the sort of place she'd be unlikely to look."

"Ha! I imagine not." The barmaid snatched up the coin and went to fetch his drink.

Best not to begin his work until she'd come and gone. A minute later a dripping pewter stein filled with sour wine not far removed from vinegar arrived at his table.

"Anything else?" she asked.

The thought of eating anything they prepared in this place set his stomach twisting. "I'm fine, thank you."

She returned to her post near the bar and Otto leaned back and closed his eyes, the very image of an exhausted husband. He sent his sight soaring through the ether and into the little tavern down the street. They had even fewer customers than this dump. Lothair and two men sat around a table, clearly deep in discussion.

Otto switched his sight for hearing and their disembodied voices appeared in his mind.

"We have another delivery tonight." Otto didn't recognize that voice.

"What does Crane want this time?" That was Lothair.

"Nothing major and the payment reflects it. I've been collecting caravan schedules for him."

"Why would a thug like Crane care about caravan schedules?" Lothair asked.

"I don't care and I didn't ask. As long as he pays in gold, I'm happy to get him whatever information he wants." It seemed Lothair was working for an information broker. Interesting.

"When are we going?" Lothair asked.

"Three bells after midnight."

"Good." Lothair yawned. "I'm going to get some shuteye before then."

The unfamiliar one laughed. "Your sweetheart wearing you out?"

Otto's fist clenched and lightning danced around his fingers. He glanced around, but no one appeared to have noticed.

"It's not Annamaria. I told you her pig of a husband came home early one day. I fear it may happen again. It's wearing on my nerves. I've got to find some way to convince her to come with me."

Another laugh from the stranger. "You think she'll move out of a mansion to live in a garret above a tavern? I doubt it's possible to love someone that much."

Otto had heard enough and severed the connection. He poured the horse piss that passed for wine on the floor under his booth and waved the barmaid over.

"Get you a refill, sweetie?"

"No, I had a question. On my way in I passed another tavern, but it appeared closed. I've been considering an investment in this part of the city and I wondered if you knew who owned it?"

"What's the name?"

Otto hadn't noted the building's sign, so focused had he been on Lothair. "I'm not sure. It has a light, stained facing and a dark-green door. Two glass windows in the front."

"Oh sure, that's The Thirsty Sprite. The owner goes by the name Allen." She cocked her head. "I've never heard his last name. Don't know how he keeps the place open; they seldom have much business. Too bad, it's a nice tavern. Nicer than this dump for sure."

"Thank you." Otto placed another crown on the table. "For your trouble. Good afternoon."

He left the bar and started for home. It was going to be a long, but hopefully interesting evening.

○

Otto stood, invisible, in the pitch-black moonless night, watching the door of The Thirsty Sprite. Three bells couldn't be far off. He felt a little bad for spies that didn't have access to magic. When no one could see you, it made sneaking around much simpler. Throw in a little teleportation to slip out of the mansion and his nighttime stalk was off to a fine start.

The hardest part had been slipping out of bed without Annamaria noticing. Otto had gotten pretty good at the various ways to use magic to blow stuff up, but he hadn't figured out some of the more subtle uses. Being able to put someone to sleep would be a useful trick. When he returned to the armory, he'd have to look closer at the other books.

The tavern door opened and Lothair, along with two other men, the same two he'd seen earlier in the day, stepped into the street. Lothair had traded his fop costume and was dressed in leather like a proper mercenary. The little group turned toward the foundry area and Otto trailed behind. No words were exchanged as they walked, at least none he heard.

They walked along for ten minutes before finally stopping in front of an alley between two foundries. A series of lights flashed before the group moved further down the alley.

Someone unhooded a lantern, revealing a group of five men. They were a rough bunch, scarred and ragged. Otto had seen better looking beggars. This lot would have fit right in with the bandits he'd helped kill this spring.

A man from each group, Otto assumed Allen and Crane, moved apart from their respective groups and into the center of the alley. Otto extended his hearing to listen in.

"You have the information?" Crane asked.

"Of course." Allen held up a scroll. "You have the coin?"

Crane jingled a small pouch. The two men exchanged items, rejoined their groups, and retreated back the way they'd come.

Otto let his spell fade away then hesitated a moment before falling in behind the thugs. He knew where to find Lothair whenever he decided to deal with him. His gut said the second group would lead to more interesting prey.

Crane and his group wove their way through twisting alleys in the poorest and roughest part of Garen. Otto had never visited this section of the city. His meager knowledge came from Wolfric's tales of youthful slumming.

He snuck by a woman in rags huddling in a doorway. How did these people survive in the winter? Perhaps the king let them starve to keep the excess population in check. That's what Father would have done, were he in charge.

At last they reached Crane's destination, a three-story tenement that appeared in danger of falling over at any moment. Lights shone in many of the windows, but he heard no voices.

Crane rapped on the door in a particular pattern, four short, two long, two short. The door opened and the whole crew slipped inside. Otto had no hope of following, but that didn't keep him from having a peek inside.

He slid into a niche between two buildings to keep anyone from sneaking up on him and extended his sight. After a blurry moment as his magical vision passed through the wooden walls he found himself in a narrow, door-lined hall. He looked inside each room in quick succession, finding nothing but one-room hovels.

The first floor was exactly what you'd expect from such a building. When the second floor yielded nothing of interest, Otto feared he'd tracked Crane home.

Another blurry moment came as he passed through the ceiling into the top level. He gaped for a moment. The top floor consisted of a single apartment furnished with enough luxury items that Edwyn would find nothing to complain about were he to visit for a night. Everywhere Otto looked, gold flashed and silk shimmered in the light of a blazing hearth.

Two doors led out of the central chamber. He looked through the first one and found a bedroom with a huge four-poster bed, a dresser, and a vanity with an oval mirror. The second door led to a large office where Crane and his men stood in front of a desk occupied by a bearded man big enough to be King Uther's brother.

The bearded man held the scroll Allen had given to Crane. Otto read over his shoulder. It was nothing but a list of caravans, their goods, and destinations. Over half weren't leaving Garenland. The rest were generally bound for Lasil, Lux, and one risking a trip to Rolan. What on earth did this man want with such information?

Otto read the scroll several more times before the man tossed it on his desk and waved at Crane. When the thug had left the room, the bearded man walked over to the far wall and tapped a loose board. A hidden door swung open.

A savage growl distracted him from whatever was behind the door.

"What is it, boy?" a voice right outside his hiding place asked. "There ain't nothing in there."

Otto ended the spell, blinked, and found himself staring into the face of a man so wrinkled he resembled an apple after a winter at the bottom of a barrel. At the vagrant's feet a scruffy mongrel snarled and bared its teeth. The stupid beast smelled Otto but didn't see him.

If the old man reached into the niche, he'd feel the invisible Otto and that would bring attention he didn't want. A tiny spark of lightning appeared at the tip of Otto's finger. He connected that spark to the dog's nose and released it.

A yelp was followed by the mutt running down the alley as fast as its scrawny legs could carry it.

"Hey, Red, come back here." The bum limped off after his dog muttering imprecations.

Otto relaxed a fraction. He'd pushed his luck as far as he dared for the moment. He'd return for a better look later. He let his invisibility fade, entered the ether, and returned home.

CHAPTER 41

olfric stood facing his father in his private study. The spicy scent of pipeweed mingled with the odor of old books. A pair of leather chairs faced a cold hearth. Neither man gave them so much as a glance.

"Father, I'm sure there are Straken spies in Garen. They must be rooted out and arrested if we're to have any hope of surviving our banishment."

"Are you still on about that?" Father sighed and looked older than ever. "I told you, there are no spies. It would be against the rules of the compact. Straken wouldn't dare risk it."

"They hate us. Why can't you accept that in their eyes the war never ended? The Lady in Red as much as admitted she had agents in the city."

Father snorted. "According to a jumped-up country noble that wouldn't recognize subtlety if it bit him on the nose. She's trying to manipulate us into doing something that will convince the other monarchs we can't be trusted to rejoin the compact."

"They don't want us back in the compact! Can't you see

Straken, Rolan, and Tharanault have colluded to get us kicked out? They want to destroy Garenland and you're letting them do it."

"How dare you!"

Uh-oh. Maybe he'd pushed too hard this time. Father's gray pallor had turned red as the heat rose in his cheeks.

"I meant no—"

"Get out! I don't want to hear your voice or see your face. Your foolish ideas will destroy us, not some imagined conspiracy."

"Father, please—"

"Out!" His father pointed at the door, his finger trembling with rage.

"As you command, Majesty."

Wolfric stepped into the hall and closed the door behind him. He rested his head against the cool stone of the wall and sighed. Now he'd done it. What little influence he'd had with his father was gone.

How could he be so blind to Straken's intentions? It almost felt like he'd rather blame Wolfric than the people responsible for their predicament. He grimaced and pushed away from the wall. As long as Father was king, Wolfric had to accept his decisions, but that didn't mean he couldn't do his best to mitigate the damage.

He gave a silent word of thanks that he'd had the good fortune to meet Otto. Whatever Father might think, Otto knew what he was talking about. He was as clever and well-read as any of the nobles from Garen. He was also the first wizard Wolfric had spoken to at any length. The more he got to know his new friend the less Wolfric understood the limitations on wizards in positions of authority. Otto was more sensible than most of the regular people he knew.

At the end of the hall leading from the royal residence to the public areas of the palace Wolfric found Hans waiting for him. He'd selected the grizzled veteran to lead the small force Otto requested to assist him in his hunt for spies.

"How went the meeting, my lord?" Hans scratched the scruff of beard Wolfric had ordered him to grow. He wanted the soldiers assigned to Otto looking more like mercenaries than royal guards.

"Badly. We're going to have to use the backup plan. Did you and your men find the armories I discovered in my research?"

"Yes, sir, though only one was usable for our mission. The others are cleaning it out and getting everything ready. I was just waiting for a final word from you before I went to join them."

"Consider it given, Sergeant," Wolfric said. "I know I've told you this before, but it is absolutely vital that no word of what we're doing gets out. If Father finds out before we have the evidence we need, the results will be... unpleasant."

∽

Otto yawned as he walked along the streets of Gold Ward beside Edwyn. They were making their way to the portal, more out of curiosity than anything. He hadn't gotten nearly enough sleep the night before. He didn't regret the loss. Otto was pretty sure he'd located one of the spies Wolfric had set him to find. Even better, Lothair was mixed up with them. He could let the Crown execute the man for him. That would be sweet indeed.

Today was the first morning of Garenland's banishment, but Edwyn wanted to try his key just to make sure Lord Valtan hadn't forgotten. More likely with no auction to attend and his business in chaos, Edwyn simply sought something to take his mind off his problems.

That plan didn't strike Otto as one with a great chance for success, but he'd offered to tag along anyway. It would be interesting to see how the deactivated portal looked in his wizard sight.

The streets of the ward were empty. None of the rich and powerful seemed certain how to handle their new circumstances. They'd best adapt quickly if they wanted to survive, at least that's what he'd been telling Edwyn.

"Did you reschedule that caravan I mentioned?" Otto asked. One of Edwyn's shipments had been listed on the scroll Allen sold to the thugs the night before. It might mean nothing, but in case it did he'd warned his father-in-law to send it out a day later than planned.

"Yes, though the caravan master wasn't thrilled."

"He doesn't have to be thrilled as long as he does what you tell him."

They found the always-bustling area around the portal as empty as the rest of the ward. You'd think everyone had up and disappeared. It gave Otto the creeps, but he quickly shifted his focus to the portal. It still seethed with etheric energy. It seemed impossible that the Arcane Lord had forgotten, but the power flow hadn't changed from the last time he viewed the portal.

Edwyn dug the enchanted cylinder out of his pants' pocket and touched it to the Garenland rune. Of course, nothing happened. The device held no magic in the first place and as far as Otto could tell it served only a ceremonial function.

Edwyn slumped and threw the rod to the ground. "It really happened. I'd half convinced myself it was just a threat, but it really happened. We'd best get home. There's much that needs to be done."

"Are you going to leave that there?" Otto pointed at the activation cylinder.

"It's useless now. Why should I bother lugging it around?"

"May I have it? As a souvenir?"

"Suit yourself." Edwyn turned for the mansion.

Otto collected the device and looked closer at the matching rune on the portal. While the portal still crackled with power, it didn't reach the activation rune. Interesting. Lord Valtan hadn't cut off the flow of power to the portal, he'd simply stopped the activation cycle from initiating.

The hint of an idea began percolating in the back of his head. He'd need to consult with Lord Karonin, but maybe they weren't as helpless as he'd first believed.

∽

Otto sat across from Wolfric at their usual table. A platter of roast beef and potatoes grew cool as the prince glowered at nothing in particular. His stomach growled but he didn't reach for the food. For the first time since he met the prince, Otto feared what his friend might do.

Finally, their gazes met and Otto risked raising an eyebrow. Wolfric gave a full-body shudder and made a visible effort to relax.

"I'm sorry, Otto. I'm in a bit of a mood today. Please, dig in."

Otto fixed himself a plate and when Wolfric didn't make a move fixed one for the prince as well. When he slid the food across the table Wolfric waved him off.

"You need to keep up your strength. Why don't you tell me what the problem is?"

Wolfric obliged him by taking a bite of meat. "The problem is the same as it has been since we returned from Lordes. Father refuses to see that the other nations are our enemy now. I've tried everything I can think of to convince him that no matter what we do they'll never let us rejoin the compact, but he won't accept it. After our last argument he banished me from the throne room and his councils."

Otto winced. That certainly explained Wolfric's anger. Perhaps Otto's discovery would cheer him up. "I believe I've located one of the Straken spies. Or perhaps I should say I've located someone's spy. I'm not at all sure who the fellow works for, though he's certainly big enough to be from Straken."

"That was fast. I didn't think we were even going to start looking until today."

"I wasn't actually hunting spies and I stumbled onto this one quite by accident. I'll be returning this evening to confirm my theory, assuming the men and dungeon I mentioned are prepared."

"Since Father refused to even listen when I brought up the spies, I had to find an alternative location to hold our prisoners. I also reassigned five men from my personal guard. They're absolutely loyal and at your disposal."

"If not the dungeon then where?" Otto asked.

"When I was reading in the library one day I found mention of old armories from before the compact. It took a bit of looking, but we found one of the empty buildings and made a few modifications. The place isn't ideal, but it should serve our needs. Would you like to see it?"

"After lunch."

Wolfric grinned and they dug in with a will.

An hour later a plain, unmarked carriage was clattering down the street toward the converted armory. They soon left

Gold Ward behind and entered the business district. Otto glanced out the window. The neighborhood grew steadily worse. It wouldn't surprise him if they ended up in the same area as the tenement where he found the spy. That would certainly be convenient.

"So you read about this place in the library?" Otto asked when the silence had dragged on for a while.

"Yes. During the war against Lord Karonin's followers, there were four of the armories in the city so guards could reach them in an emergency. The other three have either been torn down or repurposed. The one we're visiting seems to have been forgotten. You should have seen the cobwebs."

"I can imagine. Did you find any weapons?"

"No, someone cleaned the place out," Wolfric said. "I still can't believe no one turned the building into a business or something. The structure is solid."

The carriage slowed and the driver said, "Whoa."

When the carriage door opened a rough figure appeared in the opening. He wore leather armor and a pot helm, both of which had seen better days. A week's worth of beard covered his cheeks and his nose had been broken in some long-ago fight.

"My lord," the man said in a smooth, polite voice. "We've finished the final preparations."

"Excellent, Hans." Wolfric motioned Otto down. "This is Otto, your new commander. Otto, this is Sergeant Hans, the ranking soldier in the team I arranged for you. They had to swap their uniforms for this lesser equipment since we didn't want word of royal guards in the slums getting back to my father."

That explained their unadorned transport. "Good to meet you, Sergeant. Shall we have a look around?"

"I'll leave you in Hans's capable hands. I don't want to risk being spotted here. Best of luck, my friends." Wolfric closed the door and the driver shook his reins. A moment later the carriage was gone.

Otto turned his attention to Hans. "How about that tour?"

"Yes, sir."

Hans led him to a stone building that consisted of a single large room measuring around thirty by forty feet. Four men leapt to their feet and saluted, their card game forgotten.

"At ease," Hans said. "This is our new commander. When he says jump you ask how high or my boot will show you the hard way."

"Yes, sir!" came the chorused reply.

"Not much to see at the moment," Hans said.

Iron rings had been pounded into the wall and piles of manacles and chains lay on the floor opposite them. Five simple cots sat in a row as far from the rings as the room would allow. All in all, a crude sort of jail, but it should suit Otto's needs.

"Looks like you have everything ready to go. Splendid. Hopefully in a day or two we'll have someone to keep you company."

"Yes, sir. If you don't mind me asking... what, exactly, is our mission? Prince Wolfric's orders were a little vague."

"What did he tell you?"

"That we were being reassigned to your command and we should do whatever you told us to, no questions asked."

Otto laughed. "So the first thing you thought to do was ask a question?"

The sheepish expression on Hans's grizzled, leathery face made Otto laugh again.

"I thought if we understood the mission better, I'd be of more help. I intended no offense."

Otto clapped Hans on the shoulder. "You should know I'm not one of the easily offended nobles you may have encountered at the palace. We're hunting spies. Straken spies we assume, but any others we find we'll take in as well. We'll need to get them talking, one way or another."

"The walls are quite thick," Hans said. "That'll block most of the noise and in this neighborhood, no one will kick up a fuss about a few shouts."

It seemed the sergeant understood him clearly. Good, Wolfric had chosen the right men for the job.

"We're going after our first target tonight. We want him and his flunkies alive."

Hans nodded. "We'll be ready."

CHAPTER 42

Around midnight Otto teleported back to his new base of operations. He'd carved a rune in the floor and explained its purpose to the men, but they still jumped when he appeared in the corner of the old armory. A charcoal brazier burned in the center of the room, casting everything in shades of red and orange and sending smoke swirling around the ceiling.

"Ready to move out, sir." Hans touched his fist to his heart.

"Not just yet, Sergeant. I need to confirm the target."

Otto sat on the edge of one of the cots and sent his sight flying through the ether. Seconds later he reached the tenement. A few lights burned in the windows, but the top floor was dark.

His magical sight passed through the wall and into a dark room. Nothing was visible beyond the vague outlines of furniture. He ground his teeth, wishing he had some way to see in the dark. The ether responded to his will and the room appeared in shades of gray.

Otto had heard of the Dark Vision spell, but never learned

it. Perhaps simply being aware of its existence was enough to create the effect. He'd add it to his list of questions for Lord Karonin when he visited the tower again.

Recalling the layout from before, he flew through the bedroom wall and found the sleeping form of the bearded man from the previous night. So far so good, but Otto wanted Crane as well and preferably his whole crew.

He left the bedroom and went to the office. How would they carry everything back to the armory for study? There had to be fifty books on the shelves and any of them might hold valuable information. They could figure that out later.

One last thing remained to be checked. Otto went through the secret door and found a short passage that led to a ladder. A hatch at the top of the ladder opened into an aviary on the roof. Six niches each held a single gray bird of a species he didn't recognize.

Otto returned his sight to his body. "The primary target is home, but the secondary target is elsewhere. Here's the mission. We grab the primary target and bring him back here along with all written material in his apartment. There's a lot so we'll need a way to transport it."

One of the men raised his hand. "Would a wheelbarrow work, sir? We still have the one we used to lug all these chains from the palace."

"That'll be perfect. You're in charge of gathering books and other written material. Leave nothing behind."

The soldier saluted and one of the others muttered something and punched him on the bicep. A bit of good-natured ribbing no doubt.

When Otto finished describing the spy as well as Crane, Hans said, "I think we've got it, sir. We definitely want these men alive, right?"

"Absolutely. If we don't get the spy in one piece, we're back to square one. I don't want to have to tell the prince we've failed on our first mission."

"Me neither, sir. We'll get him. Just lead the way."

Otto guided them along a roundabout path to the tenement. The disguised guards didn't draw a second look in this part of the city, though a couple vagrants stared at the wheelbarrow. Otto had wrapped himself in a full-length cloak with a deep cowl so no one would be able to describe his features.

The team stopped in front of the building and one of the guards muttered, "It'll probably collapse with us in it."

"Shut it, Cord," Hans said. "Want us to break down the door, sir?"

"Let's try knocking first."

Otto tapped out the pattern he remembered from the previous night. A moment later the door opened.

A grizzled, one-legged man that made his soldiers look like posh nobles stared up at Otto. "Who the hell are—"

He fell silent as Otto's paralysis spell settled on him. Hans and another man rushed in and gagged the doorman before clapping him in irons. Otto released his spell and the group hurried up the stairs to the top floor.

They stopped at a locked door that appeared far sturdier than the ones downstairs. Sturdy or not he doubted it would stand up to a mithril blade. He drew his weapon, forced the blade into the gap between the door and the jamb, and slid it down. The lock resisted for an instant before the impossibly sharp sword cut it in half.

Hans nudged the door open and they slipped inside. They'd barely entered when a mountain of a man slammed the bedroom door open.

"Crane!" the spy shouted.

Otto flicked his ring and bound the man, but it was too late. People were pounding up the stairs and from the volume it sounded like far more than Crane and his four thugs.

"Shackle him and barricade the door." Otto slammed the door, wishing he hadn't cut off the lock. He could have barred it with a spell, but he feared he'd need all his power before the night was over. Better if they just barricaded it.

Hans took the manacles while three men set to work piling up expensive furniture in front of the door. They'd barely gotten a leather chair in place when the first heavy blow landed. Otto left the men to their work and tried to think how they'd escape the building with their prisoner, short of killing everyone between them and the exit.

"Are you okay, Master?" a voice shouted from the hall, maybe Crane, maybe not, Otto couldn't tell for sure.

Hans had the spy wrapped up and Otto let his thread vanish. The moment he did the bearded giant started thrashing and fighting his bonds. So broad were the man's shoulders that for a second Otto feared he might actually succeed in breaking the steel chains.

"What now, sir?" Hans asked. Something heavy slammed into the barricaded door, giving added urgency to the question.

"How long do you think the door will hold?" Otto asked.

One of the soldiers barricading said, "Unless they've got a battering ram, they're not getting in here any time soon."

"Alright, let's finish our inspection then I'll decide how we're going to escape."

Otto went to the office and conjured a light. The room was every bit as cluttered as he remembered. "Start gathering everything up."

The soldier he'd designated for collection duty set to work

piling up books and papers while Hans joined Otto by the wall. The dull thuds of something slamming into the door lay over everything, a constant reminder of their situation.

He studied the wall, trying to remember exactly where the release was.

"What are you looking for, sir?" Hans asked.

Otto stabbed the wall with his finger and the hidden door slid open. "That. Come on."

Another light appeared at his command and Hans drew his sword.

"Best let me go first, sir." The sergeant didn't give him a chance to protest as he started down the passage.

A handful of steps later they reached a ladder that led up to the aviary. The area wasn't any more interesting in person than it had been in his magical sight.

Hans stopped in front of the ladder and looked back.

"Up you go," Otto said.

They climbed the rungs up to the aviary and were met by the loud, angry cries of the caged birds. Up close he noticed that the cages weren't connected. That was handy as he planned to take one of them back to base. Off to one side in the corner a little table held ink, pens, and blank pieces of paper. Nothing indicated where the birds were trained to fly, though Otto would have bet his sword that the answer was Straken.

"Sir, do we have an escape plan now?" Hans asked, a little more urgently than last time.

"Yes, though how good it is, only time will tell. Grab one of those cages and let's go rejoin the men."

When Hans had taken the nearest bird, Otto sent a thread through the rest before summoning lightning. The birds fell instantly silent when the charge struck. It was a shame to kill them, but he didn't dare risk someone sending a message warning Straken that their spy had been found out.

Back in the office everything was arranged in six neat piles. Hans set the bird beside the papers and they all went out into the living room. The pounding hadn't let up, but it didn't appear the mob outside had made any progress either.

"Report," Hans said.

"They keep pounding away, but they're not accomplishing much," Cord said.

"This might be a good time for that plan, sir," Hans said.

"It's nothing complicated, I'm afraid. I thought I'd blast the men out there with lightning and we'd escape before they recover."

"Why don't you just kill them?" one of the men asked.

"Because if Crane's out there I want him alive." Otto didn't add that he had no desire to kill out of hand however many people waited beyond the door. "Are we ready?"

When everyone had their weapon drawn Otto sent two threads out into the hall. He guided them by feel until all eleven people had been pierced through the abdomen. He made sure to keep the thread well below their hearts just to be safe.

When his hands crackled with energy, he sent lightning rushing down the threads. Screams were followed by thumps and then silence. Otto sent his sight along the threads and found a heap of twitching bodies on the landing floor. They'd been using a rough-hewn post as a battering ram. No wonder they hadn't gotten through.

"It's safe. Clear the doorway and let's get going."

The soldiers tossed furniture aside and in short order the path was open. Two soldiers carried piles of paper while another pair guarded them. Otto and Hans checked the unconscious men one by one until they found Crane.

Hans snapped the manacles on and dragged him to the ground floor. Otto kept an eye on the unconscious men, but no one moved. He fell in behind the final load of papers and the group hurried back to base. It wasn't the smoothest infiltration ever, but they captured their targets and none of his men were hurt, so Otto decided to call it a win.

CHAPTER 43

Otto studied the spy they'd captured the night before. He appeared even bigger than last time he'd seen him. Noon had come and gone a few minutes ago. Hans joined him in front of the prisoner while the others indulged in their seemingly perpetual card game.

"He hasn't said a word since we brought him in," Hans said. "The other one either."

Otto looked away from the spy's angry glare and focused on Crane. The gang leader didn't look anywhere near as intimidating chained to a wall as he did when he met with Lothair and Allen.

The papers had been piled neatly a safe distance from the brazier. The bird, a gray and black creature Otto had never seen before, hopped around in its cage. Every once in a while, it let out a little squawk.

"Did someone feed that thing?" Otto asked.

Cord looked up from his cards. "We tossed it a couple crusts after breakfast."

"Good. Well, I suppose we'd best get started. State your names."

Crane and the spy offered nothing but sullen silence.

Otto shook his head. "Are you really going to make me torture you just for your names?"

When that brought more silence, he shrugged and made a show of walking over to the glowing brazier and setting the iron poker in it. While he'd never tortured anyone himself, Father had made him watch a few of his sessions back home so Otto understood the basic principles.

"Maybe we should chop a finger or two off while we wait for the poker to heat up," Hans said.

"Good idea. We can use the hot metal to cauterize the wounds." Otto glanced at Hans. "I don't suppose you have an especially dull knife we could use?"

"As a matter of fact..." Hans pulled the rustiest, most-chipped dagger Otto had ever seen. "I keep this for special occasions."

"Start with the bearded giant."

The spy clenched his fists tight and bared his teeth. That wouldn't do. Otto conjured five threads, wove them together, and inserted the tentacle into the prisoner's index finger. Muscle and bone protested, but soon enough the finger stuck straight out. Another thread paralyzed him in that position from the neck down.

"There you are, Sergeant. Take your time now, no need to rush this."

"Yes, sir." Hans stalked closer, letting the ruddy light play over the rusty dagger. The spy's eyes grew wider as Hans drew closer.

When the edge of the dagger touched his skin the man said, "Xavier. My name is Xavier. This is my helper, Crane."

"That wasn't so hard." Otto waved Hans back. "Now, why don't you tell me who you're spying for, what you've shared, and all the other juicy details of your sordid business."

"If I tell you I'm a dead man," Xavier said.

Otto glanced around the makeshift prison. "If you don't tell me you're going to wish you were dead. No, what I think I'll do is make a big show of releasing you with Garenland's thanks for all you've done. When word reaches the Lady in Red I suspect you'll be begging to return to our care."

Xavier's flinch when he mentioned the Lady answered one of Otto's questions. Maybe if he played on that fear, he'd get what he wanted more quickly than with torture.

"Take good care of this one, Hans. We don't want Garenland's new best friend injured."

"Yes, sir. What about the other one?"

"What about it, Crane?" Otto asked. "Want to tell us something useful or should the sergeant start carving?"

Crane slumped in his bindings. "What do you want to know?"

Otto conjured up his father's evil smile. "Absolutely everything."

♀

Lothair took a sip of brandy and sighed. The tavern held only a handful of serious drinkers off in the corner. The summer night was warm and Annamaria loved him. All was right with the world. A little way up from him Ulf polished the bar with a dirty rag. He must have just wanted something to do since the rag probably added more filth to the bar than it removed.

The tavern door opened and a trio of vaguely familiar men

entered. They wore rough leathers and each carried a small arsenal. Two of the thugs lugged a wooden chest between them. The drinkers in the corner took one look at the new arrivals and high-tailed it out the door.

"Where's Allen?" asked a one-eyed bruiser tattooed with an eagle on his forearm.

Ulf favored the men with a disdainful look before he yanked the pull rope. A muted bell sounded and Allen emerged from his office a moment later.

He eyed the men and frowned. "I told Crane I didn't want him or his men hanging around my place. There's a reason we meet in that alley, you know."

"We've got a problem, a big one," the designated speaker said. "Crane and our boss got kidnapped last night. We need help finding and springing them."

Allen sat beside Lothair at the bar. "Has there been a ransom demand?"

"No, we haven't heard anything."

"They're probably dead." Lothair refilled his glass and took another sip.

"If whoever grabbed them wanted the bosses dead, why take them prisoner? They had plenty of time to kill them last night, but some of our guys saw them dragged away in irons."

"Was it a rival gang?" Allen asked.

"No one recognized them, but get this. They had a wizard. Bastard zapped Crane and a bunch of the boys, knocked us all cold. We didn't even have a chance to fight."

"So you want us to find the kidnappers and help you rescue your employers?" Allen asked.

"That's right. By the time we came to they'd gone and no one dared follow them for fear of the wizard."

"That was smart," Lothair said. "Normal men taking on a wizard is beyond stupid, it's suicidal." He turned to Allen. "You're not seriously considering taking this job after what I told you."

Allen waved him to silence. "We haven't heard how much they're offering for the job. So what about it?"

The thugs with the chest set it on the floor and opened the lid. Gold double eagles glittered in the tavern's dim light. Lothair's breath caught in his throat. He'd never seen that much gold in his life.

"How much is in there?" Allen asked in a ragged voice.

"We didn't count it, but it's the boss's whole stash. It's yours when they're free and in one piece."

Allen rubbed his eyes. "How many men do you have for the assault once we find them? The three of us are no match for a wizard backed up by warriors."

"I've got fifteen men," One-Eye said. "I can call in favors for ten more. How soon will it take you to find them?"

Allen shrugged. "I have no idea. Could be a day, could be a week. This isn't the sort of thing you can predict, but rest assured we will find them. How do I get in touch with you?"

"I'll station a man in the alley every night. Let him know and he'll bring me the message."

The thugs slammed the lid of the chest and the little group left the tavern. Ulf pointed at the spot where they'd stood and dragged his finger across his throat.

"Yes," Allen said. "It would have been easier to kill them here and take the gold, but if they have fifteen more men, and those men know where their comrades went, we likely wouldn't have lived long enough to spend it."

With the glitter of gold out of his eyes Lothair returned to his senses. "We shouldn't do this, gold or no gold. A wizard makes it too risky. I told you how the noble pig bested me without even trying. Gold is useless to the dead."

"One on one, I agree, none of us would have a chance, but thirty to six? I like those odds even if one of them's a wizard."

Lothair looked away and took another drink. With his share he'd have wealth enough to support Annamaria and their daughter in luxury for the rest of their lives. It was a risk. Heaven above, was it ever a risk, but the reward…

"I'm in. Where do we start?"

༄

Otto took a bite of braised veal and sighed. Wolfric wished he could enjoy the food as much as his friend. They sat together in his private dining room with a platter of meat between them. Three days had passed since Otto captured his first spy and Wolfric was eager for an update.

It seemed the man had been remarkably forthcoming once Otto made it clear that his only hope of living a long, reasonably healthy life lay in helping them understand what his masters in Straken intended. Just because Father refused to accept reality didn't mean Wolfric had to stand aside and let Garenland's enemies do as they pleased.

"So give me the rundown," Wolfric said.

"Well, the spy, Xavier, claims he's just one of many agents that infiltrated Garen over the years. His task was industrial espionage. Not long ago agents of his stole the formula for a new steel alloy—that pleased his masters a great deal."

"I've heard nothing about any theft."

"Not surprising since he ordered his thieves to make a copy of the information and leave the original behind. And that's just the most recent action he's ordered. It seems he makes an effort to steal anything as soon as our people think it up."

"What about the other spies?" Wolfric took a bite of his food, hardly tasting it. He ate mechanically, resigned to the necessity of maintaining his strength for the long fight he knew was coming. That and it seemed to make Otto feel better when he joined in during the meal.

"How did they even sneak into Garenland in the first place?"

"I have few details. He sends reports to Straken and they send orders to the other spies. All he knows for sure is that a lot of our bandit troubles are organized by his fellow agents. As to how they entered the kingdom, that's simple: they arrived through the portal, posing as merchants or guards or whatever and simply disappeared into the countryside. It's not like anyone keeps track of who comes and goes every day through the portal."

"Another oversight on our part." How Garenland had survived this long was a growing mystery. Only the other nations' desire not to lose their place in the compact had protected them from their own foolishness. "Do you have any proof of the spy's claims? Something I could take to my father to show him I was right about Straken's intentions."

"I'm sorry, Wolfric. All we have is Xavier's word and the ledgers, which are written in code to look like a simple merchant's logbook."

Wolfric slammed his fist on the table, rattling the silver-ware. "So capturing this spy has gained us nothing."

"On the contrary. At a bare minimum we've removed an enemy from the board and gained insight into Straken's network in our country. That's the first step to rooting them out. It's only been two weeks. You need to have patience, my friend."

Trust Otto to be the calm one. Wolfric didn't know how he'd manage if anything happened to the mild-mannered wizard. "How can I have patience when Father concocts new plans every day to appease our enemies in the vain hope that they'll decide to be our friends instead? He's so invested in the compact that he'd rather see Garenland burn than risk offending one of the other monarchs."

Otto held his hands out to either side. "I'm doing all I can. As long as your father is king, we'll have to accept that we can only accomplish so much."

Wolfric scratched his chin. "Yes, as long as Father's king…" Wolfric refused to let his thoughts wander down that path, not yet anyway. If only he could find something irrefutable, Father would have no choice but to listen to him.

⌒

L othair followed Allen down a dark alley with Ulf bringing up the rear. Just enough light from the half-moon overhead reached them to reveal the crumbling stone of the building to his right. The stench that wafted up every time he took a step in the crud covering the ground made him gag. One of Allen's informants claimed Crane and his boss were being held in an old building nearby. He'd harbored a secret hope that they'd find the kidnappers in Gold Ward at some mansion.

No such luck.

They'd spoken twice over the past week to the thug, Dirk, and he said no ransom demands had been sent. That implied the kidnappers wanted something other than money, though what that could be Lothair had no idea.

As they drew closer to the kidnappers' hideout, Lothair fought the urgent need to relieve himself. He couldn't believe he was seeking out a confrontation with a wizard, not after what Otto had done to him in the garden that day. If not for Annamaria's generous act he might have been killed without even being able to defend himself.

At the end of the alley Allen paused and waved for them to stop. Lothair inched closer. Across from the alley sat a simple stone building with no windows and a single door visible. It wouldn't be an easy place to break into. The door looked nice and sturdy. Two or three men could hold that entrance for a while.

"Gonna be a job breaking in there," Lothair said.

"Assuming Crane's even inside," Allen said. "We need to make sure."

Lothair was just as happy to stay a safe distance away, but Allen was right, they needed to make sure. "How do you want to handle it?"

"Knock on the door then run," Allen said. "When they open it I'll be able to look inside. Hopefully I'll see something."

To hell with that.

"I have a better idea. You knock and I'll look inside."

Allen tapped his chest with his thumb. "I'm in charge of this job, not you."

"So that means I have to take all the risks?"

Ulf tapped them both on the shoulder and held a finger to his lips. He patted the air with his hands then pointed at himself. Lothair was still trying to figure out what the mute bartender had signed when he darted across the street, rapped on the door, and ran off out of sight.

A few seconds later the door opened half a foot and a face appeared in the gap. Reddish light leaked out. Lothair tried to see past the man but made out only a bit of stone floor. He risked darting across the alley for a different angle. Before the door shut, he caught a glimpse of chain rattling around. It wasn't much but combined with the tip it argued that this was the place.

Ulf appeared from the rear of the alley having run around the block. Lothair reported what he'd seen and Allen frowned.

"It's thin, but Dirk's getting impatient," Allen said. "We have to go for it or risk losing the job."

Lothair debated whether being wrong would be so bad. At least they wouldn't have to deal with the wizard.

CHAPTER 44

Axel and his men were three days into their patrol and they'd already ambushed two groups of Straken infantry and were in turned ambushed once by a group of rangers. He'd lost two men so far and four more bore minor wounds. They rode down the dirt track with their weapons bared. Every shadow seemed to hold an enemy waiting to attack. Every branch swaying in the breeze was a bow being drawn back.

Their trek had turned from a patrol mission to one of simple survival. Everything in Axel screamed to turn back and ride for the fort, but he needed more information. Numbers and locations of soldiers, something, anything that might give them a chance of fighting back.

Everywhere they looked, signs of enemy fighters littered the ground. Straken forces had crossed the border in such numbers that they no longer bothered hiding their tracks. Such a rapid deployment defied belief.

"How much deeper are we going?" Cobb asked for the tenth time.

"We'll keep going until we figure out what the bastards are up to."

"I should think that was obvious," Cobb said. "They're invading the northern province."

Axel scrubbed his hand across his face. "Believe it or not I figured that much out already. I'm hoping for a little more detail."

They rounded a bend and found Colten and his scouts waiting for them beside a cut in the trees. Axel guided his horse up beside them.

"Report."

"I think this is what you've been looking for, sir." Colten nodded toward a well-worn track leading off the road and down a rough trail. It looked like a skid path, and a fresh one at that. No one from Garenland was logging in this area. The nearest village was miles from here.

"I think you might be right. Let's check it out."

Cobb cleared his throat.

"Then we'll return to base."

Axel designated three men, along with the wounded, to watch over the horses. All he wanted to do was have a look around. If it came to a fight, they wouldn't stand a chance anyway.

Everyone dismounted and Colten led the way down the trail. The scout ranged about a hundred yards ahead, flicking in and out of view every few seconds. The squad slunk along behind, Axel wincing at every creak of armor.

Half an hour later Colten came running back, waving his arms, and motioning them off the trail. The squad dispersed on either side of the skid path. The scout crouched beside Axel behind a clump of young spruce.

"What is it?"

Colten held a finger to his lips. A moment later the faint thump of steps and the jingle of harnesses reached Axel. He held his breath and concentrated. Sounded like two horses and a few men.

It didn't take long for the approaching group to appear. Axel's guess hadn't been far off. A ragged man in tattered homespun led two horses hitched together. Behind him came five more equally poor men in leg irons guarded by a pair of soldiers clad in leather armor and armed with spears. Looked like a prisoner work detail.

Those men could provide Axel with all the information he needed. Axel caught Colten's eye, pointed at the guards, and drew his finger across his throat. The scout nodded an acknowledgment and tapped the archer beside him. A few silent gestures were exchanged before arrows were nocked.

As one the archers stood and loosed. Both soldiers went down, arrows sticking out of their throats. Axel and his men rushed out onto the path.

"Don't worry," Axel said. "We'll get you out of here."

"No!" the man leading the horses said.

Axel stopped in his tracks. "What?"

"The Straken soldiers have our families. If we don't return, our wives and children will be killed. They only send family men out on the work details."

The rest of the squad had gathered around the prisoners. Up close they looked even worse. Fresh lash marks showed through their torn shirts and bruises covered their faces and hands.

"What's going on out here?" Axel asked.

The prisoner slumped down to the ground and the rest joined him. Axel glanced at Cobb and made a little circle with his finger. Cobb nodded and formed the men into a defensive perimeter. Not wanting the unfortunate men to have to stare up at him, Axel sat cross-legged facing the lead prisoner.

"I'm Axel. What's your name?"

"Arik, I'm head man of our village." He stared down. "At least I was."

"Tell me everything, Arik."

"A few weeks ago, a force of several hundred Straken soldiers crossed the border and overran our village. We didn't even try to fight back and to our surprise they didn't put us to the sword. Instead they put us to work."

That must have been before the commander sent out word to evacuate. "Doing what?"

"Building a fort. The outer wall is almost up and we're starting on the fort itself. Teams go out every day to cut wood and skid it back while others shape the wood and put it together. Our families are kept under tight watch. When one of the guys bristled at the commander's orders his little girl's throat was cut. That took the fight out of us, I don't mind telling you."

"I'm sorry," Axel said. "But don't worry, we'll get word to the capital and the Straken scum will pay for what they've done to you and your families."

"Thank you." Arik stood and Axel and the others joined him. "We'll have to report the ambush to the garrison commander, but we can take our time getting back. That'll give you a few hours to get out of here."

"You're an honorable man and a good leader." Axel held out his hand and Arik grasped his wrist. They shook and Arik led his people down the trail at a slow trudge. "Time to go, Cobb."

◯

A xel guided his mount down the road toward base. Four hours had passed since they left the prisoners to make their way back to their village. The sun hung low in the sky and soon they'd have to think about finding a place to make camp. Wherever they ended up stopping, he doubted anyone would get much sleep tonight.

Axel ground his teeth and resisted the urge to thump his horse's ribs and gallop back to report in. They had a hundred-plus miles to cover and running his mount wouldn't do a bit of good. In fact, they should stop early and build a proper defensive position. He was about to give the order when Colten came racing back toward the main column. He waved his hands in a frantic attempt to warn them off the road.

Axel barely had time to react when he spotted the riders hard on the scout's heels. He dragged his sword free. "Charge!"

At this point the men were as eager for a fight as he was. A roar went up and the squad thundered forward.

Axel guided his horse a little to the side. Colten passed between him and Cobb. The moment he was clear Axel put the scout out of his mind. He focused on the first enemy cavalryman and ignored everything else.

The shining, curved edge of a saber swung at Axel's neck. He met the blow with his longsword. The weapon was deflected and he rode past.

The next man in line caught Axel's back cut in his ribs and he fell out of the saddle.

The instant he cleared the scrum Axel dragged his snorting mount's head around. The two sides had switched positions. Three of the enemy soldiers lay bleeding in the dirt. The dozen behind them stared down Axel's men.

He would have dearly loved to simply ride on, but no way

could he leave enemy forces to pursue him. Axel leveled his sword and urged his horse forward.

The two forces came together again. Axel hacked at anything that came close and didn't wear a Garenland uniform.

His sword lodged in an enemy ribcage.

He yanked it free, nearly losing his seat as the sword came loose.

A saber skipped off his leather pauldron. Axel hacked at the passing arm, drawing a scream.

When he raised his sword again, he found no one to swing it at.

Men and horses lay bleeding and moaning in the mud. The figures were so filthy he couldn't tell if any of the bodies were his men.

"Sound off!" Axel shouted.

His men chimed in, but he came up three short. Axel bit off a curse. He'd lost one of his rookies. Considering they'd had no time to prepare it could have ended far worse.

"Cobb, find our dead and finish off any Straken survivors. Scouts up the road, I don't want another surprise."

"Yes, sir." Colten led his men back up the road.

At least none of his scouts had been injured. Thank heavens for small favors. If they had to blunder around on their own he doubted the squad would last a day.

Fifteen minutes later they were on their way. Axel's hope for an early quit gave way to his more urgent desire to put as much distance between them and the dead cavalrymen as possible.

They rode until it grew too dark to see. Colten led them well off the road and the patrol made a cold camp. Jerky and their dwindling supply of water was shared out. Axel had just started on his second strip of dried meat when Colten motioned him over to the edge of their makeshift camp. Cobb joined them unbidden.

"What is it?" Axel asked.

"We need to abandon the horses and the road and continue on foot through the woods. We're too exposed out there. One of these times we're going to run into something we can't handle."

"It'll take twice as long to walk through the woods," Cobb said. "And what are we supposed to do with the horses?"

Axel had been considering their best choices and while he hated abandoning their mounts Colten was right. Sneaking through the woods was their best chance of getting out of here alive.

"We continue on foot in the morning. Pass the word. We take only what we need."

"What about the bodies?" Cobb's question came out as more of a growl. The sergeant wasn't going to like hearing Axel's answer any better than he did saying it.

"We'll have to leave them."

"Our men deserve better than to be food for the crows, sir."

"You're right, Cobb, they do, but if we don't want to join them our options are limited. My concern now is for the living, not the dead. Post guards and set the rotation. We leave at dawn."

CHAPTER 45

Lothair once again found himself standing in the dark, stinking alley watching the small stone building. In fact, he'd done little else for the past two days. Allen said they needed more information on the kidnappers' schedule before they made their move. After many hours of observation, he'd determined that the kidnappers seldom left the building and when one of them did he returned in short order.

Neither Lothair nor any of the other watchers had seen any sign of a wizard. Whether that was a good sign or not Allen hadn't decided. Lothair dared hope the wizard had been a mercenary hired for the job and was now long gone. More likely he simply hadn't returned to check on his guards and would show up at the worst possible moment for the rescuers.

Either way, they'd find out soon enough. Dirk had grown sick of waiting and ordered the attack for midnight, half an hour from now. Lothair had drawn the short stick so while the others prepared, he got stuck playing sentry. At least he hadn't been assigned to the first wave. Dirk had hired some bums for that task and gave them rusty axes to swing around before they were killed.

The midnight bell tolled and the small army emerged from the darkness, their torches lighting up the street. Pity it was a stone building with tile on the roof, otherwise they could have set the place on fire. Lothair left his hiding place and ran over to join Allen at the rear of the column.

"So are we just planning to charge the door?" Lothair asked.

"I gave Dirk my suggestions, but he's in charge of the assault. The only thing I'm certain of is that we're in the last wave."

That was the best news Lothair had heard since Allen agreed to this folly. The mini army stopped fifteen yards from the building and Dirk strode to the front of the mob.

"Hey! You in the stone building. Release our bosses if you know what's good for you." He stood hands on hips and stared at the door. When the seconds turned to minutes, he tried again. "This is your last chance to live. Send them out now!"

Several more minutes passed and Lothair said, "I fear the guards don't intend to comply."

"No kidding." Allen crossed his arms.

"Have it your way!" Dirk waved the bums on. "Chop that door down."

To their credit the ragged beggars gave a credible war cry, raised their axes, and charged. The first blunt blade hit and bounced off. Three men formed up around the door and set to chopping. The dense hardwood resisted almost as well as the stone wall.

The first three attackers tired quickly and another trio took their places. A few splinters of wood fell to the ground before they gave up and made room for the next group. The door might not be in any great danger, but the guards inside must be getting a splitting headache.

"If I'd known how long this was going to take, I'd have brought a stool," Lothair said.

"Sieges take time." Allen sounded like some old general offering profound wisdom.

"They also require battering rams and catapults, either one of which would end this side show in seconds."

"I doubt there's a functioning catapult in the entire kingdom." A loud crack sounded and Allen pumped his fist. "They found a weak spot. It's only a matter of time now."

Hopefully not too much time. Lothair doubted the city guard would look kindly on a gathering like this.

◯

When the shouting moron woke Hans from a deep sleep he assumed some drunk local took it in his head to vent his personal demons. It happened more often than he'd have guessed. The thick walls muffled the words, so he didn't catch the details of the idiot's diatribe.

Cord sat up in his cot and groaned. "What is all that racket?"

The other guys were awake and muttering about murdering whoever was out there. Hans didn't blame them. The cots made sleeping hard enough without this.

"Just relax," Hans said. "He'll wander off soon enough."

"You're wrong," said the smaller prisoner, what did Lord Shenk say his name was? Crane. "I know that voice. It's my second, Dirk. He's come to bust us out."

"That right?" Hans rolled out of his cot and started to gear up. This mission had been dull as dirt since the raid and the boys had been itching for some action. Looked like they were going to get their wish.

"Let us go now." Chains rattled as Crane climbed to his feet. "And I'll lead my men away from here. No one has to get hurt."

"You think I'd let you two go to get into heaven only knows what mischief? If worst comes to worst, I'll kill you both myself."

"That's not smart." The first blow reverberated through the door as if to emphasize Crane's words.

Hans drew his sword and pointed it at Crane. "Sit down and shut up. You're not especially valuable. Maybe if I cut your head off and toss it out there your men will take the hint."

Crane grimaced and slid down the wall. He leaned in and whispered something in his boss's ear, drawing a nod. Hans didn't know what they had planned, but they'd have a hard time doing it chained to the wall.

His men were geared up and the crashes outside grew louder by the second. That was probably just his imagination though. An especially heavy strike landed and a crack ran halfway down the door. Then again, maybe it wasn't his imagination.

"What's the plan, sir?" Jax asked.

"Simple, we hold the door. As long as we're in here we have the advantage. Only one man at a time can come through."

Cord grinned. "If they break down the door, we stack up their corpses to make a new one. Nothing to it."

Hans clapped him on the shoulder. "That's the spirit."

An axe head blasted through the wood. It wiggled and pulled back leaving a gap. An eye appeared, peeking in. Hans lunged. The narrow sword blade slid through the gap, into the attacker's eye, and out the back of his head.

He yanked the blade free, scraping the brain matter off on the wood as he retracted his weapon. "One down."

Jax crouched and looked through the opening from a safe distance. "There's at least twenty guys out there, Sergeant."

"Four to one's not so bad given our position," Hans said.

The drumbeat of axes resumed. Given the damage the door had sustained Hans doubted it would last five more minutes. They needed reinforcements. He paced to the opposite end of the building where Lord Shenk had left his glowing rune.

Hans hadn't fully understood the wizard's explanation, but somehow the rune was connected to Lord Shenk, allowing him to come and go from the makeshift prison. Maybe there was some way to contact him.

He glanced back at his men, but they were all focused on the door. Good, if he was going to make a fool of himself, he'd just as soon not have an audience. "Lord Shenk? We're under attack and require assistance."

No response from the rune.

Stupid magic. He slammed the pommel of his sword on the rune twice in quick succession.

The light wavered for a moment then resumed its steady white glow. Looked like they were on their own.

〇

Otto sat bolt upright when a vibration in the ether ran through his mind. Annamaria murmured something and pulled the covers closer around her. A moment later a second vibration struck. It didn't hurt exactly. In fact, if someone asked him to describe the feeling, he wasn't sure what he would have said. He'd never felt anything like it.

Maybe he could trace the vibrations back to their source.

He closed his eyes and sent his sight into the ether. A wavering thread still trembled. He traced it and quick as thought found himself inside the prison. In the ruddy light of the brazier Hans and his men faced a broken door. Through the numerous holes a body was visible lying on the ground.

Otto pulled back, out of the building, and took in the scene from above. A group of twenty-eight people, all of them armed, and four carrying torches, faced the converted armory. Apparently, their guests had allies who had chanced onto the prison. He couldn't allow their prisoners to escape.

A blink severed the thread and he returned his awareness to the bedroom. A quick agitation of the ether produced enough light for him to dress by. A minute later he finished belting on his sword.

Just as he reached for the ether Annamaria said, "Where are you going?"

"An emergency came up. There's been a setback in the project I'm helping Wolfric with. I need to go take care of it."

"Can't it wait until morning?"

Otto grimaced. It definitely couldn't wait until morning. "I'm afraid not. Go back to sleep. You know you need your rest. When I return I'll go to the guest suite so I don't wake you."

She mumbled something and closed her eyes. Annamaria didn't know he could teleport yet and he preferred to keep it that way, so he slipped out into the hall and rushed out into the front yard. No guards were in sight, so he entered the ether and vanished.

The next thing he knew the shouts and the crash of battle assaulted his ears. He took a second to orient himself. Hans and one of the other men, Otto couldn't tell who from the back of his uniform, stood at the shattered door and hacked at unseen men trying to force themselves through.

A loud shout from outside preceded a line of men slamming into the guards and sending them sprawling. The other soldiers sprang forward, cutting down the lead attacker and giving Hans and Cord a chance to recover.

Six attackers had made it into the prison and more were gathering behind them. Otto drew his mithril blade and poured ether into his body, enhancing his strength, speed, and toughness.

Bliss filled him and lightning coursed through his blood.

He doubted the attackers' crude weapons would even scratch him.

Otto charged, slicing the nearest man in half from his left collar bone to his right ribcage. His impossibly sharp sword cut through with no resistance.

"Lord Shenk!" Hans said.

Otto ignored him and spun, taking the next attacker's arm above the elbow.

The filthy men seemed to move in slow motion and their rusty weapons offered no protection against his blade.

In half a minute all the thugs inside the prison were dead.

He channeled lightning through the blade and hurled it at those gathered in the doorway, sending them flying.

Otto charged through behind them.

The moment he spotted their torches he sent ether into them and conjured fireballs.

Four detonations sent everyone outside sprawling.

Otto stalked through the carnage with Hans and two of his men following along behind. Whenever he found someone moving the mithril blade descended, separating his head from his body.

At the rear of the gang three figures climbed slowly to their feet. Otto raised his hand and sent three threads' worth of lightning into them. When he reached the still-twitching men he couldn't suppress a smile. Allen, the mute bartender, and Lothair. This had to be his lucky day. He'd happily wake at midnight any day of the week for such a sweet reward.

"Clap these three in irons, I have questions for them. When they're secured gather the bodies in a single pile."

The soldiers set to work while Hans followed him back into the prison. Otto kept himself upright by sheer force of will. Using that much magic in such a short timespan left his arms trembling and his legs limp. The moment he entered the building he limped over to the cots and sat, holding his head in his hands.

"How did you know we needed you, Lord Shenk?" Hans asked.

"Vibrations through the ether woke me and I traced them here. When I saw the attack I came as fast as I could."

"Huh. I guess striking the rune worked. Talk about dumb luck."

Otto looked up. "Explain, please."

Hans told him how he tried to speak through the rune then slammed it in frustration. Otto had never heard of such a thing. He suppressed a sigh. Yet another thing to ask Lord Karonin. By the time three months was up he'd have a list of questions the length of his arm.

An hour later the prisoners were secure and the dead heaped in a neat pile. Otto had gained enough strength to walk outside without stumbling.

Hans eyed the pile of corpses. "This is going to draw some attention."

"Good point."

Otto rubbed his fingers and wove ten threads of ether into the resulting heat. When he sent the flames into the bodies an instant bonfire appeared. He drew the flames together to compress the heat and hide the worst of the light. In less than an hour the attackers burned down to ash. With any luck they'd avoided notice. And even if they hadn't, he couldn't see any of the locals running to the city watch.

A final blast of etheric energy scattered the pile, adding just one more layer of filth on an already filthy section of the city. The only sign that a battle had taken place was the smashed door and they'd have no trouble fixing that. Tomorrow he'd question the new prisoners. He dearly hoped Lothair proved... uncooperative.

CHAPTER 46

Otto placed the gold ring he'd taken from the unconscious Lothair and set it dancing across his knuckles. He recognized it of course. His wife had given it to the traitor so he could sell it and use the coin to flee Garen, or so she'd said. He glared at the unconscious fool and his companions. It would please him no end to watch him and his companions dancing at the end of a rope.

He'd ordered the guards outside to give him a little time alone with the prisoners. Next he made the spy and his cohort blind, deaf, and mute. The weaving had been surprisingly simple, basically he'd extended their senses into the prison wall and left them there.

Lothair rolled over, groaned, and opened his eyes. He met Otto's angry gaze for a moment before turning his attention to the ring.

"Give that back to me."

"Traitors don't get to make demands." Otto pocketed the ring. "You should have left the city when you had the chance."

The second man, Allen, cleared his throat. "We're not traitors. We were hired to rescue a kidnapped merchant."

"No, you were hired to free a Straken spy from the crown prince's personal guards. A spy, I might add, that you've been selling valuable information to for some time. Any of your individual crimes would be sufficient to see you hung. Taken together..." Otto shrugged.

"I didn't know he was a spy." Allen's chains rattled as he sat up. "I never met the man. I always dealt with Crane."

"You intend to plead ignorance? I suppose it's your only real option but given the damage your actions caused I hold little hope for you."

The third man, the bartender, sat up as well. Something around his throat glittered in the ether. Otto looked closer, trying to make sense of it.

"Give me back my ring!" Lothair shouted.

Otto flicked his iron ring and bound the fool from head to toe, silencing him without so much as a glance. He stared at the bartender who stared back, head cocked.

"What was done to you, my silent friend?" Otto bound him as well and crouched down. Tiny runes circled his neck. He'd never seen such a weaving. "Very interesting."

A conjured thread took on the shape of a narrow blade and Otto set to slicing away the spell a tiny piece at a time. After a minute the first rune broke apart. The weaving became unstable. Ever so carefully Otto made a final cut.

The last of the etheric energy fizzled away. The bartender gave a violent cough and clutched his throat.

"What did you do to him?" Allen asked. His concern sounded genuine which surprised Otto. He'd taken the information broker for the sort that used and discarded people as was convenient.

"I'm not entirely sure," Otto said.

The bartender stopped coughing and Allen said, "Ulf? Are you okay?"

Ulf croaked something, coughed again, then said, "I'm fine." The words were thick and distorted, but understandable all the same.

Allen stared. "I thought you were mute?"

"No." Ulf's voice grew stronger by the word. "My voice was bound when the Lords of Alchemy banished me. You have my gratitude for releasing the spell."

"You're perfectly welcome." Otto backed away and released both his bindings.

Lothair surged against his chains, yanking at the wall ring and trying with all his might to get at Otto. After a futile half minute, he exhausted himself and slumped back to the floor. Lothair hung his head between his knees and gasped for air.

Otto dismissed his wife's lover from his mind and focused on Ulf. "I have so many questions, but the obvious one is: who are the Lords of Alchemy and why did they feel the need to silence you?"

"The lords oversee all the alchemists in the Celestial Empire and they gave me a choice, death or silence and banishment. I chose the coward's way out."

Otto grabbed a cot and dragged it over so he could sit. He'd heard of the Celestial Empire, but no one from Garenland had visited them since the time of the Arcane Lords.

"How did you end up with this traitor?"

Ulf shook his head. "Allen isn't a traitor."

"Thanks," Allen said.

"He's a greedy opportunist who's perfectly happy to do anything for coin, no questions asked. That he ended up working for an enemy of the Crown was simple bad luck."

"I see," Otto said. "I suppose you can't be a traitor if you lack loyalty in the first place."

"I'm right here, you know," Allen said.

Otto ignored him and continued his interview with Ulf. "Were you a willing accomplice?"

"When I arrived in Garen," Ulf said, "I'd been on the road for over a year. I was starving and alone. At the time Allen worked as a bartender in the tavern he now owns and sold secrets on the side. He offered me food and drink then convinced his employer to give me a job. To this day I'm uncertain why he did it, but I owe him my life. Where he goes, I go, even if it's to the end of a rope."

Otto knew exactly why Allen did it. He saw a chance to make a loyal ally for the price of a meal and a job. That turned out to be an excellent investment. His opinion of the information broker rose a notch. It would be a shame to waste someone with Allen's skills and connections. The fact that he was a wholly untrustworthy snake could be worked around.

"You know," Otto said. "It's possible I've been too harsh in my assessment of your involvement with Straken's spy. Perhaps hanging you would be rash."

Allen sat up straighter. "If you have an alternate suggestion, I'm eager to hear it."

"I thought you might be. Garenland has a problem. We lack a spy network, while our enemies, obviously, don't. I feel your expertise would be useful in both setting up our network and finding and destroying our enemy's."

"The three of us are at your disposal, my lord." Allen made an awkward attempt at a bow.

"Not the three of you. Lothair is going to die, whether at the end of a rope or the end of my sword, I have yet to decide."

"Ah," Allen said. "He did mention the two of you had a difficult relationship."

"Did he?" Otto's voice went cold.

"Yes, well, no details, of course. And even if he did you could count on my discretion."

"That's reassuring," Otto said, not believing a word of it. "On your feet, both of you."

Allen and Ulf clambered up.

"Face the wall."

They turned and Otto summoned the ether. He carved tiny runes in the backs of their necks, drawing pained hisses. When the designs were complete, he empowered them. A quick look revealed no flaws in his casting. He gestured again and their manacles and chains crashed to the floor.

The two men faced him. "What was that?" Allen asked as he rubbed the mark.

"I engraved a rune at the base of your neck. It will allow me to find you anywhere in the world. It will also—" Otto sent a single thread's worth of lightning racing into the runes. Both men shuddered as the current caused their muscles to spasm. "—let me do that. Or should you really annoy me I can just blow your heads clean off."

When his teeth had stopped chattering Allen said, "I believe we understand. How do you wish to proceed?"

"Go about your regular business. Keep your ears open for anything that might be of use to me. Do not sell information to anyone else. I'll be in touch."

"If I'm not to sell information how will we survive?" Allen asked. "The tavern isn't exactly profitable."

"I'm confident you'll manage. Also, I can get your annual tax bill set aside. That ought to free up some coin."

Allen's eyes widened. "It certainly will. If there's nothing else, we should get started."

Otto nodded and his new agents headed for the door. Before they could leave Otto said, "And Allen, I'll be checking in regularly through the runes. Keep that in mind should your mercenary nature start to get the better of you. I'd hate to have to end our relationship permanently."

Allen's throat worked as he swallowed. "I understand completely, my lord. I'll give you no cause to regret your generous decision."

"Excellent. Off you go then." Otto followed them out the door and when Hans looked his way said, "It's okay, Hans."

Allen struck him as a pragmatic fellow. He doubted there'd be any trouble on that front and with any luck his new agents would come up with some useful information.

For their sakes they'd better.

CHAPTER 47

For four days, from sun up to sun down, Axel and his squad followed Colten through the forest. So far, they'd snuck around six mixed companies of enemy soldiers. Axel crouched beside the scout and surveyed the current collection of Straken soldiers occupying a field directly in their path.

After a quick count he came up with twenty irregulars, a squad of rangers, and a squad of heavy infantry. Way too many for his exhausted, depleted patrol to take on. Unfortunately, there was no way for them to sneak past with such limited cover. With only a mile to go the trees had started to thin. They just couldn't catch a break.

He tugged Colten's sleeve and they slid back out of sight before scrambling to their feet and rejoining Cobb and the rest of the patrol.

"Well?" Cobb asked. The veteran had twigs and spruce needles stuck in his beard and not for camouflage.

"Another mixed unit. There's no way to get past them

unseen. We're going to have to smash our way through," Axel said.

"What's the plan?" Cobb tested the edge of his sword, sounding eager. Not that Axel blamed him; they'd been running and hiding for so long that everyone was keen to strike back.

"We hit them hard and fast. Don't stop to duel, we only need to get by. Once we're clear, run like hell for the fort. It can't be more than a mile."

Cobb grunted. "What are the bastards up to?"

"They're preparing for a siege and the commander needs to know. Keep that in mind if anyone's tempted to stop and fight."

That drew another grunt, this one more annoyed than amused. It didn't take long to explain the plan and two minutes later the patrol had gathered at the edge of the woods, weapons drawn and ready to go.

Axel looked right and Cobb nodded.

He looked left. Colten had traded his bow for a hatchet and dagger. The scout nodded his readiness as well.

Well, here goes. Hopefully some of them would survive to warn Commander Braddock.

"Charge!"

Axel burst through the tree line and ran a ranger through.

He ripped his sword free and sped on. He parried a spear thrust from an irregular and hacked the man's left thigh to the bone.

Pain flared in his side as someone gashed him.

He ignored it and pressed on.

Shouts and the clash of steel on steel sounded all around him.

All Axel focused on was the edge of the clearing, and killing anyone that got in his way.

A second irregular fell under his blade then he was through. Axel didn't even pause to look back.

He ran as fast and hard as he could, trusting that his men would follow.

If they didn't, he'd avenge them later.

An arrow hammered into a tree trunk beside him.

He sacrificed evasion for speed and kept going straight.

Axel's heart hammered and his lungs burned.

He caught movement in the corner of his vision and risked a glance.

Colten ran beside him. The scout appeared uninjured.

He didn't have breath to waste asking after the others.

The trees continued to thin until they finally burst into the clearing that surrounded the fort. Axel had never considered the collection of rough boards and timbers especially attractive, but at that moment he would have sworn he'd never seen a more beautiful sight.

Soldiers gathered on the ramparts and raised their bows.

No, no, no!

Axel waved his arms, frantically trying to keep the soldiers from shooting, but knowing it wouldn't do any good.

He had just time enough to appreciate the irony that after escaping hundreds of enemy soldiers he was about to get killed by his own men. Arrows arced into the air and sailed over his head.

Dull thunks were followed by pained screams. Another volley was launched with similar results.

The gate opened and two squads equipped with shields and broadswords emerged. They took up position on either side of the opening and motioned for Axel to hurry.

He'd have been happy to oblige if he wasn't already running with everything he had.

With a final burst of effort, he stumbled through the gates and fell to the ground in the bailey. Half a second later Colten landed beside him.

Axel closed his eyes and breathed, trying in vain to calm his thundering heart.

A second and third thump sounded. He continued counting until the gates slammed shut. The number of thumps was far too few.

"You're bleeding, Lieutenant."

Axel opened his eyes and looked up at Commander Braddock. He felt the pain then, a sharp burning along his ribs. It matched the pain in his heart for the men he'd lost. Ten men sat in the dirt around him, less than half of what he set out with.

Cobb had survived; the veteran campaigner was too tough to fall to anything less than a full company. One of his rookies sat cradling a limp arm. The rest looked exhausted, but otherwise unharmed.

"Let's get you and your wounded to the infirmary." Braddock helped Axel to his feet. "And where are your horses?"

"Heaven may know, sir, but I surely don't." Axel didn't bother giving orders. Cobb would see to the men. "We have a serious problem."

"I know," the commander said. "After you get stitched up come to my office."

Axel managed a weak salute and continued on his shuffling way. What he wouldn't have given for a hot bath and a mug of apple brandy. He didn't like his chances of getting either anytime soon.

A xel touched the freshly stitched wound on his side and winced. The fort's healer had assured him it could have been much worse. A shallow cut along his ribs was nothing more than an inconvenience. Easy for the healer to say, he hadn't narrowly avoided getting his guts spilled by a Straken soldier.

The commander's door stood open when he arrived. Braddock sat behind his desk and stared at an unrolled map. A spare chair had been dragged in from somewhere.

Axel knocked on the door frame. "Sir?"

Braddock startled and looked up. "Come in and close the door. How's the wound?"

Axel obliged, dropping into the chair he assumed had been brought for him. "The healer assures me I'll be fine."

"That might be overly optimistic given our situation." Braddock spun the map, allowing Axel to read it. "Your patrol was the last to return, again. Everyone else encountered resistance fifteen to twenty miles out and retreated at once. What about you?"

"If you ignore the rangers we attacked five miles out, then yes, that's where we first encountered trouble. I considered making a quick retreat, but I deemed it more important to find out what the enemy's up to."

"And did you?"

"To a degree." Axel tapped one of the villages on the map. "Straken is using our people as slaves to build a fortification here."

"Damn it! I knew some of them didn't escape when we sent word. What sort of fortification?" Braddock asked.

"I didn't dare get close enough for a firsthand look, but the worker we questioned said a palisade had been constructed and a fort set in motion. We also encountered enemy positions here, here, and here." Axel tapped three locations between a mile and two miles from base.

Braddock frowned and spun the map back around. "We're being encircled. The Straken commander must not want word getting to the capital.

"The bastards must have crossed the border as soon as Uther returned from Lordes. That's the only way they could have made this much progress."

Braddock nodded, but before he had a chance to speak the door burst open and a scruffy rookie barely Otto's age burst in. "We need you on the wall, sir. Now."

The two men leapt to their feet and followed the young man out of the fortress and up on the wall. At the edge of the clearing hundreds of soldiers had emerged from the woods, fully surrounding the fortress.

The Straken forces stayed out of bow range, seeming content for the moment to let the besieged soldiers see the force they faced. Axel tried to count them but gave up when he reached three hundred.

"Ten to one you think?" Axel asked.

Braddock pursed his lips. "At least. I wonder if the other forts are in equally bad positions."

"Excellent question. Do we know how big Straken's southern army is?"

"No." Braddock's disgust came through loud and clear. "Garenland hasn't made a proper attempt to scout the enemy since the compact was signed. Apparently, everyone assumed peace would last forever."

"So much for that theory. What now?"

"Siege protocol. Assign someone to inventory food and weapons. I want a company on duty at all times watching the enemy. The next move is theirs."

The next move wasn't long in coming. Two hours before sunset three men crossed the clearing, one of them carrying a white flag. From a distance he couldn't make out much detail, beyond the fact that the enemy leader was as tall and broad as all the high-ranking Straken soldiers he'd ever seen. Must be something in the water over there.

Axel had managed a few hours' sleep before rejoining the commander on the wall. He'd also checked in on his men and found them battered, exhausted, and itching to kill some Straken soldiers. He knew just how they felt.

"Do you know him?" Axel asked.

"Can't say as I do." Braddock shaded his eyes. "He's brave, coming within bowshot after everything his men have done. I've a good mind to feather him and talk to his second."

Axel would have been happy to carry out the order, but he knew his commander wouldn't give it. No good military man would shoot a person advancing under a white flag, and Braddock was as good as they came.

The Straken delegation stopped fifty feet from the wall. "Shall we not speak face to face like gentlemen?"

"I can hear you fine from up here," Braddock said. A good man, but fortunately not a stupid one.

The enemy leader shrugged. "As you wish. This won't take long in any case. I offer you one chance to surrender. You will be taken as prisoners of war. On my honor, no harm will come to you."

"As if a citizen of Straken knows anything about honor," Axel muttered.

"Steady." Braddock gave his arm a warning touch. "Do you require our answer now?"

"I should think the answer was obvious, but very well. You

have until the sun rises. If you and your men aren't standing, disarmed, in front of your open gate, I will take it as a no." The enemy commander turned on his heel and marched back the way he'd come.

"Generous bastard," Axel said. "Can I assume we aren't going to accept his offer?"

"You can. In fact, I want a double guard posted tonight in case they try anything while we're thinking it over."

CHAPTER 48

Sometime during the night, a squad of rangers tried to climb the fortress wall. They found forty armed and angry soldiers waiting for them. When Axel rose before dawn their bodies were lying on the ground, soaking the dirt with their blood. If nothing else the late-night raid settled any debate about the enemy's intentions, not that Axel had harbored much in the way of positive feelings for them.

One of the soldiers on duty kicked the nearest body. "What should we do with them?"

"Strip their weapons and toss the bodies over the wall. We don't want that filth stinking up the base."

That brought a round of smiles as the men set to work. When the sun cleared the horizon ten bodies littered the ground in front of the gate. Axel stood atop the wall and watched the enemy camp come awake. There were certainly enough of them. He hadn't seen the inventory yet, but hopefully they had enough arrows to go around.

Cobb appeared at the top of the stairs, a steaming bowl in his hand. "Figured you'd forget breakfast."

Axel accepted the bowl and took a bite of the hot oatmeal. He smiled at the sweet finish. "Did you put honey in this?"

"Just a bit. I can't eat that stuff plain."

"Thanks."

"How's it looking?" Cobb asked.

"We're certainly popular. I estimate Uther sent three full cohorts to kill us. You can't help feeling honored."

Cobb grunted. "If this is an honor, I could do without it."

"Indeed." Out in the field soldiers were gathering. The commander emerged from his tent along with his flag bearers, one of whom carried the white banner from yesterday. The idiot couldn't imagine they'd negotiate after his attempt with the rangers.

"Find the commander and get him up here." Axel marched to the area above the gates, five archers falling in behind him.

"Can we feather the son of a bitch this time?" one of the archers asked.

"If he's foolish enough to come within range, by all means."

As he drew closer, the enemy leader met Axel's gaze. He stopped, the hint of a smile playing around his lips. A knowing nod was offered as he spun and retreated back to his men. It appeared he wasn't as stupid as Axel had hoped. Pity.

"Spread the word," Axel said. "They'll be coming before long. Tell the archers to pick their targets. We can't be wasting arrows."

The soldiers saluted and dispersed to pass on his message. Axel held his place. He didn't know where they'd come from, but this was as good a place to wait as any.

"What's all the fuss?" Commander Braddock asked as he marched down the wall toward Axel.

"The enemy commander seemed to want to pay us a visit, but when he saw the archers with me he changed his mind."

"It seems we face a prudent enemy." Braddock grinned. "That might work to our advantage."

"I'm glad something's working to our advantage."

A great roar went up across the field as scores of Straken soldiers charged the wall carrying crudely made ladders.

"To the walls!" Braddock shouted. "Archers, fire at will!"

Arrows rained down from the towers. Soldiers fell, but the mass of enemies kept coming. At that moment Axel would have given a great deal for a moat.

The first ladder slammed into the wall a hundred yards from the gate. Men swarmed to it and quickly shoved it off the wall.

Seven more clattered into place.

Axel ran to the nearest just as the first enemy soldier's helmet came into view.

His longsword caved the helmet in along with the head under it.

His heart racing, Axel tried to shove the ladder over.

He didn't have leverage or strength enough.

More enemies started up the rungs.

He strained harder.

Come on, damn you!

"I got you, my lord." Cobb grunted and pushed.

Colten and another of his men arrived a moment later and between them they pushed the ladder clear, sending the Straken soldiers crashing into their fellows down below.

They had no time to bask in their accomplishment. A shout from down the wall drew Axel's attention. A Garenland infantryman went down with an arrow in his chest, creating an opening for one of the enemies to reach the top of the wall.

Axel charged.

If they allowed the Straken forces a foothold in their defenses the fort was doomed.

The soldier met Axel's overhead chop with a solid parry. Cobb's sword darted in around Axel, slicing into the enemy's guts and sending him toppling down into the bailey.

More of the defenders swarmed the ladder. Soon enough it and the soldiers climbing up crashed back down.

Another shout went up from the enemy and the attackers withdrew, though they left a satisfying number of their comrades behind. Braddock marched up carrying a bloody sword.

"We survived the first wave," Axel said.

"That wasn't even a real attack." Braddock waved his dripping sword. "Their commander was just testing to see how we'd react. Next time they'll come in earnest."

"That many more targets for the archers, right Cobb?" Axel asked.

Cobb grunted, seeming disinclined to play along. Axel didn't blame him. If the Straken commander sent his full strength against them Axel didn't know how they'd manage to hold them back.

∽

The enemy came at them a little after noon, two hundred men carrying fifty ladders. They attacked from every direction, forcing the defenders to spilt their already meager force. The shouts of the attackers rattled the walls and put Axel's men back on their heels. The commander had assigned Axel to oversee the defense of the gate while Braddock defended the rear of the fortress.

They came in numbers that made Axel despair. Only iron

will combined with the knowledge that if his men saw any weakness they'd lose heart kept Axel's expression stony. He could despair later, assuming they survived.

"Archers, loose at will. Infantry, to the walls. Prepare to repel attackers."

The walkway rattled as Axel's forty soldiers ran to their assigned positions. Everyone had trained for this and the earlier victory gave the men confidence.

Hopefully it would be enough.

Axel drew his sword and gripped the hilt until his palm ached. Out in the killing field the enemy fell one after another to his archers, yet it appeared their numbers remained undiminished.

The first ladder reached the top of the wall ten yards from Axel's position. Three infantrymen rushed to shove it over. Axel smiled when it struck the ground. Only forty-nine more to go.

The bulk of the enemy reached the base of the wall and fifteen ladders went up at the same time. Axel ran to the nearest. Enemy arrows struck all around him. He reached out to push and nearly got punctured for his trouble. Two infantrymen went tumbling off the wall with arrows jutting from their chests.

"Focus on the enemy archers!" Axel shouted to his own bowmen. "We'll handle their irregulars."

A face appeared at the top of the ladder. Axel punched it.

The Straken soldier lost his grip and went tumbling to the ground, thoughtfully taking one of his comrades along for the ride.

Axel took his momentary reprieve to shove the ladder clear.

His whole world narrowed down to kill, shove, kill, shove.

Axel had no idea how long he spent running up and down the wall, hacking at anyone wearing the wrong uniform. It felt like hours, but was probably only minutes.

He'd barely paused to catch his breath between ladders when a cry went up from the left-side gate tower. "Battering ram!"

Axel glanced at Cobb who nodded. He left his trusty sergeant in charge of the defense and ran to the gate. A group of thirty burly fighters had emerged from the woods carrying a crude battering ram. Little more than a log with a point hacked into it and rough shields nailed in front of the bearers. It didn't look overly impressive. Nevertheless, if they got up a good running start it still might damage the gate.

"Focus your fire on the ram!"

A volley of arrows streaked toward the approaching force with little effect. From their high angle most of the shots stuck in the top of the log or clattered off the shields. Axel's string of curses proved as effective as the arrows.

"We need to get lower." Axel pointed at three archers. "Come with me."

They ran along the wall, down the nearest steps, and across the bailey to the gate. Axel grimaced at the risk then proceeded to unbar the gate and winch it open three feet. The archers shot as fast as they could. Every second Axel expected the ram to strike home and smash the gate all the way open.

The bows fell silent. "The ram's down, sir."

Axel wasted no time closing and barring the gate. That had been too close. "Return to your posts."

He followed them back up on the wall. The ram lay on top of thirteen dead bodies ten feet from the gate. The rest of the bearers had been shot down as they fled. He would have liked to set fire to the ram, but fire arrows were useless against the green wood. What they really needed was a few gallons of blood of the earth.

"Lieutenant!" A shout was carried from soldier to soldier down the line.

Axel grabbed the nearest man. "What is it?"

"Commander Braddock is down, sir."

"They're retreating," Cobb said.

"It might be a feint. Everyone stay at your posts. I'll check on the commander." Axel left Cobb in charge and ran down to the far end of the compound. Fifteen men stood in a circle. "Back to your posts!"

They all looked at him, their faces long and ashen.

"Now, damn you!"

They shuffled back to the stairs revealing Braddock's broken, bleeding body. Three arrows jutted from his chest and right leg. The fortress's chief healer, Dokken, knelt beside him and frantically bound a wound in his side.

"He lives?" Axel asked.

"For the moment," Dokken said. "Though heaven knows how. We need to get him to the infirmary where I can work."

"I'll take his legs."

Between them Axel and Dokken wrestled Braddock into the fortress, down a short hall, and up onto an operating table. Two injured men lay moaning softly in cots off to one side. Other than those unfortunates they were alone.

"You'll have to help me," Dokken said.

Axel knew nothing about healing and hated being around the sick and injured. "I need to get back to the wall."

"I can't do this alone. If you don't help me he's going to die."

Axel's jaw clenched until it ached. "What do you need me to do?"

An hour later Axel emerged from the fortress, exhausted,

his arms scrubbed raw from trying to wash off Braddock's blood. How the commander managed to survive Dokken's crude attempts at surgery beggared understanding.

A gathering of anxious soldiers waited in the late afternoon sun. Their expressions ranged from terrified to angry to desperate. Hope was in short supply.

"He's alive." Axel answered their unspoken question. "For how long I can't say."

"We're doomed," someone said.

Murmurs ran through the gathering. If Axel didn't do something quick he was going to lose them. Once despair set in they'd have no chance of holding the fort.

"Quiet! Before he lost consciousness, the commander came up with a plan." That perked everyone up. "We're going to send for reinforcements. Colten!"

His scout elbowed his way to the front of the gathering. "Sir?"

"If we lowered you over the side of the wall after dark, could you sneak through the enemy's line?"

"No problem, Lieutenant. I watched them for a while last night. The enemy spends a lot of time laughing and eating by the fire and very little effort watching us."

"Why should they?" came a bitter reply. "The best thing we could do for them is try and break out."

Axel didn't recognize the voice, but he found no fault in its assessment. "Exactly, that's why they'll never expect one of us to try and slip out. If you hurry you can reach General Varchi in four days."

"If I steal a horse, I can make it in three," Colten said.

"Get some rest. You'll need it."

Colten headed for the barracks and Axel left the muttering crowd to check out the enemy's position. It looked like they'd had enough for today. Fires flared to life and Axel would have sworn he smelled meat roasting.

Cobb stopped beside him and stared out over the enemy encampment. "So the commander came up with that plan before he passed out, huh?"

"As far as the men are concerned. If you've got a brilliant tactical suggestion, I'm listening."

Cobb grunted. "I've never been much for plans. You think the kid will be okay?"

"I think Colten's liable to be the only one of us that survives. I figure with travel and muster time we need to hold out at least ten days for reinforcements and that's if everything goes perfectly."

"When's the last time anything went perfectly in the army?"

"Exactly."

CHAPTER 49

Colten tried to follow Lieutenant Shenk's order and rest, but he found sleep refused to come. Instead he tossed and turned in his bunk and tried not to think about that fact that all his comrades' lives depended on the success of his mission.

Oh, he'd sounded confident enough when the lieutenant asked if he could do it, but deep in his heart Colten didn't know if he was up to the challenge. There were a lot of enemy soldiers out there and plenty of rangers mixed in with them. If his woodcraft was less than flawless, they'd find him and hunt him down like a dog.

A mixture of relief and anxiety washed over him when one of the rookies, a boy not much younger than Colten himself, shook him.

"It's time, sir." The candle in the boy's hand trembled, casting wavering shadows all around the barracks.

Colten tossed his blankets aside and rolled out of his cot. "Lead the way."

The rookie seemed frozen in place. "Do you really think you can sneak past all of them?"

Colten puffed out his chest. "You'd be more likely to notice a mouse than me in the woods. I'll get to the general and be back with help before you know it."

He tried to sound confident and thought he pulled if off reasonably well. Maybe if he said it enough times he'd believe it himself. Not that Colten wasn't confident in his abilities, but he'd never had so much riding on his shoulders.

He followed his guide through the dark barracks, between cots, some temporarily empty and some permanently. Like he needed more reminders of what his failure meant. Outside, Lieutenant Shenk and Sergeant Cobb were waiting. Cobb handed him a light pack which he slipped on.

"Ready?" Lieutenant Shenk asked.

"Yes, sir." That came out pretty steady, but the way his commander looked at him Colten suspected he hadn't been as convincing as he hoped.

"Remember." The lieutenant put his hands on Colten's shoulders. "I chose you for this mission because you're the best scout in this outfit and maybe the best in the legion. Trust your instincts and do what needs to be done. We'll be waiting for you when you return with the general."

Colten's resolve hardened. "Understood, sir. Anything else I should know?"

"There's a letter of introduction in your pack that'll get you in to see General Varchi along with a week's supplies. Good luck."

Cobb led him up on the wall where three men waited beside a long rope. The soldiers picked up the rope and Cobb tossed the end over the wall. He gave Colten a thumbs-up and grasped the rope at the head of the group.

After one last deep breath Colten climbed over the side and shinnied down. The moment he reached the ground the rope disappeared back into the fort. He resisted the urge to look up and stalked into the night.

The stars provided just enough light for him to see the first sentry. The irregular leaned on his spear and stared into the night, every so often fighting back a yawn. It appeared the enemy planned to make the first part of his mission as easy as possible. Good of them.

Colten fell to his stomach and inched closer. Even this half-asleep fool would notice if he just walked past. Foot by agonizing foot he crawled past the guard and deeper into enemy territory. When he was fifty feet from the perimeter he stood and strode confidently onward. His scout uniform and the enemy ranger uniform weren't so different that he'd draw attention in the dark. His safety now lay in looking like he belonged.

He kept his distance from any fires or gatherings, returned several friendly greetings, and hurried on to the edge of the camp. Ten more yards and he was home free.

"You there, what are you doing?"

Cursing his luck, Colten turned to find a bearded figure in an officer's black, fur-trimmed uniform marching his way. He brought his right fist to his heart in a salute while his left hand reached for the dagger strapped to his belt.

"Just going to water the flowers, sir."

"Use the trenches, that's why we dug them," the officer said, as if he'd ever dug a latrine trench. "What unit are you with?"

He'd almost moved within range. If Colten struck there could be no mistakes. The sound of a struggle would have every soldier in a hundred yards on his tail.

"Second Rangers, sir," Colten said, offering a silent prayer that they had such a unit.

"Second Rangers?" The officer stopped three feet away. "What are you doing over here? You people were assigned to the northern wall."

Shit!

Colten tightened his grip on the dagger. "I was asked to deliver a message to the second cohort's commander."

"That's m—"

Colten drew his dagger and slashed in one smooth move cutting deep into the enemy's throat. Blood spurted and the dying man crumpled to the ground without a sound. Colten waited a few seconds to make sure he was dead then ran for it.

He needed to put as much distance between him and the enemy camp as possible before daybreak. As soon as the body was found the enemy would be after him.

○

Colten leapt from the branch of an old spruce to the branch of a twisted pine. For the past half hour he'd been traveling through the trees in the hopes of throwing off any pursuit. He didn't even know for sure anyone was after him, but it seemed impossible they weren't. The sun had risen four hours ago. Some soldier must have discovered the body of the officer he killed by now.

If he'd killed the cohort's commander that might have bought him an extra hour or two while they sorted out who was now in charge, but he didn't dare assume any more than that.

When he'd gone a good third of a mile through the trees, he climbed back to the forest floor and broke into a jog. The summer heat hadn't fully faded yet and he wanted to make as much headway as possible before it grew too uncomfortable.

As he ran, Colten racked his brain trying to figure out where he might find a mount. There were some farms between legion headquarters and base, but at best he'd end up with a draft horse and he could probably make better time on foot. In his wildest hopes he'd encounter a patrol from one of the other forts and they'd escort him to headquarters.

That dream was doomed to die. If their fort was besieged the others probably were as well. At best they might have struck on the same plan as the lieutenant—Colten knew better than to believe Commander Braddock thought this scheme up —but that was a dim prospect.

Noon arrived and with it the full heat of the day. He stopped long enough to drink from a stream and eat two strips of jerky. Colten figured he'd covered fifteen miles, a tenth of his journey. Not bad, but not nearly good enough. Thrashing through the trees was too slow. He needed to risk the road if he wanted to arrive in time to help his friends. On his own he should have time to hide from any approaching threat.

Determined on his course, he ran for the nearest road, the main supply road if he wasn't mistaken. He burst through the tree line ten minutes later and turned south. The dirt track ran straight to Army Headquarters.

An hour or so before dusk he spotted a heavily laden supply wagon. Four horses pulled it along at a steady, if slow, pace. Two men sat on the bench seat, one of them armed with a crossbow. A crossbow that rose and pointed at Colten's chest when the man carrying it spotted him.

The driver pulled back on the reins. "Who are you and what are you doing on foot out in the middle of nowhere?"

"I'm a scout with the Second Legion. Our fort is besieged. A

Straken force has crossed the border and seized half the northern province."

The crossbowman's aim never wavered.

"Who's your commander?" the driver asked.

"Braddock, sir. Though he was badly injured and Lieutenant Shenk has assumed command."

The driver pushed the crossbow down. "I know Braddock and I've heard of Shenk. We'd best turn around and head for home. Need a ride?"

"Angels bless you, sir, I do. And as fast as possible."

"Well, cli—" An arrow in his throat silenced the driver.

The crossbowman raised his weapon, fired over Colten's head, and leapt into the back of the wagon ahead of two more arrows. Colten glanced over his shoulder. A squad of rangers stood at the edge of the woods. Five of them had bows and one lay on the ground with a crossbow bolt sticking out of his chest.

Colten ran for the wagon. An arrow grazed his left arm as he dove over the sideboard. The crossbowman grunted when he landed on him.

"Friends o' yours?" the crossbowman asked.

"No, though I dare say they're looking for me." More arrows slammed into the wagon. "I don't suppose you have a sword?"

Colten's companion popped up, fired his weapon, and ducked back down. "Right side wrapped in oilskin. Find it fast. They're coming."

Colten dug frantically until he heard the clang of weapons. He groped around and his hand settled on a leather-wrapped hilt. He yanked the weapon free just in time to slam it back down on the head of the ranger that appeared beside the wagon.

The crossbow clunked again and a bolt went through the face of a ranger on the opposite side. Colten risked a peek around the seat. The rangers had their swords out and were running toward the wagon. He stood up now that there was no danger of arrows and prepared to meet death on his feet. Colten's only regret was that he failed to get help for his friends.

"I'm Colten."

The crossbowman stood next to him, reached around, and pulled a long-handled axe from beside the wagon seat. "Grubber, supply company, Second Legion. Let's show these sons of whores what a legionnaire can do."

Colten grinned and readied his borrowed sword. If he was going to die, at least it would be beside a brother.

The first ranger reached the wagon and leapt at Colten. His counter slash sent the airborne enemy sprawling in the dirt. Two more circled, looking for an opening.

At his back Grubber roared and leapt out of the bed.

What was he doing? They had the advantage of height as long as they stayed put.

Four rangers surrounded Grubber who swung his axe like a madman. The heavy weapon crashed through the first ranger's block and caved in his chest. The backswing took another ranger's hand off.

Colten had no more time to watch. The rangers circling the wagon separated and leapt, one right next to Colten and the other at the tailgate.

He stabbed the nearest one through the gut and spun to find the second man standing in the wagon bed. So much for his advantage. At least he still had reach on his side.

Colten circled, careful not to trip on the supplies cluttering the wagon.

He feinted a thrust then blocked a cross slash. He tried to think how best to handle his opponent when the ranger shuddered and a bubble of blood formed at his mouth.

The bubble popped and the ranger collapsed, revealing Grubber's axe in his back. Grubber himself stood on the ground surrounded by dead bodies. He had a shallow cut on his thigh and another on his left bicep, but other than that he appeared unharmed.

Colten stared for a moment. "Are you sure you're in supply? Seems like you'd be more use on the front lines."

Grubber grunted and set to cleaning his axe on a dead ranger. "I was housecarl to a nobleman once upon a time. When a stray arrow struck him down, his father demanded my head. General Varchi convinced him demotion would be enough. So instead of fighting like a real warrior, I haul them supplies."

"Your misfortune was a blessing for me. I'm on my way to Army Headquarters. I would be grateful for your company."

"My delivery seems to be canceled. Very well, I'll go with you."

They set out after binding Grubber's wounds. All the horses had been killed in the attack, yet even though he was still on foot, Colten felt he had a better chance of succeeding in his mission.

CHAPTER 50

After three exhausting days with no more than five hours' sleep combined, the dark stone of Army Headquarters rose ahead of them. Colten hadn't been so relieved in his entire life. He staggered toward the front gate on limp legs. Beside him Grubber trudged along at the same inexhaustible pace he'd maintained since the first step of the journey together. If the former housecarl felt as tired as Colten, he didn't show it.

When they reached the main gate, the portcullis was down. A guard shouted for them to identify themselves and once they had he climbed down to face them from behind the iron bars.

"What's your business here?" the guard asked.

Colten shrugged off his almost empty pack and pulled out the scroll Lieutenant Shenk prepared for him. "I bring urgent news for the general. I have a letter from my commander."

The guard read the note, then read it again. Why didn't he hurry? Nothing but grit and a refusal to embarrass himself at headquarters kept Colten on his feet.

At last the guard said, "Raise the gate. I apologize for the extra scrutiny, but we've heard some crazy rumors and the general said better safe than sorry."

When the portcullis had clanked up enough for them to duck under, they stepped into the fortress and for the first time in what seemed like forever Colten felt safe. Now if he could just find a cot or even a quiet piece of floor to sleep on he'd consider his life complete, but first the message.

The guard led them into the fortress. After many twists and turns, all of which were a blur to Colten's sleep-addled brain they reached a closed door.

Their guide knocked. "Messenger to see you, sir."

"Send him in."

The guard pushed the door open and motioned them in. Colten staggered through and remembered to salute the man behind the desk. Lieutenant Shenk's message came spilling out in a rush of words. Colten wasn't sure any of them made sense or were in the correct order.

"Slow down, son," General Varchi said. "Have a seat, take a breath."

Colten fell into the proffered chair, grateful beyond words. He was vaguely aware of the general sizing up Grubber. The two men exchanged words, but Colten failed to comprehend any of them.

A savory scent brought Colten back to his right mind. His eyes opened and a warm bowl was placed in his hands. He stared into the bowl of beef stew like it was a divine revelation. He ate, choked on a potato for a second, then plowed on. In short order the bowl was empty.

Food and rest restored his energy and he realized he was sitting and eating while completely ignoring the general. He scrambled around, looked for a place to set the bowl, found nothing, and tried to think of the best way to apologize.

General Varchi chuckled. "Calm down, soldier. Grubber has given me the gist of the situation. Your fort is besieged by Straken soldiers and you've come to get reinforcements. That about sum it up?"

"Yes, sir." Colten breathed a sigh of relief. The general didn't seem upset with him. "I don't know how long my friends can hold out. If we hurry—"

General Varchi raised his hand, silencing Colten. "I'm sorry, but without the king's permission I can't mobilize the Northern Army."

Colten stared without comprehension for a moment. "Our comrades are dying as we speak, sir."

"I understand, believe me I do, but I answer to the king and he's ordered us not to escalate our differences with Straken."

"Differences? Is His Majesty aware that several Straken legions have crossed the border, enslaved citizens of Garenland, and killed his soldiers?" Colten's voice rose with each word, but he couldn't help it. His friends were dying and the general was murdering his hope.

"I'm not certain he is." General Varchi didn't seem put out by Colten's tone of voice. "But he will be once you tell him."

Colten was struck dumb for a second. "I'm going to tell him?"

"That's right. Lieutenant Shenk's brother, Otto, is great friends with the crown prince. You will seek out Otto and he'll take you to Prince Wolfric, who will arrange for you to see the king. Once the king hears your report he'll have to order the army to deploy. It will mean an extra day, but we have no other choice."

Colten squared his shoulders. If he had to convince the king to save his friends, he'd damn well convince him. "Can I trouble you for a horse, sir?"

W hen General Varchi said Otto Shenk lived in a mansion in Gold Ward he hadn't been kidding. Franken Manor was bigger than a fortress.

"Nice-looking place," Grubber said. For some reason the supply officer had offered to ride along with Colten. While he didn't know why, Colten appreciated the company.

Thunder rumbled and the sky grew darker by the moment. Colten guided his mount up to the wrought iron gates. A pair of mercenaries moved to block his path. He clenched his jaw against the anger that filled him at yet another delay.

"Do you have business here?" the nearest mercenary asked.

"I have a message for Lord Shenk from General Varchi." Colten presented the sealed scroll the general had given him before showing him out of his office.

"We'll see that he gets it." The mercenary reached for the scroll, but Colten pulled it back.

"My orders are to deliver it personally. Is Lord Shenk in residence?"

"He is." The mercenary nodded to his partner and they opened the gate. "Go to the main entrance, the butler will summon him for you."

"Thank you, from myself and the general." Colten and Grubber rode through the gates and trotted up to a set of doors that looked strong enough to withstand a battering ram.

As they dismounted Grubber said, "This place would make a good fortress if it didn't have so many windows."

Colten tied his horse to an iron post set there for that purpose and climbed the short flight of stairs to the door. He pounded on it and a moment later a slender, bald man in a black uniform opened it. He had to be the butler. The bald man looked Colten up and down with a little sneer.

"Yes?" the servant asked.

Colten resisted punching the snooty prick in the face by the narrowest of margins. "I have a message for Lord Shenk from General Varchi. Before you ask, I have orders to deliver it personally."

"Stay in the foyer. I will see if His Lordship is free." The butler marched out, nose in the air and back stiff.

"I've met friendlier executioners," Grubber said as he took in the opulence surrounding them. This one room held more wealth than Colten had ever seen, but he had no patience to soak it in. Every minute he wasted was another minute his friends fought alone.

After a blessedly short wait a young man in black tunic and gray trousers with a sword belted at his waist emerged from deeper in the house. Eyes far too hard and angry for one so young bore into Colten.

"You have a message for me?" Lord Shenk, for he could be no other, asked.

"Yes, my lord." Colten handed him the sealed scroll. He had no idea what the general had written, but hopefully it would do the trick.

When he'd finished reading Lord Shenk said, "Is my brother well?"

"He was uninjured when I left, my lord. Now... I have no idea."

Lord Shenk nodded. "Follow me. I'll introduce you to Prince Wolfric. I warn you, the king may not live up to your expectations."

Colten wanted to ask what he meant by that, but the

nobleman was striding past and out the door. The two soldiers fell in behind him.

The journey to the palace was a blur for Colten and before he got his bearings, he was in the presence of Crown Prince Wolfric. The prince received them in a simple salon with a pair of chairs, a cold hearth, and a table with wine and glasses. Both soldiers took a knee before the prince.

"Straken is moving faster than we feared," Lord Shenk said. "The border forts are already under siege. These men are witnesses. Surely your father can't ignore their testimony."

"A month ago, I would have agreed," Prince Wolfric said. "But now? I don't know."

Colten couldn't believe what he heard. His Majesty wouldn't leave his loyal soldiers to die, would he?

"On your feet," the prince said.

Colten stood, but kept his gaze locked on the prince's shiny black boots.

"Are you prepared to tell my father what you've seen on the border?"

"Yes, Your Highness," Colten said, his voice trembling. "I have traveled far and faced many dangers to get help for my friends. I am prepared to give testimony before man, angel, or demon if that is what it takes."

A strong hand grasped Colten's shoulder and he dared look up. The prince smiled and his eyes twinkled. "I see why General Varchi sent you. If you cannot convince my father, no one can. Come, court is in session. The Merchants League is here to petition the king. We shall do what we can to speed matters along."

And they were off again, through halls and corridors, past statues and tapestries worth more than Colten could imagine. At last they stopped before a set of closed double doors. Two guards in mail and carrying poleaxes moved to block their way. Colten didn't know how they dared, but His Highness didn't seem troubled.

"An urgent matter has come up, gentlemen," the prince said. "Whatever Father may have said, I assure you he'll want to hear this."

The door guards exchanged looks, clearly trying to decide which was the safest route, turning the prince aside or ignoring the king's orders. After a moment of silent debate, they pulled the door open.

"Best remain here, Otto," Prince Wolfric said. "You're still not in Father's good graces."

Lord Shenk bowed and withdrew, settling in on a bench off to one side of the entrance. Colten focused solely on his breathing in the hopes that he wouldn't pass out in front of the king. Prince Wolfric marched down a wide, red carpet that ran between row after row of benches.

Hundreds of people filled the throne room, the soft murmur of their voices along with too much perfume filling the air. At the front the king sat on his throne and listened to a fat merchant in silk robes complain about losing his caravan to bandits. The king met Colten's gaze and the scout looked away at once.

A hush fell over the gathering and Colten raised his gaze. The king had gotten up from his throne and father and son locked stares. Colten shivered at the intensity both royals showed and gave silent thanks that neither of those looks was directed at him.

"I thought I said I did not wish to see you," the king said.

"You did, Majesty, but information has come to my attention, information you need to hear." Prince Wolfric bowed to his father. "I apologize for disobeying, but this is too important for our differences to get in the way."

The king huffed and sat back down. "Very well. Despite our disagreements, I respect your judgement. If you feel it is of sufficient import, I shall listen."

"Thank you, Father. Colten, please relate your story to His Majesty."

Colten bowed to the throne. "Majesty, my name is Colten, scout of the Second Legion. I serve at one of your border forts. We are besieged, Majesty. Legions of Straken soldiers have crossed the border. My brothers fight to hold out, but without reinforcements they will surely fall. Many have died already, but if the Northern Army marches at once there may be hope of rescue. I beg Your Majesty to authorize reinforcements."

"This can't be right," the king said. "Straken wouldn't risk breaking the compact. And if they have we have all we need to convince the other monarchs to restore our portal. I must prepare letters. This is just the break we've been waiting for."

Colten didn't understand what was happening, but it didn't sound like the king intended to dispatch the Northern Army. He risked everything to speak again. "Majesty, what about my comrades? They are in desperate straits."

"I can't risk being seen as escalating the conflict. That might be all the excuse the others need to deny my petition. The Second Scout Division must retreat." The king rose and swept out of the throne room, leaving Colten to stare at his back.

He'd failed and his brothers would die.

CHAPTER 51

Otto ignored the glowers of the door guards and ended the spell that allowed him to listen in on Wolfric's attempt to convince the king to act. Though he greatly respected his friend's gift of persuasion, he'd held little hope of the king changing his mind on fighting Straken. Regaining his position within the compact was all that mattered to him and nothing would convince King Von Garen to do anything that might put that in danger.

It was with considerable relief that he got up off the hard bench and joined Wolfric and the two soldiers.

"Why would he do nothing for my comrades?" Colten asked. "His Majesty says they must retreat, but the fort is surrounded. They have—"

"Quiet," Wolfric said. "Criticizing the king won't be well received in this part of the castle."

Wolfric led the way back to the salon they'd used earlier and away from any curious ears. Otto forced himself not to smile at the firm set of his friend's jaw. It seemed the prince had come to a clear understanding of what needed to be done.

Now it would only take a nudge or two to get him moving in the direction Otto needed.

The moment they reached the salon Wolfric slammed the door and poured himself a glass of wine. When he'd drank half of it he turned to Otto. "Father's going to write letters. Letters! By the time he gets answers, assuming he ever does, the entire northern province will belong to Straken and their armies will be within striking distance of the capital."

Otto nodded, pretending he hadn't been listening in to the conversation. "What do you want to do?"

"I want to order the Northern Army to retake our territory and drive Straken back across the border, but I can't because General Varchi is loyal to my father. I'm helpless to do anything!" Wolfric threw his half-full glass of wine against the wall.

"I beg your pardon, Highness," Colten said. "But can nothing truly be done for my friends?"

Wolfric hung his head. "I'm sorry, soldier, but as long as my father is king, my hands are tied."

"Perhaps not fully tied," Otto said. "I can rescue them if you wish. We may not be as close as brothers should be, but I have no desire to see Axel's head on a spike."

"You can save them, alone?" Wolfric met his gaze. "How?"

"Magic. I'll need royal dispensation to wield offensive spells, but if you give me permission, I'm confident I can get the survivors back safe. I can also take a look at the enemy forces and see what we're up against."

"You have my permission," Wolfric said. "However, we can't bring them here or to the Northern Army's headquarters. Word of their arrival will reach my father at once and that will lead to questions I'd prefer not to answer."

"I know a place," Grubber said. The man had been so quiet

Otto almost forgot he was present. "There's an old trading post ten miles from headquarters. We used to ride past it every time we made a delivery. It'll be tight, but if we augment with tents it should work."

"Excellent," Wolfric said. "You and Colten will have to arrange whatever supplies you deem necessary through the civilian channels and transport them to the trading post. Everything must be ready before Otto arrives. Go now. There's no time to waste."

"Yes, Highness." Grubber tugged Colten's sleeve and headed for the door.

The scout held his ground and turned to Otto. "Please hurry, my lord. The fort is in desperate straits."

"Don't worry," Otto said. "I'll be there before you know it."

Colten saluted and let Grubber lead him out. When they'd gone Wolfric said, "The way Father's going we won't have a nation left to defend by the end of the year. The merchants complain of constant bandit attacks and seizures by soldiers at the border. How long before Rolan decides if Straken can take our northern province why shouldn't they have our southern province?"

Otto held his hands out to either side. "As you've told me many times, as long as your father is king our hands are tied. I have to go. Whatever you decide must happen, you have my full support."

Ether flowed into Otto until they became one. He turned his consciousness north and searched until the resonance between him and his brother vibrated in his chest.

An instant later he appeared in the pouring rain. Thunder cracked and a shout rang out. Soon Otto found himself surrounded by armed men. At the center of the group, his green cloak dripping, stood his brother.

"Hello, Axel. I got word you needed a hand."

"Sheathe weapons," Axel said. "It's only my little brother."

"That's some greeting considering I came all this way to save you."

Axel barked a laugh and his men dispersed. "Let's get out of this rain."

Otto followed his brother into the fort and shook off the water that had soaked his tunic. A quick glance revealed nothing impressive. The building was as roughly built as Otto had expected. Straken would gain little here.

"I trust Colten arrived safe," Axel said.

"Aside from a little nick on the arm he was fine. He was worried about you though. It seems you inspire great loyalty in your men."

"Fat lot of good it did. Where's my relief force?"

"I'm it. The king refuses to mobilize the Northern Army."

Axel threw up his hands. "What sort of sick joke is this? There's over a thousand Straken soldiers out there now and the bastards just keep coming. If not for this rain we'd all be dead now. We're just lucky the commander doesn't want his men getting wet."

Otto smiled as he felt the electricity crackling in the ether. "This storm, dear brother, is what will allow me to save you all. I trust you have wounded."

"Thirty walking and an even dozen that can't get out of bed."

"Make them ready to move. Don't take too long, Axel. If the storm ends, we're doomed."

"I guess I don't have a choice. I'll need an hour to rig up stretchers. How the hell are we going to outrun that army carrying wounded men?"

"The army will be otherwise occupied. I'll meet you on the wall in an hour."

Otto spent the hour preparing. He managed to weave twenty-two threads before the resistance grew too great. He was getting stronger all the time. When he finished, he left the fort and climbed the wall, an etheric shield protecting him from the rain. He'd have to release it eventually, but why get soaked until then?

Out in the enemy camp lights glowed inside many tents. That was a lot of targets. He'd have to be judicious in how he deployed his threads.

"We're ready." Axel stomped up beside him. "Time to work your miracle."

"Which tent belongs to the enemy commander?"

"The biggest one, naturally."

"That's what I assumed, but I didn't want to take chances."

Otto tagged the largest tent with a thread, then repeated the process with four more in that encampment. They walked along the perimeter of the fort and Otto tagged more tents as he went. He saved five for the area directly in front of the gates. That portion of the camp needed to be fully neutralized.

Otto grinned. This was going to be an amazing show. "Ready?"

"For what?"

"A miracle." Otto threw his hands into the air and the threads connected to the tents flew up into the sky. A moment later twenty-two lightning bolts flashed down as one. Blinding light turned night into day and even though he expected it Otto had to look away.

"The angels be merciful," Axel whispered.

The lightning had done its work. Tents and bodies smoldered. Enemy soldiers staggered around in a daze. The area in front of the gate looked like a giant fist had slammed into the camp. Nothing moved. No wonder offensive magic had been made illegal. He never would have dared put on such a display without Wolfric's permission. With anything less than royal dispensation, if word got out, Otto would soon find himself lacking a head.

"We should go before the survivors collect their wits." Otto found he barely had breath to speak. A casting of that magnitude, even if he only directed the power, exhausted him. "I won't be able to do that again for a while."

CHAPTER 52

W olfric waited outside his father's private office and ground his teeth. Three days had passed and still no word from Otto. Worse, the merchants grew more restive by the day and Father refused to even hear their complaints. Instead he'd locked himself away to work on his useless letters. His father had always been a man of peace and diplomacy, but this was ridiculous.

When Garenland was a member of the compact, Father's inclinations served them well. Now that action was required, he seemed unable to change strategy. In fact, Wolfric feared something in his father's brain had broken when the other monarchs voted against him. That failure destroyed something and only getting Garenland back in the compact would restore it. If the king had to destroy his country to do it he appeared ready to do so.

Wolfric refused to let that happen.

At last the office door opened and Father appeared in the gap. He hadn't shaved and his eyes appeared sunken in and his cheeks hollow. A sour smell wafted out. Had the servants not emptied his chamber pot?

"Come in, son, come in."

The door opened wider and Wolfric stepped inside, careful to breathe through his mouth. Scores of wadded-up pieces of paper covered the red carpet. More scraps littered the mahogany desk. Father hurried over and picked up the topmost piece.

"I know we've quarreled, Wolfric, and I regret that, but the news you brought regarding Straken's brazen acts make up for everything. That was the final piece I needed to complete my argument. I've been laboring nonstop on a missive that will be certain to convince my peers of Garenland's righteousness. Read it. I'm eager for your thoughts."

Wolfric accepted the paper and read paragraph after paragraph of beautifully written and reasoned arguments. Despite his fears, it appeared Father's mind was still working properly. That almost made his refusal to accept reality harder to swallow. If he were mad or impaired in some way Wolfric could forgive his failure, but the king wasn't mad, he was willfully, arrogantly blind.

His people were attacked on all sides and the king wrote a letter to people that had conspired against him already. There was no way around it. Father had to be removed from the throne if Garenland was to survive.

"It's beautiful, Father. The finest you've ever written."

"Thank you. I knew you'd appreciate it. Have my scribes make five copies and dispatch couriers at once. Send out an announcement that I will speak to the people to reassure them that matters are in hand, one week hence in the central plaza. You will make the arrangements."

"Of course, Father. I'm sure it will do wonders for the citizens' morale to know their king is working hard to keep them safe."

The king beamed. "You echo my thoughts perfectly. Garenland will soon put this wretched episode behind her and we'll enjoy even greater prosperity. There was a time I feared for you, my son, but now I see that when the time comes you will make a fine king."

Wolfric bowed. "Thank you, Father. Your confidence brings me joy beyond measure. I go to make preparations. You should rest now. You've earned it."

Wolfric backed out of the stinking office and strode away. He had many preparations to make. Father was right about one thing. When the time came, he would make a fine king.

〇

Annamaria bustled about her bedroom, fluffing pillows, smoothing the sheets, and generally making sure everything was perfect. A quick squirt from an atomizer filled the room with a light, floral scent. She hadn't seen Lothair in weeks and the lack of news was driving her to distraction. He'd never been gone for a day, much less longer. What could have happened?

On top of that Otto had disappeared, off on some task for Wolfric days ago and he hadn't been seen or heard from since. All she got was a note from the palace delivered by a nervous boy, who knew nothing beyond their address.

Why were all the men in her life abandoning her? True, since she'd convinced Otto the child was his, she'd begged off sleeping with him, claiming it was too uncomfortable in her condition.

Perhaps she should have played along a little longer, gotten him completely wrapped around her little finger. She shuddered at the thought of him touching her.

No, she'd done what she had to in order to assure her daughter's future. Besides, Otto hadn't uttered a word of complaint and he'd done everything he could to keep her comfortable, at least when he wasn't off working on whatever task Wolfric had set him.

She sat on the edge of her bed and rubbed her slightly round belly. At least her daughter was developing well, or so the midwife assured her. That was what mattered most. Lothair would return to her in time, she only needed to remain patient. He loved her and would never abandon her.

Never.

A faint knock was followed by Mimi poking her head in. "Lord Shenk has returned, miss."

Relief at seeing someone and disappointment that it was the wrong someone warred within her. Disappointment lost the battle. She smoothed her dress and swept out of the bedroom.

"Where is he?" she asked.

"The dining room, miss. Lord Shenk appeared hungry and very tired."

"Thank you, Mimi." Annamaria left her maid and glided along to the dining room.

Mimi hadn't exaggerated. Otto had dark ridges under his eyes and stubble covered his cheeks. His normally crisp tunic appeared slept in and the less said about his hair the better. Whatever he'd done, it appeared to have taken a toll.

He must have sensed her approaching and looked up. "Annamaria, you're looking a bit frazzled. How's our daughter?"

"Growing nicely according to the midwife. You're looking rough around the edges as well."

"Wolfric seems intent on running me ragged." Otto offered a weary smile. "Clearly having a wizard at his disposal is something he plans to take full advantage of. Will you join me?"

"Thank you." She smoothed her skirt and sat across from him. "Though I've already dined."

A servant emerged from the kitchen carrying a plate loaded with a thick roast beef sandwich. Otto tucked in and ate with enthusiasm.

Halfway through he looked up. "You appear pensive. I know I haven't been around much lately, but I promise I'll think of something to make it up to you."

Annamaria managed to smile for him. Poor, clueless Otto, he had no idea her melancholy had nothing to do with his absence. Her betrayal seemed especially cruel to her just then. He'd tried so hard to do right by her, but she simply felt no connection to him and doubted she ever would.

Otto finished his meal and went straight to bed. He clearly needed the rest. She considered offering to lie down with him but didn't have it in her. With her husband home there was no chance Lothair would show up today. It was all she could do not to cry.

◯

Otto met Wolfric in their usual dining room. They ate in silence, each lost in their own thoughts. For his part Otto kept replaying the day before over and over in his head. Lothair's loss was starting to wear on Annamaria. Seeing the strain it caused brought him bitter joy. He'd let her wonder a little longer before returning her ring.

He often fantasized about looking into her eyes and watching her heart break. Perhaps if he ruined her as she had him, they could be a proper husband and wife, united in pain and hate.

When the food was finished Wolfric sighed. "We have much to discuss. Can you fix it so no one can overhear?"

"Of course." Otto wove a dome of ether around the table from which no sound could escape. This was the moment he'd been waiting for. Wolfric must have finally reached the correct conclusion. Nothing else would explain his desire for such security. "Go ahead."

"Father has written a letter to the other monarchs explaining Straken's actions and how they prove Garenland should be returned to the compact." Wolfric shook his head. "He pretends they didn't know what Straken intended from the start."

"You don't seem confident in his plan."

Wolfric barked a laugh. "No. Father has become a danger to Garenland. When we were still a part of the compact, he served the kingdom well as an administrator and diplomat, but in this time of war his inability to change course will destroy us. He must be removed."

At last! As long as the current king sat on the throne, Otto would never be able to move the kingdom's wizards out of their second-class status. Doing so went against the laws of the compact after all.

"Removed how?" Otto asked.

"In six days, he plans a speech in the central plaza. I've been tasked with making all the arrangements. If I put people loyal to me in key positions it won't be difficult for an assassin to sneak close and strike." Wolfric ran his fingers through his hair and down his face. "How did it come to this? He's my father.

Despite our differences, I love him, but failure to act will endanger the nation."

"I know the perfect person to serve as your assassin," Otto said. "Of course, he'll be killed immediately after the act and found carrying Straken documents."

"That will galvanize the people into action."

"Yes, especially when you capture and hang a pair of Straken agents, say a day or two later. It won't be difficult to claim that the other nations were allied to our murderous northern neighbor. You'll have all the excuse you need to conquer the whole of the continent. Instead of King Wolfric, you'll be Emperor Wolfric."

The prince grinned. "I like the sound of that, but there's no way we can defeat the combined might of the other nations."

"On the contrary, we have a resource that the others lack: wizards. Everyone else either murders or enslaves their wizards, we treat them with at least basic dignity. You can build on that."

"I'm not sure I follow you. We may treat them better than the others, but Garenland still imposes many limits on our wizards. According to the law you should have been executed many times over. Why would the wizards of Garenland fight for me?"

Otto smiled. This was it. "Because you're going to offer them something they haven't had in six hundred years, true freedom and equality. Restore their full rights and promise to do the same in any country we take over. Do you think there aren't parents in Straken that hate Uther for killing their children? How many of Rolan's wizard-slaves would chew off their left hand for what you can give them? We'll have an army of wizards eager to sign up."

"How will we control them?" Wolfric's smile curdled. He knew the histories as well as Otto. "Isn't there a danger of them taking over?"

There was a huge risk of that, not that Otto would say anything to confirm his friend's fears. He had to allay Wolfric's concerns quickly, before they sank in too deep.

"Wizards in this day and age could never rule like they did in the time of the Arcane Lords. One, there aren't enough of us and two, wizards of this age are weaker than they were. What we can do is act as a lever, multiplying the strength of your regular troops."

"How so?"

Doubt was turning into belief. So far so good.

"I've been studying wars in the age of wizards," Otto said, warming up to the subject. "Imagine your legions wading into an enemy in disarray after being hit by half a dozen fireballs. Or maybe a volley of arrows being knocked from the sky before they can strike home. An army with those advantages would be invincible."

"Someone would have to train them," Wolfric said.

"I can handle that. In my researches I found a book of war magic. Many spells are complex, beyond my skill at this point, but many more are of only modest difficulty. I could get the first group ready in a month or so and send them on to the northern campaign. Straken could be driven back across the border before winter."

"I'm convinced." Wolfric's smile had returned. "But I can't do this alone. I plan to name you High Councilor at the same time I grant the wizards full rights as citizens. Having a wizard as my primary advisor should make a show of good faith, don't you think?"

"Indeed. I will do my utmost to live up to your trust."

Otto strove to keep a calm facade, but inside he was doing backflips. Everything he needed to meet Lord Karonin's requirement for further training had been laid at his feet. If his plans worked out he'd make Wolfric emperor of the continent and himself the most powerful wizard in the world.

CHAPTER 53

Otto sat in a beat-up wooden chair at their makeshift prison and studied a book he'd retrieved from the armory. It dealt primarily with controlling others with magic. The simplest way was to seize control of the target's body directly with a number of threads and manipulate them like a puppet. The process appeared simple enough, in fact it reminded Otto of the spell he used to send his dagger flying around his room only on a larger scale.

He turned the page. As easy as it would be, that sort of spell wouldn't work in this circumstance. If any wizards attended the king's speech, they'd see the threads connecting him to Lothair and even the dimmest of them would understand what was happening. In the worst-case scenario some noble-acting idiot might sever the threads and free his assassin. That would be a debacle beyond comprehension.

No, he needed a more subtle means of control. Otto flicked a glance at Hans and his men. None of them had complained about the lack of action since they captured the spies. Soldiers were probably used to long periods of inactivity.

JAMES E WISHER

The title on the next page brought him to a stop. Psychic Programing, that sounded like exactly what he needed.

"How long are you going to keep us here!" Lothair shouted and rattled his chains.

The other prisoners looked at him as well. Otto marked his page and closed the book.

"Not much longer."

"You're going to release us?" Xavier sounded so pathetic a momentary pang struck Otto. Then he remembered this man was responsible for a fair portion of Garenland's troubles and the pang vanished.

"Indeed, the hangman is eager to make your acquaintance."

"Please, I'm sure if you contacted my superiors an arrangement can be made."

"Really? What do you suppose the Lady in Red will offer for a spy whose identity has been exposed? Will she convince Uther to withdraw his armies back across the border? Or perhaps she'll free the innocent men and women taken prisoner and used as forced labor. You know her better than I, but she didn't strike me as the sort to make such a generous gesture."

Xavier sagged in his chains. "No, she isn't."

"I thought not. I'll have silence from you three. Nothing says you need your tongues when you hang."

Otto returned to his book. The programming spell seemed doable. It involved two steps followed by the command implementation. Considering the king intended to give his speech in two days Otto needed to get started.

After one final perusal of the spell he went over to Lothair, crouching just out of his reach. His wife's lover stared daggers at him. A flick of Otto's ring froze him in exactly the perfect position. Next, a disk of spinning, glowing energy appear in front of Lothair.

As the prisoner stared, Otto sent threads into his brain. He imprinted an image of the king in Lothair's psyche along with a dagger plunging into his chest. As soon as he finished the image vanished.

Otto didn't get frustrated. According to the book he needed to imprint the desired action over and over until it stuck. Otto intended to keep at it until he succeeded. This was the final piece of the puzzle. Wolfric had made all the other necessary arrangements. Otto needed only to provide the assassin and the king was doomed.

᧧

It was the day before the speech and an exhausted Otto had been called to the palace by Wolfric. As he trudged down the hall to the prince's favorite salon Otto tried to contain his excitement. After twelve straight hours he'd finally imprinted the task he wanted in Lothair's brain. Not much else remained. The man was now a weapon, honed and ready to strike.

Though he'd done more powerful individual spells, he'd never sustained a magical flow for such an extended time. The process wearied him more than calling lightning or teleporting and not by a small margin. All Otto wanted was to crawl back in bed, but if something had happened and Wolfric needed him he didn't dare ignore the summons.

Wolfric was probably eager for a status report. Otto should have informed the prince of his success, but he'd opted for sleep instead.

A guard waited outside the salon door, which was odd. Why would Wolfric feel the need for protection this deep in the palace? Otto hadn't heard of any threats against the prince. Perhaps he was just being extra careful with their moment of triumph so close at hand.

The guard opened the door without comment or salute. Stranger and stranger. Inside he found Wolfric seated with a nearly empty glass of wine in his hand and a nearly empty bottle on the table. Nothing good ever happened when Wolfric drank too much.

Somehow Otto found the strength to weave the silence spell around the room. When he'd finished Otto sat in the empty chair. "You summoned me?"

"We have to call it off," Wolfric said. "I've thought of nothing else for the last six days and I simply can't go through with it. Despite everything he's still my father."

This couldn't be happening. Otto refused to believe it.

All his work and planning was about to fall apart because Wolfric was struck by a sudden bout of conscience.

"What happened to doing the right thing for Garenland? If your father lives, the kingdom dies."

"I know!" Wolfric slammed his fist on the table. "But there has to be some other way, some way to convince him that I haven't thought of yet."

Maybe Otto still had a chance to salvage his plan. "What if, instead of killing him, I had the assassin wound him, seriously, but not fatally. The king would be out of commission for weeks, even with magical healing. If I'm not mistaken the law says in that event you'd be in charge until he recovered. You could drive Straken out of the country and when your father recovered present it as a fait accompli. Perhaps he'd be angry, but I doubt he'd invite them back."

"But if he's wounded badly enough to put me in charge he might still die."

Otto threw up his hands. "He might. He might die in his sleep tonight, sparing us the need to make a decision. I have no certainties to offer you, my friend. There's risk in every direction and I can't weigh those for you."

Wolfric drained the dregs of the wine. "I know. You've been a great friend and I appreciate your support more than I can say."

The prince closed his eyes and took a deep breath. This was the moment of truth, Otto felt it in his bones. He didn't dare speak for fear that any word might nudge Wolfric in the wrong direction.

"Very well, a wounding only. Perhaps being nearly killed by a Straken agent will show my father the folly of his course."

Otto wanted to leap from his chair and thrust a fist to the sky. Instead he nodded, his expression solemn. "As you wish. I'll be in the crowd to make sure nothing vital is hit. Of equal importance is to make sure your men know the assassin has to die."

"Have no fear. I've made that perfectly clear to the guards." Wolfric rubbed his eyes. "For better or worse we are set on our course."

⟳

Otto and Edwyn rode along the cobblestone street toward the central plaza. The carriage rattled over the occasional bump drawing a muted curse from the driver. The temple bells sounded eleven times. The king wasn't due to speak until noon, but Edwyn wanted to get good spots. Since Garenland was cast out of the compact fifteen caravans had been destroyed or seized by soldiers just over the various borders, including two of Edwyn's. The master merchant was eager to hear what the king intended to do.

Annamaria had begged off attending, claiming she didn't feel up to it. That was a pity. Otto had hoped to see her face when her lover got run through by the king's guards. Ah well, life was full of disappointments.

"What do you think His Majesty intends?" Edwyn asked for the tenth time that morning. He'd dressed in his finest white silk robes and gold rings decorated each of his fingers.

"I don't know what the king plans. While Wolfric and I are friends, I'm not part of their inner circle. The contents of the speech will be as much of a surprise to me as it will be to you."

A quarter mile from the plaza the carriage stopped. Otto peeked out. Ahead of them a line of people and carriages had formed. It appeared Edwyn wasn't the only one that wanted to find a good spot.

Otto sighed and closed his eyes. He hadn't taken time to check on Hans's progress. The sergeant should have a disguised Lothair in position by now. Otto had prepared false Straken documents and placed them in an inner pocket of Lothair's cloak. It had been simple enough considering how many papers they'd seized.

Otto extended his sight through the ether. Seconds later he found Hans, Cord, and Lothair exactly where they were supposed to be. The soldiers had swapped out their disguises for proper uniforms which no doubt made the task easier. Lothair stood with a slack expression, his eyes glazed over. He'd remain that way until Otto set him loose.

He shifted his view and found the royal procession on its way. A lot was riding on Wolfric seeing his part through. If the prince had gotten cold feet again the plan was finished.

Otto hated it when things were out of his control, though at this point he should have been used to the feeling. His whole life felt out of his control. Soon enough he'd put an end to that. When he gained the power of an Arcane Lord, no one would control him again.

Otto and Edwyn found a place right at the front of the gathered crowd along with other members of the merchant class. All around them murmurs filled the air as everyone speculated about the king's plans.

Two men wearing tabards with the royal griffin blew trumpets. The crowd fell silent as the king's herald announced, "His Majesty King Von Garen."

The king walked through an aisle made of palace guards and took his place beside the herald who bowed and stepped back. His Majesty looked as strong and confident as Otto had ever seen him. No sign of the uncertain, weak man the prince had described earlier. Whatever his frailties, the king did a fine job hiding them this day.

Wolfric joined his father and stood to his right and a step behind, looking every bit the loyal, loving son. The prince's gaze ran over the crowd, finally settling on Otto who offered a faint nod. He watched for some sign Wolfric had reconsidered the new plan, but saw nothing, thank heaven for that.

"Good citizens of Garenland," the king said. "We have been through a frightful time these past weeks, but I have good news. Straken has overplayed its hand and given us everything we need to restore our place in the compact. Earlier this week I sent letters to the other monarchs informing them of Straken's actions and demanding satisfaction. Rest assured when my peers learn the facts they'll be swift in their condemnation."

"A letter," a hard-faced woman to Otto's left muttered. "What good's that going to do?"

"It'll probably end up in the royal garderobe," another said.

Variations on that theme filled the air around him, confirming Otto's theory that the people wanted action not words. It also reassured him that the plans he and Wolfric had made would be met with support.

"Take heart, my friends," the king went on. "Soon our brief nightmare will be over."

From the middle of the crowd someone shouted, "What about the bandit attacks?"

"And the border taxes!" another added.

An angry ripple ran through the gathering. Otto needed to act before the crowd did his work for him. He sent his thoughts racing across the crowd to where Lothair waited.

Do it now!

His mental command stabbed into Lothair's brain.

Lethargy vanished as his programing kicked in. Otto withdrew his awareness and turned to watch the show.

Lothair crashed through the crowd like an out-of-control carriage, shoving people aside as he forced his way to the front of the gathering.

Angry shouts filled the air.

The king looked on in obvious confusion.

A skinny merchant and his wife staggered forward a little to Otto's left.

"What is going on?" Edwyn asked.

"I have no idea," Otto said. He moved a little ways further from the gap. No need to be too close to the action.

Lothair appeared a moment later, his dagger bared.

When the first person spotted the naked weapon a scream went up. People started pushing and shoving. Otto ignored them all, instead focusing on Lothair. A single bound carried the custom-made assassin past the guards' half-hearted attempts to stop him.

The king's eyes bulged as the gleaming dagger descended.

Otto used a single thread to redirect the blade, so it struck the king to the left of his heart. Lothair ripped the blade free, snarled, and drove it home again. This time Otto dragged it down to plunge into the king's stomach.

Before Lothair could pull the dagger free for a third strike two spears pierced him from behind. Blood gushed from his mouth and he collapsed to the ground, his weapon clattering a few feet away.

"Someone fetch a priest!" Wolfric shouted.

That was Otto's signal. "Let's see if we can slip out of here."

"An excellent suggestion." Edwyn turned back toward the waiting carriage, his face ashen. The master merchant clearly hadn't seen much in the way of combat. That was about to change for everyone.

Garenland was going to war.

CHAPTER 54

W olfric knelt beside his father and tried to staunch the bleeding. Where was that blasted priest? He'd never expected such savagery from Otto's assassin. It was a miracle the dagger had failed to kill his father instantly. Of course, Otto had said they'd only wound the king and if there was anyone in the world he could count on, it was Otto.

Father opened his mouth, but no sound emerged. Wolfric took his father's hand and got a weak squeeze in reply.

"Excuse me, Your Highness."

Wolfric looked up to find a severe, middle-aged man in black robes standing over him. For the briefest moment he imagined Death himself had appeared to claim his father. That was ridiculous and a second look revealed the sword-shaped medallion around the priest's neck identifying him as one of the Sword Lord's followers. Their church wasn't known for their healing prowess, but right now Wolfric wasn't in a position to complain.

The priest knelt beside him, ignoring the blood soaking his

robes, and raised his hands. For long moments nothing happened, but eventually the king's breathing grew easier and the flow of blood slowed until it stopped altogether.

"The damage is severe, Highness, but he will live. I've stabilized him enough that he can be moved. I recommend returning him to the palace at once."

"Understood," Wolfric said. "Guards! Prepare a stretcher for the king. Bring the assassin's body. We need to figure out who sent him."

There was a chorus of "yes, sirs" and ten minutes later they were on their way. The guards carried the king back to the palace and into his bed chamber. Every step of the way Wolfric stayed on one side and the priest on the other. Despite the jostling and rough handling his father never made a sound. Wolfric didn't know if that was a good sign or not, but at least Father didn't appear to be in pain.

When the guards had cleared the king's bedchamber leaving Wolfric alone with the priest he asked, "What now?"

"Let me work." The priest had his eyes closed and his lips twisted in a scowl.

Wolfric fell silent and watched his father's chest. Magical healing never ceased to amaze him. As he sat there the deep stab wounds closed, leaving only faint scars.

Half an hour later the priest sighed. "I've done what I can, but there are no guarantees. Do you understand, Highness?"

"I do and thank you. Can you stay with him for a little while? I want to check on the assassin."

"Of course, take your time." The priest pulled a chair over beside the bed and settled in.

Wolfric took a moment to wash his hands in a basin of water before stepping outside. The ten guards stood at rigid attention. They were all his chosen men, loyal to the death, and well aware of what had happened.

"You all did a wonderful job, but it isn't over yet. Stay here and guard the door until I return. Where was the assassin's body taken?"

"We left him in the yard, my lord," Commander Borden said. "Captain Kelten was eager to examine him."

Wolfric nodded. Better if someone else found the papers Otto had planted on the man. "I'm going to see what he discovered. I'll return shortly."

"Yes, my lord." Borden and the others saluted.

Wolfric left the guards and marched toward the main entrance. Everything was going according to plan, but he still felt sick. Seeing his father like that twisted him up inside. It didn't help that he had given the order.

Damn Straken and the rest! If they hadn't betrayed Garenland none of this would have happened.

He reached the yard and found a powerfully built man of middle years wearing the black and gold tabard of the palace guard bent over the assassin's body. He straightened at Wolfric's approach.

"Find anything, Captain?"

"Papers, Your Highness. The assassin's from Straken. This was clearly a suicide mission and the bastards wanted us to know they were behind it. You almost have to admire the sheer gall of the act."

"My father lies in his bed hovering near death." Wolfric didn't even have to feign the rage he felt. "I assure you there's nothing about this I admire."

"Of course not, Prince Wolfric. I meant no offense." Kelten bowed his head. "What are your orders?"

"Seal the palace. No one in or out for the rest of the day.

Send a messenger to the Sword Lord's temple and let them know that their priest—"

"Marcus, my lord," Kelten said.

"That Marcus will be staying at the palace tonight."

"As you command, my lord." Kelten hesitated then asked, "We're going to make them pay for this outrage, are we not?"

"We are, rest assured. Before I'm finished all of Straken will bleed."

○

Otto lay in bed beside Annamaria and stared up into the dark. After the attempted assassination he'd seen Edwyn safely home then set out to get a feel for how the city was reacting to the attack. After visiting six taverns, three inns, and a pie vendor he felt he had a fair grasp of things. Anger and outrage were the common emotions, along with a desire to do something about it.

He couldn't help smiling. Straken and their allies had set a low simmer of anger running through the country and Otto had turned it up to a boil. Now he and Wolfric needed to direct that anger in the proper direction, a direction that would leave them as rulers of the continent.

First, however, Otto had to finish what Lothair started. He closed his eyes and extended his sight. The palace was well within his range, especially given how much his power had grown. His awareness soared above the streets, through halls, and finally into the king's bedchamber.

Otto stared down at the unconscious king. He looked far older than his fifty-three years. In a chair beside him Wolfric slept with his naked sword in his lap. He looked every bit the distraught son.

Perhaps he even was. The prince's desire to call off the attack seemed genuine, though Otto hadn't had much difficulty convincing him to go through with it in the end. No doubt Wolfric would be grief-stricken when his father died in his sleep, but these things happened. Even magical healing wasn't perfect.

Now for the tricky part. Otto had little practice manipulating the ether from a distance, but since he could see it with his extended vision there was no reason his plan shouldn't work.

He moved in closer to the king, going so far as to slide his sight inside the dying man's chest and draw his focus down to the smallest level. Conjuring light inside a living body was another first for him, but it worked. The king's steadily beating heart appeared inches away.

Otto forged a tiny claw and grasped a single speck of blood. With slow, deliberate care he built a clot. He had no sense of time as he worked, one cell at a time. In the history of the world he doubted anyone had ever been murdered in such a tedious fashion.

At last he had a fair-sized dam built and the flow restricted. A little way up the vessel he built another clot, half the diameter of the artery, and set it loose. It struck the first damn he'd built, fully cutting off the flow of blood.

Otto withdrew his awareness, content to let the king die unwitnessed. When his sight returned to his body Otto let out a soft breath, rolled over, and went to sleep. Tomorrow promised to be an interesting day.

○

Wolfric stared at his father's cold, dead body. The wounds were gone, a testament to the skill of the priest, but he'd died all the same. Marcus knelt beside the body, his hands extended over the king's still chest.

After an interminable stretch the priest stood and shook his head. "A blood clot, Your Majesty."

Your Majesty. That was Father's title, not his.

When Wolfric made no comment Marcus went on, "With serious wounds like your father suffered, it's not uncommon for a stray clot to make its way to the heart. Sometimes new blockages form even after the healing is complete. Your father wasn't a young man and the stress—"

"Get out." Wolfric didn't blame the priest for his father's death, but he couldn't spend another second listening to the man's jabbering.

Marcus bowed and withdrew, leaving him alone with his grief. He and Otto had done this. He could get as angry as he wanted, but there was no one else to blame. They killed the king, not with their own hands, but with their deeds.

Wolfric sunk to his knees beside the bed. "I'm sorry, Father. I didn't think you were strong enough to do what Garenland needed. I will try to be worthy of your sacrifice."

He fought for a moment to collect himself then went to the door. Captain Kelten waited just outside. "Send a message to the Franken estate summoning Otto to the palace. When he arrives bring him here."

"Here, Majesty?"

Wolfric cocked his head. "Was my order unclear?"

"Not at all. It shall be done." Kelten bowed and hurried off to see to his task.

An hour later the door opened and Otto strode in. If the death of the king bothered him, he showed no sign of it.

"I'm sorry for your loss," Otto said when the door had shut.

Wolfric crossed the room in three angry strides, grabbed Otto by the front of his tunic, and slammed him into the wall.

"We did this. It's our fault he's dead." The prince bounced his friend's head against the wall with each shouted word. Any moment he expected the door to burst open and armed guards to appear, wondering what was happening.

"No," Otto said with total calm, as if Wolfric's manhandling him was a minor annoyance. "Straken killed him with their invasion and treachery. Rolan and Tharanault killed him with their jealousy and greed. Lasil killed him with their indifference to what was right. Lux killed him with their cowardice. And Markane killed him with their supposed neutrality. There's plenty of blame to go around, my friend. You could even argue the king's unwillingness to do what was necessary to protect Garenland killed him."

Wolfric lowered Otto to the floor and staggered to a nearby chair. "I know they're to blame as well, but we—"

"We did what was necessary for the many to survive. Your sacrifice will be remembered as a turning point in the history of this great nation. But only if you don't squander the opportunity it's given you."

Wolfric took deep breaths and latched on to Otto's words. His friend was right. What was done was done. Father's death would be meaningless if he failed to pull himself together.

"We will have a proper funeral," Wolfric said. "I will make a speech denouncing Straken and their cowardly assassination of my father. All the plans we made will come to pass and those that betrayed my father and his dream of a peaceful world will rue their decision for all time."

"May I suggest hanging the spies right afterward as a symbolic first blow to our enemies?"

Wolfric smiled for the first time in two days.

〜

Two days had passed since Otto's visit with Wolfric and the time for the funeral had arrived. There had been a few minutes when Wolfric grabbed him that he'd wondered if he'd need to protect himself, but the prince, now king, had come to his senses. Otto could hardly wait for the funeral to end so the real work could begin.

As soon as the announcement regarding the wizards' new status was made, he'd return to the tower and Lord Karonin. Hopefully she'd explain how everything in the armory worked. Considering how many enemies Garenland faced, they'd need every weapon they could get their hands on and he wasn't certain even that would be enough. If the wizards in the other kingdoms didn't rise up against their oppressors, Garenland might be in trouble.

Otto smoothed his black tunic and adjusted the position of his sword. They'd need to get going soon, but before they left the mansion, he had one more bit of personal business to take care of.

"Otto?" Annamaria emerged from the walk-in closet dressed in a simple black dress. Her stomach had swelled as the pregnancy progressed, but she still looked beautiful. "Could you button me up?"

She spun around and moved her long, blond hair out of the way. Otto smiled and obliged her. When the last button was hooked, she turned and kissed his cheek. "Thanks."

"My pleasure, darling." Otto reached into his pocket and

pulled out the ring he'd taken from Lothair. "In all the excitement I forgot about the surprise I picked up for you."

"What surprise?" Her eyes widened when she saw the ring.

"I was walking through the city one day and a flash caught my eye. I saw it in the window of a pawn shop. What are the odds of me stumbling on your ring after all this time? It had to be fate. As soon as I laid eyes on it, I knew I had to return it to you."

Tears ran down her cheeks as she accepted the ring. "Is he dead?"

"Who?"

She met his gaze, hate twisting her beautiful features. It was the sweetest sight he'd seen in many weeks. "Lothair."

"Lothair?" Otto favored her with a look of wide-eyed innocence. "Surely he's alive and well far from Garen."

Her fist clenched around the ring. "You owe me the truth."

Otto laughed. "The truth? Are you even aquatinted with the word's meaning? You've done nothing but lie to me since the day we met. 'Take this ring, Lothair, and use it to pay your way clear of the city.' What you meant was take this ring, it's my promise that we'll be together again soon. How long did you wait after the wedding to invite him back to your bed?"

"It was no lie. I never expected to see Lothair again. He snuck onto the grounds one day while you were at the palace. I knew what we were doing was wrong, but I didn't care." She raised her head and met his angry glare with pride. "I love him and I always will."

"If you say so. I wish I'd known your plans. I'd have let Stephan have his way with you. At least then the child growing in your womb would be related to me."

She flinched as if he'd struck her. "How long have you known?"

"Since the night you told me. I felt the child in the ether and found no connection. Blood calls to blood, my dear wife. It didn't take long after that to track down your lover."

"Is he dead?" The words barely escaped her lips.

"Very." Otto shrugged. "Turns out not only did he have a taste for other men's wives, but he was also a Straken spy. He murdered the king before the palace guard cut him down. I believe his head's decorating the wall. You might get to see him one last time before the ravens strip the flesh from his skull."

"I hate you!"

The door opened and Mimi came in. "Miss? Is all well?"

Otto turned his back on Annamaria and smiled at Mimi. "She just got a bit of bad news, nothing to be concerned about. And don't worry, I don't plan to see you put out on the streets for your part in deceiving me. Your first loyalty is to your mistress, as it should be. Though I trust you won't feel the need to keep anything else from me."

Mimi stared at the floor. "No, Lord Shenk."

Otto patted her head as he passed by. "That's good. Help her finish getting ready. We don't want to be late."

෨

Otto sat amongst a select group beside Wolfric on a raised platform. The king's body lay in a gold-inlaid oak coffin filled with flowers, both as tribute and to hide the worst of the stink. They'd decided to hold the funeral in the central plaza, on the exact spot of the attack.

It was a powerful bit of symbolism. Otto was impressed Wolfric thought of it given his state of mind. Hopefully he'd made peace with what they'd done and was ready to begin the important work of destroying their enemies.

373

Beyond the platform, as far as he could see in every direction, people had gathered to honor the king. He spotted Edwyn and Annamaria in the front row. His loving wife refused to meet his gaze. In time she'd accept her situation, or she wouldn't. Otto no longer cared either way. He was finished with the woman. Mastering his magic was all that mattered.

Wolfric got out of his chair and stepped up beside the coffin. Otto activated the spell that would send his voice out over the crowd so everyone could hear.

"People of Garenland, I stand before you on this sad day that we may mourn my father together. He was a good man, too good for the world he found himself in. He had faith in the system that had served us so well for so long. His faith was betrayed by those too greedy or too lazy to compete with us on an even playing field. Our enemies conspired against us and struck powerful blows, first ousting us from the compact, then invading our northern territory, and finally murdering my father, your king."

A murmur went through the crowd. Wolfric was hitting the tone perfectly and the people were eating it up. If he kept going like this, they'd be begging him to go to war.

"My people, I know you to be generous and honorable, quick to forgive and slow to anger. But there can be no forgiveness for what happened here. Our anger is deep and abiding and nothing short of the defeat of all our enemies will satisfy it. The forces arrayed against us are great and only the efforts of all the good people of Garenland will allow us to see our foes laid low. To that end I'm announcing that all the laws limiting the freedoms of Garenland's wizards are hereby revoked."

Otto fought to keep the smile from his face. Out in the crowd people were looking around, not certain what the announcement meant. Wizards had been second-class citizens for a long time and it would take a while for people to fully accept the new reality.

"As a sign of good faith, I'm naming my dear friend Otto Shenk, a wizard himself, as my high councilor. Otto, come up here."

He stepped up beside Wolfric and bowed. "I'm honored, Your Majesty. I promise you won't regret your generous appointment. To my fellow wizards I say this, the king's offer is true and from the heart. We need you; your country needs you, now more than ever. I will be overseeing the training of any who wish to join our fight. I beg you to step up and do your part. Not just for Garenland, but for all the mistreated wizards everywhere. We will see them all free and safe."

Wolfric laid a hand on his shoulder. "Today we bury my father and mourn our losses. Tomorrow, Garenland goes to war!"

Wolfric thrust a fist in the air. Otto and the others on stage followed suit. The crowd roared and pumped their fists. It was an excellent start.

When they hung the spies later in the day the people would drink up their first victory. Once they finished, nothing short of divine intervention would stop Garenland from conquering her enemies.

CHAPTER 55

O tto emerged from the ether and found a scowling Lord Karonin floating in her mirror. He bowed. The hidden tower appeared exactly as it did the first day he arrived. The day that changed his life forever. The cold stone was spotless and not a mote of dust hung in the air.

The place was timeless.

"Has it been three months already?" Lord Karonin asked

"No, Master, but I have made a good start on your task and I hoped you might be willing to help me with the next phase."

"Tell me."

"I've convinced Wolfric to remove all the restrictions on Garenland's wizards and I've set the stage for the conquest of the other nations. Once that's done their wizards will be freed as well. I'm now the second-most-powerful man in the kingdom. I'll have no trouble maneuvering things to our advantage."

"Impressive. It seems I chose well when I made you my apprentice. How did you manage all this?"

"It was easy. All I had to do was kill a king."

Lord Karonin laughed long and loud. "You will make a fine Arcane Lord. Ask your questions. I shall tell you everything."

Otto grinned, eager to begin. "How about we start with those giant suits of armor?"

AUTHOR NOTE

Hello everyone and thanks for reading The Hidden Tower. I hope you enjoyed getting to know Otto and those around him. With the danger in Straken ramping up, the danger only increases going forward.

I hope you'll join me for the next book in the series, The Great Northern War. It tells the tale of Garenland's invasion of their northern neighbor and the rise of the War Wizards.

You can find links to all the bookstores here. www. jamesewisher.com/books/the-great-northern-war

Thanks for reading.

Chains of the Fallen Arc:

Dreaming in the Dark

On Blackened Wings

Chains of the Fallen Omnibus

The Aegis of Merlin:

The Impossible Wizard

The Awakening

The Chimera Jar

The Raven's Shadow

Escape From the Dragon Czar

Wrath of the Dragon Czar

The Four Nations Tournament

Death Incarnate

Aegis of Merlin Omnibus Vol 1.

Aegis of Merlin Omnibus Vol 2.

Other Fantasy Novels:

The Squire

Death and Honor Omnibus

The Rogue Star Series:

Children of Darkness

Children of the Void

Children of Junk

Rogue Star Omnibus Vol. 1

Children of the Black Ship

ABOUT THE AUTHOR

James E. Wisher is a writer of science fiction and fantasy novels. He's been writing since high school and reading everything he could get his hands on for as long as he can remember.

To learn more:
www.jamesewisher.com
james@jamesewisher.com